MW01616842

SAVING EMMY (SPECIAL FORCES: OPERATION ALPHA)

HELLFORCE SECURITY: ALPHA TEAM, BOOK 2

RAYNE LEWIS

This book is a work of fiction. Names, characters, places, and incidents are products of the author's imagination or used fictitiously. Any resemblance to actual events or locales or persons living or dead is entirely coincidental.

© 2021 ACES PRESS, LLC. ALL RIGHTS RESERVED

No part of this work may be used, stored, reproduced or transmitted without written permission from the publisher except for brief quotations for review purposes as permitted by law.
This book is licensed for your personal enjoyment only. This book may not be re-sold or given away to other people. If you would like to share this book with another person, please purchase an additional copy for each recipient. If you're reading this book and did not purchase it, or it was not purchased for your use only, please purchase your own copy.

All cover art and logo © Copyright 2021
By Rayne Lewis
Editing by Rebecca Hodgkins
Cover by Lori Jackson
Proofread by Turn The Pages Proofreading

Dear Readers,

Welcome to the Special Forces: Operation Alpha Fan-Fiction world!

If you are new to this amazing world, in a nutshell the author wrote a story using one or more of my characters in it. Sometimes that character has a major role in the story, and other times they are only mentioned briefly. This is perfectly legal and allowable because they are going through Aces Press to publish the story.

This book is entirely the work of the author who wrote it. While I might have assisted with brainstorming and other ideas about which of my characters to use, I didn't have any part in the process or writing or editing the story.

I'm proud and excited that so many authors loved my characters enough that they wanted to write them into their own story. Thank you for supporting them, and me!

READ ON!
    Xoxo
    Susan Stoker

To J, my very own Alpha hero, who believed in me way before I believed in myself. You are my rock when I need to stand, my shoulder when I need to cry and my wings when you lift me to soar to heights greater than I ever imagined.
Loves.

To my team of Smutties, who are to blame for this entire venture.

PROLOGUE

The midday sun blazed above and beat down on the crude rubble of the village. Houses, if they could be called that, lay in ruins. Decrepit, crumbling stone structures that looked as if they belong to a bygone era lined the dust-clad roads from biblical times. The air hung heavy with earth and staleness, a scent and taste that was indescribable to anyone who hadn't experienced it. Hundreds of years of death and woe wove its way through the stench of desolation. Though the sun shone above, dust covered the horizon muting the pristine blue skyline and marred it with a darkened haze of brown and orange, matching the unforgiving ugliness of the mood of war.

Moon dust, what soldiers called the fine powder that got everywhere, lined her nostrils, a smell that was constant and always present, collected in every pore and crevice. There was no escape from the grit that clung beneath the necklines, gloves, and tight-laced boots, coating her battledress blouse and trousers a lifeless gray against her normal khaki Kevlar vest. She watched from her perch as the fine chalk dust stirred and swirled, settling beneath the feet of the squad moving in tandem from decimated shack to mud-laden stone shanty, looking for those who weren't the occupants.

Lying prone on the rooftop, she watched and waited, being the eyes for her brothers below, alert to anything that moved, though the dust lay dormant and dead around the ruins settled in silt from the desert haboob that rained through the day before. As long as she lived, she would never forget the intense sand and ultra-fine dust storms that darkened the summertime day into a haze of a modern day apocalyptic movie thriller. Darkness fell when the dirt bellowed, consuming everything in its wake, only to pass, blown away by the curtailing winds in the hot, dry desert air.

She swallowed the grit lining the roof of her mouth. Sweat trickled from the crest of her brow and stung the corners of her eyes, though she was immune to the urge to wipe it, not chancing any small movement to give away her cover.

A billow of dust rose from behind the abandoned row of houses to the east, resurrecting the bleak, barren wasteland deserted weeks ago. No soul of good intentions marked this godforsaken village. Evil intent bore their presence.

She sighted-in the lone boy, navigating over the rocky terrain and stones of once-there-buildings, tracking his journey and noting his attire. A relic of a rifle slung across his chest and a brown leather satchel held tight to his side. Leaving the rifle to sway and fall, the boy cradled the satchel as if it were a newborn child. Zeroing in on the boy through the refraction of the high-powered scope, she reassessed her judgement noting the boy more resembled a young man—fighting age of ISIS insurgents or those trying to show their allegiance to the terror group. She radioed to the Ranger squad breaching compounds just a few houses to the north of the young man's position.

Dead.

Tracking his movements, he hunkered behind the remains of a burnt-out car.

Crouching, he opened the satchel.

Radioing to base, she got the green light.

Control yourself. Calm yourself. Clear yourself.

Time didn't exist. Peripheral vision dimmed. The rushing of blood timed to her heartbeat filled the void of nothingness in her ears.

Exhale. Two...Three...Fou—

The sharp crack of air splitting as her round left the gun and parted the atmosphere. The sound coupled with the smell of metallic sulfur—burnt earth if you will—that was a familiar, oddly settling and pleasant scent to her senses.

The lethal bullet marked for the insurgent sailed through the air on trajectory and route to its intended target.

As if sensing its approach, the young man's head turned in time to meet his demise.

Eyes.

Widening eyes.

Wicked, diabolical eyes scorched her soul and stained her memory.

The body fell, muddying the stale grey dust to a crimson quagmire.

Ember lay prone, on an exhale, in the hot desert sun.

CHAPTER 1

PRESENT DAY

The emergency vehicles were all around her, though the sirens were now silenced, but the lights still flashed.

This is bad.

Oh, God, so bad.

"Gunshot wound to the chest and head. This was no accident." Sheriff Richards looked at the victim lying face up, barely recognizable, and shot the Ranger a side-eyed glance, discreetly motioning him towards the woman.

"Ma'am, I'm going to need you to step to the side. Ranger Matthews would like to talk with you."

How could this be happening? Her world was spinning out of control and nothing was making sense. She saw the sheriff's mouth moving, but no sound came out, as if someone had pressed the mute button on her life and there were no subtitles.

"Ma'am," he stiffened his tone, "I need you to go with Ranger Matthews."

The sheriff stood in front of her, yet she couldn't comprehend what he was trying to tell her. *What is he trying to get me to do?*

Somebody turned off the mute button, but the volume was

just above a whisper. With all the sensory overload, the lights, the previous sirens...the man lying dead twenty feet away with half his cranium missing, she was having trouble tracking. His blood-soaked t-shirt was now more crimson than white.

Was this shock? Was her PTSD resurfacing? Was this a battlefield flashback?

Sheriff Richards placed his hand on her shoulder and upper arm and turned her away from the horror show playing out in front of her. His deep, commanding voice was a bit more forceful and authoritarian. "Ma'am."

It snapped Ember out of her head and she brought her eyes to the grey-haired man beside her. "Yes?" She heard herself speak, knew the words were her own, but her body stayed frozen in place, like an invisible carbonite slab cocooning her in an alternate universe. Her eyes darted about his face as she tried not to look at the chaos taking place around her.

"Ranger Matthews will take you to the station and will need your statement."

She turned to see the Ranger holding out his hand to her, but her feet were lead weights rooted in place. Could she go willingly? Before she made the decision, one hand led her by the forearm away from the scene while the other rested on his utility belt and the light glinted off the set of handcuffs.

Oh, shit, this was BAD!

On the edge of town stood a nondescript building. If there were a sign out front it would read Hellforce and it would be the most accurate description of the men inside. Six highly trained, former military Special Forces operatives willing to bust through the doors of hell in some of the worst, darkest, most dangerous hellholes on the planet, raining brimstone on those on the other side. Each of them willing to risk it all to bring home victims subject to the most vile, depraved, violent atrocities imaginable.

Hellforce was King's dream, vision and reality. His team of Deltas—Slate, Cypher, T-BAR and Trip—rescued King and

Arctic when their SOF team was ambushed in the foothills of Afghanistan after hitting a roadside IED. And now six worked as one. They knew what it took to get a mission done and they were stellar at mission execution. Each looking out for the other with little disregard for their own safety knowing their brother would have their six. They were brothers.

Slate was about to jump off the loading dock at Hellforce and onto the blistering hot asphalt when his cellphone peeled out familiar beats. *Ember. His Red.* A smile crept across his face. He loved hearing her ringtone. She was his longtime, childhood friend. He'd known her practically all his life. It was Ember and her family, mainly her father Mitch, who played a pivotal role in shaping him into the man he was today.

The thought drew him back to the past, at the age of five, when he lost his father to cancer. After that Eli was lost as well. He was a little boy, alone, and only his mother to fill the shoes of both parents. In kindergarten, he'd met the girl he loved to this very day, though she was oblivious to his true feelings. Ember was the girl with fiery red hair. His Red. His Emmy. It was as if the setting sun had reached out and touched each unmanageable strand on her head. They were coppery-orange, unlike most Irish gingers who had a lighter, blonder orange. Ember's locks were, well...like embers. The blazing red-orange of stoked coals; the type that burn hot in the belly of a fire. Yup, that was his Emmy. She was fiery and magnificent.

Ember's parents had befriended his mother, giving a middle-aged, widowed, unskilled, inexperienced woman a job at their hardware store. His mother and Susan became best friends and formed an unbreakable bond. Ember's father, Pops, took Eli under his wing, fishing, hunting, camping, teaching him a multitude of trades and skills, growing a bond a father and son would've shared.

A second instrumental chorus sang out from the phone and he was jerked to the present as the memory faded. Reaching into the side pocket of his cargo pants, his gloved hand fumbling, the incessant melody continued to sing from the speaker as he tried to pull his phone out. Biting the tip of the gloved finger, he pulled it off just as the phone fell silent.

Damn it!

The "missed call" icon displayed across the screen. He swiped it and entered his security code. With his thumb hovering above Ember's contact, he was about to dial her back when Arctic burst through the dock doors with a hurried, bleak expression on his face.

Beelining straight to Slate, he motioned his thumb over his shoulder, "Boss wants everyone in the conference room, pronto."

"What's up?" Slate's adrenaline piqued in his veins.

"Now, Eli."

Eli? Rarely did the team use given names. With the exception of business meetings with clients or formal events, the guys monikers were more their identity than the name on their birth certificates.

Arctic's face paled and for a moment Slate thought he detected a hint of fear. Before he could question it, his phone pinged with an incoming text. Looking down, the message notification backlit across his locked screen; it was Ember.

Three words made his blood run cold.

"I need you."

CHAPTER 2

Nerves made Ember's body quake uncontrollably.

Breathe. Deep breaths. Deep Breaths. Breathe.

She told her lungs to cooperate but they had other plans. Her legs trembled as she sat in the dank, over-lit office that felt like it was closing in on her. The overhead lights glared harshly on the sharp angles of the room. She was going to be sick. Bile churned in her stomach and she fought it from rising up. Closing her eyes, willing the sickness away, all she saw in the absence was red.

Blood.

Dark, stained crimson blood.

Screwing her eyes tighter, willing the memory away, it only intensified the images. She couldn't quell them and bile pushed its way up again.

Her eyes shot open and she squinted against the blinding light. Looking down, her fingers wrapped around her phone and her knuckles turned white from the punishing grip. She loosened them to keep it from shattering. Glaring at the screen, she mentally willed it to ring.

"We'll only be a little longer, then you can make another phone call. I know this is nerve-wracking, but there's a lot going on here." Ranger Matthews smiled a tight smile, but all she wanted was her phone to ring. "Just sit tight and we'll get your statement."

Just sit tight? Really? Sit tight. How was she supposed to sit tight? *A man took one to the chest and was missing half his face, and I'm supposed to "just sit tight?"*

A man entered the room wearing a starched white shirt and crimson red tie. The tie made the memories resurface, and Ember felt ill again. The lines of his shirt were crisp, and the harshness of the overhead lights seemed to make the whiteness electrify and glow. With papers in one hand and a coffee in the other, he offered the steamy brew to her.

"It's station coffee, so I apologize in advance. It's thick as ink, over-brewed, and will probably eat the plating from a spoon."

Ember knew the lighthearted joke was for her benefit, to break the tension that hung in the air, but all she could manage was a tight smirk. "Thank you," she said as he handed her the cup.

"Would you care for cream or sugar?"

She could feel the warmth of the brew beneath the cardboard sleeve. "No...no cream, no sugar." Taking a sip of the black ink, she held back the grimace that tried to surface. Setting the coffee on the edge of the desk, she glanced down at her phone again. *Please, ring!* While pleading with the inanimate object, she missed the conversation around her.

"Ms. Hayes?"

Ember looked up and the man repeated his question. "Will your lawyer be joining us? I was told you called him when you arrived."

Still finding it hard to believe the shitshow she was living, she found her focus vague and hesitated. "Um...yes. Yeah, he should be on his way. I'm sorry, I didn't catch your name?"

"Detective Washburn," he held out his hand to her. Guessing her follow-up question, he said, "FBI."

FBI. Oh, shit.

Shit, shit, shit.

A heavy knock came from the office door and all heads swiveled in its direction. Ember shrugged a sigh of relief. *It's Miles.* Miles was here.

Miles Harrington entered the already cramped office and Detective Washburn rose along with the Ranger, offering an outstretched hand.

"Detective Washburn, FBI."

"Ranger Matthews." Matthews gave a shake and a nod.

"Miles Harrington, pleased to meet you. I'm Ms. Hayes lawyer," he announced after the men exchanged pleasantries.

Miles put his hand on Ember's shoulder, giving it a light squeeze, while looking for a place to sit. Washburn retrieved a folding chair from the side of the filing cabinet and offered it to him.

"Thank you," Miles said as he unbuttoned the top button on his suit coat before sitting, "I understand there was an incident?"

An incident? A parking lot fender bender is an incident. This...this, is a fucking nightmare. Ember couldn't keep her inner dialog from running. In all her life, she never thought she'd be involved in a shooting investigation on U.S. soil. When she was serving overseas in Iraq, this was a weekly occurrence. But here...at home...in Texas, it never crossed her mind. Which was why she was having trouble processing the scenario. She'd seen the casualties of war. Lost friends who served right beside her. She knew death and had stared it in the eye too many times to count.

Through a sniper's scope, she got an up-close-and-personal viewing every time she squeezed the trigger. One minute the target was there.. the next, she was watching them fall lifeless to the ground. Sometimes headless. So, why was this so terrifyingly difficult?

She felt the slow burn of tears threatening to surface. *Push. Them. Back. Soldier.* She chastised herself.

She wasn't an emotional girl. Never had been. All the years of training had taught her how to push her emotions aside and focus on what mattered.

End goals.

"...and then we'll need her statement, and she'll be free to leave."

Ember focused her thoughts and came back to herself. How long had she been pulled into her memory? *Focus. What was the conversation, and what did I miss?*

Miles again put his hand on her shoulder and lightly squeezed. "Do you think you're able to do that now?"

Do what? She scrambled. *Oh, the statement.* "Yeah, I can do that." Her head nodded yes, but her emotions told a different story.

Miles sensed the contradiction.

A vibration hummed beneath her palm. Looking at her phone, she noticed a message had come in while she was lost in her thoughts.

ELIJAH: *On my way.*

Three words settled her heart.

Wait, what? On his way? On his way where? Here? Is he coming to the station? How does he know I'm here?

Staring at her, Miles lifted her phone from her hand, waiting for her to notice him. She lifted her head and met his warm eyes.

"You don't have to do this now. They have your earlier statement from Sheriff Richards. We can schedule an appointment to come back once you're ready and not dealing with shock."

Shock? Is this shock? She didn't do shock.

"Ms. Hayes?" Ranger Matthews interjected, "Would you like to reschedule? Detective Washburn and I can come to your residence when you're ready."

Just as she was going to decline, the office door swung open and the most beautiful sight graced the entryway.

"Red, are you all right?" Eli took three quick strides to her chair and knelt on one knee, balancing himself effortlessly.

Behind him, taking up every inch of the doorframe, was Henry Clark, Elijah's boss, King. King gave a chin lift of recognition to Ranger Matthews, which Matthews returned with a nod of understanding. Then he did the same to Richards. King turned and pulled the door shut behind him leaving Ember in Slate's care.

The already cramped office was really closing in on her now, but Ember didn't care. They could be shoulder-to-shoulder, wall-to-wall, and it wouldn't matter. Elijah was there. A calm fell over her as Eli grasped her hand, caressing her knuckles with his large, calloused fingers. She focused on his hands. He had a working man's hands. Large, meaty, gorgeous, calloused hands. For their size, they were surprisingly gentle. How many times had his hands comforted her? Wiped her worry away with a gentle touch? Caressed her after returning from the horrors of the sandbox? Elijah, her rock and refuge. Her friend.

"Red? Come back to me." Eli's breath fanned her face, breaking her focus on his hands, and she raised her eyes without raising her head, peering at him through heavy, lidded lashes.

Her facade was cracking along with her voice. Barely above a whisper she spoke, "I want to go home."

Eli tipped her chin with his fingers, "Okay, Red. I'll take you home." From his squatting position, Eli looked to the man beside her.

Miles Harrington hadn't had a chance to introduce himself but he nodded back, "We'll have someone come by her place. Call me when she's ready."

Looking to his right at Washburn, Eli raised his eyebrows in question. Washburn looked at his watch and answered, "That'll be fine with me. Whenever she's ready." He added a smile for reassurance.

Turning his final gaze to the Ranger seated behind the desk, he gave Eli a nod also, then retrieved a business card from his top pocket. Washburn did the same. Taking both cards, he handed them to Eli.

Eli stood in one swift motion and offered a hand to Ember. Tucking a loose tendril of hair behind her ear, she took his hand in hers and quickly stood, scooting the chair with a screech across the linoleum floor. She blankly shook the hands of the men around her then turned to leave. Eli wove his fingers into hers like they had done hundreds of times before. No thought. No plan. Just a gravitational pull to the familiar.

Before they exited the tiny office, Washburn called her name. "Ms. Hayes? I'm going to have to ask you to please stay away from the range. It's being processed as a crime scene at the moment but should be finished up by this evening." Ember nodded and rubbed her arm, warding off a chill though it wasn't cold in the office. She was anxious to exit the room.

"If you need anything from your office call me and either I or one of the other Rangers can escort you to your property. Your employees have been sent home for the day." He continued, "The firearm has already been taken into evidence and will be processed. The victim, Gabriel Dorian, will be taken to the Medical Examiner's office, and the shooter, Husani Bazwar, is already in custody, and tomorrow will be awaiting arraignment. We'll keep you informed of any revelations in the case."

Ember nodded a second time. With her voice trapped in her throat, she managed, "Thank you, may I go now?"

He nodded. "Yes. Call us when you're ready and we'll come by," Washburn replied. "Mr. Harrington, can you join us then?"

Her lawyer nodded in agreement.

"Thank you," Ember repeated, her voice timid and not at all like herself. She looked from the three men and then up at Eli.

"Come on, Red, I'll take care of you."

And, with that, hand in hand, they exited the office.

The car ride home was deafeningly silent. The continuous hum of the truck's engine brought all around solace. Eli looked over at Ember. She had her head pressed up against the window, lost in thought, watching as the mile markers carried her closer to home. The sunlight coming through the window caught the depths of her hair, making it blaze brighter than its normal radiance. He reached over and grasped her delicate hand, lacing his fingers with hers, entwining them with a light squeeze of reassurance. Ember didn't take her head from the window but returned the squeeze. That one little gesture let Eli know that she knew she wasn't alone. She was safe. But he could see by the crease in her brow that her mind was reliving and recalculating today's sequence of events. It was the soldier within her.

With his eyes back to the road he, too, reflected on the moments just hours before.

Slate was about to dial Ember back, when Arctic came bursting through the doors onto the loading dock, telling him King wanted everyone inside. Slate sensed a hint of fear on his friend's face and then he got Ember's text.

RED: *"I need you."*

Those three words made his blood run cold. About to call her, Arctic's next words made him look up.

"Ember's fine."

How Arctic knew what Slate was thinking didn't surprise him. Working together for the last five years at Hellforce, the guys knew each other better than they knew themselves. On missions, they often had to communicate in silence using hand gestures and cues, and each of them knew how to read each other's emotions, so Arctic must have read something Slate didn't realize he was giving away. He saw his friend's head nod in reassurance.

"Where is she?" The words were calm, calculated, and Slate's feet were on the move before he finished the question. He stormed off the loading dock, pushing through the doors Arctic exited moments ago. He was on autopilot. His mind on the mission only.

Get to Ember.

Barreling down the corridor leading to the fitness gym, Slate marched at a fast clip with Arctic fast on his heels. He practically threw himself through the heavy gym doors and into the cage room. He entered his personal cage looking for his truck keys. Not finding them, he patted his pockets, double-tapping his Glock holstered to his left hip, a habit formed during his time on the teams. Pinching the pocket below his holster, he hit paydirt and pulled out his truck FOB. Grabbing his wallet from the pullover he wore during his early morning workout, he headed towards the door.

"SITREP," Slate barked to his teammate and headed for the hallway leading to the parking lot.

"Slate." A hand fell hard on his left bicep and shoulder. Slate spun around with such speed and force, Arctic ducked back a few steps in anticipation if Slate threw a punch. "Whoa, buddy," Arctic raised his hands in a surrender. "Conference room. King's been contacted. She's fine. Take it down a few notches. I'm a friendly." Arctic let out a breathy chuckle to defuse the situation and pointed towards the conference room. "Answers. There." He sidestepped Slate and headed to the room down the hallway.

Slate steeled himself, inhaling sharply through his nostrils, feeling the calm of emotional armor come over him. Cool. Calm. Collected. He needed to be centered so he could focus on the mission.

And the mission was Red.

"A fucking homicide!" Slate bellowed through gritted teeth. "At Ember's range? You've got to be fucking kidding me!" Slate kept his composure but shook his head and fisted his hands at his sides.

The minute he stepped into the conference room, spotting King on the landline and seeing the concentrated looks blanketing his brother's faces, he knew something big was about to blow wide open. Trip told him the information they knew so far while the rest of the guys huddled up around him. Slate let out another expletive. At his outburst, King's stare met his and Slate saw it in King's eyes; King was pissed. Taking a few strides farther into the room, he moved swiftly towards his boss, closing the gap between them. King kept his eyes on Slate, relaying to him that he had things under control. King could say more with his eyes than Webster's dictionary could ever convey. Years of battle had forged King into an iron master of all things chaos.

"Okay, thank you, Tex...I appreciate the heads-up." King hung up the receiver with a little more force than necessary. "Just spoke to Tex and Ranger Matthews—"

"Where is she? What happened?" Slate cut his boss short but asked in a cool but urgent tone.

"Shooter at her gun range. One dead, one in custody."

"And Red?"

King continued, ignoring the interruption, "Tex got a heads up from our mutual friend, Beth, who lives here in Texas. She *monitors* the police radio chatter and knows Ember's connection to Hellforce. Ember's at the station with the authorities waiting for her lawyer to show, so she can give a statement. He's probably on his way for legalities to protect the range...and Ember," King added when Slate's nostrils flared.

Slate didn't voice out loud that *he* would take care of Ember. He knew to the depths of his soul he'd keep her safe and protected. "Was she there? Did she witness the shooting?" Slate ran his hand across the back of his neck then rubbed his scalp, feeling the dampness of perspiration dance on the ends of his short hair. He wanted to leave now but needed to get as much information as possible before going to her.

"She was on the premises. Security vid's been turned into authorities already. Premises will be on lockdown, most likely 'til this evening, depending how fast they can wrap things up. Cypher's gathering the footage with his "voodoo cyber powers," 'cuz you know how deep you have to dig to get it from the Feds. When he gets it, we can get a better idea of what went down."

"Tex is gathering all the information he can on the victim and the shooter. We should know things pretty quickly."

King picked up the phone again and dialed Mary, his assistant and wife, telling her to forward his calls to voicemail and to cancel the rest of the day's appointments and virtual meetings. "We'll head to the station," he glanced to the man at his right, "Trip, follow me, I'll need a lift back here." He turned to Slate, "I'll get you in to her," then he motioned to the door.

The rest of the men stood waiting for instructions. "The rest of you," King said without breaking stride, "there's a truck to unload."

A formidable groan grew from the men, more for show and humorous childish defiance than not wanting to finish the job in the midday Texas heat.

~

The memory faded as Eli pulled into Ember's driveway, turned off the engine, and looked over at her. Her head still leaned against the window and their fingers were still entwined, resting on the center console. Loosening her grip, Slate felt the loss of her immediately as she pulled her hand from his and squeezed her fist a few times, bringing back the lost circulation. She unfastened her seatbelt but didn't reach to open the door.

The air hung still in the truck as she sat for a moment staring at the dashboard then turned to him, "Thank you for coming to get me, Eli," she said with a little lift of a smile.

"Always, Red. I'll always come back to you." Slate opened his door and jumped down from the truck's height, then made his way to Ember's side. He opened her door and helped her out. And, without another word, just like always, they made their way to her house, hand in hand.

CHAPTER 3

Mitch and Susan Hayes sat on each side of their daughter, the three-cushion couch barely fitting the trio. Slate sat in the chair adjacent to her and leaned in with hands clasped and forearms resting on his thighs. In the kitchen, his team waited silently, listening from the room as Detective Washburn and Ranger Matthews went over Ember's statement.

Two hours after Slate drove Ember home, she called Ranger Matthews and asked if he could come to finish the questions. She apologized for not giving the statement at the station, but now that she was in the familiar comfort of her own surroundings and felt more at ease she wanted to get it over and done with.

"I was in the office going over paperwork, trying to catch up on things before the weekend," she told Washburn as she wrung her hands. "I wasn't working the front end, so I didn't see him come in."

"Him?" Matthews asked, writing old school on a notepad and glancing up in between questions. "Mr. Bazwar or Mr. Dorian?"

"Mr. Bazwar...I didn't see him come in, but I saw him at the...scene...the crime scene." Ember closed her eyes and immediately drew in a sharp breath. Instantly, his face was there. Cold, evil, haunting eyes blazing with hatred. A memorable but unrecognizable face. *Why was he so familiar, yet unplaceable?* Why had he sneered at her with a devious almost demonic glare when they arrested him? And why was he also gleeful? The memory burned in her mind and twisted her stomach.

Her eyes shot open and she started to tremble. Her mother placed a hand on her knee and her father placed a hand on her back, rubbing small intricate circles, trying to soothe her. Slate wanted to reach over, to be the one to soothe her, but right now she needed her parents. She needed the loving support they'd always provided her.

Slate stayed seated, his eyes trained on Ember, searching for any signs of the stoic, take-no-prisoners, hard-as-nails girl he knew. At the moment, she was MIA. Ember never cracked under pressure. She was always calm and collected in situations of danger or chaos. Her moniker, Diamond, proved just how hard she was.

Diamonds were formed under pressure and never cracked. They could cut through anything, just like Ember. But, Slate also knew that diamonds were precious and rare, a beauty of nature and a treasure to be sought. If ever a moniker encompassed every characteristic of a person, it was Ember's.

"I was already in the back when he came in." Ember continued, her eyes tracked, searching her mind, "I didn't...see him..." her voice trailed off lost in thought.

"And Mr. Dorian? Did you see him?"

"Yeah, I saw Gabriel," she answered.

Hearing her address the victim on a first-name-basis grabbed Slate's attention. His interest piqued but he kept his posture and emotions in check. He gave nothing away. *Intelligence gathering 101. Never show interest in details. Show no emotion. Never offer information. Keep the person talking. Let the story play out before asking the next, or follow up, question.*

She went on, "I spoke to him when he arrived. He comes in a lot...often...I see him a lot." Frustration bloomed in her expression. Her thoughts were jumbled, and it was clearly irritating her. Slate had never seen her have a problem articulating her thoughts. She was clearheaded, cool under pressure. Her mind a steel trap.

One of the attributes of every great sniper, second to being a solid shot, was the ability to recall the target, details, descriptions, times and atmosphere. Every minute detail had to be absorbed, logged and recalled, because along with taking out HTVs came a shit-ton of paperwork.

"How often?" Matthews asked.

"Um...I'd say once, maybe twice a week...sometimes more, sometimes less." She mindlessly rubbed her palm on her knee.

"Were you friends?"

Ember thought for a minute, rolling the question around in her head. A minute too long for Slate's liking.

Matthews softened his tone. "Did you see each other outside of the range?"

"We'd get coffee...I mean, not *get* coffee, but...we both like the same coffee shop down the street and we'd sometimes both be there...at the same time. Like, we'd get coffee, and we'd see each other and sit down and chat for a bit."

Matthews' looked up from his notepad at Ember, "Were you involved in a relationship?"

Ember blanched, reeling back from the question.

Slate stood abruptly, gaining everyone's attention. "I think she could use a break." His tone was supposed to come off as comforting, but even he could hear the overwhelming alarm in it. His gaze fell on Ember. She looked frazzled.

"That's okay, Elijah. I really just want to get this done. It's been a long morning." She squeezed and rubbed her temples with her thumb and middle finger.

Feeling slightly embarrassed, Slate nodded and sat back down, placing his forearms on the chair's armrests and trying to appear nonchalant. *Does Red have an attraction to Gabriel Dorian?* Jealousy coursed through him.

Ranger Matthews settled his attention back on Ember waiting for her to answer the question.

"No," she said, shaking her head slightly, "we weren't in a relationship. We were just acquaintances who happened to like the same coffee spot."

A rush of relief came over Slate, which was ridiculous. Ember wasn't his. Hell, she didn't even know he wanted her, had wanted her for as long as he could remember. Since the day he first laid eyes on the girl with the fiery red hair. His kindergarten crush. She never noticed he'd crushed on puppy-love and never moved past it.

He knew she didn't see herself in the same light as others. She was immune to her own beauty, seeing herself in some type of alternate universe where men didn't give a second glance whenever she walked into a room, which was the furthest thing from the truth. All the years seeing and labeling herself as a tomboy had somehow hidden her femininity from herself. Ember may have been a tomboy when she was twelve, but those days were long gone. Slate saw how other guys looked at her. How postures seemed to straighten and voices got a little deeper, more husky, when she walked into a room. Everyone saw it...well, everyone but Ember.

The motion of everyone standing shook him from his reverie. The interview was over and Ember looked relieved. Slate stood as Detective Washburn took a few steps towards the front door.

"Please, don't hesitate to contact either one of us if anything else comes to mind." Ranger Matthews said holding out his hand first to Ember and then to each of her parents.

"I told you just about all I know, but if anything comes to me..." she let the sentence trail off.

With that, Matthews, Washburn and Harrington exited the house.

Ember wrapped her arms around her middle as she leaned into her father's side. He held her, placing a kiss atop her head, and she nestled in a bit closer. Mitch's eyes met Slate's and he gave the slightest nod. His arms fell away from around his daughter and she was swept into a hug by her mother.

Slate excused himself, heading to the kitchen to talk with his team. The guys were in mid-discussion when he entered.

"Any information yet?" he asked quietly while coming around the table to Cypher's side, who had his laptop open, scouring the contents of the screen.

"Still digging, but Tex found some things I want to delve a little deeper into before I get ahead of myself," he said without his eyes leaving the screen.

"Were you able to get the security footage?"

Cy mockingly scoffed as if insulted. "Got it right away." He continued typing.

"He hasn't gone over it yet," King broke into the conversation, "but we'll brief back at HQ and hash out the information there." Then, before Slate could ask, King added, "There's got to be something other than just a random, accidental shooting at a range. Something's missing, not adding up."

Slate nodded in agreement, "My gut's screaming, I just don't know at what yet. Everyone and their brother has a gun in Texas and an accidental shooting is *rarely* accidental."

Around the table, the guys nodded in agreement.

"Gut's always right. If anyone's learned that, it's us. Never failed us on the battlefield," Trip said.

Arctic and King exchanged solemn glances, both knowing when they were ambushed as Deltas their guts knew something was amiss, though upper command ignored them and shit went sideways.

"Agree with you brother," T-BAR answered Trip. "Something's off."

"We'll find it. Just going to take some digging. Tex and I pulled background checks, credit scores, and bank records, both on Bazwar and Dorian. Usually financials give you a better picture of someone's personal life...better than interviewing their own mother. Debt, gambling, prostitutes aren't things privy to a mother, or even if they are, not something she'd likely disclose to strangers, but Big Brother will lead you down some pretty shady alleys."

All heads turned as Mitch walked into the kitchen.

"Susan and I are going to be heading out. Ember said she wanted to be alone right now." Then he added, "Not the advice I would suggest."

The men agreed.

"Was wondering if I could have a word with you, Eli?"

Slate nodded as the rest of the guys stood from their chairs.

"We'll see you at the office. No rush. We'll be on this the rest of the day; just come in when things settle down," King told Slate.

He nodded once and threw a chin lift at the rest of the team. They reciprocated.

Before the men could leave, Mitch stopped King with a light hand to his forearm. "Anything yet?"

"Not yet."

"On the trail?" Mitch looked King in the eye. Being former military, he knew King's experience was more than regular Army, and knew that Slate, being Delta, meant that King and the boys were more than mere soldiers.

"Marching the path." King returned.

Mitch nodded in a sign of appreciation and King nodded in return. They shared a mutual look of respect then King led his team through the kitchen and out the front door.

Mitch turned to Slate who stood a few feet away. "I need you to stay with Ember. The last thing she needs right now is to be alone...even if she thinks that's what's best."

Slate agreed one hundred percent. Even if her father hadn't brought up the suggestion, there was no way he was going to leave her alone.

"I agree."

"You know she's going to ask you to leave?"

Slate nodded.

"And then, demand that you leave?"

Slate nodded again.

"She's a stubborn one."

Slate nodded a third time.

"Must get that from her mother," Mitch said with a chuckle.

Slate chuckled, too. "I'm going to have to politely disagree with you, Pops. That trait is all your DNA."

Mitch nodded his head in agreement, then sobered. "Are you ever going to tell her?" He asked with knowing in his eyes.

Slate looked down at his feet and shifted from side to side.

"You've loved her for as long as I've known you, and that's a really long time."

Slate didn't look up.

"Sooner or later, you're either going to have to tell her, or you're going to have to let her go. I would hate for you to miss the opportunity when it's always been yours."

Slate lifted his gaze to Pop's. Opening his mouth, the words wouldn't seem to come. Mitch had been the father Slate thought he lost. He'd taught Slate to shave, drive, change a tire, and most importantly, how to treat a lady. Mitch's influence shaped Eli's decision to join the Army, entering the same branch as Pops. In the honor of his father, and Pops, he wanted to serve his country as well as his community.

"As military men, we're always looking for the sure thing. We have a plan A, and a plan B, C, D, and on, and on. But, you also know that sometimes we have to go with our gut," Mitch paused, "even if it scares the shit out of us. When the gut tells you to go, you go."

Slate knew he had a point.

"And," he added, putting a hand on Slate's shoulder, "you know as well as I do, we're not promised tomorrow. That goes the same in life and in love. Don't wait until tomorrow's passed and you're left wanting the opportunity back."

Slate was at a loss for words. Rarely was he ever speechless but getting this somewhat unconventional blessing from the man he'd looked up to his entire life, made a lump form in his throat.

"I would like grandchildren someday, and I can't hedge that bet on Rhys, or heaven help me, even worse...an unknown guy out there somewhere who probably eats kale, wears Birkenstocks, and weaves his own hemp shirts." Mitch shuddered.

The levity of the moment made both men laugh.

"You're a son to me, Eli. Let's just make it official sooner rather than later." He said it with a slap on Slate's shoulder as he turned to leave the room. He paused and over his shoulder he added, "Take care of my baby girl."

And he left.

CHAPTER 4

Eli steadied himself in the kitchen. Mitch's declaration had his thoughts rattled and he had to center himself before going to Ember. On one hand, he wanted to stride right into the living room, take Ember up in his arms, plaster his mouth to hers, and carry her off to the bedroom. It was all very, *Officer and a Gentleman*-ly, but he would *never* want to impersonate a *squid*.

Eli shuddered.

Delta's had their limits. Impersonating a seaman was a line in the sand.

But, on the other hand he wanted to tread lightly because she was in no state of mind to have him taking advantage of her vulnerability. He ran his hands over his face and short-cut beard, took a deep cleansing breath, then headed out of the kitchen into the living room but didn't see her.

Her home was small so he knew she couldn't have gone far. He'd been there a thousand times and he knew the layout. Heading down the short hallway, he looked into the bathroom as he passed. Seeing it vacant, he continued to the guest bedroom which was empty as well. He stopped at the end of the hallway. This room, however, he'd never been in. He stood outside her bedroom door and swallowed. Hard. Rapping lightly on the slightly ajar door, he pushed it open.

Ember was lying on her side, uncovered, in the middle of the queen-sized bed with her eyes closed. She didn't open them as he entered, nor did she say anything. Eli walked to the side of the bed and gently sat down. Her hands were under her pillow but as he sat one hand came out, reached down, and grasped his.

There it was. The sign that said she knew she was safe, that she wasn't alone.

For being in the friend zone, they held hands a lot. It wasn't a lovers' gesture, but it was a gesture of love. Eli thought back and could remember the first time he held the hand of the girl with the fiery red hair.

Kindergarten had just started, and he was transferred from an overcrowded classroom into Ember's classroom. He was shy and started to cry because he didn't know any of the other kids. He was alone again. A few boys started teasing and picking on him because of his tears. He tried to pull them back, but the taunting and teasing was endless and just too much for a little boy to take. He'd just lost his father, and his mother for the first time started to work, and he barely had time to spend with her. She worked the early shift as a baker at the City Bakery, and then worked the afternoon shift as a custodian at the hospital.

The boys circled around him and chanted, "Cry baby! Cry baby!" while rubbing their fists in front of their eyes, mocking him as he wiped the tears pouring down his cheeks.

Then out of nowhere a fury of fiery red hair stepped in front of him, reared back and punched the main instigator square in the nose. The boy fell backward, grasping his face and began to howl and cry. The mass of hair turned around...and there she was. Emmy. His Red.

Reaching out, she grasped his hand, linking her tiny fingers in his and walked past the other boys still standing there trying to figure out what happened as their friend lay crying on the floor. Looking back, that was probably the first time his heart knew he loved her. Of course, being five, *he* didn't know he loved her, but his heart sure knew. From that day forward, they held hands all the time. No one dared to make fun of them...seeing the end result of the last boy who teased. Ember and Eli were peas in a pod, clasped together by the hand.

~

With her eyes still closed, Ember said, "I thought you left, Elijah."

Eli held her hand and slowly rubbed her thumb with his.

"How'd you know it was me and not a crazed burglar?" he said with a chuckle.

"If you were a burglar, you wouldn't be sitting on my bed. And also, I can smell you."

Eli scrunched his brow and took in a deep breath trying to catch a waft of something rank or off-putting. He smelled nothing. "I showered," he said a bit defensively.

Ember gave a breathy giggle, "You don't stink. I can smell you."

Still confused, Eli replied, "Sorry, Red, not tracking."

Ember huffed and came up on her elbow. "I. Can. Smeelll. You! *You*. Your smell. I can smell it."

"Sooo, I smell." Eli said it more as a statement than a question.

"Yes."

"And what, per se, do I smell like? And, don't say 'you.'"

Ember smiled and scooted farther back on her mattress, then patted the empty space beside her. She said nothing, but Eli knew what she wanted. Hesitating, he lay down in the spot she just vacated. He could feel her body heat still trapped in the comforter beneath him. It radiated into his back. As wrong as it felt, he liked it, which unsettled him. His heartrate ticked up a notch...or five. He steeled himself, not wanting to show any signs of his heart slamming into his ribcage.

He could do this. *So, I'm lying in my friend's bed. Ember is my friend. That's cool. Just my friend...it's just Ember...not the girl I've been pining over for almost three decades. Play it cool, Ryan. Play it cool. Elijah Ryan and Ember Hayes...just friends...laying in a bed.*

Oh, who was he kidding? *I'm in Ember's bed!*

About to sit back up, Ember curled herself up into his side. He unconsciously lifted his arm and settled it behind her neck. She threw her leg overtop his and rested her cheek on his pec.

Eli tensed for just a second but caught himself. What should have been terrifying, felt...natural. His heart was still beating out of his chest, like a racehorse in the final stretch of the Kentucky derby, and he knew Ember could probably feel it through his t-shirt. But it felt right. Like an extension of holding hands.

Does she feel the same as me? Has she been pining for me as long as I have for her?

They had shared a kiss, once, back in high school. *Maybe she wants me, too, but is afraid to put the question into the universe. Should I ask her?*

His thoughts were running wild. His mouth opened to ask the question he was dying to ask, but Ember's voice filled the moment.

"Mmmm, this feels good." She settled herself into him. "I'm glad we are such good friends."

Friends. There it was. The answer to his question. Back to the friend zone. His heart deflated. *Friends.*

"So...you smell." Ember picked up the conversation from before the death-defying bed cuddle.

"You don't have to keep saying it," he quipped.

"But, you do." Eli could hear the smile in her voice.

"Liiiike?" He asked while drawing out the word.

"Like you. A man. Earthy. Clean. Powerful. Calm." Her voice softened, "Safe."

"I don't think some of those are smells?" He furrowed his brow with his questioning voice.

"Yes, they are."

"Um…" his furrow deepened.

"Most smells are linked to memories. They can be more powerful than sight or sound," she paused, "when you're near, I can smell my childhood."

Eli took in a heavy breath.

"I can smell the principal's office after I nailed Tommy Fleck in the nose in kindergarten," she chuckled. "I can smell the tree-house where you cut my hair after Becky Steltzer put chewing gum in it and I cried. I can smell the thunderstorm at the camp-ground, the first time my parents let us pitch our own tents, and I was so scared and snuck into yours in the middle of the night."

Eli smiled at the memory.

"I can smell the first car ride with you after I got my license. I can smell our first dance. Our graduation day. The first letter you sent to me during my basic training, where I was so homesick, I wanted to go AWOL." She took a long breath. "I can smell the day you returned from Iraq and told me your contract was up and you'd be closer to home. The list is endless, Eli."

Ember lay silent for a moment, "Every one of those smells, they're my safety...because they were all with you." She inhaled deeply, pulling this moment into memory. "I don't need eyes to know when you're near, Eli. A hundred people in a room and I could seek you out blindfolded. Believe me, Elijah, every smell is you."

He lay frozen, not wanting to break the reverence of the moment. Every memory was a moment that he could see clearly in his mind. Listening to her list off the moments they'd shared, he could smell them as well. And, that smell was now Ember. Never again would he be near her and not smell every moment they shared.

A slight snore came from Ember. With that last inhale of this moment, she must've fallen asleep. He knew he had to get back to his team but nothing was going to tear him away from this place. This memory. The moment he knew he was going to make Ember Hayes his.

Slate texted the guys to let them know he'd be back in the office in the morning, but he wanted to be kept informed of any revelations that surfaced. He trusted them wholeheartedly and knew they'd alert him the minute they knew something. But, right now this was where he had to be. He knew he could call Ember's sister, Rhys, to come stay with her, or her best friends Maven or Mary. Her parents would come back in a heartbeat if he called them, but he wanted to be the one there. He *needed* to be the one there. No way he was leaving her.

They lay snuggled together for a few hours. The adrenaline crash had come and taken its toll. Ember slept soundly and occasionally stirred, but stayed close to his side and clutched his tee in her fist every so often. He loved the feel of her body wrapped around his, their limbs entwined with one another. When she'd first snuggled into him, terror was his initial feeling, which melted into comfort, which immediately melded into home.

Yes, home. Ember was *his* home. And, he was *her* rock. The place *she* could always come back to. The place that kept *him* safe and grounded. *She* was his refuge. As *he* was hers. Both islands to unburden themselves. They'd shared a lifetime together. There weren't many times he could think back upon and not have Ember somehow woven, connected or intertwined in the memory.

Ember stirred in his arms, breaking his reflections, then bolted upright into a sitting position, gasping for breath and holding her chest. Her eyes landed on his, and he didn't see fear in them; he saw terror. Pure unadulterated terror. She frantically searched for her bearings, trying to find her ground.

"You're fine, Red. You're safe." Eli sat up, speaking in a stern, commanding but comforting voice.

Searching her surroundings, it took her a second to assess the situation and come back to herself. Her breathing evened out and her eyes searched his.

"That's it, Red. Come back to me. You're home. You're safe." He put his hand in hers and caressed her delicate fingers with his own. "Come back to me, Red," his voice low and soothing, beckoning her to come to safety. He tucked a tendril of her hair behind her ear.

"It's him." That's all she said, her chest not heaving as it was a minute ago.

"Who?" Eli questioned in a softer tone.

"I don't know."

Ember was searching her mind. Eli could see the mental torture she was experiencing, and all he wanted to do was sooth her and make everything alright.

"Bazwar. I know him."

"You know him? What do you mean, know him?" Eli was mentally logging every emotion crossing her face and every word she spoke, "As a customer?" he questioned.

"No," she shook her head, still searching her memory, "I've

never seen him at the range." She corrected herself. "Well, not until today."

Her mind was clearing. Eli could see the soldier inside her taking command. Decompartmentalizing the situation and examining every detail. Recalling facts and analyzing them. Ember the woman and Ember the soldier were one in the same, but when shit hit the fan, the warrior in her came out with a vengeance.

She stood from the bed and walked around to the back, pacing and concentrating deep in thought. She pinched her bottom lip with her thumb and forefinger, pulling it slightly, puckering it in frustration. "I've seen him. I've seen those eyes. The hate in them," she paused, grabbing a hank of her hair and twisting it around her finger, "the fear in them." She paused and took a few steps back in Eli's direction, the space between them still wide.

"The gym? The store?" Eli stood and threw out suggestions, but Ember ignored them as she searched for the memory. Recall was ace with Ember. She didn't have an eidetic memory like Cy, but it was pretty damn close. The girl could recall almost anything.

She stopped pacing. Her eyes focused on nothing while her mind was working, recreating, sensing the moment in her memory. She fiddled with her bottom lip, biting it and caressing it with the upper flesh.

Eli wanted to be that lip. *What the fuck! Not now.* What was he doing? Ember was in a moment of crisis and he was thinking with his dick. Calming himself, he looked away.

"I'm blank," she said in frustration, lifting her head and taking in Eli. "I'm never blank. Why can't I place him?" She caught his eyes when he shortened the gap between them, fright and frustration was one in her expression. "I've seen those eyes. I've seen them!" The last words were more of a soft plea than a hard fact statement.

Eli leaned into her and wrapped her into his arms, enveloping her against his steel chest. Bringing her into his body again was glorious. They'd hugged often and held each other in an embrace, but this was different. Was the surfacing of his feelings changing the dynamics between them? Would this spin their relationship beyond the friend zone, or would it demolish the structure between them and ruin their friendship?

He tamped down his thoughts, focusing on Emmy. She was his priority. He had to put Eli the man pining for the girl in his arms away, and bring out Slate, the Delta Force soldier, who could objectively help her figure out who Bazwar was. He needed to compartmentalize the situation; put his feelings in a box, shut it into a deep, dark closet, and slam the door. Lock it and hide the key. He had to keep his shit tight. Stifle his feelings. If or when the setting presented itself, he would seize the opportunity. Until then, the box wouldn't see the light of day.

CHAPTER 5

Ember stood in his embrace for what seemed like an eternity. An eternity Eli would gladly spend with her. Unconsciously swaying with her, Eli's mind went back to the first time they'd swayed like this. Back to a day he replayed often. The day he should have made Emmy his. Whenever *their song* played on the radio, Ember often brought up the memory, reliving the embarrassing story of her father's mischief, scheming, and ultimately what was unknown to her—the best, and worst, night of Eli's teenage years.

The past

It was prom night. Senior Prom to be exact. Ember was working in the barn, her chores were done, but she wanted to get a few more bales stacked to make the morning chores easier. She bent to pick up the next bale when she heard her father's approach.

"There's my baby girl," she could hear the love in his voice, and though she was seventeen, she loved that her daddy called her, *baby girl*.

She heaved the large bale up and over, settling it with a

heavy thud on the rising stack. Brushing her hands together and then wiping them on her dust-clad jeans, she turned to see her father with an ear-to-ear, Cheshire Cat grin across his face. *Oh, shit!* She knew that grin. She knew he was up to something, as the smile only shone when he had mischief planned.

It was the same smile he wore when Ember was ten and he taught her how to peel the tape off the Christmas presents to sneak a peek at what was inside. The secret to the *007* mission: her mom reused the wrapping paper from year to year, and with that being the case, it didn't matter if the paper got a little torn when peeling the tape. It could always be blamed on last year's frenzied excitement of unwrapping gifts. No one was the wiser and each year she and her daddy would bring Christmas early and open each gift whether it was theirs or not. Leave it to her dad to know their spying game wouldn't be discovered and would live on to be played each year. If her mom ever knew, she never told.

It was also the smile he wore when he let her play hooky from school and convinced her mom that *he'd* stay home with her and nurse her back to health. And by "nurse her back to health," he meant a day of fishing, taking the horses on trail rides, maybe ATVing across the pastures or just a day of daddy/daughter time lounging in PJs, eating junk food while watching reruns of *Walker Texas Ranger* or *Riflemen*, and hoping mom didn't come home unexpectedly.

Yup, she knew that grin. But the sinking feeling in her gut told her that she was *not* going to like what he had in store.

He walked closer. In his hand he held a large, flat, rectangular box. "Have a seat, honey." He motioned to the single layer of bales she hadn't stacked yet.

"What are you up to?" she asked slyly, pulling off her gloves and taking a seat.

He sat beside her and stared at the box a moment before looking over at her. "You know I love you, right?"

Oh, shit. That's not a good preface to a conversation.

"Yeeees," she said it, holding the word a bit longer for dramatic effect.

He paused. "I think I may have done you a disservice," he said while running his palm over the box.

"Let me guess, you're not my biological father." Ember joked to cut the seriousness of the moment. Her deadpan humor was a trait of her father.

"No...I mean *yes*. Yes, you are definitely my biological daughter. If not, I have a long-lost twin somewhere, because no one could have given you those baby blues except me. Every time I see them, it's a carbon copy of my own DNA," he said, chuckling under his breath.

"Well, mom *would* have a lot of explaining to do if these aren't yours." Ember fluttered her eyelashes at her dad, tilting her head as if to say *Look at these beauties!*

"Don't even joke. Your mother's off-limits when it comes to your sarcasm."

There was a silence in the air, and the seriousness was back. The mood hung thick in the air.

"What'cha need, Daddy?" Ember put her hand on her dad's knee and waited for him to gather his thoughts.

"I wanted a boy."

Ember furrowed her brow, tilting her head in question, and waited for her father to continue. "Go on..." she held onto the statement while trying to figure where he was going with this.

"When your mother and I found out she was pregnant with you, I knew, I *knew* I was going to have a son. Guaranteed! I just knew it. Someone to play ball with; someone who would like the same sports teams as me; a son who would be my shadow and grow up to be just like his old man." He paused a moment to catch his breath. "I wanted a son to fix cars, build things, ride on the ATVs. Someone to work right beside me in the hardware store and hopefully run it when I taught him all the things I knew and the day would come to pass it on to him. I wanted a protege, a legacy."

His voice slowed after the rambling of the long, drawn out declaration. He continued, "The moment I knew I was going to be a father, with a son of my own, I had big plans ahead."

"You're not making me feel very good dad...kinda feeling like a disappointment here." Ember said the words with sarcasm. "Is there a reason you're tearing my soul out?"

Not looking at Ember and speaking more to the ground, he gave a little chuckle, took a deep breath, and continued without answering her rhetorical question. "Every father wants a son. I don't know if it's primal, or just a man's psyche, but it's true. I wanted a boy, like my father and his father before him. Hayes Y chromosomes live on!" he said with a grin.

Ember cleared her throat and questioned, "You gotta a point?"

"The moment you were born, when they put you in my arms and you looked at me with my very own eyes, none of that mattered. Not one single thing I thought I needed mattered from that moment on." He smiled. "The love that I didn't know I was missing shattered all the things I thought I wanted."

He went on. "I knew that I would do *anything* for you. You had my heart from that day and every day since. You had me wrapped around your finger as tight as I was wrapped around yours." His smile lit his face as he looked over and saw Ember smiling back. She felt moisture in her eyes and blinked it back. "And, I did get my *boy*, just not in the packaging I thought it would come in." He bumped Ember with his shoulder and she laughed at his lame dad joke.

"So, where's this going, and why are you monologuing the story of my disappointing gestation?"

"My point," he paused, looking over, getting her full attention, "is I raised you just like I would have if you were a boy. Didn't matter you were a girl, you were my shadow. Everywhere. Couldn't even go to the bathroom without you waiting on the other side of the door." He shook his head, "You love the same sports as me; you love the outdoors as much as your old man; you're an amazing marksman," he corrected himself, "marks-*woman*."

"Thank you," Ember interjected, noting her father's faux pas.

He went on, "You hunted and camped...worked beside me, absorbed everything hardware and you're only seventeen."

"Does this mean you're giving me a raise?" she quipped half-jokingly.

"A lot more to learn, little lady." He raised one eyebrow while giving her a stern look.

Ember mimicked her father, mirroring him by raising the opposite brow at him.

"Anyway, all these years, I taught you like you were a boy…"

"Ah—"

He cut her off, "*Not* saying girls can't do these things, but in the years that you were imitating me, I never gave you the tools to be a 'girl.'" He made quotation marks in the air with his fingers.

"Look, I love that you're a miniature me. Not sure how happy your mother is with that, but that's not the point. But, it's oddly satisfying to see myself in female form…"

Ember raised the same eyebrow to her father in question of his possible Freudian slip. "Something you want to tell me, Dad?" She said in consternation.

"There, right there, that's what I mean. Female body, projecting me." They broke out into a fury of laughter, slowly catching their composure. "My point," he went on, "as a dad, I couldn't be prouder of you. But, there are some things in a young woman's life that need to be experienced."

"Such as?"

Her father thought for a moment and said, "Learning to put on make-up."

"Hate that, not doing that, next," she said with a deadpan face.

"Um…" he searched his thoughts, "buying their first bra."

Ember hooked her thumb under the neck of her sweat-stained tee and beneath the strap of her sports bra, pulling it upward, exposing it. "Got it covered."

"First date…"

Ember fell silent.

"First kiss…"

She looked away from her father and off into the distance of the dimly-lit barn.

"First time she brings home a date, and a father gets to put the fear of God into the young man that dares to approach his princess with the desire of deflowering on his mind."

"*Dad!*" Ember slapped his arm and blushed as red as her hair.

Softening his tone, he said, "A girl's last high school dance."

Ember tipped her head, schooling her father. "You know I'm not going."

Her father didn't say a word, but handed her the box.

"Dad? What is this?" she asked while looking at the box.

"Open."

She inhaled deeply, rolled her eyes and took the box with trepidation.

"Dad..." The word, more a whisper than a sound.

Her dad waited her out, anticipating her opening the box.

Blinking her eyes closed and shaking her head, she slowly removed the lid. Removing the tissue paper, she paused a moment seeing what lay inside. She threw her head back, looking at the barn rafters, and let out a single word. "Da-aa-ad!" She gave a fake, breathy, three-shudder breath, shaking her shoulders for full effect. "Dad, *no*...why? What is this?" she pleaded.

Her dad waited for her theatrics to dwindle before answering, "Humor me. Go inside, clean up, and put on the dress."

"No, Dad. I'm not going to some stupid prom." She looked down at the light pink dress, "And, *pink*! Really?"

"Ember." He waited until her eyes met his. "Please, for me. Please."

Ember saw the pleading in his eyes though he didn't show it in his voice. She shook her head and looked back down at the pink nightmare laying in the box. "I'm not going to the prom."

Her dad sat silent.

"I'll humor you, old man," she shook her head back and forth slightly, "but, promise, I won't have to go to the stupid school dance. *Promise.*" The last word was a stern plea. She held out her pinky which her father wrapped around his and they shook on it, just like the pinky promises he made with her as a child.

"Wrapped around my finger," her dad said with a grin and tightened his pinky around hers.

With that, Ember stood, hoisting the box under her arm with no finesse and headed out the barn doors towards the house.

Mitch watched her leave, and when she was out of sight, he

laid his head in his hands and breathed a sigh of relief. He needed to give her this moment. Even if it meant she was kicking and screaming the entire way.

~

After taking the world's quickest shower, Ember stepped into the floor-length, formfitting dress. It hugged the developing womanly curves of her youthful body quite nicely. It was the lightest hue of pink—more of a crepe pink, than a *pink*-pink. Nothing that would make her want to vomit, so it was doable.

In all truthfulness, Ember was kind of hoping to go to this dance, her Senior Prom, a milestone of high school most got to experience. But, of course, she was non-existent to the boys in her grade. None of them paid her any attention.

Not true. She corrected her thoughts. Elijah was the only boy on the planet who knew she existed, probably the only one in the universe, and she was hoping he would've asked her to the prom. But, he had to work and wouldn't be able to go even if he wanted. He worked constantly, taking any hours he could get, always asking her father for extra shifts his co-workers didn't want. Ember knew he was most likely saving for college, and he helped his mom with the bills even though she, too, worked at the hardware store. But, he didn't want his mom to have to scrape by to make ends meet, so he helped her every chance he got. Not only financially, but fixing her clunker of a car, doing chores around the house, yard work, running her errands. He was the man of the house before he was eighteen.

Ember fingered the bodice of the dress and looked at her reflection in the mirror. This was the girliest she could remember seeing herself. God's honest truth, she really liked the color—it actually complemented her hair instead of contrasting with it as was the case with almost any color palette she wore. She pulled the elastic tie from her hair's messy bun. She kept her hair up in the shower, not wanting to have her masses get wet. The fiery curls cascaded over her shoulders and around her face, framing it, making the paleness of her ivory skin seem a bit more rosy. She would do the dress but would draw the line on make-up. Make-up and girly-girl was her sister Rhys' thing. Ember didn't do makeup, and she'd refuse if that was her father's next request.

She turned in the mirror to see the back of the dress. The smooth material clung to her ass. An ass Ember wasn't aware she possessed. It was always buried beneath denim or sweatpants. Not exactly flattering and accentuating to her derriere.

Also, inside the box, she'd found a strapless bra and matching lacy panties. Her boobs were a little too full to go braless and her black sports bra was not going to cut it with the cut and straps on the bodice. Reluctantly, she had to wear the new one. And when she slipped on the lacy panties, she despised the instant wedgie it gave her.

Feeling as ready as she was ever going to be, she left the bathroom in search of her humiliating doom of modeling the dress for her parents. Luckily, Rhys had already left for the dance, so Ember was thankful she wouldn't have to endure her sister's incessant ridicule of all the fashion faux pas she was committing. She loved her younger sister—the two were surprisingly close— but Rhys was over the top and a drama queen. Ember thought of her as valley-girl-meets-the-Kardashians. Heaven help the poor sap who ended up with her. Ember shivered at the thought of the poor man.

She navigated the stairs, lifting the dress knee-high and unlady-like to make sure she didn't fall ass-over-tea-kettle down the steps. Although, if she did take a dive down the staircase, maybe it would get her out of having to parade the stupid thing. As tempting as it was, she carefully continued her descent of the stairs.

Entering the living room, her mother rose at the sight of her with a hand cupped over her mouth as she inhaled sharply. Her dad sat stoic, his eyes taking her in from head to toe. She was sure she wasn't striking the correct pose as she stood, posture slumped like Quasimodo, and her arms dangling at her sides. More in the likeness of a wet cat than a prima donna.

Her mother came to her and Ember was afraid her mom was going to burst into tears. "You look stunning, Ember," she said in a tone on the verge of cracking, "absolutely stunning. Turn." She motioned with her finger, circling it in the air.

Ember complied, turning in the most ungraceful circle, continuing the dog-and-pony show.

"So pretty." Then her mom scampered out of the room saying, "Shoes. Gotta get the shoes."

Ember turned to her father, who was still sitting, and mouthed the word *Shoes?* His eyes were still soaking her in. "Dad, I don't need shoes. I'm not leaving this house." Her voice was serious and tinged with a bit of anger.

Mitch stood in one smooth motion and slowly approached his firstborn. No words were said; he just drank her in. Putting both hands on her nearly bare shoulders, he closed his eyes and tipped his forehead to hers. She stood in silence giving this moment to him. Without lifting his head, he whispered, "You're beautiful, baby girl. Nothing but absolute beauty."

Ember felt the rush of tingles in her nose and behind her eyes. She wasn't a crier, but this moment, with her daddy, could have opened floodgates if she allowed it. He pulled back and placed a chaste kiss on her forehead, lingering a bit longer than necessary.

"Daddy? You're making this really awkward. Even more awkward than the awkward it was to begin with."

She could feel her father's smile against the crown of her forehead.

"Thank you, baby girl, for giving this moment to your old man."

Ember blinked away the moisture pooling in her eyes.

"Shoes, I got shoes!" Her mom entering the room broke the awkwardness Ember was experiencing.

Her mother laid a pair of low-heeled, white satin shoes at her feet and Ember stepped into them, thankful they weren't the skyscrapers Rhys wore. Sprained ankles weren't in her forecast. Ember stood, not sure of the purpose of the whole show, when her mom pumped a tube of mascara in front of her, holding the wand out to Ember's eyelashes.

"Mom! No. No make-up." She looked over to her dad and saw the plea in his expression. Surrendering in defeat, she fluttered her lashes at her mom and endured the torturous primping. Before she could step back though, her mom swept a brush across her cheeks, painting them as well.

"Okay, enough!" Ember said stepping back, careful not to trip on her dress.

"Okay. Okay. I'm done." Her mom waved her hands, "I'm done." Ember didn't think she could endure any more. "You look beautiful, sweetie," her mom said as she held up a hair clip and gave her daughter a hangdog look.

"Fine," she said with a huff, and her mother pinned up one side of her red locks.

Her mom stepped to the side and sprayed a mist of perfume in the air above Ember's head, and the light fragrance danced down over her body. Ember gave a stink-eyed glare and her mother sweetly smiled back at her.

Mitch joined their little huddle. "Stunning. Absolutely stunning. My two favorite girls in the world." He wrapped them both in his embrace.

"What about Rhys, dad?" Ember asked, knowing she was calling him out.

He chuckled, "I mean, my two favorite girls in *this* room." Ember laughed when her mom gave him a disdainful glare.

The doorbell peeled throughout the house, and her parents gave each other a knowing look. The Cheshire grin made another appearance. *Oh shit!* Ember felt a jolt of panic course through her. No way was she going to the stupid prom.

From the living room, she heard the front door open and shut in the foyer. Whoever it was just let themselves in. She was about to voice her defiance when her body went stiff and her jaw went slack.

Standing in front of her was Eli. He was dressed in a black suit, coat buttoned at the waist, complete with a crepe-colored bow tie that matched the pink of her dress. His hair looked freshly cut and his short beard trimmed tight and neatly groomed. For an eighteen-year-old, he grew a sexy-as-fuck beard. He was gorgeous! Knock-down, wet-your-panties gorgeous. The full grin on his face slowly fell when he took in the sight of her. The shock of seeing him rose to self-consciousness, as she tried to figure out what made his smile flatten. She pressed her hands to her stomach, flattening the material under her palms, and then skimmed the waistline down the sides of her hips and then down the lengths of her upper thighs.

Her parents left the room, her dad slapping Eli on the shoulder as he ushered Susan in front of him, and it was now just them. Eli and Ember. She stood awkwardly, imagining her self-consciousness was easy to read.

He closed the gap between them, gently putting a hand on her jaw and lightly caressing her cheekbone. "You look beautiful, Emmy," he said, staring into her eyes and giving one more swipe of his thumb, then lowering his hand.

"Emmy? You haven't called me that since grade school." Her cheeks deepened with a faint blush.

"I guess it just popped out. Didn't even think about it." He fumbled, "Here, these are for you." He handed her a freshly picked bouquet of wildflowers, some still with their roots and dirt dangling from them. "Sorry, they're not the prettiest things, but I forgot a corsage...and I didn't have time to stop and get you flowers, so...yeah...I picked them in the field before I came in." He gave a little one-shoulder shrug. "They're actually pretty sad." He reached for them with embarrassment to take them back.

"No!" she said, pulling the bouquet out of his reach, her voice a little more forceful than she meant, "I think they're precious," her tone quieted, "they're beautiful."

And they were beautiful, roots and all. Anyone could buy a dozen roses or an expensive bouquet, but Eli took the time to gather these, even if it was spur of the moment, because he knew she'd like them. They were the most precious thing anyone had ever given to her.

Her mom rushed back into the room, digital camera in hand, "Almost forgot, gotta get a picture!" Her exuberant happiness and glee were a bit too cheery for Ember.

"Mom!" Ember whined. "Really?"

"I promised Elijah's mom I'd get a picture." Her dad tried to feign an *I'm sorry* look, but his stifled grin betrayed him. He was loving this.

"*One* picture. And don't show any of your friends!"

"Geez, a mother can't have any fun, can she?"

"Not at my expense." Ember volleyed back.

Her mother took pictures, *a lot of* pictures. As many as Ember assumed were taken at a Hollywood movie premier. The type where the actors are blinded by a barrage of flashes...Yes, that many pictures.

"Okay, that's enough," her father said, as her mom took one more. "Leave the kids be."

Ember's eyes met her father's and she silently thanked him.

"Have a nice night, kids." Her father nearly pushed her mother out of the room, and Ember stood in mortification.

"Well, that went well." Eli laughed.

"That's your definition of *well?*"

"Could have been worse."

Ember shamelessly shook her head. "Yeah, the house could have started on fire, and we all could have perished in a fiery death. That would have been about the same."

Eli laughed at her over-the-top comparison. "I'm actually glad she got so many pictures. I can't wait to get copies."

Ember's heart bloomed and she too couldn't wait to see them.

"Shall we go?" Eli motioned his hand towards the foyer, and Ember's eyes rounded.

"Go where? I'm not going to the school. Please, say we're not going to the school." The fear rose in her voice.

"Nope." With his voice softened and leaning into her ear, he spoke softly, "We're going somewhere way better."

"Where?"

Eli lifted one brow and took her hand in his, lacing their fingers, a gesture Ember loved. It settled her nerves. She trusted him implicitly, so she followed him out the door into the unusually warm springtime night.

CHAPTER 6

The past

Eli opened the door of his truck and helped Ember into the cab. Usually, she just jumped up onto the seat, but the task was a bit more difficult and daunting in the formfitting dress. As she raised her foot onto the running board, the slit running up the side of her dress exposed her pale ivory thigh and Eli had to hold back the gulp that lodged in his throat. Ember was unaware she was making this menial task of getting into his truck a major boner show. If Eli wasn't able to tamp down his raging libido quickly, it was going to be a real embarrassing night.

Before tonight, she was still the girl who liked *boy* things. Playing in the dirt, catching frogs and swimming in the creek on a hot summer's day after fishing from its banks. Camping, hunting, bikes, skateboards and fast cars. She could fix damn near anything. Girl knew more about hardware, plumbing and Do-It-Yourself projects than half the men in rural-town Texas. Though she still loved all those things, she never realized, somewhere along the way, that tomboy grew into a pretty young girl and then into a stunningly, gorgeous lady. It was a pity she never knew how he loved her through all those stages.

The minute he'd taken in the sight of her in the house, Eli

had stepped forward, closing the distance between them, oblivious to anyone else in the room but her. She was magnificent. Strikingly beautiful. Sophisticated.

The simpleness of the dress set off her curves, and her hair, falling in tendrils framing her face and pulled back to one side, was a sight that Eli burned into his mind. Never again would he be able to unsee this gorgeous girl...no, not a girl...she was a young lady. All woman.

Eli had never seen a more beautiful sight in his life. It was a bit of a shock to see the tomboy he grew up with transformed into this beauty with just the simplicity of so little. So little, that was so much. She didn't need a face full of make-up or an over-the-top dress to make a stunning statement. He knew it was the same Emmy in front of him, his best friend, but the femininity standing there was Emmy 2.0.

Ember situated herself in the seat and Eli shut the door, thanking God that the PG-rated peep show was over. He walked around the front of the truck and hopped in, settling onto the bench seat, gave the ignition a start, and the engine came to life with a roar.

"Where're we going?" Ember asked again.

Eli just turned to her, grinned, put the truck into gear and pulled forward. But, he didn't head out on the driveway. Instead, he pulled the truck around back behind the house, through the expanse of prairie grass, and up along the side of the barn. He shut down the engine and turned to Ember.

Reaching across the seat, he laced his fingers with hers. "I know you didn't want to go to the prom, but I really wanted to take you. Actually, I was dying to take you, but I would never ask you to do anything that makes you uncomfortable." He paused, thinking about his next words. "We've shared everything, Emmy. Everything from kindergarten to now has been experienced with you. Every field trip, every camping and hunting trip, even the skiing trip when I broke my leg. You stayed with me until our parents came and then you refused to leave when I had to stay the night in the hospital." He chuckled at the memory. "We've always been together. Next is going to be graduation and then we're off to new adventures. Even the same college. I want to do everything with you, Ember. That day will be here before we know it, so before that happens, I need to have this night with you." His eyes were laser focused on hers, and he swore he could see into the depths of her soul. "Please, Emmy, do this with me. Dance with me. I need this moment with you."

~

Ember sat speechless. This was Eli. Her best friend. It was true; every moment she could recall had been with him. She realized she needed this moment with him as much as he needed it with her.

"Yes, Elijah. I'll dance with you."

That was all he needed before opening his door, making his way around the truck then opening her door, hand held out, to help her down.

They walked hand-in-hand to the barn, and Eli slid the heavy door open. Ember looked inside and saw that he must've set things up prior to coming inside the house. White twinkling Christmas lights hung haphazardly from the rafters as if strung in a hurry. A lantern sat on the ground between two hay bales. An ice cream pail filled with ice held a variety of children's juice pouches, and a plate with grapes, strawberries and cheese with an assortment of chips sat on a paper plate under a covering of cellophane. A small radio, set to a country station, also sat on the same bale. Ember giggled at the makeshift prom setting.

"Had to compromise on a tight budget," he said, reading her expression.

"I love it!" Not one false word left her lips.

He shrugged and led her over to a vacant hay bale.

"Would you care for some punch, m'lady?" Eli said, gesturing to the makeshift ice bucket, imitating a horrendous French accent.

"Why, thank you, kind sir. That'd be absolutely mav'ulos!" Ember used her strongest southern drawl, laying it on thick.

He pulled out a juice pouch and stabbed the straw through the silver foil packaging, and presented it to Ember over the length of his forearm like a maître d'. "Only the finest for you," and they both laughed.

"I thought you had to work?" Ember questioned while taking a sip off the tiny straw.

"I did, but I have some pull with the boss." He winked at her then punctured the straw into his own juice pouch.

"Really?" She pulled her head back, feigning surprise.

"Ends up, when you tell the boss you want to take his daughter to her own personal prom, he looks very favorably on you." Eli reached over and uncovered the paper plate, "Hors d'oeuvre?" He offered the plate of sad appetizers.

Ember took a few grapes and popped them in her mouth. "So, you did this all yourself?" she asked, taking in the setting.

Well, I did get some help from your mom," he said as he pointed to her dress. And, your dad took me to his tailor and hooked me up with this." He pulled the lapel of his jacket. "He even taught me to tie a real bow tie. Said every man should tie his own; never use one of those pre-tied adjustable ones."

"Well, you're very dapper, Mr. Ryan." Ember smiled while looking him over.

Eli grinned, then took Ember in once again, from head to toe. "You look absolutely beautiful tonight, Emmy. I mean, you're beautiful all the time, but tonight, you look," he paused, "like the prettiest thing on earth."

The moment hung between them, neither saying anything to break the splendor of the confession. Ember wasn't sure how long they sat there staring at one another—could have been seconds, maybe hours—but Eli broke the moment when he stood and walked over to the radio, turned up the volume, and sent the speaker into the beginning guitar riffs of Brad Paisley's "She's Everything." Turning, he held out his hand to Ember and asked, "Dance with me?"

She rose, wiping her backside free of stray hay and took his hand in hers. Eli pulled her into his body and she went willingly. He held her right hand in his left and his other hand wrapped around her waist, skimming her lower back, almost resting on the top of her lace panties beneath her dress. She was now grateful for the skimpy scrap of material, because she knew her everyday casual underwear would be granny-panties compared to the light lace, and he would've definitely felt those bloomers through the thin material of the dress.

She laid her head against his chest, hearing his heartbeat beneath her cheek. It was strong and beat out a rhythm that soothed her soul. Eli tipped his head and slowly inhaled, taking in the scent of her hair. It was all Ember. He wished he could bottle it and that way she would always be with him.

Slowly, they swayed to the song, Eli sang softly and every word of the song was felt in his heart. He wanted to tell her that every note of this song was for her and that she was his everything. She was everything to him.

The song drew down, but they stood still in each other's arms, caught in the depths of the other's gaze. They were standing so close. Eli tucked a tendril of fiery red hair behind her ear, the escaped curls embodied an emblazoned halo around her head. He gently brushed his thumb over her cheek. Just grazing her skin, sending tingles over her body, and she felt the hair on her arms come to life. His hands cupped her face, gently, lightly, with a barely-there touch. Then, hesitantly, Eli leaned forward. Slowly. Intimately. Reverently.

Inhaling through her nose, Ember smelled a hint of the spiciness of his cologne and the scent that was all Eli. Her heart beat erratically and her breath shuddered in her lungs. Their lips parted, and slowly, their mouths met. Her top lip over his; his suckling her bottom. Slowly, tentatively, just a single kiss. Time came to a stop. The cosmos stood still.

They each pulled back, barely, with their lips slightly agape, but lingering close enough to feel each other's presence. Their lips brushed again and parted once more. Without hesitation, their tongues intertwined. Their lips molded and tongues danced. He deepened the kiss, pulling her into his soul, further into the depths he thought he'd never explore.

It was her first kiss. She'd waited for this and it was more than she ever could've imagined. The taste of his lips washed across her palate. There was no floor; there was no ceiling, just them. Two souls crashing together as if pulled by some force of nature, pushing them, ravishing them into the throws of passion.

Ember felt herself shimmering in the afterglow of what neither of them expected, yet felt so natural. Inevitable.

What am I doing? Is this really happening? This is Eli. This. Is. Eli. I'm kissing Eli? OMG, this is weird. Eli's like my brother. Am I kissing my brother? Oh, God! This needs to stop!

Hesitation ensued. Eli was waiting for her to recoil, but she stayed in his arms. This is what he waited for, what he'd imagined in his dreams. She gave as good as she got. He was kissing Emmy, his Red. He loved her. Down to the marrow of his bones, he knew Ember Hayes was his. His past. His present. His future. There was no turning back. Be it the gods, or fates, or karma or whatever spiritual pull was in the universe, he was kissing his forever!

Then Ember pulled back with such force, she almost lost her balance, surprising Eli

"We can't do this Elijah," she said with heavy breaths, her hand going to her lips feeling the swell of their kiss. She started to pace away from him, but he stopped her with a hand on her upper arm.

"Emmy, wait. Wha—"

"You're my friend Eli, my best friend. We can't do this. I don't feel that way about you." Her words came out on heaving breaths.

Cold. Water.

Her words drenched his soul. Blanketing him, shivering to his core.

"I mean I love you in a brotherly/sisterly way." She tried to laugh off the moment, but it fell short. "I mean, come on, Eli. You're like my brother," she paused for a moment oblivious to the destruction she was laying on him. "Like you said earlier, we've grown up together. We've known each other since kindergarten. We're not," she pointed back and forth between them, "this."

So, there it was. The truth Eli didn't want to face. The truth that Ember and Eli were just that.

Ember. And. Eli.

There would never be an *us* with them. He was relegated forever to the friend zone. A truth that tore his being. He internally steeled himself, not wanting to show his vulnerability, when in truth, he wanted to wail away at the cruelty of it all. Show how much her words were tearing his soul, the very soul that would always belong to her, though she would never claim possession of it.

Eli heard the nervous tremble in her laughter. Not wanting her to feel embarrassed, he joined in the denial, though each word was a dagger to his heart.

"No...No, yeah, you're right. I'm sorry about that." He rubbed the back of his neck, one of his nervous ticks. "I...we, ah, yeah...we never should have done that." He laughed a breathy laugh, hating himself with every word.

"Right? That's just crazy." Ember's mood lightened, though the nervousness was still there. "Please, Elijah, tell me you don't hate me."

The shocking question took him by surprise. "Why would I hate you?" he asked, shaking his head in disagreement.

"I don't know. I guess...I...um."

He waited to hear her reasoning. What would make her think he could ever hate her?

"I guess, I don't want you to be mad."

His next words made him sick, but he had to give them to her, if anything, to get her off the hook of any guilt she was putting on herself. "Em, don't worry. I'm not mad. It was a mistake. Guess we just got caught up in the moment. I mean," he swallowed the bile creeping up with each word, "that kiss...it didn't mean anything."

He could physically see the relief come over her and her shoulders fell as she chuckled, getting the pent up nerves out. "Yeah, not like you haven't kissed lots of girls before."

It wasn't a lie, he had kissed girls before, not a lot, but he had his fair share of girls he dated, but none even came close to the explosiveness of the kiss he shared with her. And, he knew none would ever come close to it again. The lies were killing him, but he would say them if it meant it would soothe her conscience.

"Yeah, lots of kisses. Like I said, just got caught up in the moment." The constant rubbing of his neck quelled the shivers crawling up his spine. He hated himself for even venturing into the realm that was Ember Hayes. The dynamics were forever changed, and he knew that path to calling her his was never going to change. She didn't see him in the same light. But, he vowed, Ember Hayes would own his heart until his dying day, until he breathed his last breath. He couldn't live with her, so he would figure a way to live without her. Even if it killed him to set her free.

She let out the breath she was holding. "We'll probably look back and laugh at this moment. It'll be hilarious. One of the stupid moments of regret." She laughed.

There would be regret all right. His regret. The regret that the only girl he loved, didn't love him back.

CHAPTER 7

Present day

"So, he's lawyering up? What the fuck!" Slate paced the office floor, piss and vinegar running through his veins. After the morning he spent with Ember, he was not taking this situation lightly. "What kinda lawyer defends a piece of shit like that?" He turned and faced the group of men sitting around the conference table. "I'm all for innocent 'til proven guilty but this," he made an open hand gesture with both his hands, "this case is cut and dry. He walks in, goes to the range, sets up next to the guy, then turns and shoots him. Double-tap." Slate rubbed the back of his neck and then drew his hands down his face.

"Just 'cuz he's lawyered, doesn't mean he'll get off. Justice takes time and more time means we have more time to dig," Cypher said, looking up from his computer.

"Justice is better served in the dark hours of night," Slate said under his breath as he picked up a bottle of water and drank half of it down.

"That's not what we do!" King said standing up straighter, one palm still leaning atop the table. He marked Slate with a hard stare. "We aren't vigilantes. We work within the confines of the law."

"Well maybe we shou—"

King cut him off giving a swift jab of his finger in his direction, "You need to take a walk!" His eyes told Slate he was at his tipping point. "I know you're pissed, hell, we all are, but your bullshit attitude isn't helping." King pointed to the door, "Walk it off, come back in ten." He pinned him with his stare, telling Slate he'd better take the walk.

Slate drank down the rest of the water, all the while not taking his eyes from King. He was pushing his luck because King was a take-no-bullshit-from-no-one kind of guy, and it didn't matter if you were friend or foe. If Slate wanted to rumble, King would be the last guy he'd want to go a round with, but he'd take his chances. Tossing the empty bottle into the recycle bin, Slate headed out the door.

"Who pissed in his Wheaties?" Trip questioned with a laugh, swiveling his chair to face King.

"Damn, I know it's his woman, but guy's gotta chill." Arctic chimed in. "For all we know, this could just be a crazy, with a gun and a delusion, trying to get headlines on the news. I mean, half the time we hear about shooting incidents it's 'cuz some whack job wants infamy."

King stood to his six-foot-two height, rubbing the tattoos on his forearm, the tattoos that hid the hideous scars of the mangled mess his arm once was. "Nah, this isn't a call for infamy," He pondered his thought while stroking down the length of his beard, "this is just cold-blooded murder. We just need to find the *why*."

The *why* was always the hard part. Execution of a mission, that was the easy part. Get in, get the bad guy and get out.

Simple. Easy-peasey.

Most times, the *why* was already a given when missions were sanctioned through Homeland Security or some other alphabet agency. People above Hellforce's pay grade already knew the who, what, where, when and why, they just needed the boogiemen to finish the deed for them. Go into places the US military couldn't.

Although the team dealt with a number of security needs, K & R was their forte. The number of people who went missing, got abducted, kidnapped and/or held for ransom was astounding. The average person had no clue what a common occurrence it actually was or how often it happened. When law enforcement was under-staffed, underfunded and overwhelmed, that's when people turned to the private security firm. The boys of Hellforce weren't in the yellow pages, you couldn't Google them or even look them up on Facebook. Hellforce was a company that worked in the shadows.

Most of their clientele came from law enforcement or other agencies who contacted King. He had discretion over what cases they took. King weeded through the files and took the most desperate ones. K & R was the most common case. Kidnapped victims taken to a shithole, third world country had very little if any chance of ever seeing their home soil again. Women and children sold into sex slavery happened more often than people fathomed. It was out of the hands of local and state law enforce-ment, and the feds had so much red tape that resources allocated to them were often wasted on paperwork and time constraints. No, Hellforce was more of a "get in, get out, silent night warriors," and no one was the wiser.

And, Hellforce was known far and wide to get the job done. No terrorist, sex trafficker or other scum-of-the-earth wanted to look in their closet, or under their bed, and find Hellforce. Nope, being boogiemen was where Hellforce reigned. They were one of the most sought out elite private security firms.

T-BAR, rolling a stress ball between his hands, also turned his chair to face King, "So, what do we know so far? The security vid shows Dorian walks in at eight-seventeen a.m., shoots a few rounds, doing his thing, is clearly focused on his own tasks, paying no mind to anything else around him."

"That was his first mistake. Dude had his music bluetoothed into his CAPS, had no clue of his surroundings," Arctic added.

"Like we say in the field, 'Dumb will getcha dead,'" Cypher said.

All eyes landed on T-BAR.

"Fuck off, all of you!" he addressed his new found audience. "I got my shit tight," he pointed around the table, "I've saved your sorry asses a lot! You all should be thanking me for my bravery and courage. Slap that medal and tab right here." He slapped his hand over his left pec.

"Yeah, medal for douchery valor and half-thought, crack-pot ideas. Sure, I'd pin that shit on you all day!" Trip quipped.

T-BAR threw his pen at Trip, who caught it in midair. Both brothers smirked at each other, playing off the banter.

Cypher leaned back in his chair, abandoning his laptop, and squared off with T-BAR. "Explain your moniker."

T-BAR side-eyed his friend.

"Go ahead, speak to the class. What's your brave and courageous nick?"

"Maybe he's wearing stolen valor? Wearing that brave and courageous moniker without living up to its high expectations." The guys laughed at Trip's jab.

King shook his head at the idiocy of the men he called brothers. Just like any brothers, the jabs and ridicule were endless. Especially with this group of guys who weren't bonded by natural blood, but bonded by blood, sweat and tears of brotherhood. Being the boss was hard at times because it also meant being the "parent" of adolescent assholes.

"Cut the bullshit," King stood upright and crossed his arms. "T-BAR, we all know you ain't right. Somehow, somewhere along the line you got your head whacked too hard too many times and things are just rattlin' 'round up there, half-firin' and your logic takes a hit and suffers."

He was interrupted by Trip. "Yeah, who else in their right mind would tackle an S vest, wrestle for the detonator, all the while hobbling on a fractured femur? It's literally a one-legged man in an ass-kicking contest." With the exception of T, the group broke out into hysterics. Even King threw his head back and roared.

"Again, saved all your sorry asses!" he said as he pointed out each man around the table. "Pin that shit right here." He continuously tapped his pec.

"That-Boy-Ain't-Right, Bronze star, coming up." Trip quipped with snark.

T-BAR stared down his friend, "Sure the fuck ain't pinning

any Bronze stars on your plate, *Trip*!" The name was said with emphasis, all the guys busting out in laughter even more.

"Hey, it didn't go off, so I saved all *your* sorry asses on that one."

"Tripping over a tripwire when *you're* EOD, now that's a fucked-up way to get a name for life." Arctic bellowed, "never gonna change that bitch!"

Trip had tried to get his moniker changed many times, without success. His original nickname was Ripper. Badass. Trip had no qualms about ripping the life and souls out of the world's worst pieces of shit that abused, used, raped and killed innocent women and children. But, ever since he tripped over that damn tripwire, the guys started calling him Tripper, which over the years got shortened to Trip. Some days, he jokingly wondered if it would've been better that the wire would have tripped than to take one more day of the guys ribbing.

"This is the life I've chosen?" King muttered, as he tried to rein in his disorderly children. "Enough, play nice. Fuck-off time's over. Heads back in the game," King said, trying to stifle a grin.

Just like a petulant child, Trip threw his empty water bottle at T-BAR.

King gave him a glare and asked in all seriousness, "You need a time-out or go over my knee, son?" On the last word, King let out a laugh.

"Sorry, Dad." Trip gave the apology in a sullen teenager voice.

Slate walked in and all heads turned.

"You good?" King questioned.

"Five-by-five." Slate answered, taking the vacant chair next to Cypher.

"Dad yelled at us," Trip loudly whispered, so they all could hear.

"I swear, Trip, I will take you behind the woodshed and tan your ass. Beat that smartass snark right out of you."

Trip avoided eye contact with King and busied himself with the pen and paper in front of him.

"'S'what I thought." King got the final word which meant they were getting back to business, but no one missed the smile that crossed King's face. Trip constantly chapped King's ass but there was no doubt that King loved the smartass banter from his guys.

"Sooo," T-BAR drew out the word, "as I was saying, Dorian's in at eight, shootin' rounds, no clue of happen'ns around him. Bazwar comes in thirteen minutes later, blasts him in the chest and noggin then stands around waitin' for the po-po."

"Geez, was that read off the official report." Trip laughed at his own joke, until he noticed King eyeballing him. "Sorry," he whispered, bringing his eyes down, as he scribbled on his paper.

"Doesn't try to flee. Complies to Ty's demand to stay on the ground until cops arrived. Seems like he wanted to be found out. Something doesn't add up." Arctic added.

Heads nodded around the table.

"Bond? Slate asked, looking around for someone to clue him in, in case the information was already discussed when he was on his mandatory stroll.

"One-mill," King stated.

Slate snapped the pencil gripped in his hand. His pisstivity level cranked up a few notches regarding the low bail amount for what was at least Murder Two. If Bazwar walked on bail, Emmy could be in danger, something it seemed his team wasn't concerned about. They weren't witnessing her mental state, which Slate thought was on the edge. Emmy had been a wreck when he left her that morning. Her friend, Maven, was spending the day with her, probably doing girly-shit, like watching Master Chef marathons, so he knew she was in good hands. She didn't do *girly*, but Maven had a way of bending Em's will and letting her pamper for a day It'd be a good way for her to relax.

Ember was experiencing this situation unlike her usual self, almost like she was spooked or haunted. She'd seen combat, and by that Slate knew she'd *seen* combat. Through a sniper's scope she'd experienced the kill unlike other soldiers. It wasn't down range, it was up close and personal. Every dispatch was a file stored in a sniper's memory bank. So much had to be detailed and debriefed, making it almost impossible to disassociate the dispatcher from the *normal* civilian society expected them to mold into once off the battlefield. If society could peek into the mind of a sniper, first, they'd be horrified, and second, they'd understand why so many vets chose to live in no-man's-land, away from societal pressures and cultural lemmings. Sadly, some chose to check-out completely. It was the main factor for why snipers only lasted an average of five years in civilian life after leaving the military. Most snipers' mental health, too often, went unchecked.

Slate watched Ember like a hawk. No way would he allow her to become a statistic. She'd only been out of the military a little over three years. After college, she gave service to her country and transitioned back to civilian life unbelievably well, though she had a rough start initially before King's help, after suffering from PTSD.

Slate came back to the conversation. King was waiting on him trying to gage him. Slate shook off his reverie and joined into the brief.

"One mil and he's out. No fuckin' way that's happening." Slate took a second and then added, "Bail *can* be raised, after arraignment, if we can find and bring more evidence to raise the charge." Slate laid out the facts that they all knew, but he needed to reiterate it for his own wellbeing. "Premeditation. When did he purchase the firearm? Did he recon the range? Did he post any warnings or confess his plans on any social media platforms?" His voice was steel as he continued, "Cy, there's gotta be something you can pull, dig, hack, something's gotta be out there. You and Tex can find anything. Get him on the horn!" His adrenaline was rocketing.

"Doin' my best, buddy," Cypher gave him a nod. Slate knew Cy was digging and scouring every inch of the web, dark web, hell, probably even Narnia, looking for anything that could be used.

King picked up the line and dialed Tex.

"King." Tex's unmistakable southern drawl lit up the conference room coming over the table speaker.

"Any new news since we last spoke?"

"I'm afraid not. I'm still scouring."

"We're going over the file you and Cy put together but other than that, we're no further along on our end either. The only revelation is the bond was set."

Tex let out a low grumble from the back of his throat. "I saw that. Pretty low."

"I don't like it any more than you do, but low is normal. Not a flight risk, no priors. We knew it was going to be a low bond." Slate was about to lose his shit, but King kept control of this brief, keeping the ball rolling. "Though, the charge will most likely be raised to Murder One, first degree, if they can establish it was pre-meditated. If a plea is offered, it could be lowered to the standard that the prosecutor would settle. Murder One, premeditation, is hard to prove. Especially to a jury of twelve."

It wasn't the answer Slate wanted to hear. His anger rose a notch. "Has it been posted?" He asked through gritted teeth.

Tex answered, "Hasn't been posted yet. Doesn't look like it'll be posted. The family is small, and there's no other relatives here in the States that would be able to help them post it."

"Assets to secure the bond?" Slate clenched his fists, wanting to know if there was any possibility of this guy bonding out.

Cypher interrupted, "According to the bank records I *borrowed*…"

Tex chuckled on the other end of the line.

"…it doesn't seem the family owns anything worth enough to hold the bail bond."

"According to the police report, Husani Bazwar immigrated here last year with his mother, two brothers, and one sister," King informed the group.

"No father?" Arctic questioned, while looking at the file in front of him. "Don't see any listed."

All the guys looked at Cypher then volleyed to the tabletop speaker.

Cypher glanced at the computer, but Tex's voice answered, "No...none listed on the ICE forms. All inquiries of the contacts back home on the initial paperwork said the father was killed in a home invasion by a local rebel group seven years ago, probably a small rebellious sect in the area. After the robbery, the home was occupied by the group for a few months, eventually taking control of the small village."

"One of the family members...I think it was the mother's relation," Cypher tapped a few keys and scrolled through a few documents, "ah...give me a sec...here, the woman named Faaria, said, 'the family was forced from their home, mother and daughter, but her four sons were forced to stay with the group in the home.'" Cy's brows came together as he read the statement again to himself. He was about to question it out loud, when Slate broke in.

"Four sons?" Slate questioned, straightening in the chair, "the Immigration form only has three sons listed."

Cypher rechecked the information. "Three sons. Husani, Omar, and Rafi. Says it right here in the report from this Faaria woman."

Tex chimed in, "And intel on the family's relatives revealed Faaria was killed by an insurgent sect six months after the family immigrated while waiting to immigrate herself."

King picked up the phone. "Mary, I need some things added to the profile pack..." he paused, "Cy will forward the info. Need it in the files as soon as you get it in order." He paused again. "...Yup...ok...Yes, I picked them up this morning..."

King turned his back to the guys and murmured into the receiver, "No, I don't know if it was with the others...how am I supposed to know, I don't look at them, I just pick them up..." He turned his head and side-eyed to see if the guys were listening. "...Yes, I'm still here...I *am* listening...like I said, I *don't* know if the yellow sundress was in the bunch...I just pick up the shit on the hangers and I move on with my day...no, I'm not yelling, I'm explaining..."

A rumble of light laughter and snickers came from behind him. King lowered his voice almost to a whisper. In a wispy tone he said, "I'm sorry, didn't mean to call your dresses 'shit'...you'll just have to wear something else...yes, the peach one's fine, I like your ass in that one...yes...ok...I gotta get back to work..." His voice fell even lower, "I know, I love you too, Sugar."

If King would've made kissy noises the room would have lost it.

King turned around and eyed the table of men, daring anyone to make a sound. All was quiet. Even Trip didn't mutter a single word, though by the look King saw on his face the with-holding was killing him.

Tex snickered over the line and muttered, "Welcome to the club, King."

King ignored the jab from his friend, the only friend who could get away with the remark, and continued, "Mary will update the information files. Tex, any info you get send it through the usual channels to Cy. Cy," he pointed to the laptop, " anything you can pull from there and send to Mary, do it now. Anything that's *borrowed* that can't be sent, do your 'thing,' and get the info to the usual server, and we can get it from there to hardcopy."

Slate began to delve into the file folder in front of him. Each team member had one with the pertinent information gathered so far, and Mary kept everything up to date. Cypher, of course, didn't bother with paper files as he *found* information his own way. No one asked questions, they were just blessed to have him, and his *skills*, on the team. With Cy and Tex on the prowl, they'd turn up something.

"Anyone spoken to the immediate Bazwar family?' T-BAR questioned.

"Family was questioned yesterday about the shooter, Husani, the eldest son. The second son, Omar, wanted to translate for the mother during the interview and was quite upset when the investigators had their own translator. And the daughter, Temi-rah, wasn't able to be questioned alone. Omar stood sentry over her the whole time claiming customs practice, having to be accompanied by a male relative. Ranger Matthews said they tried to get the family to come to the station to give a formal statement, but the brother refused." King looked down at the file in his hand and added, "Says here, the youngest son, Rafi, was very upset and nervous when he was questioned."

"You thinkin' normal child anxiety? He is only six." Arctic said, "or, you thinkin' he was too scared to speak with the detective?"

"Talked to Matthews and he said Omar would barely let the younger boy speak," Arctic answered.

"My money would be on intimidation from his brother. Kid

may have heard or seen something, but is scared to death to say anything." Trip spoke while skimming the file.

"You got any digging on the middle son, Omar?" King asked Cypher.

"Searching as we speak."

King nodded at him and then turned back to the team. "I wanna get a lock on the family. Find out who they know, where they go, where they frequent. I want to know everything. Absolutely no interference with the ranger's investigation. This is in-house. I'll give Matthews the heads up, as usual, that we'll be doing our own discovery."

"Got a lot on my plate, but when one of our own is the target, it takes top priority. I'll be searching for leads if I can find any. Slate, give my best to Ember."

"Will do, Tex." Slate gave the speaker a chin lift as if Tex could see it.

Tex disconnected the call.

King's cell rang and he excused himself from the group.

"How's your girl?" T turned to Slate, asking with genuine concern.

Slate didn't rebuke the fact that she wasn't *actually* his, but he rubbed his neck and answered his friend. "Not good. Something's off, but I can't pinpoint it." He let out a defeated breath, "I've never seen her like this. I don't understand what's going on inside her head. Last night, she settled down and seemed to be past the initial shock, but this morning she was jacked. Nervous, drawn out, jumpy." He rubbed his short beard. "It's not like her at all."

The guys around the table were in agreement that wasn't like the hard-as-a-diamond Ember they all knew. Ember was a non-official part of their group. She didn't join in on missions, but since she and Slate were best friends, she spent a lot of time with the team, be it at the bars hanging out and shooting pool, cook-outs, get-togethers or late night bonfires, they'd all become friends with the spitfire that was Ember. She was part of Team Hellforce by proxy.

Slate went on, "We all know what it's like on the battlefield. We've all seen the ugliness of war, carnage the average person wouldn't be able to process. Saying we're a special breed is pretty damn accurate. We're all able to take in the horror show and still somehow function on a day-to-day basis."

"Slay a guy in the morning and back to base for lunch at noon," T commented.

"Exactly. And, there's always the times when we struggle." Slate paused, looking down at the table, "But, we work through it."

"You think she needs a shrink? Someone to debrief?" Trip shook his head side-to-side to emphasize no judgement on his next point, "No shame in that game. We've all needed it at one time or another."

They may've been hard-as-steel, badass motherfuckers, but they all knew too well that everyone needed help now and then, and they were smart enough to ask for it. They were familiar with the results of fellow Deltas and soldiers who let their pride get in the way of taking or asking for help.

"I suggested it to her this morning." Slate continued the conversation waiting for King to return.

"How'd that go over?" Trip asked.

Slate chuckled. "Like a fart in church." The guys laughed. "She said she's fine. Just a little shook up."

"You don't believe that, do you?" Arctic raised a brow.

"Nope."

The guys were in agreement; if Ember was showing signs of not processing the situation it was more than being a little shook up.

Cy chimed in. "Talked to Pops?"

All the guys knew Slate's history and the fact that Ember's dad filled the needed role of a father figure as he grew up. All the guys called him Pops. Ember's father had brainstormed a few missions with the group and King valued his expertise. Mitch Hayes, being former military, had the respect of the team.

"No, not yet. Going to touch base with him today...after this." He motioned, circling his finger around the room.

"Pops'll be able to figure out what's going on. If his girl's hurtin', he's not gonna let that fly." Trip reassured him.

King returned to the room.

"Slate, I need you to steel your shit." King pinned him with a look that told Slate he wasn't going to like what was about to be said. "The Bazwar family's MIA. Matthews just gave the heads up."

Everyone turned to Slate.

King kept an eye on him knowing he was going to fly off the handle, but Slate sat stock still, only his face hardening at King's words.

"MIA. No fucking way!" Arctic growled.

"What the fuck?" Cypher added.

"How's that even possible?" Trip added to the melee of the reactions.

Slate's interjection was cool and collected. His focus became lasered. "Friends, employers, neighbors, any of them questioned?" he clipped.

"Don't know. Just came down the pipeline. Matthews thought Cy could do his *thing* and begin looking into the circles around the family. We can move faster than their office. Red tape's choking them." King looked at Cypher to affirm his statement. "We'll create a circle of persons associated with each family member. Employers, former employers, friends, schools. Any angle we can explore—"

"Ember needs twenty-four seven," Slate said to King, more as a demand than a statement.

"Someone's on it." King said like he knew what was coming. He knew Slate; knew his men better than they knew themselves, so he'd geared up for a fight on his hands. "Matthews has someone on their way to her now."

Surprisingly calm, Slate stood with a relaxed demeanor. "Not. Fucking. Happening."

"Slate. Sit," King demanded. "This is by. The. Book." He punctuated the last statement, planting his finger hard against the tabletop with each word.

"You gotta be out of your fucking mind if you think I'm gonna trust *anyone* else and put her safety into someone else's hands other than mine."

Slate usually wasn't a hot-head, but King knew when it came to Ember, Slate would storm the gates of hell to protect her. So,

King knew he'd want to step-up and take the lead on Ember's protection detail.

"Well?" Slate waited

"Slate, stand the fuck down. Don't put me in a position and force my hand."

"You'll have to fire me before I'll allow this shit to happen. Ember's mine. *Mine*. I'll take leave if I need to. I'm on her protection detail and—"

"No-can-do. Matthews' orders. He doesn't want our team getting too close and interfering," he paused. "That means especially you." He pinned Slate with a pointed stare. "You're sidelined—"

"What the fuck does that mean!" *There* was the Slate King was expecting to surface. "He singled me out?" The fury was contained, but venom lit every word.

"No," King's composure went from friend to boss, "I did."

Slate's blood pressure was about to blow.

He knew King would most likely be the victor, but if he wanted to go a few rounds, Slate would welcome the fight.

The two men locked eyes waiting for the other to blink.

The rest of the guys froze in their seats, not wanting to spook prey nor predator, not being able to distinguish either. Tension was volatile. No one toed with King. They all trusted his rationale and leadership. This was uncharted and dangerous territory.

"I need you level headed. Do. Not. Interfere." King was clear. It was an order.

"Like you didn't interfere with Mary?" Slate's words hit their intended target.

King's mission of vengeance went FUBAR when he attempted to dole out justice on Mary's abusive brother after she was hospitalized. The mission of *justice* went off the rails and earned King a bullet to the heart and lung. It was still fresh in everyone's memory.

King's eyes lit. Hellfire blazed within them. The boss was gone and King, warrior, defender, protector and husband was now in control.

"Step off, Slate." Three words conveyed a warning not to go

any further. "I will not have my *employee*," King enunciated, punctuating the hierarchy, "defy orders. You will *obey* direct orders and not deviate from an order from upper command. You work here, you follow the rules."

Slate burned with rage, but his facade was composed.

"Don't fuck with me, Ryan." Addressing Slate by his last name and not his moniker hit its mark. Slate was relegated to employee, not a teammate.

Slate calmly stepped back as King tracked him with a punishing stare. "Fuck you, King. I don't fucking work here."

With those parting words, Slate turned, walked out the door. and off the premises of Hellforce.

CHAPTER 8

Slate had been gone a month. The dynamics in the office were off and everyone felt it. Like missing a limb of one's body, the loss was glaringly obvious but nobody talked about it. Especially to King. King was a good man. The team stood behind him with every decision, but this time the fissures were deep; not everyone agreed with his decision to let Slate walk and to stay gone. He left and never looked back.

Cypher cleaned out Slate's cage and boxed up all his belongings, which was another glaring reminder every time the guys entered the room. Slate's cage, first in the row, sat empty. Each morning, of each day, the wound was ripped open as they filed in, putting their things in their cages. And every evening, the reminder stayed with them when they picked up their belongings and headed home. It was a reminder that their body was broken, and just like an amputee, the loss of the limb was always present.

King interviewed a few prospects to join the team, but hadn't solidified a hire, so the possibility of the brotherhood becoming one again was slim, if nonexistent.

Slate was gone. The team was divided. And, because it was divided between Team King vs Team Slate, it went way beyond what the guys thought would be a mere spat; a lover's quarrel. Everyone was sure that once cooler heads prevailed, Slate would return on his own, or King would call him back. Such was not the case on either side.

They'd been on a few missions since the *breakup*. And, that's what it was; a breakup. One lover scorned; the other refusing to admit fault. *Pride will always be the longest distance between two people*. Whoever coined that phrase hit the nail on the head. And, although the missions were successful, mistakes were made and injuries resulted. Severe injuries.

The team was uneven and second-guessed each other, and although trust wasn't completely lost, the faintest hint of doubt was causing fractures to become breaks.

~

Cy stood outside King's office and steeled himself to talk with his boss. After the devastating last mission, King knew he had to bring a new guy onboard, even if it was on a temporary basis, until he could permanently fill Slate's spot.

He was tempted to call upon his friend Keane "Ghost" Bryson and his team of retired Deltas, the group he knew from his days back on the teams but instead called his friend and buddy, former Army Captain Chase Jackson, who sent one of his operators, Apollo "Creed" Winters, to temporarily come onboard Team Hellforce. Chase and his wife, Sadie, ran Zion Task Force, a private security company in nearby Killeen.

Creed knew the ropes, had team dynamics, got along with the guys, and the team was melding. But, things weren't meshing the way they did with the old team. He'd only come on board last week, and Cy knew there was always an adjustment and break-in period when someone new joined a group; especially a group that was as tight as theirs. It had to be difficult to come onto a team where guys had previously served together, bled together and saved each other's lives countless times.

Cy was hopeful, but skeptical, things would work out. He didn't know if it was so much the fact that the new guy wasn't fitting in, or the fact that he wasn't Slate. He was hoping once Slate heard King was looking to get a new guy, he'd give King a call and see if the two could come to a mutual understanding, and the Hellforce family would be reunited.

But, Slate hadn't contacted King, and King hadn't contacted Slate, so the breakup was still on.

Cypher knocked on King's office door and peered in, "Got a minute?"

"Sure, got plenty of time. What's on your mind?" King put down a folder, probably a potential case file for a future mission, and leaned back in his chair.

"Slate—"

"Don't have time for this." King picked up the folder and studied it.

"King—"

"Shut the door on your way out," he ordered without lifting his eyes.

Cypher stood his ground. Taking a moment, he measured his words, "You know, King, I've never questioned your judgement. Never disobeyed an order. I've always trusted you knew what was best, and we all fall into order because you never steer us wrong."

King looked up, meeting Cy's stare.

"But, this time...this time, I have to respectfully disagree with you."

King folded his arms on the desk in front of him and leaned forward, presenting a man who didn't want to be fucked with.

"You're my boss, so I respect you, but I can't agree with you on this one."

"That's fine because it's not your decision. Doesn't concern you."

"That's where you're wrong."

King stood, arms crossed over his broad chest, his forearms straining against the rolled-up sleeves of his button-down shirt. He waited for Cy to sound off.

"You know as well as I do that we're *all* affected by the decisions *you* make. You know the team's falling apart. You *see* that the team is falling apart." Cy's gaze locked on his boss. For a second, King's eyes fell downcast at the declaration of the hard truth but came back up when Cypher continued. "Mistakes are being made, King. You and I both know it. Hell, T for damn sure knows it."

At the last statement, King closed his eyes and rubbed the tatts on his forearm.

"Look, I know your job is hard. I wouldn't want it, God only knows why you do." King's eyes came back to his teammate, "It's gotta suck to be the one responsible for the lives of all of us when you send us out. And to have that burden has to weigh heavy on you. I *know* it weighs heavy on you. I get it. I would never disparage your commitment to what you ask us to do." Cypher paused a moment before adding, "but, King, we can't continue like this. One of us is coming back under the stars and stripes if we continue on this path."

King's expression hardened. Cypher knew he was thinking of his former Delta team. The one on which he and Arctic served together. Seven men went out and only two returned. The other five weren't as lucky.

Five men gave the ultimate sacrifice.

Five men buried beneath the flag.

Twenty-one guns and flag-draped caskets.

Cy couldn't imagine what it would be like to lose one of the men he called brother, let alone all of them.

The two stood in silence. Cy waited for King. He'd said his peace. It would be King who'd steer the direction of the team, because Cypher didn't know if he could continue in the same direction if things didn't change. He wouldn't abandon the team, but he would need to take a different position, maybe an advisory position behind the scenes, but he couldn't continue in the field. He knew his words were true and not just a low blow, but one of them would be coming home in a bag if they continued making the drastic mistakes they'd made on the last mission.

"I'll call Slate."

That's all King said. He sat and picked up the file he was looking at when Cypher first entered his office. Cy nodded and turned to leave.

As he reached the threshold, King's voice sounded. "Thanks for your honesty."

Cy turned around. "I know you do your best, King. I never

question your integrity or devotion to us or the job. You're one of the most upstanding men I know, and I'm damn proud to call you my brother and fight beside you." King looked up, and Cypher continued. "I know you and Slate have pride, hell, we all do. In our profession we need it, or we'd never take on the next mission. Pride isn't a bad thing," he paused, "until it is."

King nodded in agreement, and then said the words Cypher had rarely heard him say, not because of pride, but because they were rarely true. "I may have been wrong."

King tossed the file onto the desk, leaned back, and let out a breath. He scrubbed his hands down his face and the length of his greying beard. Leaning forward and resting his forearms on the desk, he unconsciously rubbed his left arm. Cypher knew it was a nervous habit. He rubbed his burned and scarred arm when he was deep in thought or irritated, which with the group of men he oversaw and parented, was about ninety percent of the time.

"Close the door on your way out,"

Cy pulled the door closed as King reached for his phone.

CHAPTER 9

"Gyrating dicks or angry Brit? You decide." Maven looked at Eli and Ember sitting next to each other on the sofa.

"Definitely *not* dicks!" Eli said definitively. "Whatever we're deciding on, the answer is always, not dicks."

"Okay, angry Brit, *with* a dick it is then." Maven plopped down in the oversized chair and took the remote from Ember.

"But, Magic Mike is a classic!" Ember whined.

"A classic? For real? Do you even know the definition of classic?" Maven schooled her best friend.

"Well...it will be."

Maven rolled her eyes at her bestie.

Ember continued, "This movie will one day be studied, dissected, and examined in future cinematic classrooms all over the world."

"You've cracked, my friend. No one is going to be studying Channing Tatum's crotch for cinematography class. The only ones studying his crotch will be the lucky Mrs. Tatum...and also the other three bazillion people who watch the movie."

"Can we be one of those bazillion? Please?" Ember gave a pleading look.

"Eli doesn't want to watch greased-up abs and sweat-clad men parade their toned, tanned, ripped, muscled bodies across a stage, pumping, pulsating, and grinding to hard beats of music..." Maven's breathing sped up, so that her chest was starting to heave with every panted breath. "Oh, my...I need a panty change!"

The girls broke out in hysterics while Eli was left wondering if Maven really was going to jump up and dash to the bathroom. He wondered if she kept a spare pair for emergency use in her purse. She used the phrase so often, he didn't know any more if it was a joke or if she actually got that worked up. He shook the disturbing thought from his head. He was glad to see Emmy getting back to her old self. She still had anxiety and an occasional nightmare, but over all, she was getting back to the girl he always loved.

∼

After a four-hour marathon of reality cooking, Ember announced she was hungry.

"What food are you in the mood for?" Slate asked from beside her.

At the same time, Ember and Maven both answered, "Mexican!" Then looked at each other and broke into laughter.

"Oh, shit." Slate put his head back against the headrest of the couch. "It's Monday!" He uttered in defeat.

"Yassss!" Maven sang.

In perfect unison the girls rang out, "Margarita Monday!" falling into another fit of laughter.

Eli was not up for Margarita Monday. "Maybe we could order Chinese? There's a place that just opened, and I've been dying to try it out. Heard great things about it." Eli tried to make a convincing argument but knew it was a futile attempt.

Maven put her hand on her hip and glared at him. "Nope. Nope...can't let you do it. Not gonna let you do it. You are not breaking our sisterhood of Margarita Mondays."

Eli knew it was a last ditch attempt, but he really didn't want to babysit while Maven and Emmy got sloshed, three-sheets-to-the-wind. "But, I really have a taste for Chinese," he tried in his most convincing tone.

"Okay—"

"Really?" Eli's brows came up in astonishment.

"You didn't let me finish," Maven huffed. "I was going to say, okay, you...go get Chinese, and we'll," she pointed back and forth between herself and Ember, "we'll get Mexican." She looked oddly satisfied.

"But, you two get blitzed. You can't drive," he pointed out the obvious.

"Well, no shit, Sherlock!" Maven looked at Eli like he was a dumbass. "That's why you'll be dropping us off before you go get your food and picking us up after."

He watched as Ember sat quietly enjoying the dramatics that never seemed to disappoint when it came to Maven and Eli. Maven adored him but loved to give him a hard time, just because she could. And, Eli allowed it, because one: Maven was her best friend; and two: he adored Maven as well. No way would he ever take shit talk from anyone else.

"You really want that margarita, Emmy?"

"Yes!" Maven answered for her.

Eli gave Maven a stink-eye stare and then turned his attention back to Ember. Ember nodded.

"Told you," Maven said, matter-of-fact.

Eli ignored her and spoke to Ember, giving a defeated breath, "Chimis or fajitas?"

"Yes!" Maven did a little happy dance in the middle of the living room. Eli rolled his eyes at her. She grasped his face with both her palms and planted a kiss on his forehead. "You're the best!" she crooned, giving him a wide smile. "I'm always telling Em what a great catch you are," she said, which made Eli's heartbeat jump a notch. "But she's gonna miss that train if she holds out. There's gotta be plenty of passengers riding that rail." Maven wagged her eyebrows at him, and Ember gave her an *oh, please* look.

If only they knew the truth. There'd been no passengers to ever climb aboard the Eli Express. Not that Eli was a prude. He'd never judge anyone for whomever they decided to sleep with, but he never found the one he wanted to make that forever bond with.

Well, that was a lie.

The girl he wanted to purchase a ticket for the Eli Express was sitting right beside him. She was the only one he ever loved, so she was the only one he'd ever consider. He dated plenty of women, but most just wanted to purchase a ticket, ride the rails and abandon the train at the next station. Eli wanted more than that. Call him old-fashioned, but he wanted his first to be his only.

Too many people looked at sex as a physical, recreational activity, and he guessed if it was just sex, that's all it could be considered. But, he knew when the day came that he made love to his forever, that it would be so much more than just a meaningless hookup. It would be a bond that'd tie him to her for a lifetime.

"Hello? Earth to Eli!" Maven waved her hand in front of Eli's face. "We gonna get grub, or are you going to sit there being a space cadet the rest of the night? Need to know, or I gotta call us an Uber." Maven loved to rattle Eli.

But, Eli gave as good as he got. He stood up and stretched. "Space cadet? Kettle, meet pot. Thought maybe *you* could call a spaceship if you needed a lift to your home planet 'cuz God knows you ain't bred on Earth."

Maven stuck her tongue out at him, but he grabbed the tip before she pulled it back in her mouth.

"Awe, that's not nice, Mavey." Eli tsked as he held her captive, like a brother torturing his little sister.

"Lhhet ith gooo!" Maven screeched.

"Say you love me," Eli taunted.

"Nether!"

"Say you love me. Just three words...that's all I need to hear."

"Ellli!" Maven tried to plead for him to let go.

"Come on, Maves...I know you want to say it."

"Emmmba, helth me!" she whined.

Ember stood next to Eli, grinning. "I think you need to say it, Maves."

"I donth wanth thu." She feigned crying.

Ember taunted her. "The sooner you say it the sooner we'll be drinking margaritas."

The words barely left Ember's lips before Maven blurted, "I lovth ooou!"

"Awe, that's so kind of you, Maves. I love you, too!" Eli let go of her tongue.

"Bastard." Maven ran her tongue over her teeth, giving him an evil eye.

"Wow...such a potty mouth," Eli teased. He made a show of wiping off his hand on his jeans.

Ember grabbed her purse from the front table. "Don't know what I'm going to do with you two."

"You can start by kicking him to the curb." She motioned to Eli.

"Weren't you the one that said I was such a great catch?" he questioned Maven as he held the door open.

"You'd never be my catch, Eli. You're my best friend," Ember answered, giving him a wide smile.

All humor left Eli's face.

Maven cut Eli a glance, noting his silence, then huffed to Ember, "Hey, I thought I was your best friend?"

"Everyone's allowed to have two best friends, 'cuz they're two different categories...dicks and chicks," Ember said straight-faced.

Both the girls broke into laughter, and Eli shook his head following the two out the door.

It was going to be a *long* Monday.

While babysitting Ember and Maven at their favorite restaurant, El Molcajete, where Margarita Mondays often got out of hand, Eli sat sentry over the woman who drank enough booze that both were feeling the early effects as they sipped.

Usually, it was a gaggle of three—Ember, Maven, and Mary—but with tensions between King and him running high, the girls decided it would be just them. They were drinking margaritas out of what could only be described as a small-sized fish bowl. Ember sipped the last of her first drink while Maven had one down and was working on a second.

"I don't know why they just don't make the entire glass out of a salt mold. You know, like one of those salt blocks 'deerses' lick. It'd be so much better." Maven's words slurred a bit as she spread her wisdom to Ember who was nodding along at the crap flowing out of her best friend's mouth. "I mean," she paused searching her thoughts, "I have fifty-four ounces of 'rita here, and by the fifth sip," she popped the *P*, "I'm out of salts. I mean, I turn the glass," she studied the drink, turning it to show her thought process, "but once I'm back to start...here's no more salts, and I gots lots of 'rita left to go." Her words were relaxed, as was she. Fifty-four ounces plus of strawberry margarita had her feeling pretty good.

Eli glanced at his watch willing the time to go faster. As a Delta, he had an enormous amount of patience, but a man had his breaking point. Sitting recon for days in the remote Afghani mountainsides, no problem. Sitting recon over two slightly inebriated women, one who matched herself with the likes of the great thinking philosophers, Socrates and Plato...Slate would take the mountainside any day.

"Hey girls, wha'cha got going on here?" A woman's voice came from across the bar.

Eli went on high alert, even seeing the girls clearly knew the woman.

"Imogen!" Maven squealed, almost toppling herself off her barstool as she rushed to embrace the pint-sized woman. Maven was usually high-energy, but with a few drinks in her, the girl was wound like a top. Ember climbed off the bar stool and made her way to the huddle.

"Did you come to eat or drink? 'Cuz if you came to drink, better order now, 'cuz Maven's drinking the bar dry."

Imogen took in Maven and grinned.

"Oh, you hush, boo. You're a lush, too," Maven giggled at her rhyming words. "You'd think she was a teetotaler she's sipping so slow." She tried to hide the words behind a side hand, but it was obviously meant for Ember to hear. Maven smiled at her bestie.

"Where's Mary?" Imogen scanned the empty stools nearby.

Mary had introduced Ember and Maven to Imogen after she

got the job at Hellforce, explaining to the girls how it was Imogen who pep-talked her and worked her up with enough confidence to get the job. Since then, the group were regulars at the coffee shop Imogen owned.

"She's not joining us tonight."

"Married life, huh?"

Eli kept an eye on the group from his table in the corner. He could see Ember's discomfort with Imogen's question. She probably didn't want to go into detail about the break at Hellforce with Slate and King and that it had slowly bled into her friendship with Mary.

"Eat or drink? Which one you doin', Immy?" Maven slurred a little over her friend's name.

Imogen looked crestfallen and defeated. She quickly masked it and answered in a cheery tone, "I was supposed to be meeting a date here, but he's a half an hour *late*." She did air quotes around the last word. "And, he's not answering any texts or calls." Her voice feigned an upbeat tone, but her sullen look gave her away. "I don't think he's so much *late*, as he is not coming."

Her friends did what friends did best and consoled her.

"Oooh, ghosted." Ember tipped her head to the side. "That's too bad, Immy. I'm so sorry."

Maven shook her head, "His loss." She swung her arm around her friend's shoulder, pulling her into a side hug. "That's fine. Who needs men?" She threw a disdainful look over at Eli. "I don't have a man, and I'm perf'ticly happ-ly." Maven tripped over the last words. "Ember doesn't have a man, and she's happier than anyone I know."

Looking over at Eli, she gestured to him. "Eli doesn't have a man," she leaned in closer trying to whisper, but her judgement in volume was impaired, "but, I don't think he swings that way." Her brows pulled in on themselves. "But, he's cranky all the time, so I don't think he counts in this scenario." Her bubbly composure came back. "Like Meatloaf sings, 'Two out of three ain't bad.'" She sang the last words and the girls burst into side-splitting laughter. Even Eli had to chuckle at Maven's exuberance. He was happy to see Ember laughing again. With Maven's crazy antics, never knowing what the girl was going to do next kept Ember's mind off the fact that she could be in danger.

"My God, girl!" Imogen said to Maven. "How much have you drank?"

Maven held up one finger.

"Only two?'

Ember raised Maven's second finger. "Yeah, two fifty-four ouncers."

"Damn, girl. Why aren't you on the floor?" Imogen chuckled.

Maven shrugged and led her friend over to an empty stool. "This round's on me. What'll it be?" She laughed, again at her rhyming words.

Slate approached the group and pinned Maven with a stare, his eyebrows raised, "No more for you." His tone held a stern warning.

Maven huffed. "You're not my dad."

"I may not be, but I *am* your ride home and I don't need you puking in my truck."

"I promise I won't puke." Maven held up three fingers in the sign of the Girl Scout promise.

"You're not a Girl Scout, and I'm not going to chance it." He gestured to her drink, "Finish up the fish bowl you have in front of you, and we'll call it a night."

She pulled her face back then turned to Emmy. "Such a buzzkill." She pointed in Slate's direction and poked his chest. "That should've been his nickname in the Army, Buzz Kill."

"Drink up." Eli pushed her drink towards her and waited for her to comply.

"Yes, Sergeant Kill." She saluted him and took a long pull from her drink.

Eli turned to the newest member of their clique. "Hi, I'm Slate...um, Eli," he corrected, extending his hand to the newcomer.

Imogen eyed him up and down and took his proffered hand. "Imogen. Single and looking. And, you look fine!" She perused him once again.

Slate smiled. She was barely five feet tall, standing on her tiptoes and cute as a button.

"Nope. Can't have him, Immy," Maven said matter-of-factly. "He's Emmy's." She got a shocked, confused expression on her face then repeated, "Immy, Emmy...Immy, Emmy," then chortled.

Ember reeled back, "He's not mine!" She looked over at Eli. "Eli's my best friend..." She corrected before Maven was going to butt in, "My best guy-friend. We grew up together," she told Imogen.

"Dicks and chicks...separate best friends," Maven added as clarification for Imogen.

Imogen scrunched her face, seemingly baffled, but didn't ask.

"Imogen owns Brews & Books, the coffee and bookshop downtown." Ember told Eli.

He nodded, knowing of the little shop. "It's nice to have met you, Imogen," giving her a genuine smile. He pointed. "I'll just be over there." Then he walked to the table where he could see the ladies but still give them room to finish having girls' night without hovering. Seeing the group prattling on and laughing with each other, he thought about his team—well, his former team—and wondered what they were up to. He hadn't heard from them, with the exception of his best friend, Cypher.

Cy was keeping him informed of their findings and what was happening with the situation concerning Bazwar. Last he heard, Bazwar wasn't talking and his bail hadn't been posted. The fact that the Bazwar family was still MIA had him on edge. Although Dorian was the target, Eli had a gut feeling Ember was a target as well. His gut wouldn't settle, wondering if Ember was still in danger.

He hadn't spoken to Cy in the last week. He knew the guys had taken a mission and returned, but he wasn't privy to any details. His mind ached at the fact he hadn't joined them. Never had he missed a mission in the five years since he'd joined Hellforce. But he didn't regret his choice to leave to keep watch over Ember. He couldn't live with himself if he stayed on the job and something happened to her. He wasn't chancing her safety to anyone else. He'd rather die than to see one hair on her beautiful head hurt.

His attention was drawn back to the three friends as Ember threw her head back and laughed and the others giggled. They were talking about God only knew what, and it made him miss the guys even more. If not on a mission, once a week they got together for beers, or a cookout, or had evening bonfires just sitting around shooting the shit. They saw each other every day at work, but it was nice to have time outside the office where they could just be guys and not worry about the next mission or prep that had to be done.

Forty-five minutes later the girls called it a night and he was heading back to Ember's house, three ladies in tow. Imogen had come to the bar in an Uber waiting on her no-show date. She made a phone call home, to whom Eli didn't know, but she continued girls' night without a care in the world, seeming to have the weight of the world off her shoulders. There was no way Eli was letting the slightly tipsy woman catch a ride with a stranger. Maven had insisted that she continue girls' night back at Ember's house, though by the sounds of soft snoring coming from the back seat, he had a feeling it would be a pajama party and not an extension of Margarita Mondays. Eli's watch would extend overnight.

CHAPTER 10

It was Tuesday morning, and Slate was taking in some indoor target practice at Ember's gun range. Usually, he practiced daily with the guys at Hellforce and today, he was missing his brothers. He was getting up the nerve to bite the bullet and call King. He was still pissed and thought King was wrong which had him hesitating to make the call. If given the chance to redo the situation, he'd still make the choice of protecting Ember over his job, but he'd come up with a plan, a way to still keep watch over Ember and also return to the team—that is, if King would have him back. That was question number one. And, question number two—would King be willing to allow Slate's plan?

If King would even talk to him.

At the moment, Ember was in the office having lunch with Maven. It'd been two weeks since she'd been back to the range. He knew returning was hard for her, but it wasn't as bad as he'd imagined. Being back to work, keeping herself busy, kept her mind busy as well. She'd had a few flashbacks, which was the thing that concerned Slate the most, but it wasn't unexpected. It was more frustrating for her. She said Bazwar was a feeling of déjà vu. The haunting look in his eyes was something she couldn't explain. She *knew* those eyes.

Slate entered Ember's office when his phone rang. King's name came across the display and he hesitated to answer. He paused. He wasn't mad at King; he was upset. The fact that King thought he couldn't separate his heart from his head showed how little faith King had in him.

If anyone knew that your heart could mess up an objective, it was King. He knew firsthand that a heart needed to take a backseat when the one you love was in danger, but he went rogue when it was his love, Mary, who was on the line. Telling Slate he wasn't able to compartmentalize was a slap in the face. King was a hypocrite.

King knew Ember was Slate's, though not in the official manner, but he knew, so putting her safety in someone else's hands was never going to sit well with Slate, and King knew it. Yes, his heart may be in the game, but his head was leading one-hundred percent. His mind led before his heart. It always would. He was hyper-vigilant and would squash any threats that dared to make themselves known. With King sidelining him, the bond of trust was broken. A team didn't work without teamwork, and the number one virtue was trusting the men around you. King didn't trust him, so he walked. It was not a hot-headed decision. It was a rational one. His mind and gut told him Ember was in danger.

If orders had come from Ranger Matthews, then Slate would have taken it up with him and his team would've had his back. He would have found a way to skirt along the boundaries while not interfering with the investigation. Matthews would know; no matter what orders, Hellforce wouldn't lie docile. Matthews knew from King and Mary's case that fact was true. Hellforce would walk through fire to rescue one that was theirs. But, the decision to sideline him didn't come from Matthews, it came from King. So, again, King was the hypocrite.

"You going to answer that, or are you ghosting your pimp?" Maven was her normal snarky self. He shot her a mocking glare and Maven rolled her eyes. "Answer it and make a few bucks." Maven laughed at her own joke and Ember giggled at her friend's banter.

Slate answered with one word, "King."

His voice was steady and sure. It'd been a month since he

heard from his former boss, and he was curious as to the aspects of the call.

King responded in the deep timber of his voice, "Slate."

Dead air hung between them; each waited for the other to speak.

"How's Ember?"

The question caught him off guard. King probably knew how she was doing. Hell, Slate was certain of that. King knew just about everything that was happening around him and with his men. He probably even knew what Ember had for lunch. It was scary how intuitive he was, and how he got his knowledge and information, Slate didn't want to know. It would be one of those *If I told you, I'd have to kill you* type of scenarios.

The fact that Ember was King's first concern softened his demeanor. "As well as can be expected." Slate kept his reply short. He didn't want to spend this call chatting, he wanted to know why King was calling.

"That's good." King wasn't chatty either.

The tension was thick on both sides. Neither had animosity, but both felt jilted.

"I need to talk to you."

"We need to talk."

Both men spoke at the same time.

Again, silence hung on the line.

"King." Slate paused. "I'd like to come to the office and hash some things out."

King was silent. Slate hoped he was considering the meeting rather than thinking of a way to tell him to go to hell.

"I'm free this afternoon."

"An hour?"

"Sounds good."

"Approval at the security desk, so I can get a visitor's pass?"

"Never a visitor, Slate. Door's always open to family."

King's words had Slate letting out the breath he didn't know he was holding. It also gave him a glimmer of hope that King would hear him out and consider his proposal.

〜

Walking into Hellforce after a month felt like coming home. Just like a vacation, leaving was nice but coming home was always comforting. Protecting Ember wasn't what Slate considered a vacation by any stretch of the imagination. It was far from relaxing. The opposite, in fact—hypervigilance was far from calming or relaxing.

Slate showed up a bit early but didn't go to King's office right away. He walked into the ready room where the cages were located. Slate stopped still in the doorway. Seeing his cage empty put a pit into his stomach. Cy had cleaned it out for him after the fallout. Slate had never seen it empty and the finality of his decision hit home. He was no longer part of the team.

But, it wasn't seeing his empty cage that brought that feeling into reality and his stomach roll. It was the cage at the far end of the room that dropped the floor out from under him. The cage that previously held backup and extra supplies was now filled and organized like the rest of the cages.

The new guy. Slate's replacement. He swallowed hard. Anger flushed through him, not at the new guy, but at the fact that he was replaceable. Cy told him King was considering new prospects to join the team, but Slate thought King would at least wait until his body was cold before burying him and bringing in the new guy.

But in reality, Slate knew missions didn't wait. A full team had to be at the ready. The safety of each brother was taken up by the guy who had his six. Each man for himself didn't work on a team. No, Slate knew they needed a six-man team. Each brought their own specialty to the group and all the cogs had to mesh for a mission to execute and succeed. But, the sight of his brother's new teammate hammered the final nail in the coffin of his new-found reality.

Slate was now just Eli.

"Good to see you, brother."

Slate turned to see Cypher enter the room. A smile crossed his face as the two gave each other a fist bump and a side armed man hug.

Cy patted him on the back, "How's Ember? She here too?"

Hearing Ember was on his best friend's mind was a comfort.

Whether he was on the team or not, didn't matter, his brothers would always have his back and the backs of those they loved.

"She's doing well. She's back at the range."

"Protection?"

"Pops is there and Maven the hellcat is with her, too. That woman would make any terrorist turn and run."

Both laughed. Cypher knew of Maven's fierce attitude, and knew no one would want to go toe-to-toe with her. She was barely over five feet tall but was a force to be reckoned with.

"She lookin' for a job?" Cypher joked and then his joke hit home.

Both men fell silent, both feeling the awkwardness of the fact that Hellforce would fill any position needed, including Slate's.

"Sorry, man," Cy said with sincerity. "I didn't mean..."

"No, no...that's fine. I know you didn't."

Slate motioned to the newly occupied cage at the end of the row. "New guy." It was a statement rather than a question.

Cy followed his direction and looked at the cage. "Yeah, name's Creed."

"Good guy?"

"Pretty decent. Takes orders, follows without question. Takes command if needed."

Slate donned a stiffened smile.

"I can hate him if you need?" Cypher gave a half-laugh to quell the anxiety in the air.

"Naw." Slate rubbed the back of his neck. "Maybe just slight him a little." He laughed knowing Cy would have his back if he asked his friend to disavow the newbie.

"Creed's on loan from Zion."

Both Hellforce and Zion had backed each other when needing manpower. But, Slate wasn't familiar with Creed, his replacement.

Slate looked around the room, "How'd the last mission go?"

Concern crossed Cypher's face and he hung his head, shaking it in memory. Drawing in a deep breath, his gaze came to Slate's. "T-BAR..."

The sound of his name must've summoned his teammate. T rounded the corner and entered the room. Slate's breath hitched at the sight of him. His eyes met his friend's eyes, or at least, his friend's *eye*.

T-BAR was now missing an eye.

He wore a black patch over his left eye that, in all honesty, made the six-foot-three, two-hundred-thirty pound man look lethal; more badass than usual. But, he was sure optics weren't of T's concern. Slate's eyes immediately went to the eyepatch but didn't miss the six-inch gash across his bicep. Luckily, his right bicep wasn't inked. Slate knew T was waiting to get a new piece eventually, but the pink scar against his tanned flesh was unmistakable. And, he also didn't miss the jagged, shiny scar down the left side of his neck.

"What the fuck?" Slate glanced from T over to Cy, and then back to T, waiting for an explanation.

T-BAR focused on Slate. Side-stepping him, he headed towards his cage.

Slate again looked at Cy. Cy shot him a *don't go there* look and shook his head slightly.

Slate disregarded the warning and stormed over to T who busied himself, paying no attention to his former teammate.

"What the fuck, man? What happened to you?" Slate knew the guys got busted up on missions. It was collateral damage of the job. But T looked bad. For him to have three substantial wounds, at least three Slate could see, told him that a scuffle had taken place on his own.

T didn't acknowledge his friend.

Slate stepped into the cage, keeping a distance from him but blocking the entrance, forcing T to confront him. T-BAR stood. The man was like a brick shithouse. Every inch of the man was toned and bulk muscle.

"Step aside." The two words were lethal.

Slate ignored him.

T-BAR hardened his stare. Even with one eye the man looked deadly.

"T, straight up." Slate stood his ground. He wasn't going to move. He'd have to be moved if T wanted to pass, a feat he knew wouldn't make T break a sweat. Again he asked, "What happened? You're my friend, talk to me." The honesty in his plea made T answer.

"You didn't have my back."

Ice went through Slate. He and T were usually paired on missions. Though everyone on the team watched out for one another, T and Slate teamed together.

Slate didn't say a word. Couldn't say a word. The bluntness in T's statement hit him in the gut, knocking the voice out of him. He opened his mouth, not sure what to say, when T interrupted him.

"Move or be moved."

Slate blinked a few times, feet rooted in place, weighing his options. He knew he could give T a run for his money. The two sparred together weekly. Even with his injuries, Slate had no doubt T would still be a force to reckon with, but what would it prove? It wouldn't force T-BAR to talk, so it was futile.

Still staring at his friends, Slate stepped aside, clearing the door.

T didn't waste a second stalking past him and exiting his cage.

Cy stood by the door to the room's entrance and didn't say anything when T exited, charging into the hallway.

Slate's gaze met Cy's. Cy's mouth flattened in a straight line and he shook his head.

Slate knew he'd fucked up.

CHAPTER 11

Not too many things could rattle Slate.

"You didn't have my back."

T's words dropped like an anvil. The rage and fury on his face was raw and palpable. Slate's mind reeled. He failed his teammate.

Cy walked over to Slate and put his hand on his shoulder. "Not your fault, man. He's looking to lay blame, and right now, he's pinning it on you."

"How'd...what the fuck happened?" Slate's heart rate ticked up.

"Got called out a week after you left. New guy wasn't hired yet." Cy crossed his arms settling in, and continued the story. "It was a quick, get in get out hostage retrieval. CIA intel...we were fed bullshit, as usual, and from the time we touched down 'til the time we left, everything was FUBAR. The cartel was heavily armed and were waiting for us. We breached the front compound and things went smoothly until we met the second force of resistance, then all hell broke loose. We were out-manned.

"T's gun jammed, and before he could pull his Sig, two guys were on him. Knifed him in the arm and again in the neck." Cy paused, "Got his right thigh as well. He was able to kill one, but the other got him in the lung. It collapsed and he was helpless."

Helpless. The word made his stomach flip. He would've had T's six if he'd have been on the mission.

"We all had our hands full in our own fights and couldn't get to him." Cypher looked at his boots, reliving the moment in his memory. "We tried, but like I said, we were outnumbered with our own hand-to-hand."

"His eye?" Slate didn't know if he wanted the answer to his question.

"Got jacked with the butt of his own rifle by the guy on top of him. When he figured it was jammed, guy mustn't have known it was non-op and turned it on T. T took a blow to the face...got his eye." Cy paused, the gravity of the memory weighing heavy.

Slate closed his eyes when he asked, "Blind?"

He could taste the guilt in his words, hear the guilt in them as well. It was as if each syllable was poison. T-BAR losing his sight would mean he could no longer be an active member on the team. Being operational meant being one-hundred percent, physically as well as mentally, capable to take care of yourself and those around you. He would either have to work behind the scenes, in an advisory position or tech capacity, but field missions would be a no-go.

Slate was waiting for Cy to answer. When he hesitated, Slate met the grief on Cy's face. Cy was coaxing the end of his nose in a repeated motion, a tell that was his nervous tick.

"Blind?" Slate's voice hardened.

"Don't know, man." Cypher's words tinged with uncertainty.

"Come again?"

Cy adjusted his stance, balancing his weight from one foot to the other. "Don't know yet. Had a detached retina and an orbital fracture that needed surgery."

Slate, being a medic, knew the extent of the damage without his friend simplifying, but Cy did anyway.

"Got his eye socket cracked, and the eye nerve to the brain...fucked it up."

The layman's terms put the injury into perspective. T most likely was off the team.

"So, he's blind." Slate's statement rolled his stomach.

"Don't know yet, Cy repeated himself. "Doctors fixed what they could, now, just a waiting game. He could see just fine," Cypher shrugged one shoulder, "have a little blurry vision, double vision…"

"Or he could be blind." Slate's words were concrete.

"Don't hang on that. Speculation isn't gonna heal it any faster." Slate knew his friend's words were to comfort him, but Cy rubbed his nose again which told Slate Cy was worried about T's outcome.

The silence hung between them.

"Did you dispatched the son-of-a-bitch?"

Cy nodded, "T was out of commission. King got to the guy and ended him in one twist."

That sentence sent satisfaction into Slate's gut. Contrary to belief, no man in the field wanted to take a life if it wasn't necessary, but when killing was at the mercy of saving a fellow teammate, no man had qualms about it. None whatsoever.

Knowing King, when in rage, his deadly factor ticked off the charts, Slate knew King would have no qualms saving his teammate. King was the boss and team lead, but being alongside brothers always trumped being the boss when it came to being an operator.

King got his hands dirty, and soul blackened, along with his men. He wasn't a cake eater, managing a mission from three thousand miles away giving directives and second guessing decisions, while not physically being in the fight. No King was beside them every step, on every mission.

Cy's phone rang, giving an end to their conversation. He excused himself, and Slate stood alone in the silence of the room collecting his thoughts. He couldn't let his emotions get the best of him. He locked them tight and headed to King's office.

Slate rapped on the doorframe of King's office. The door was open and he had to stop himself from just waltzing in. He wasn't on the team anymore, which meant King wasn't his boss, so open-door office policy no longer applied.

King, on the phone, motioned for Slate to come in. He wore a dark blue business suit, a crisp white shirt, with a blue pinstripe tie which was rare. Very rare. Only a handful of times a year rare, which told Slate that a meeting with the alphabets and/or men who wore stars on their shoulders probably happened in the office earlier.

Yes, *they* came to King. King *didn't* go to them.

He was not a man who extended his services, or his men, to just anybody for any mission. It wasn't about money. King could make a fortune ten-times-over, taking any and as many jobs that were offered to him. But, King wasn't offered or given jobs. No, King *chose*, and chose carefully, the jobs he and his men executed.

"...again, it doesn't matter to me..." King glanced up at Slate then back at his desk and brought the phone closer to his mouth, "...I know we had Mexican food the last three nights, so a fourth night will be absolutely fine...Mare..." King swiveled in his chair and then walked over to the window, essentially getting distance between him and Slate. "...Mare, just 'cuz I don't have an opinion doesn't mean I don't care...*not mattering* and *don't care* are two different...don't cry..."

Slate felt awkward listening to the conversation between King and Mary, but he couldn't distance himself any farther, so he pulled out his phone and busied himself.

"...I'm sorry...I absolutely have an opinion, and I would *love* to have Mexican again for supper...yes, I'm sure...extra spicy...got it...I'll pick it up on my way home...no, I'll remember...okay, gotta go...love you, too, Sugar."

Slate heard him end the call but didn't want to be caught eavesdropping, so he continued futzing with his phone until King spoke.

"Take a seat." Unlike the phone call, his voice hardened and his pitch was deep as usual. Gone was King, pussy-whipped phone husband, and back was King, stone-cold boss.

Oh, God, did I just think those words? Never in a million years, even under the most inhumane torture, would he ever let King know his thoughts had conjured up the words, "pussy-whipped," as an adjective to describe him. Slate's mind raced for another word, panicked...*ah...concerned husband, yeah, that's better...concerned husband.* His mind sighed in relief and was apologizing for even thinking the vile words, "pussy-whipped."

Slate took the seat in front of the desk as King settled back into his chair.

The vibe in the room was tense. Both men sat facing each other, neither one sure if the other was going to speak first.

King won the coin toss.

"You wanted to talk?" He leaned forward with his forearms braced on his desk, hands clasped together. Relaxed, but formidable.

King's size was impressive. For a moment, Slate wondered if he needed to order a special reinforced chair to hold his massive frame. All the men at Hellforce were big—none lacked any bulk —but King, King was huge. An image of the superhero, Mr. Incredible, formed in his mind. Steeling himself, he cleared his throat, hoping to disguise his musings.

He centered himself. Humbled himself. T's words rolled through his mind. *"You didn't have my back."* The words stabbing each time they presented themselves, almost buckling Slate at the knee. Listening to Cy retell the details of the mission and how T had no one at his ready, watching his six, Slate had a come to Jesus moment. He had a difficult but powerful realization. His decision, though meaning to be selfless, put his team, his brothers, literally at death's door. Which made him more determined to get King to agree to his proposal.

Slate met King, eye to eye. If there was one thing he knew it was that King could smell bullshit from a mile away. He wanted King to know there was no masking or deception in his words. He held King's stare. "I'm sorry."

Two words. Wholehearted and sincere.

King's posture didn't change. His face didn't disclose a single reaction. He sat.

Slate felt the temperature in the room rise, the awkwardness of no reaction made him want to squirm, but he sat still waiting for King to make the next move.

But it didn't come.

King sat.

Slate tried not to swallow but the visceral reaction couldn't be stopped.

King waited.

"I fucked up."

King waited. Unmoving.

"Damn it, King!" Slate stood from his chair and paced to the window.

King didn't track his passage. Eyes forward. He sat.

Slate paused at the window hoping King would say something. Anything. With long strides, he paced back to King's desk, hoping his former boss would make eye contact with him.

But he didn't.

Slate rubbed the back of his head and squeezed the base of his neck. "I'm sorry, King. I fucked up," The words were a strangled plea. "What more do you want me to say?"

Still unmoving, King spoke. "Sit."

Slate hesitated, waiting for him to continue the sentence but nothing came. So, like an obedient, disciplined child called to the principal's office, Slate made his way from the side of King's desk to the chair he'd vacated in front of King.

And, he sat.

And, he waited.

He knew King had the upper hand. King could wait a man out for days, probably weeks, if the human body would let him. He had the patience of a praying mantis. Like a Siberian tiger stalking its prey, King could wait. And, he did.

King took a measured breath, then exhaled as slowly as he inhaled, eyes dead set on Slate.

Breaking the stare, King loosened his tie, looping it around his hand a few times, then set it on the corner of his blotter. Methodically, he placed his hands on the edge of his desk and pushed back, smoothly rolling his chair from beneath his mahogany desk. Standing, he side-stepped his chair and rolled it back into place. He removed his suit jacket, placing it neatly over the back of the chair, then unbuttoned the top two buttons of his shirt and straightened his cufflinks, pulling each one into submission.

No words were said. Slate waited.

King strode around front, putting his massive frame between the desk and the chair where Slate sat. Every inch of space was occupied by this man. Leaning back against the desk top, King crossed one foot over the other and folded his hands at his waist. He was a force not of intimidation but of strength.

Slate went to stand, not liking to be towered over.

"Sit."

One word. One command.

Like an obedient dog, Slate sat.

King locked eyes once again, then spoke. "You saved my life."

Slate was silent waiting for King to elaborate, which he did.

"I was at death's door, cashing in, and you saved my life. Not once, but twice. I wouldn't be standing here if you first hadn't saved me on that mountainside and then at the warehouse."

The memory washed over Slate. The day he and his team of Deltas saved King and Arctic in the remote hills of Afghanistan. He could taste the air, that distinct taste that only men who wore the uniform or lived there knew. He felt the weight of his gear, bulky and heavy, strapped to his body. He heard the guttural, agony cry Arctic let out as the men lifted the burnt, torn remains of the armored Humvee off his legs. He saw King's stare. The haunting, empty stare of King's blue eyes and the fear that raged within them before they drew blank. A death stare looking back at him.

No life. No soul. Blank. Empty. Dead.

And suddenly, his memory met the same blank eyes as he rolled King's massive bulk over the night he was shot, point-blank at the warehouse

King cleared his throat, breaking Slate from his reverie.

"When you joined this team, I told you I needed you. You were one of the best damn operators I knew."

Were and *knew*. Those weren't the words, past tense, he wanted to hear.

"I told you when you joined this team, that you were not an employee, you were family."

King paused so long, Slate didn't know if he was waiting for him to respond. Then, King continued. "You hurt me….walking out that door, you hurt me. Family doesn't abandon family."

97

Slate had the thought come to mind *family also doesn't turn their backs on family* but he remained quiet.

"I, too, was wrong."

The words hit Slate like a brick wall. So much so that Slate recoiled in his chair.

A soft chuckle came from King and Slate looked the man in the eye.

"I know. Words you probably never heard me say." King rubbed his left forearm beneath his white dress shirt. The arm that bore the horrific burned scars of that day they first crossed paths in the Afghan mountains. "But, I'm a big enough man to admit when I've fucked up."

King was a man of few words. He wasn't flowery, he wasn't poetic, he wasn't long-winded. He was pithy. The only time he got long-winded was when he was chewing the team's asses for some asinine thing they'd done, which was more often than not, so maybe that meant King *was* long-winded.

King's voice kicked him out of his thoughts. "I always knew I owed you a marker. But, this isn't it. This isn't a boss correcting insubordination for a past debt. This is one brother coming clean with another brother. I want you back on the team." King corrected himself, "I *need* you back on this team." Correcting himself one last time, he said, "*We* need you back on this team."

Slate took in King's words. Not just mere words to his ears, they were words to his heart; his soul. He knew he'd fucked up. He told himself he was walking away to protect Ember, that *he* had to do it to protect her. King lost faith in him but, as King's words settled in his soul, he realized *he* failed King as well. He, too, lost faith in his boss, his brother and teammate. He should have known King would never put Ember in danger. King would've had her six because she was Slate's. And, because she was his, she was theirs. Just as Mary was theirs. Each man would walk through fire to protect Mary. They *did* walk through fire and hell to protect her by protecting King that night at the warehouse. How could he expect any less than that from King?

Yes, he fucked up.

"What about the new guy?" Slate wanted back on the team but wanted to make sure the new guy wasn't slighted.

"Creed? We'll keep him on until we know the outcome of T's situation. Then plan accordingly." King continued, "Creed can go back to Zion if T comes back, or he can stay on if he'd like."

That realization soothed as much as it stung. Slate's gut soured and churned, because if T wasn't able to come back it would shatter not only the team, but it would decimate their friendship.

CHAPTER 12

Ember didn't like this plan. No, scratch that, she hated this plan. It was too early to discuss this plan...it wasn't even sun up. The range wasn't open yet, and this was not the way she wanted to start her day.

"Why do I have to go to the office with you every day? Why can't I just stay here in my office?" Ember's voice was working up to a whiney, shrill level even to her own ears. "I mean, we have security and every person in this place is strapped. I'm strapped," she tapped the H&K holstered to her hip. "Someone would have to go through a hail of gunfire to get to my office. If anyone asks for me, I'll be super vigilant."

Slate scoffed and ran his hands over his neck. "You think someone's going to come in and politely ask you to step out of your office? You think this is the Old West, gunfight at high noon, OK Corral? There's myriad ways someone can get to you."

Ember gave him a disdainful look. She didn't like Eli belittling her. Of course she didn't think someone would just walk in, ask for her, and announce they were there to hurt her.

Mitch joined in. "I think it's a good plan, honey. Are you safe here? Probably. Will you be safer at Hellforce? Absolutely. Should you take a chance? Absolutely not."

"But what about the range? I just can't just up and leave. I have to be here to manage things."

"You have a competent, reliable staff. Most all your accounting, payroll, ordering and purchasing can be done online," her father added. "There's almost nothing that can't be done, office wise, remotely. All staff can do training classes, firearm sales, and background checks. You've trained them well. Rely on that training. "

Ember paced her small office. Her father and Eli were overreacting. She couldn't deny she felt like there was more to this than just a random shooting. Her gut said she hadn't seen the last of the Bazwar family. But, she was never one to run and hide. She wasn't a coward, and she could take care of herself. She didn't need to be sheltered by Eli and his friends. If hell was going to come knocking, then she would be geared up to face the devil.

"I'm not going to run and hide. You both know that's the last thing I'd do. I've been in tighter spots than this, and I've always held my own." Ember felt the fire burning within her. "Thank you, but I can take care of myself."

"We're not asking you to run and hide. We're asking you to be smart and safe. And yes, you are competent and capable. You've proven that over and over, time and again. And, yes, you have been in more dangerous spots than this, but you've also had a team at your back." Her father took a moment to let his words settle. "You're a warrior, you always have been, but you don't have to be an army of one. Please, baby girl. I need you to do this."

"Your staff took care of things while you were gone earlier for two weeks, and they managed just fine. King will set you up with an office at his place. You'll be able to run things just like you do from here." Eli gestured around the room with his hand. "And, for anything that you can't do there, we'll make time for you to come back during the week." He hoped Ember would do the right thing and take King up on his offer to give her an office space at Hellforce.

"Baby girl, even the devil himself isn't crazy enough to come into Hellforce. It's the safest place for you to be right now."

Ember mulled it over in her head. From an office standpoint, there really was no difference where she worked. Paperwork was paperwork, whether it was done from the range office or a remote office. But, this was *her* range. *Her* business. *Her* dream. She built the business and wasn't going to let someone make her run from it. The fire built inside her and was now raging.

"No!" She spat out the word. "I'm not leaving. You two are blowing this whole situation out of proportion. You're conjuring up demons where there aren't any. I'm not in any more danger than any other random person on the street." She felt the anger radiating throughout her. She wasn't letting their paranoia run her out.

Mitch looked to Eli and gave him a nod. Eli pulled a piece of paper from a manila envelope. Walking over to Ember, he handed her the photocopied letter.

Ember lifted her eyes to him. "What's this?"

Eli pushed the paper towards her gesturing her to take it. She grasped it, holding Eli's stare. Her dad had his eyes on her and she knew whatever this was, she wasn't going to like it.

"Wrong one gone. Resemblance dead. Next not wrong. Take from ours, we take from yours. No shadows dark to hide. Time is patient. Both you and loves no more."

"What the hell is this?" Ember read it again, confusion marring her face.

"This came to the range."

"What? When did this come in the mail? Why didn't I see this?" Ember was trying to make sense of the situation. "Who opened this?"

Eli shook his head. "It wasn't mailed. It was left yesterday on the sales counter up front."

Ember read the note again. "This doesn't even make sense. It's gibberish. It's not even a poem. Probably someone being a dick...trying to pull a prank." She turned to her father, looking for agreement. She didn't find it with him.

"It's no joke, honey."

"Why wasn't I made aware of this? Why didn't anyone tell me?" Now, she was pissed.

"John found it on the counter. He thought it was just trash until he read it, and then he showed it to me." Her father shifted his weight. "Ranger Matthews came and took it into the station for examination and processing. This is a copy."

"Again, I wasn't told about it?" Her voice was laced with ire.

Her father showed no remorse. "I didn't want to worry you. Like you said, it could have been a prank."

"Could have? And, is it?"

Eli rubbed the back of his head and caught the look from Mitch, jockeying to see who would tell her.

"Well?" A single word filled with scorn as she volleyed back and forth between the two men. "Stop whatever you two are hiding and just tell me!"

Slate spoke. "Husani Bazwar's brother, Omar's prints were found on the face and back of the note."

Ember staved off her rage and adrenaline filled her. She kept her bearings, staying in control of herself. Her eyes darted between Eli and her father. "No mistake? Are they positive?"

"The prints match. No doubt about that. They match his prints on his immigration form. Matthews would like to comb the security footage and see if they can make an identification of anyone dropping that on the counter." Mitch pointed at the letter she was still holding.

"If Cy could get a copy of the footage as well..."

"You mean he hasn't helped himself to a copy yet?" She pinned Eli with a look of ire.

Eli didn't say anything, but shook his head no. He, as well as everyone in the room, knew Cy could get a copy if he wanted, but his team wouldn't do that without her consent since this was personal.

She looked back at the letter in hand. "I'll get the footage," then added, "for Matthews and Cy."

Her father took her by the shoulders and held her in front of him. "Please, baby girl. I'm not above begging. Please, just tell me you'll at least try the arrangement at Hellforce. I need to know you're safe."

The plea in her father's eyes was heart wrenching. She wanted to say no, she could handle this on her own, but she knew in all honesty she needed to have someone at her back. At least until the Bazwar family was found, she would give this to her father.

"Okay, Daddy."

The words were a blessing to his ears. He knew Eli and all the men at Hellforce would protect her.

"I'll work remotely until the family is found, then I'm coming back here. I don't run. I'm not going to let fear run my life."

Taking his hands from her shoulders, Mitch engulfed her in a hug. "Thank you, baby girl."

"This is only temporary," she spoke into his chest.

Neither her father nor Eli responded.

Eli broke into the conversation. "Do you need to box any of this up?" He scanned the office, looking at the various things she may need to bring.

"I'll get a box and we can load up the essentials. I'll send the security footage before we leave."

～

"Omar Bazwar made four stops to the range prior to dropping off the letter." Cy had gone over the security footage and swept from the date of the shooting to when the letter was found. "All the same week before he dropped the note."

"No one found it peculiar that the same guy browses the counter and makes no purchases?" Arctic questioned from the table discussion.

"That's not all that uncommon," Ember said. "We have some customers who come in multiple times before making a purchase. The decision to have or carry a firearm isn't made lightly. I actually prefer customers that come in multiple times and customers that ask a lot of questions."

"So, a looky-loo wouldn't have raised any flags with the staff?"

"No, happens all the time," she answered.

Cypher pointed to the wall where the security footage was projected. "If you watch him," he pointed to Omar, "he enters and kinda hangs back while the other customers are being helped. Then, he walks past the counter and is looking down the back corridors. Seems odd to me." Cy switched the video to the next visit. "See...here, again, he wanders around before browsing the cases. Seems to me that if you're coming to purchase a gun, or are considering it, you'd go straight to the case." He let the footage play out a little longer. "This guy," he points to a sales rep, "he addresses him multiple times, and Omar refuses the help."

"That's Marcus. He was the one that remembered Omar coming in on the day the letter was found." Ember watched the footage intently. "He said Omar told him he was just browsing. Matthews came in and questioned Marcus, and he said he definitely remembers him."

Cypher changed the video, and again, Omar wandered throughout the sales floor.

"The front end isn't that large, so he has to imagine he'd be seen by someone." Trip said.

"There were a lot of people in the second and third video, and it was really busy the day he dropped the note, so maybe he thought he wouldn't be suspicious. I mean, we see him because we're looking for him, but on an average day, in shop, we see so many faces they kinda all blend together with one another," Ember spoke while watching the video.

"He has to know there are security cameras watching like hawks." Slate added.

King piped in, "He's an amateur. Probably hasn't thought his plan through."

"Those are the easiest to catch." This came from T-BAR who for the most part was keeping to himself. "Too many mistakes...leads us right to them."

Slate and T hadn't spoken since his return, and King assigned them to neutral corners. Slate figured King didn't want animosity between them boiling up and all hell to break loose. T was holding his own, but Slate wanted to have a face-to-face with him. Slate knew the talk would come sooner or later, but he wasn't going to have the discussion in front of Ember. She was already placing the blame of T's injury on herself because

Slate left to protect her. That thought was bullshit, because Ember didn't make his decision when he walked out. That was on him.

"This is the day he dropped the letter." Cy was pointing to the screen. "When he wrote it, probably wore gloves, but, see...he pulls the paper out already folded in half —"

"No gloves." A few guys said in unison.

"Dumbass," was Trip's contribution to the conversation.

"That's why no prints were found as they normally would, say if you were writing a letter, you'd have palm prints, smudges, partials. His prints would be all over the face of that thing." Arctic was thinking out loud.

King swiveled in his chair. "Majority of the prints were on the folded face. Wrote the letter with gloved hands, folded it, didn't wear gloves after that. It's an imbecile criminal."

The new guy, Creed spoke up, "Unless he wants to be caught?" He let the question hang in the air.

"Naw. He's just stupid," Slate added.

"Would have been pretty suspicious if he'd have been in the shop with latex gloves on." Trip huffed a quick laugh, "Or any gloves in ninety-degree Texas heat."

"Question now, where is he? And, where's the family?" King asked, running his hand down his short beard.

Trip raised his brows. "If we can figure that out, then we grab 'em and nab 'em, then make him talk. Don't let him clam up like his brother."

"If only," came Arctic's response. The guys in the room gave head nods and murmurs of agreement.

"Gotta do this one by the books, boys. I promised Matthews no interference."

"Why would he expect that? Does he know us at all?" Cy quipped back, giving the room a well-needed chuckle.

"Serious as shit, boys. By. The. Book." King punctuated each word and leaned into the table giving a glance to each of the men, and Ember, sitting around the conference table. "Don't want this fucked up. Recon only. Call in what you see. Do not handle this ourselves."

"Can we be concerned citizens making a citizen's arrest?" Trip laughed.

"Yeah, citizens who carry a Carbine as their EDC, no questions asked!" Creed added, while everyone continued to laugh.

CHAPTER 13

Ember stayed in the conference room for a bit while the analyticals continued and the men discussed strategies. She breathed a sigh of relief knowing she had seven men on her six. She really had to pee, so she slipped from the room, no one noticing her make her pee-getaway.

Ember made her way down the hallway to the closest bathroom, thinking about how she was going to set up her office in the space King had given her. Her space was right next to King's office, and sandwiched on the other side was Slate's, which gave her a sense of comfort knowing if someone *were* stupid enough to come to Hellforce to find her, they'd be meeting King before they got to her, and Slate would be right behind him. That is, if they could get past the other six just-as-deadly men in the surrounding offices.

She pushed open the door to the bathroom and was met with a sound that almost turned her stomach. Someone was puking.

Ember stood in the bathroom entrance, not knowing if she should turn back around and give the poor person her privacy, or if she should offer some help or assistance. The latter won out.

"...Um, is everything all right?" Her words echoed in the cavernous space of the stalls. "Are you okay?"

Another gut-wrenching heave came from within the first stall.

Ember stifled a grimace. She waited until the remains of someone's breakfast emptied into the toilet. "Do you need help?"

Heaving pants came from within the stall. "Nope..." The words were strangled and nasal, "I'm good."

Ember didn't think the woman on the other side of the metal barrier was all that good. "Ah, are you sure? It sounds like it's the opposite of good. I can get someone—"

"No, no...I'm alright. I'm fine." The sound of toilet paper being spun off the roll was loud in the large space. "Just need a minute."

Ember paused, waiting to see if the woman was going to empty anything else into the bowl. The voice was clearly in distress, but also seemed familiar. She could be any one of the number of women who worked in the building, so Ember took a chance. "Um, Mary?" She drew her friend's name out.

There was a lull before a response came. "Yeah?"

Ember let out a breath. "Is everything all right? Did you eat something bad?"

No response.

"Do you have food poisoning?"

"Um...no." Her response hung in the air.

"Do you need me to get King,? I can—"

"Oh, God, no!" Mary almost shouted. Her voice rang off the tiles.

"Are you sure? You sound absolutely miserable."

The toilet flushed and Mary scurried until she righted herself, the metal partition forbidding her much room and not nearly enough privacy.

Ember recoiled in her mind when Mary came out from the stall. She looked horrendous. She was sweaty and her face was pale and flushed at the same time.

Straightening her skirt and righting her top in a frenzy of motion and nerves, Mary asked, "How do I look?"

Ember stood and stared.

When her response didn't come, Mary staggered to the sink

and looked in the mirror. "Oh, God..." She franticly tried to finger comb her hair.

"You don't look...that bad."

Mary shot her a look through the mirror. Suddenly, one hand flew over her mouth as the other grasped her stomach. She raced back into the stall not bothering to shut the door behind her.

Ember entered behind her friend, reached over her bent posture, and held Mary's hair.

Mary's dry-heaves sounded guttural and Ember felt bad for her. She didn't know what to say so she just waited until the heaving stopped.

"Oh, God...I'm going to die," Mary said with panting breaths, resting her head over her crossed arms. "Oh, God, this sucks!" She pulled a handful of toilet paper from the roll and wiped her mouth. She reached back and took her hair from Ember's grasp. "Thanks...you're a great friend."

Ember moved out of the stall, over to the sink, and wet some paper towels with cold water. Mary emerged, looking even more sickly than before. Ember handed her the towels and waited with her hip against the vanity top.

"Oh, whew...thanks," she said, taking the wet towels and patting her forehead then her neck.

Ember eyed Mary, waiting for her to talk.

Mary met her eyes in the mirror, but still said nothing as Ember noted the indecision in her gaze. Was she trying to make something up?

"Are you..."

"Don't say it! Don't even utter the words." Mary closed her eyes as she pleaded.

"...pregnant?" Ember couldn't stop the word from rolling off her tongue before Mary's mournful plea.

"Oh, fuck!" Mary sagged against the counter with her arms locked and head hung. "Now you did it! You uttered the words and now you did it!"

Ember shifted her weight to the other hip. "Um, I'm pretty sure it was King who did it...if my assumption is correct."

Mary shook her head. "Fuck!"

Ember tried to tread lightly.

"Is this a bad thing?" The question was curious.

Mary filled her cupped hand with water and rinsed her mouth, sipping and spitting, and didn't answer.

"Is this an unpleasant thing?" Ember tried again.

Mary winced. "No, it's not unpleasant.

Ember flattened her lips in confusion. "No, it's not unpleasant? That's a double negative," Ember tried to lighten the mood and raised her eyes to the ceiling. "So, two negatives negate each other, so...it's not a bad thing? But, the not, negates the unpleas..." Ember closed her eyes and shook the rambled grammar from her thoughts. "Um, kinda sendin' mixed messages, Mare." She knew her ramblings worked when Mary cracked a grin.

Mary stood, shoulders slumped in front of her friend, with a goofy grin on her face though she also looked like she wanted to sob. Ember waited for her to say something. Between the cryptic sentence and now the mixed facial features, she didn't know what to expect.

Mary started to sob. It began slowly and then morphed into a shoulder-shuddering cry.

"Oh, it's okay, hun." Ember took Mary into a hug and Mary almost fell into her. She didn't know if it was okay, but she didn't know what else to say. "Babe, listen, it's okay. I'll help you through this. Anything I can do, you got it."

Mary sobbed into Ember's shoulder and then uttered the muffled words, "I'm so happy."

Ember paused, thinking she may not have heard her friend right or maybe this was another cryptic message, because Mary's emotions were all over the place and definitely sending mixed signals.

She pulled back, noticing Mary had ugly-cried onto her shoulder and now had snot leaking from her nose. Ember pulled a few paper towels from the dispenser and handed them to her. She vigorously wiped her nose and blew into the paper. Composing herself, she stared at Ember.

Ember raised her brows.

"I think I may be pregnant."

Ember waited for her to continue.

Mary smiled another goofy grin.

"This is good?"

Mary nodded her head, the grin getting bigger and goofier than before. "I think so."

"And, King? Is he happy?"

Mary's face fell and she again looked on the verge of tears.

"No, no, no, nooo...not gonna do that again. Happy, you're happy, no tears." Ember didn't want to go another round with Jekyll and Hyde.

"King doesn't want a baby?" Was this the source of Mary's tears?

"He doesn't know."

"He doesn't know if he wants babies?"

"No, he doesn't know."

Ember shook her head and looked Mary directly in her face. "No, no more cryptic grammar. Look at me, Mary. Are. You. Happy?"

"Yes."

"Is King happy?"

"He doesn't know. I haven't told him."

Okay, now Ember was getting somewhere. "Have you taken a test or been to the doctor?"

"No," she looked at Ember and then added, "and, no."

"So, no test; no doctor?"

"Yes."

Oh, my God. It was like Abbott and Costello's *Who's On First.* Ember wanted to shake her friend, but then had second thoughts because she didn't want to hurt the baby that may or may not, be gestating.

Ember drew in a breath and smiled back at her friend.

"Do you need me to go and get you a test?"

Mary nodded.

"Do you want to take it here?"

Mary desperately shook her head no.

"Do you want to take it at home?"

Mary shook her head in the negative. "I don't want to take it at home. I don't want King to know."

"Okay, so not here and not at home." Ember paused and then asked, "Do you want to come to my house and take it? Give you privacy?"

Mary nodded and wiped her nose again, "Will you stay with me while I take it?"

"If that's what you want, then, yeah, I'll be there."

"Thank you. I've been a wreck."

Ember wanted to say, *"No, shit,"* but thought better of it.

"When do you want to do this?"

"Right now?" It came out as a question, but Ember took it to mean sooner rather than later.

"Okay, where's your car keys? I'll grab them while you stay here and...freshen up."

"I don't have my car. King drove me in today."

Shit. That was a problem. She would have to ask Eli if she could use his truck. *Damn!*

"Okay..." she looked around. "I'll go get some keys and we'll head out." She turned to leave but then turned back to Mary. "Don't you have to let King know you're leaving?"

"Can you just tell him we're leaving for lunch?" she pleaded.

Ember looked down at her watch. "It's only nine-thirty."

"Shit."

"Can't you tell him you're not feeling well and need to go home?"

Mary laughed, which Ember liked, because it meant she wasn't on the verge of crying. "You ever seen him when I'm sick?" Mary laughed a little harder. "Man practically sets up a triage unit in the house to assess my degree of illness and then plays nursemaid until I'm back up to par. I've had a hell of a time trying not to puke at home. I hold back until I'm here at work."

Ember had to laugh because all she could picture in her head was a big, strapping King in a little nurse's uniform waiting on Mary hand and foot.

"I'll just tell him we're having a girls' day." She added, "Not a total lie."

Mary looked relieved as Ember headed towards the door. "Be back in a snap." She quickly hurried out the door.

~

Ember barreled out of the bathroom and collided into a chest of steel. "Whoa!" Slate stopped her from crashing into him and Ember let out a little screech. "Where's the fire?"

"What'cha doing here?" she asked in a startled breath, steadying herself.

"Didn't know you'd be gone this long." He checked his watch. "You've been gone for twenty minutes. Came looking...to make sure everything's all right."

"I'm fine." The words came out in a rush.

Slate tucked a stray tendril of hair behind her ear. Her red locks were on the verge of frizz because of the hot Texas morning.

"Ya sure? 'Cuz you seem kinda jumpy."

She tried to relax. "No, everything's fine. Perfectly normal. Peachy."

Now, Slate knew something was amiss. He eyed her with suspicion.

Ember smiled a smile she hoped didn't look too forced. Eli knew her like the back of his hand. She never could get away with lying to him. He could always tell when she was pulling a fast one. She had to say something quickly to keep the questioning off herself. She blurted the first thing that came to her mind. "I need to use your truck."

Eli *loved* his truck and never let anyone use it. "Why do you need my truck?"

Ember tried to think of a reason, but her mind was blank.

Slate waited for her to answer. She watched him assess her body language.

"I want to take Mary for lunch." *Oh, double shit!*

Slate repeated the gesture she had done with Mary and looked at his watch. "It's only a little past nine-thirty."

She could feel a bit of perspiration breaking out on her upper lip and hoped that her forehead wasn't glistening as well. She was painting herself into a corner. *Think, think, think. He's going to know you're lying.* Her conscience was screaming at her and she was warring with it to shut the hell up and let her think.

"Girl'sday!" Ember blurted out the words so fast they came out as one word. *Triple shit!*

She knew that he knew she was lying. She had to pull this off. Mary was going to burst into tears, sobs, and possibly histrionics if she failed to get the keys.

"Girl's day with who?" Eli's suspicion was palpable.

Stay calm. It's not a lie. "Mary." She could do this. She had to keep her calm. She was a former sniper. She knew how to collect herself. She just had to dig into the mindset that this was a mission. Plain and simple. Nice and easy.

"Where's Mary? Didn't see her at her desk."

Shit. Shit. Shit. Stay calm. Tell him the truth. "In the bathroom." *Nailed it!*

Eli pointed to the door behind them. "This bathroom?"

Truth. "Yes."

"Is she all right?"

Panic! "Yes." *Nothing unhealthy about possibly being pregnant, right?*

Eli stepped around Ember and knocked on the door. "Mary?"

There was no reply.

He knocked again, this time a little more forceful, the sound echoing in the hallway. "Mary? Are you in there? Is everything all right?"

Shit. His voice was loud and carrying down the corridor. If he got any louder it would bring the guys out of the conference room. That was the last thing Mary needed.

Eli looked over at Ember.

Panic was trying to seep in, but she held it at bay. "Maybe I'll just go in and make sure she's okay." Ember didn't see any other way to quench this fire. She tried to move around Eli, but he stood his ground in front of the door, not moving an inch. He was a wall.

He knocked a third time, this time so hard she was almost certain everyone in the building heard it. Her heart was beating against her ribs. She wasn't sure if the sound was coming from Eli's knuckles or from inside her body. Hell, she could feel every knock as it reverberated in her chest.

"Mary, if you don't open the door, I'm going to have to come in to make sure you're all right."

Shit. Damn. And shit again!

Eli waited no more than three seconds and then pushed open the door.

Mary was standing at the sink, composed, pulled together. Ember let out her breath in a woosh.

Mary turned around and met Eli's gaze.

"You all right?" He asked.

"Yes, I'm fine." Mary stayed poised.

"You didn't answer." Eli was studying every inch of her, measuring every reaction.

"Kinda hard to answer when you're in the middle of taking a sh— "

Eli didn't let her finish the sentence. "Okay, okay. Got it." He shook his head, probably to clear out the mental image. "You could have at least yelled or something."

Ember held still.

"Ready to go, Em?" Mary was pulling off this nonchalant attitude so well, she could have won an Oscar.

"Can I have the keys?" Ember held her hand out, palm open, waiting for Eli to hand them over.

"Nope."

"What do you mean, 'Nope'?" Ember felt the panic flow again but tamped it down. She didn't want to prolong this and have Mary possibly burst into sobs.

"First, no one drives my truck, and second, wherever you need to go, I will drive you. I don't want you traipsing all over town when you're supposed to be in my protection."

Shit, that threw a wrench into their plan. Ember tried to think of an excuse but couldn't conjure anything concrete, so she went with, "How is it a girls' day if it's me, Mary and Eli? You have an 'outtie' when you need to have an 'innie,' for it to be girls' day."

Eli looked confused for a moment but caught on to her jest.

"The same way you and Maven have Margarita Mondays. I stay within seeing distance and you girly it up."

Shit, shit, shit! He had a point. Mondays were sometimes

spent with Eli and the Hellforce boys. The boys shot the shit over beers while the women sat at the bar and 'rita-ed.

"Our girls' day is at my place. No girly spa or nails, just me and Mare watching chick-flicks on Netflix and eating junk food."

"That's fine. I'll just bring the laptop and catch up on things I missed while being gone this last month. You and Mare can have the living room, and I'll work in the dining room."

Fuck! They were screwed. No way Eli was going to let them out of his sight. And, how was Mary supposed to pee on a stick with him hovering at her house? She had to go with it, because if she suddenly changed her mind and told him she didn't want a girls' day, his suspicion would skyrocket, and he'd start asking questions.

"That's cool." Ember hoped he bought it, because she was using every bit of cool she could muster.

"Okay. Meet you back up front. Just gotta tell the guys I'm taking off."

He gave her a tight smile, turned and gave Mary a wave, then he was out the door.

Ember and Mary stared at each other, then Mary clapped a hand over her mouth and beelined it into the stall.

Shit!

CHAPTER 14

"Flaming Cheetos or BBQ chips?" Ember held up a bag of each and asked Mary which one they should get.

"Um, both!"

Ember rolled her eyes and added both bags to their already overloaded grocery basket. Each woman had one slung over the crook of her arm and the contents were a cumulation of items— lemon cookies, peanut butter, jalapeno peppers, mini bagel pepperoni pizzas, dill pickles, popcorn, beef jerky, cheesecake, and a giant size Swiss chocolate bar.

"Ooh, and ice cream. We need ice cream." Mary's eyes widened with desire for the frozen glory as she headed for the freezer section.

Eli glanced down at the assortment of random items with confusion. "This is what you're eating?" He grimaced. "Is this some kind of food punishment, lost a bet, type of thing?"

Mary was on a mission several aisles ahead of them, already scoping out the selection of ice cream. "Yes! Jackpot."

Ember heard Mary's excitement and made it to her friend's side. She had to second-guess Mary's pick. "Mango Habanero Coconut Ice Cream. Eww! Mare?"

"Doesn't that sound delish!"

"Sounds like a stomachache if you ask me," Eli said as Mary

placed it in her basket. "Anything else you need? Like maybe some antacids?"

Ember glanced at Mary. Both were trying to figure out a way to get to the personal care aisle without him on their heels.

"Ooh, do you know what I could *really* go for?" Mary urged.

Eli raised his brows waiting for her to blurt out some insane item like stewed oysters or pickled eggs.

"Steak!"

That got Eli's interest. He liked to cook, but the grill is where he was master. Seeing his face light up, Ember knew she had him.

"Why don't you head to the meat department, and we'll finish up our shopping," Ember said when she saw the excitement of reigning over the grill in his eyes.

"You got more shopping to do? You mean this isn't enough junk food?" Eli questioned.

Mary shifted from one foot to the other trying to hide her nervousness.

"Just gotta get a few more things then we'll be done. We'll meet you at the meat counter." Ember gave Eli an agreeable look, hoping he would leave.

"Okay. I'll head over there. Don't be too long." He turned and headed off.

When Eli walked away, Mary shrugged in relief. "Wasn't sure he'd leave. Let's go, gotta make this quick."

Both women beelined for the personal care aisle. When they got to the right aisle the selections overwhelmed them.

Ember took two pregnancy tests off the shelf to compare them. "So, what do you want, Mare? Blue line, pink line, double line, plus sign?" Then, she looked at another on the shelf, "This one actually tells you in words, pregnant or not pregnant." Ember put back the ones she was holding and took two more off the shelf. Reading the back of the boxes she tried to figure out which was best.

Mary stood, reading the box over Ember's shoulder. "Never realized there were so many choices. Does it really make a difference?"

Ember held up a test and showed it to Mary, "This one says it can tell before a missed period. Have you missed a period?"

"Kinda...I'm never regular, so it's actually been a few months."

Ember gaped with astonishment, "Whoa, you're just checking now?"

"Well, yeah," she said while perusing the shelf, "I'm never this late, my boobs hurt, and I've been on a roller coaster of emotions this last week. King probably thinks I'm a bitch."

Ember stayed silent. She hadn't seen Mary in the last month with things on the rocks between King and Eli. She had kept in touch through texts, but Mary never said anything about feeling out of sorts. "Sorry I haven't been there for you, Mare. I wish I'd have known."

"Not your fault. Things were contentious with the guys, and I wanted to be neutral. Didn't want to get in the middle of the spat. I tried to talk King into talking to Eli, but he's bullheaded. Every time I brought it up, I was met with a pissed-off husband. Figured they'd make up eventually, but it just took longer than I thought."

"I'm so glad things are back to normal." Ember looked from Mary back to the shelf of tests. "Eli wants to talk to T, but T's been keeping his distance."

"Yeah, King's making them play nice, but they really need to clear the air."

"Let's just hope they can."

Both stood silent thinking of the situation with T-BAR. A lot hinged on the outcome of his recovery.

Mary looked over the shelf of options and said, "Let's just pick one."

Ember held up the one in her hand, "Let's take this one. It has actual words on it, and we won't have to second-guess the test."

"And, it's a multipack so I can double-check. Be twice as sure."

Ember handed Mary the box. She hid it beneath the bag of extra-spicy Jamaican Jerk beef jerky.

They started down the aisle towards the meat counter when Eli rounded the corner, meat packages and other items in his hands.

Ember's heart skipped a beat and Mary said under her breath, "Oh, shit!"

"You two ready? I've been waiting fifteen minutes and you never showed. Why are you over here?"

Mary reached over to the shelf, grabbed a random package, and held it up, "I had to get," she looked at the box in her hand, "um, an economy pack of super-flow tampons." She tried to hide the confused and muddled look on her face.

Eli scrunched his face, "Okay, didn't need to know that."

"Perfectly natural thing, Eli," Mary said as she put the box in her basket, hoping that the bag of jerky hid her secret beneath it.

"I know it is," Eli tilted his head a bit, "nothing I'm embarrassed about. Bought them myself many times for my mom, but I just don't need to know the flow cycle of my friend and boss' wife."

"You've bought tampons for your mom?" Mary said, a little too much surprise in her voice.

"Yeah, why not?"

"Well," Mary paused, "just guessed...not many guys would do that."

"Like you said, a perfectly normal function of nature. If I can buy toilet paper, why not tampons? Girls buy condoms even though men use them."

Mary thought about that, pursed her lips, and nodded her head in agreement.

"Unless you want to talk about your cycle some more, are you two ready to go?"

"Yes!" Both women said in unison and then laughed at each other's quick reply.

The trio headed to the checkout line. Eli got into the shortest line since there were only three open registers.

"Gonna go to the self-checkout," Mary said, imploring Ember with a look that was practically telepathic.

"Don't like those things," Eli remarked. "Never work for me, and then I end up taking twice as long, waiting for an employee to come fix or override the register."

"How did you survive the Army?" Ember asked in mockery. "You can execute a mission flawlessly, in the dark of night, in unknown terrain but can't check out your own groceries?" She laughed at his shit-ass grin.

"Maybe if I shopped with the team at my back, then I could checkout flawlessly as well?" His smile lit up his face.

Ember thought he had a great smile. In fact, she absolutely loved his smile. "Well, you can stay in this line, I'm going to checkout with Mary." She stepped out of line and headed towards her friend.

Eli stayed where he was and Ember was relieved that he didn't follow. She was still within his sight, so she figured that was good enough for him to feel she was still safe.

Mary put her basket on the shelf next to the register. "Oh, my God," Mary said out of the side of her mouth, "that was so close."

"I know, right?"

"Don't need these tampons, but I just grabbed the closest thing on the shelf."

Ember laughed at the irony of the situation. "Kinda counter-productive to be buying a pregnancy test and tampons, hey?" She chuckled when Mary laughed.

"At least it wasn't a mega pack of vaginal yeast cream. Think Eli would have turned green in shock if I'd had that in my hand." Both girls broke into laughter at the thought.

They checked out their items, making sure the test was at the bottom of the bag, then finished bagging up the rest of the groceries.

Eli walked over. "See, Emmy, same wait time and I didn't have to do the work."

That gorgeous smile was back on his face.

"Okay, all set." Mary picked up her bags, as did Ember.

"Lord, that's a lot of junk food." Eli eyed their bags.

"That's the rule for a great girls' day."

"Yeah, followed by a night of heartburn and upset stomach."

They all laughed and headed for Eli's truck.

Back at the house, the trio carried their bags into the kitchen. The girls lingered in the living room, not wanting to unpack the bags on the counter next to Eli, who was preparing a marinade for the steaks. Mary was nervously chewing her nails while Ember searched for a chick flick, one that Eli, hopefully, wouldn't want to watch.

"How am I going to do this? He's going to be hovering around this place all day. And, the bathroom's right down the hall off the living room." Mary was talking just above a whisper. "Why'd you have to buy a house with only one bathroom?"

Ember looked over at Mary, gauging if she was joking or was on another emotional rollercoaster. Mary had a grin on her face and Ember breathed a sigh of relief. No way could Mary break into tears in front of Eli if she wanted this to remain a covert op.

"Why did you have unprotected sex with your husband if you didn't want to get knocked up?" Ember laughed at the comeback, but Mary wasn't laughing. She had a quivering chin and her eyes were shiny.

Oh, shit. Not here. Not now.

Ember was about to console her friend, when Mary rapidly blinked the wetness from her eyes.

"Mare, I'm sorry, I was just…"

"You think I am?" She swallowed and whispered, "Pregnant?"

"One way to find out and that's to get Eli out of the house."

From the kitchen they could hear Eli whistling a tune and rustling around in the paper bags. "Do you want this junk food out on the counter or on the table? Where should I put this?"

Oh, shit! Eli was in their bags. Both Mary and Ember spring boarded from the couch and raced into the kitchen. Their hasty entrance had Eli turning around.

"Don't touch those!" Mary pointed a finger with a demand so forceful, Eli removed his hand from within the bag, his eyes widened.

"I mean," Mary stammered, looking for another explanation, "um…"

Ember chimed in, "We'll just take the bags into the living room." She grabbed the bag Eli had rummaged in. "That way we won't have to leave the couch while our movie's on."

Mary followed pace and took the other bag from the counter.

"Don't you have to put the pizzas and ice cream in the freezer?"

Mary reached into her bag and pulled out the box of mini bagel pizzas and container of ice cream and put them in the freezer.

"Is everything okay?" Eli asked.

"Peachy," Ember answered. "Are you going to start the grill?"

He washed his hands then shut off the faucet and reached for the towel. "Yup, on my way to do that next."

"Grill may need to be cleaned." Ember was praying it needed a good brushing so it would keep him busy.

"Great." Eli rolled his eyes.

They took the bags into the living room and Eli headed out the patio door to deal with the grill.

"Fuck. How fast can you pee?" Ember shot Mary a wide-eyed expression.

Mary tore through the bag and pulled the test from the bottom. They both headed for the bathroom. "Lock the door," Mary told Ember, as she opened the box and pulled out the instruction pamphlet. The pamphlet was small but unfolded to the size of a 1980s state map. "Oh, shit...how complicated is this?"

"Kinda thought it was pretty much straight forward. Just pee on it and read it."

Mary searched the paper and found the section of instructions. She paraphrased while reading out loud. "Remove from foil...remove end cap...hold at downward angle...urinate for ten to fifteen seconds," Mary lowered the sheet, "who pees for fifteen seconds?" She continued reading, "Replace cap...lay on flat surface...wait three minutes."

Mary turned the huge instruction sheet over a few times, "Why do I need a paper the size of Texas to tell me seven steps of directions?" She attempted to fold the sheet back up, but gave up when it wouldn't fold nicely.

Ember took the paper from her. "Pee, lady. We don't have time to fold this map."

There was a knock on the door. Both girls froze in place.

"Em, are you in there?" Eli's voice came from the other side of the door.

Ember looked at Mary, shock and surprise on her face.

"Emmy?"

"Answer him," Mary mouthed.

"Yeah," she paused, "I'm in here." She stared at Mary.

"Grill won't start, you're out of propane."

Hallelujah! The grill gods were on their side, meaning Eli would have to run and get a new tank.

"Oh, that sucks." The girls had huge grins stretching their faces. "You gonna go get a new tank?" Ember could feel the glee radiating from her chest.

"No. King's picking one up. He's on his way over."

Fuck!

Ember closed her eyes and Mary sat down on the toilet lid. *What the fuck were they going to do now?*

"Why's King coming over?" Mary blurted out then threw her hand over her mouth. Ember shook her head.

"Why's Mary in there with you?"

Ember's eyes remained closed and she hung her head.

"I had to...show her something." The excuse rolled off Mary's tongue before she thought of what she was saying.

Ember's eyes popped open and she mouthed, "What the fuck?"

Mary shrugged and mouthed, "It just came out."

There was silence from the other side of the door. Then, Eli questioned, "Um, is everything okay?"

"Yeah, everything's fine, just give us a minute." Mary strained her face and hoped he wouldn't ask any questions.

Silence hung in the air. The awkwardness was palpable.

"Okay...just do...what you're doing," Eli's voice was hesitant. "I'll be in the living room."

Both girls waited until they knew he'd left the hallway.

"Oh, my god. 'You had to show me something,' what the fuck?" Ember said in hushed tones.

"I panicked."

"I think we should just ditch this plan and you can take it later."

Mary's face started to contort. Ember hoped it wasn't water works.

"I don't think I can wait." Mary stood up and urged Ember to not abandon the plan.

"Too risky, Mare. King's on his way and he can sniff out deception like a bloodhound. If you take this and try to keep the results from him, he's going to know you're hiding something."

"What if it's negative?"

"What if it's not?"

They stood at an impasse.

"It's your choice, Mare, ultimately your decision. I'm just trying to avoid a possible clusterfuck when King gets here."

Mary knew Ember was right. King would know something was up the minute he laid eyes on her. And, with her emotions like a whirlwind, she couldn't hide anything.

"You're right. I'll have to wait, but the 'not knowing' is going to kill me."

Ember took the test, put it back in the box, and placed it in the vanity drawer.

"Safe keeping for now," Ember said as she turned to open the door.

King arrived within thirty minutes, propane tank in tow, and six men behind him.

Mary and Ember watched in horror as their plan to take the test later was now completely out the window. Slate, Cy, Arctic, Trip, T, and Creed went out on the deck while King attached the new tank to the grill. The guys were unloading packages of burgers, brats, buns and an array of salads and extras that had Mary on the hunt for something spicy.

"There." King wiped his hands on his thighs as he stood. "Steaks will be grilling in no time."

"Didn't know the crew was coming." Ember stated to King when he opened the grill to inspect the grate.

"Guys can use a break. They need some time together outside

of work." King fiddled with the grate. "Thought this would be a good time to get team comradery back in swing."

Ember couldn't help but think this was the worst time to have her house teeming with the team, but she kept the thought to herself.

King continued, "Things gotta get tight. Between looking for the Bazwars and leaving for a mission at the end of this week, the guys have to bring their bond back together. Things can't continue to go FUBAR in the field." He adjusted some knobs and pushed the ignitor, bringing the grill to life. "Voila!" King bellowed in satisfaction, "Bring on the meats!"

Ember didn't know the guys would be leaving on a mission. It put a pit in her stomach every time they left. She knew the guys were competent and kicked ass every time they went out, but it still made her worry every time. Until their boots made it back to US soil, she wouldn't breathe easy.

The guys were kicking back with beer, burgers, and steak, and everyone was having a pretty good time. T-BAR was hanging back but still enjoying the get-together. Eli wanted to get him alone, hash out whatever was building between them, but T was steering clear of him.

Ember noticed the new guy, Creed, was melding well into the group. He seemed like a great guy. At six-foot, two-hundred-twenty-five pounds, with a tight fade, brown eyes, a hint of scruff filling in his jaw, and smooth tan skin, he was a fine speci-men. Not that she was looking to hook up, but some lucky lady would definitely have some eye candy on her arm.

"Can we talk?" Eli came up beside her, startling her from her reverie.

"Sure, what's up?

"Can we go inside?" Slate looked concerned, and Ember knew he wanted to talk about T-BAR. Eli told her earlier he was concerned T wasn't going to want to air their grievances.

"Sure." She threw her paper plate in the garbage and followed him through the sliding glass door into the house.

Eli didn't stop in the living room, but started down the hallway, Ember following, not sure where he was going. They came to her bedroom door, and Eli asked, "Is this all right?"

She nodded in concern and pushed it open, entering, with Eli behind her. He shut and locked the door which put Ember on alert. He crossed the room and sat on her bed. She looked at him quizzically when he tapped the comforter beside himself, wanting her to sit. She did as he wanted wondering what was on his mind. What would call for this much privacy?

Eli pulled in a deep breath and took Ember in, studying her face with curiosity. He took her hands in his, rubbing the backs with his thumb and slowly caressed them. Ember braced for what he would say. She knew this wasn't the conversation about T-BAR she was expecting.

"You know you can come to me with anything, right?"

Ember furrowed her brow, "Yesss."

"And, you know I would never judge you or condemn you...ever."

Again, she answered him, "Yesss."

"And, you know I'd be there for you no matter what." Eli's eyes were wrought with kindness and every word was sincere.

"Elijah, what's this about? Kinda confusing me here."

He swallowed, his Adam's apple bobbing in his throat. He looked deep into her eyes and said, "You don't have to do this alone. If whoever it is won't stand by your side, I will."

Ember furrowed even more, her face squeezing tight in confusion. "What are you talking about, Elijah?"

He methodically rubbed her hands with his thumbs; his palms now dappled with a hint of sweat. "If you're pregnant, you'll have my support throughout your pregnancy and after the baby's born," his voice was strong and confident, "I'll be by your side."

Ember's mouth dropped, first in confusion, then in shock. *Holy shit! Eli knew about the test!* And he thought it was hers.

"One hundred percent, Em. I will be there if you have to do this alone. You *will not* be alone." He stared into her eyes, and she knew he meant every word. "One hundred percent. I will be there. *Whatever* you need. *Whenever* you need. Midnight cravings...on it. Late night or early morning feedings...there for you. Last-minute diaper runs, dirty diaper changings, cranky baby can't sleep...I'm there for it when you call."

Ember broke out in laughter. So much so that her eyes started to tear. She couldn't control the laughing fits that rolled up out of her chest.

Eli sat. Confused. Concerned.

It took a bit, but Ember got herself under control, wiping her tears as best she could, getting Eli into focus. "Oh, my god, Eli. You think I'm pregnant?" She bubbled up some more, her eyes brimmed again. "You think I'm having a baby?"

Eli let go of her hands. His forehead creased trying to make heads or tails out of Ember's reaction. "It's okay, Emmy. It'll all be okay," he took in another breath, "I saw you looking at the pregnancy tests at the store. I knew that's why you didn't want to check out in line with me." He cleared his throat. "You and Mare in the bathroom together solidified the fact that I know you don't want to do this alone." He took her hands in his again. "You'll have me and my mom, Mary, King, the guys, and I know your family will stand behind you through everything. One hundred percent. You're my girl, Emmy. If the guy's a piece of shit and won't man-up, know you'll always have me. You always have."

Ember's heart melted at his heartfelt declaration but she had to let him know the truth. "I'm not pregnant, Eli. I'm not having a baby." Ember watched as a mixture of relief, surprise and a bit of confusion hovered over his expression. "The test was negative?"

"No." she squeezed his hand, still in hers. "The test isn't mine...it's Mary's."

The surprise on his face was gold! "It's Mary's?" He blinked a few times, letting the statement register. "Oh, it's *Mary's*." He let out a single laugh and shook his head.

"Yeah, she didn't want to take the test alone. She was sick in the bathroom at work this morning and that's why I wanted to leave. But, then you had to be, *you*, and shot that plan all to hell."

He laughed, then sobered, "What about King?"

"He doesn't know yet. She hasn't taken the test."

Eli's face melted into happiness for his friend.

"Damn, King with a kid, that'd be something else."

"I guess Mary's been on a roller coaster lately."

Eli's expression brightened. "All the phone conversations King's been having with her lately. Makes sense that Mary was out of sorts. She's usually laid back, and she and King never used to bicker, at least not in front of friends."

"I can't believe you thought I was pregnant." Ember scoffed at Eli.

"In my defense, the crazy combination of junk food and then seeing you examining those test boxes, gotta agree with me that I was in the right frame of thinking."

"And, you didn't once think I was helping out a friend?"

Eli rubbed the back of his neck and chuckled.

"And, who do you think the prospective father would be?"

Eli sat silent, looking sheepish as he floundered in embarrassment.

"Gosh, I'm with you, like twenty-four seven, Elijah. If I was getting it on with anybody, it would be you." Ember laughed at her innocent jab, but the look on Eli's face stopped her in her tracks. Both sat in the awkwardness of the moment, neither knowing what to say in response to her joke.

He rubbed his neck again and stood from the bed. He held out a hand for her and she stood as well.

Eli leaned over and gave her a chaste kiss on the forehead. He lingered a minute and said, "I still would have been here for you," murmuring the words against her flesh.

Ember felt his lips as he said the words in earnest. A feeling came over her, one she'd never felt with him. It hit her soul and tingled throughout her body. Earth-shattering.

He stepped back and started for the door. Ember stayed at her bedside relishing in the new sensation.

Eli waited at the door, "You coming?"

Ember shuddered the breath she didn't realize she held and walked over to him. Eli took her hand in his, just like always, interlacing their fingers without thought or hesitation, and they left the room to join the rest of the gang.

Eli followed Ember out through the patio door expecting the gang to be caught up in conversation, finishing up the last of the burgers and salads. Instead, all eyes were glued to Mary as she held something up in her hand.

The group stood still, shocked and silent.

Mary repeated the words she'd announced just before they came out the door.

"I'm pregnant."

King stood from his seat in silence, holding Mary's eyes. No one dared move or make a sound. He slowly made his way over to his wife, never taking his eyes from hers. Stopping in front of her, he said three words. "Is it true?"

Mary handed him the stick that read *PREGNANT* and waited with bated breath.

King took the test from her and read the result to himself.

In one swift motion, he planted his lips on hers, pouring his soul into her. He broke the kiss and steadied his wife. Then, he dropped to his knees, placing his hands on either side of her waist and reverently kissed her stomach. He kissed her flat belly with so much emotion, everyone around him felt it.

He lifted his tear-stained eyes to his wife and mouthed the words, "Thank you!"

It was official.

King was a Papa!

CHAPTER 15

Slate was in the ready room going through gear and packing his bag for the next day's mission. They were off to Yemen on a K & R. His mind was heavy. His focus was on the mission and the plans they had gone over repeatedly, each detail committed to memory. He focused now on what needed to be packed and what needed to be on his person to make the mission a success.

He also had T-BAR on his mind. Things hadn't aired out between them, and Slate wanted to get things squared before he left. T was sitting this mission out due to his eye. He was still wearing the eye covering, and his quality of vision was still unknown.

And, because T was on his mind, so was Ember. King put T on protection duty for Ember until they returned. Slate knew T would protect her with his life, wouldn't let anything happen to her, but he still was worried. Maybe it was a primal, caveman-ish, *man-protect-woman* impulse, but unless he was the one protecting her, he worried about her. When mission time came, he had to put his trust in his brother because his mind would be nowhere else but on the task at hand; a successful mission.

He packed his things, as always being meticulous in what he was taking. Everything had a purpose. A need. Want had no place in a man's carry. Each extra ounce became a pound on a long hike. The terrain was going to be hell. They'd be hiking in from a distance and each guy knew his strength and limits, so packing was essential to get the right balance. Extra provisions in case of a delay, but not too many. Extra medical supplies, but not everyone carried the same supplies to balance out the overage they needed. Overcalculating led to extra weight and valuable space within each man's ruck. Under-packing led to disaster. Between each man's MOLLE and their ruck, they could be carrying anywhere from sixty to one-hundred pounds. But on this mission, it would be a light pack for each man.

Trip and Arctic entered the room joking and bullshitting as usual. Usually before a mission, the high of anticipation was in the air and everyone felt it. It was a great feeling. A feeling that they knew success was imminent, and they were going to be the team of six-becoming-one, to deliver nothing less than perfection. Every guy knew the high and it was towering over Hellforce and piquing in the air. The team was riding the hype of pre-mission bliss. Success was the only objective.

"Gonna need to pack light. We're in for an eight-mile hike before we even get on-site." Arctic gestured to Slate's bag as he headed to his own pack.

"We do five-mile runs every day. Not gonna even break a sweat on this mission," Trip bantered to Arctic. "If you're worried you might break a nail, if you want, I'll run with you in a fireman carry." Slate laughed under his breath knowing Arctic hated to be needled. "Or, if you're too delicate for that, I can carry you in a threshold carry...you being the bride, of course." Trip laughed when he saw the muscle in Arctic's jaw flex. He loved to lay it on Arctic, because he knew how much he hated to be the butt of a joke or prank, but Arctic always laid it back on his teammates.

"If anyone's being carried *bitch* it's you," Arctic seethed, which only made Trip and Slate laugh harder.

"No way, man. Don't need your groping, wandering hands anywhere near me Unless I'm bleeding out or missing a limb, don't put your meat hooks anywhere near me."

Arctic fell silent and a coldness came over him. The turn was stealthy and deadly. His eyes glazed and pierced into Trip. He entered the supply alcove and the world outside him fell dormant.

"Hey man, it was just a joke." Slate tried to ease the situation, but Arctic didn't counter.

The room went cold and the high riding in the air was squashed, snuffed out in an instant.

Trip's ribbing took Arctic back to Afghanistan. Slate and Trip sat uneasy in the ready room waiting for his reaction. They both knew how bad things went that day when they came to his and King's team's rescue. It was a bloodbath with Arctic and King being the lone survivors.

"Sorry, man." It was a lame apology, but it was all Trip could come up with.

Arctic turned and plastered a thin-lipped grin on his face, not masking the grim emotion of turmoil, sorrow, and anger behind it. "No harm, no foul. It's all good." Arctic clapped a hand on Trip's shoulder and gave Slate a curt chin lift and left the room.

Slate let out a breath and shook his head, reading the truth behind Arctic's reaction. "It's been five years, and he still hasn't dealt with it."

"He dealt with it his own way, pushing it deep and locking it up."

Both men felt their teammate's hurt and knew Arctic was a powder keg waiting to explode. No one knew when, they all just knew he was a ticking time bomb.

King sat at his desk, browsing the internet, a high filling his heart. Since the cookout, he hadn't stopped smiling. Mary was having his baby. He was going to be a Papa! Nothing could have prepared him for the love he already had in his heart for his unborn child. Mary told him that it was probably only the size of a pea, but that didn't matter. His heart was overflowing. After taking his wife home and making passionate love to her, King spent the rest of the evening online looking up pictures and information about the gestation of the baby and all things prenatal.

Mary was second-guessing this whole venture when he started telling her what her diet and calorie intake needed to be and how many hours of sleep she needed and so on. She was ready to throw his phone out the window so he'd stop obsessing over every detail. She knew he was doing it out of love and excitement, but if she thought King nursing her back to health when she had a week-long cold was bad, she wasn't sure how she was going to survive the next eight months of an overprotective, over sheltering King.

T-BAR knocked on the door and entered his office, and again, congratulated King. "Swear you're going to have permanent smile creases on your face."

King's smile widened, creasing the lines around his eyes. "What can I do for you, T?"

T-BAR took a seat. "Since I'm sidelined, was wondering if there was anything you needed me to take care of here while you and the team are out?" King knew T was frustrated that he was sitting this mission out. He was angry that his future at Hellforce hung in the balance. He hated that things were out of his control; couldn't stand the uncertainty of it all. He always had a plan, but a plan without the team was never an option.

"Things are pretty buttoned up here." King sat back in his chair. "Until we get back, not much will need attention."

T nodded.

"Ember's your priority." King stroked his short beard. "Got a feeling that Omar Bazwar won't lay low much longer. He was ballsy enough to step foot in her business, not once, but four times before he left the letter. Tells me he's determined to get her attention. We've seen these types of people before. They become obsessed with getting a reaction. When that isn't satisfied, they up their game. He's been laying low, and my gut tells me that's not going to be the case for very much longer."

T agreed, adding, "The obsession manifests until they're out of control if they don't get the reaction they deem acceptable."

Slate walked into the office as T was finishing his statement. King looked up and T turned in his chair.

"I was just leaving." T started to stand when King told him to sit. T stood anyway.

"I can come back," Slate told the two, and he turned to head out the door.

"Both you two, I need you to stay."

T and Slate stood, arms crossed over their chests, waiting for King to continue.

"Need you boys to talk." King stood from behind his desk, his chair creaking from relief of his weight lifting.

"Not a good time, boss." T shifted from one foot to the other.

Slate ponied up. "T, I think we should talk. I want to talk," he told his friend.

T stared at Slate but Slate wasn't holding back. He dropped his arms from his chest and put his hand on his brother's shoulder. T stepped back causing Slate's hand to fall.

"I fucked up." Slate said the words in earnest. "If I could do it over, I'd still choose Ember over my job, but I wouldn't have abandoned my team. I would've found some way to protect her and still go on the mission. I would've called King sooner before the mission. I would've done so many things differently. But, hindsight's twenty-twenty. Things can't be changed. The past is set. All I can do now is make amends."

King came around his desk, to his office door, and turned to his men. Everything that was good at Hellforce was because of his men. Because of the sacrifice they were willing to give for a single cause, and the sacrifice willing to be given for the man to the left and the man to the right. King knew Slate was eating himself alive with guilt for T's injuries, and the fact that T's future ultimately was in limbo because of his actions.

King looked them in the eye. "When a rift can't be mended, a wound can't heal. Pride is the poison poured into an open wound and allows it to fester. When allowed to fester, decay and rot set in, eating its host, spreading, growing, destroying a healthy body in its wake. Before you know it, it can't be stopped. A small cancer has eventually eaten everything that was good, and the good is now tainted and will never be whole. It's beyond repair. If only the small cancer was cut out at the beginning, the good, the whole, the rest would have been saved. But, because it was left untouched, nothing good remains or will remain. You can either decide to have a healed scar or an open wound. Decide now. The scar can be small, or the wound can be fatal."

Both men stood in silence letting King's words sink in. What he was saying was absolutely true. Slate wanted to heal, wanted a scar over a wound, but King didn't know if T was at the same impasse. After all, T was the one suffering most. His future was the one affected. Slate had told King that if T-BAR couldn't return to the field, Slate was willing to end his career, too, if it would appease his friend. Ironically, and eye for an eye. He would leave when King could find a good and competent replacement. He wouldn't make the same mistake twice and leave his team in the lurch.

King's next words were directed to T-BAR. "If you're going to blame Slate, then you're going to have to blame me as well. I fucked up, too. I didn't handle the situation the best way. I lost faith and ultimately made the bad call and let him walk." He looked at Slate. "And, after making that mistake, I let my pride fester and didn't call him to make amends. We've talked this out," he pointed between Slate and himself, "now, I need you two to do the same. We share the blame. Nothing we say at this point is going to make a difference to the future of your eye. What *is* going to make a difference is the way we continue from here on out. We're either going to mend this rift and have scars to show for it, or we're going to ignore it and let the decay eat us whole until we have nothing left and can no longer function as a team."

King let his words hang in the room. Neither man said a word—just stood and let King's words penetrate.

"I blame you." T's words hit Slate in the gut. Not that he didn't already know T blamed him, but to hear it made the truth knock the wind out of him. Slate's gaze fell to the floor at his feet.

"I blame you," T repeated. "But, I forgive you."

Slate lifted his eyes to his brother. King saw the truth in them —the words brought no solace to his soul.

"But, not all blame lays at your feet," T continued, sucking in a cleansing breath. "I fucked up as well. I shouldn't have flanked on my own. Not without cover. I should have stayed with the numbers. We all know that. We've trained that way, and I should have known better. I should have let the fight come to us as a group, not abandon and take on the fight on my own. I know we all had our own battles raging, and we could've fought better as a team."

King and Slate said nothing and let T-BAR unburden himself. He continued, "And, I made the mistake of not having my Sig holstered at the ready. Had it strapped but not accessible, and we all know that leads to failure when every second counts. If I would have had it ready, when my rifle jammed I could've pulled it and taken out one if not both of the men on me."

King didn't know T hadn't had his sidearm accessible. Made sense now why he hadn't pulled it.

"And this," he pointed to his eye," I blame myself more than I blame you." He looked from Slate to King. "Pissed off at myself more than you know. Was about to let the cancer fester until your words. Blame, hate, punishing my team isn't going to make this change. Won't affect the outcome."

Slate rubbed the back of his neck and King rubbed the tats on his left forearm. They were all feeling the same. They all felt blame, and they all would've made different choices, but they were also experiencing another sentiment; forgiveness.

King studied his men. Was it going to feel like shit every time Slate saw T's eye? Yes. Was he going to be crushed if T could no longer be on the team? Yes. Did he know his brother genuinely forgave him?

Absolutely.

CHAPTER 16

The guys had been gone four days. Ember worried about the boys and would finally breathe in relief once they were back on US soil. T spent the last two days helping her at the range. She met with some sales reps earlier in the morning, and now she was straightening out inventory in the back vault when T started to talk.

"Gotta see my doc today, at one. Going to get the dressing removed, and they're going to check my vision." He didn't turn to talk to her, just kept stacking boxes on the shelves.

Ember didn't know how to respond to that. *That's good* or *Hope it goes all right* really wasn't a great response to what was at stake. She had a feeling T must've been feeling nervous; he was never chatty.

"Thought you could drop me off and might want to stop and visit your dad while I'm at my appointment." Ember heard a bit of trepidation in his voice. She didn't want to point it out, knowing T was probably feeling vulnerable. "Don't want you to be bored waiting on my ass." T took off his hat and put it back on, pulling the brim down and adjusting it comfortably to rest on his forehead. "Not sure how long I'll be. Wouldn't want you just sitting around."

Yup, he was nervous. Ember sensed he wanted her to go along, but didn't want to ask outright and show his hand. His uneasiness punctuated in his offering for her *not* to come along. She didn't want him to go alone, so she put the ball back in his court. "I think I'd like to go along...if you don't mind."

T didn't respond.

"I mean, I wouldn't want you to get bored being alone, so I might as well be bored with you, right?" She chuckled hearing it fall flat, "I mean, I'd feel better if I could tag along."

He knew she was agreeing to go for his benefit without saying it. She was skirting and dancing around the elephant in the room to save him face.

"Wouldn't you feel more comfortable hanging with Pops?"

Em loved hanging in the hardware store with her dad. Even though she knew all things hardware having grown up around it, she always seemed to pick up a little morsel of knowledge every time she was around him. She wouldn't mind hanging with her daddy, but she needed to go with T instead. "Nah, he's been busy lately. Been working the afternoon and evening shifts. Maybe we can stop by the store after your appointment." Then she added, "Seeing as all goes well."

T stopped all movement mid-air and then continued stacking the boxes of ammo. She noticed the stutter in his movement. *Shit! Why'd I have to add that last bit?*

Awkwardness sat between them for what seemed like an eternity but in reality was only a few minutes. Both worked in silence until all the boxes were stacked.

Trying to fill the void, she asked, "Wanna hit the range?"

Throwing lead and burning bullets was always a tension reliever for her. She spent time with the guys shooting at her range or at Hellforce. It was always fun to get a little friendly competition going, especially with T-BAR. T, being the sniper for the Hellforce team, gave Ember an unspoken bond with him. She loved all the guys on the team. They razzed her like a little sister and respected her as a former soldier. But, T and she connected unlike any of the others. Some siblings bonded over shoes and fashion, Ember and T bonded over steel and lead. They knew each other's unique skill, and they knew each other's demons, an unfortunate bonus that came along with each sniped kill.

T rested his hands on the shelf, staring forward, and Ember could see the muscle tick in his jaw and flex at his temple.

"Got a new rifle that I'm dying to try. My .338 is—"

"Can't." T-BAR's clipped word cut her off.

Ember didn't understand. She waited a moment for him to continue, but he didn't. "Can't? Can't what?" Her question was sincere.

T adjusted his hat again and straightened the already perfectly stacked boxes on the shelf. He concentrated on aligning the boxes. "Haven't shot since...the eye." He gestured to his covering but didn't break concentration with the shelf.

Ember didn't know. Slate hadn't said anything, but then again, she hadn't shot with the guys since the whole meltdown at Hellforce. She still didn't understand though. She'd known people who lost vision in one eye who were able to continue shooting. Trying to nudge him to have a little fun and relax, she pushed and feigned concern and arrogance, trying to get a rise out of him. "Ah...don't want to lose to a girl? I can understand your insecurities to have—"

"I'm fucked!"

The crisp words startled her. T was facing her now and she could see the spent anger and hurt in the expression he was poorly masking. "Dominant eye." He pointed at his eye covering.

Ember thought back to times they'd shot together and realized he was left eye dominant. *Shit!* Why hadn't that occurred to her? She closed her eyes a moment and hung her head. "I'm sorry, T." It was a breathy whisper but she understood his frustration. How a loss of the dominant eye was a marksman's nightmare. His perspective and perception was lost. Both eyes were crucial when shooting, so T's dominant eye now gone was devastating.

On a mission, both eyes were crucial for peripheral vision. Although some novice shooters tended to close one eye to focus and bring a target into sight, closing one eye on the battlefield could bring about certain death. Both eyes open allowed a shooter to see a target and also see their peripheral surroundings, or any threats coming from either side. Closing one eye compromised fifty percent of the field of vision. Losing a dominant eye was a killer. Little could be done to compensate. It would be a whole new world of training to be cross-eye dominant.

"Can't hit the broadside of a barn." T tried to lighten the mood by exaggerating. The deep rise and fall of his chest showed he was holding his composure. He bit the corner of his straight, pursed lip and ran it through his teeth.

"I am sorry, T." Ember repeated, a little louder this time, and her honesty could be heard in her words. "It's my fault." Her eyes were still closed and she shook her head. "Not being a martyr here, I'm saying it really is my fault. Not directly, but it is." Every time she looked at his patched eye, she couldn't help but think the decisions that led to T-BAR being alone on that mission were her fault.

It seemed everyone was harboring some degree of guilt and blame.

She felt his arms wrap around her. "None of that, love," he said firmly, his slight British accent making the word "love" more tenderhearted. "None of this is your fault. A lot of us made mistakes, bad calls and bad judgments, but *not one* of those things falls on you."

"You say that, but it *is* my fault. It all leads back to me." Her arms hung at her sides and the top of her head was pushed against his sternum. "Not playing emotions here, just hardline facts." Ember wasn't one to throw herself a pity party or to garner attention by playing *poor me, I'm a victim* games. She was a strong woman who didn't have to wrap insecurities into fishing for sympathy.

He didn't break his hold but loosened it a little. "Did *you* quit your job at Hellforce?"

Ember didn't say anything.

"Were *you* too stubborn to make amends?"

Again, Ember stayed quiet.

"Did *you* make the bad judgement call to flank away from your teammates' cover?"

Ember shook her head.

T stepped back, forcing her to look up at him.

"Did you jam my rifle or not have my sidearm accessible?"

She stared up at him.

T tilted his head slightly to elicit a response.

"No," she said softly.

"Did you attack me?"

"No," she spoke a bit louder.

"Did you jack me in the eye with my rifle?"

"No!" She practically yelled in frustration.

"Then, stop it!" T-BAR yelled back at her. "You didn't do a damn thing to make this happen," he pointed at his eye. "A lot of us made mistakes, none of which you asked any of us to make. You aren't Slate. You aren't King. You aren't the bastards that wailed on me. You aren't me, and you sure the hell aren't to blame for any of this, so get that right out of your head!" T's breathing was heavy. He was controlled, but his temper was seething. He ran his hands down both sides of his face, smoothing out his mustache and the short stubble of his five o'clock shadow that appeared by noon. He brought himself into check. His voice softened. "You're carrying guilt that isn't yours to carry. Why take a burden that isn't yours?

"It's not going to change anything. It's not going to heal this. It's only gonna make you feel like shit." He shifted his weight. "I don't blame you. Don't blame yourself." They both stood facing each other. "Come here." T held his arms out and waited for her to embrace him. She went willingly. "I know you feel like this is your fault, and *believe me* when I say it absolutely isn't."

He rested his chin atop her head; T being six-three towered over her short five-foot-three frame. "I spent a lot of time pushing and assigning blame. Hell, I blamed everyone at some point or another. Comes down to a lot of bad judgement, but no way do you factor into the equation."

Ember leaned into him and quietly listened. Without lifting her head, she asked, "T?"

"Yeah?"

"What if it doesn't get better?" She reached up and clung to his forearms. "Your eye, I mean."

"I've spent a lot of time thinking about that exact scenario. In the chance that my vision doesn't recover, or recover enough to rejoin the team on missions, where does that leave me? Hellforce isn't just a job, it's *who* I am, not just what I do or an extension of myself. Just as in the Army, being Delta is *in* me."

"God, I feel bad even saying it. Stupid superstitions. I don't even want to put the thought into the universe." Ember couldn't look at him. She felt an ache in her heart on his behalf. She knew what it was to be a soldier. She knew, through Slate, what it took to be the ultimate elite, to be Delta. Soldiers weren't made; they were born. Truth to the fact that T joined Hellforce when he could have gone back into everyday civilian life after leaving Delta. It's who he was down to the soul and marrow of his bones. A protector of the innocent. If he couldn't return to the team, Ember didn't know how he'd carry on.

"It's the mantra that never leaves my mind." He stood still, running the question over in his thoughts. "I asked King the same thing."

"What'd he say?" Ember spoke into his chest.

"Don't be an idiot."

Ember jerked back and his arms fell away from her. Her petite frame stood like a giant; all sass and no bullshit. Her brows furrowed in anger and confusion won out. "Excuse me?" She put sass on that, tipping her chin down and raising her brows. She better have heard him wrong, for his sake, because there was no way those words just came out of his mouth. She may be small, but she was feisty.

T held himself, a smile eating up the expanse from ear to ear.

Light dawned and she realized he was referring to King's reply to his question and not calling *her* an idiot. She did her best not to smile, pursed her lips hard and squinted her eyes.

T mimicked her stance and sour-puss face.

She tried but couldn't hold the ruse any longer and burst into laughter. "Damn it! You're an ass!" She threw a jab at him with her finger landing square on his chest, as he still had a grin plastered across his face.

T let out a laugh that came from his toes, up through his chest, and out of his mouth. His head thrown back to the rafters, he laughed. It wasn't that funny, but damn, it felt good to see T laugh. It'd been such a long time since he laughed, genuinely laughed, that the sound just belted out.

Ember was now laughing because he was laughing, not even sure what they were laughing about, but it was good.

Finally composing themselves, she asked again, "So, what *did* King say?"

"He really did say, 'Don't be an idiot,' but after that he said not to worry."

"Easier said than done."

"Yeah…but he said I'd always have a place at Hellforce. Might not be in the field, but he'd make sure that I was involved on some level of the missions, be that consulting, logistics, strategy, tactics, basically everything I do now, except I won't board the bird."

That thought hung in the air between them. King would make sure he was still on the team…still involved, just not in the manner of execution.

"And you'd be good with that?" she asked with hesitation.

Having T plan and organize was great and all, but execution of a mission was where the guys crushed it. As Eli had told her many times, execution was the reward of the job and also a labor of love. Not to be misconstrued between the reward of mission execution and the reward of financial benefit. She knew the guys made a big bank, and King took care of his men both in the field and in the pocket. Each man earned an exorbitant amount of money for risking their life each time they set foot in places worse than hell.

But, even without the payday behind each mission, the guys would do the mission regardless. Just as when she was enlisted, it wasn't about a paycheck. It was because each man believed in the cause. And, her friends did the job to free one more child from the sex trade, to keep one more woman's body from being defiled, to bring one more captive home to their family. The mission didn't depend on a dollar amount. The mission to free the innocent was priceless; an unmitigated love of the job.

T-BAR mulled the question over in his mind, just as he did when King gave him the reassurance. Would he be okay being behind the scenes? *Could* he be okay behind the scenes? Would not being an active part of the mission still be satisfying? As much as it killed his heart to not be next to his brothers in the thick of the fire, it would kill him even more to not be with his brothers at all. Period.

"Don't borrow trouble." Ember's voice broke him from his thought.

"What?" T hadn't caught what she'd said.

"Don't borrow trouble. My dad always says it to me. Says I'm an over thinker," which she knew she was, "and I bring worry where it doesn't belong. Guess we shouldn't think about what *could* happen, until we know what *will* happen. We should wait and see what your doctor says."

T sat on the thought.

Ember continued, "'Today is the tomorrow you worried about yesterday.' Mom would tell me that when I'd overanalyze and overthink trivial things. I think it's a quote from Dale Carnegie. Mom always had a saying for everything. Took me forever to figure that one out. My adolescent brain trying to untangle that, whew...like a tongue twister for your mind."

T gave her a chaste kiss on the forehead. "Guess we'll find out at one o'clock. Until then, it's moot."

Ember and T sat in the tiny exam room, the sterile smell of anti-septic in the air, the telltale smells of a doctor's office. The examination chair was rather comfortable with padded faux leather with armrests helping him relax. "At least I'm not on a flat exam table with the white crinkly paper," he said. "Reminds me of a meat market butcher's paper."

Ember sat against the wall in the most uncomfortable plastic chair studying the posters of eyeballs, muscles and lenses. For something that seems so simple, the human eye was extraordinarily complex. The intrinsic nature was fascinating for an organ most took for granted, because it's just...there, not really appreciating it until it's not. She stood and fingered the pamphlets on the wall rack, *'You May Have Cataracts'* Hmmm. *'What You Should Know About Glaucoma.'* Interesting. *'Macular Degeneration & You: Knowing the Early Signs and Premature Blindness.'* Well, that just sounded terrifying.

The room was silent; no chit chat or small talk. What could be said that wasn't going to make the uncertainty more prevalent? Both had the same question running on a loop in their minds, so they just waited...and waited some more.

"Wish they'd just get their ass in here and get this over with," T spoke first. His impatience was rare. The man had the patience of a saint, which let Ember know by his outburst he was hanging by a thread. His head fell back against the headrest and he closed his eye. By the bate of his breath, she knew he was cadence breathing, a controlled rhythmic breathing to clear his mind. She could only imagine the anxiety welling within him. With their skill set, controlled breathing was a technique that was second nature. Controlling your breathing; elementary. Matching your breath with your heart rate; Breathing 101.

She left him in his trance and turned back to the wall of booklets. 'Answers to your Questions About Astigmatism' hmmm...interesting. Just as she grabbed the pamphlet the door opened and the doctor entered. Ember froze like she was caught by the principal doing something forbidden. The doctor gave her a genuine smile. T's head came forward, and he straightened in his seat. The moment of truth was upon him.

"Mr. Kingston, good to see you again." Ember didn't know if that was Ophthalmology humor or if the doc just didn't realize what an asinine greeting it was. T shook her outstretched hand quickly as if wanting the introductions and pleasantries out of the way so they could get down to brass tacks and learn what his future held.

Ember took her seat in the torturous chair and waited to hear the verdict. She glanced over at T and gave him a quick wink and a smile.

T, being an ass, motioned towards her with his patched eye, mimicking a wink beneath the wads of gauze that covered it, making her giggle. Even at this tense moment, T still had his humor, although Ember guessed it was more of a nervous humor to cut the tension they both were feeling.

The doctor crossed the room and dimmed the lights to a minimal glow, using the opaque filter covering the overhead lights. The room sat in a translucent dimness but with enough light to clearly distinguish their surroundings.

Guessing what they were thinking, the doctor said, "So the light doesn't intensify the sensitivity of your sight."

His sight. Did the doc know more than she told T-BAR after his surgery? Was she sending an omen of T regaining his vision, or was she just hoping, like they were, that T would have vision once the gauze was removed?

But, even if he regained his sight, in order to get back on the gun, T had to retain 20/20 vision. It was an absolute in their profession. No wiggle room. A sniper had to have an eagle's eye to sit on the rifle. A scope was no good if you couldn't see through it. You needed the ability to see a gnat on a target's shoulder in order to have perfection as a sniper. No shot was worth taking without absolute certainty that it would be precisely on target.

"We'll remove the bandage and let your eye get adjusted to the sensation of the open air and the darkened light before you open it. I want you to keep both eyes closed. Don't open your right eye as your left eye adjusts. When I tell you, you can then open it slowly, letting in as much light as you feel comfortable. No race. No time limit. Just as you feel comfortable, that's the pace I want you to go." Her voice matched the softly-lit room.

She went to the small sink in the corner, washed her hands and dried them thoroughly, then donned a pair of purple medical gloves. Ember thought the color was calming, better than the boring off-white latex she'd seen other doctors use. She was wondering if the calming effect of the color was the reason they used them, or if that was just the color the gloves came in.

The doctor took a seat in front of T, and it broke Ember out of her idiotic wonderings about the purple gloves. T took in a deep breath when the doc asked, "You ready?"

"Yes." Both T and Ember answered in unison causing the doctor to laugh.

"Okay, then. Let's get this dressing off and we'll see if you can see."

The waiting was agony.

T's body tensed as the doctor used a solution to peel the tape off his skin. Ember assumed it was dissolving the adhesive. It looked painful, but T didn't flinch. After she removed the tape, she removed the protective plastic shield that was holding the gauze to his eye. Ember felt her heart rate increase. The anticipation was killing her. She couldn't imagine what T was feeling.

T wanted to rip the damn thing off and open his eye. The painstaking time the doctor was taking was worse than the torture he and the team received overseas. He cleared the memory from his mind and concentrated on the moment in front of him. He kept his breathing paced and kept his adrenaline from spiking. In a few moments, would he see? *Breathe, two, three, four. Out, two, three, four. Slow and Easy.*

"Just going to remove the gauze, and we'll have you adjust to the diffused light. Keep your eyes closed." The doctor removed the top layer of padding and then slowly peeled away the pad of gauze against his eye, revealing a lubricated film over his eyelid and surrounding his eye.

"Is there going to be any scarring, Doc?" He didn't care about scars. Hell, he knew scars were the badge that you survived something bigger than yourself.

"Don't worry T, your beautiful face is still flawless and you'll still have ladies beating down your door to get into your drawers." Ember kept the mood light. "Although, by the number of girls that have notched your bedpost, I think your mug is about the last thing they're concerned with."

T laughed and the doctor chuckled. When he'd first learned he had an orbital fracture and needed surgery to repair it, he envisioned a gnarly, jagged scar across his eye.

The doc followed up, "The small incision made by the surgeons left a one-inch scar on the outer corner of your eye, but cosmetically, it will heal and be unnoticeable to those who aren't the wiser."

T-BAR felt the coolness of air across his cheek and over his eye. The pressure of the bandages being removed was a sense of relief. He wanted to jack his eye open and look around the room.

"Okay," The doctor said in her gentle tone, "everything looks good, nice and healed. The incision looks great." She examined around his eye, the bruising almost gone, dulled to a yellowish-brown. She lightly patted and pushed around the socket, asking him if it hurt here or there. So far, everything seemed to be going well.

"Things look good, Mr. Kingston. Before you open your eye, tell me, do you see any sensation of light or are things still dark?"

T took a minute to explore the sensation of what he may, or may not be seeing. "I think I sense light...faintly."

The doc hovered her flat palm in the air in front of T's right eye and then moved it away from his face to the side. "Do you see a change in the sensitivity of the light?" She moved her hand a few more times, giving T time to notice if he could sense a change. He heard Ember hold her breath.

～

Ember watched as the doctor hovered her hand in front of his eye.

"It's dark now." T spoke with a calm timber. There was no sense of hesitation or nervousness.

The doctor removed her hand. "And, now?"

"It's lighter."

The doctor kept her hand away from his eye. "How about now? Any change?"

A shot of adrenaline spiked in Ember's stomach. The feeling of driving country roads over hills, experiencing the excitement of the rise and fall came over her. *Ooh, fake out!* Ember knew the doctor was testing to see if T really was sensing a difference or if his mind was imagining the change in light, guessing it's presence and absence.

Immediately, T said, "No. It's still light."

Ember wanted to howl with excitement that he had some

sense of sight, even if it was just light sensitivity. His eye was recognizing the changing difference. The doctor handed him a tissue and told him he could start to open his eye, keeping his good eye closed.

He pulled in a deep inhale, and Ember saw the flutter of his eyelid slowly start to lift.

~

T felt the pit in his stomach sitting like a lead weight. He tried to open his eyelid, but it felt like it was fused together. The sensation was strange. He pulled with his upper brow, and squinted his good eye tight, willing his injured eye to open.

Utter darkness.

Then...light. Blinding, piercing, hot-white light danced in his vision as he fluttered his lid. His eye started to water.

"That's good. You're doing well." For a moment, T forgot the doc was even there. "Use the tissue if you need to dab the tears. Don't apply any pressure, just lightly dab." T inwardly laughed. She sounded more like a mother coaxing her child than a medical doctor.

The waiting was agonizing, but the sensation of actually seeing, *something*, had him in knots.

It took a few minutes but, wincing, T opened his eye completely. His eye darted around the room searching for something to come into focus.

The silence in the room was deafening, hanging there, mocking time, as everyone waited for him to say something.

"Mr. Kingston?" The doc was about to ask a question but T beat her to it.

"Colors. I can see shapes and colors...but it's murky." He paused, trying to focus on anything.

The doctor grabbed a few medical swabs from a sterile packaging. "Close your eye, please." Her tone was motherly. Soft and light. "This may feel a little scratchy, but I need to remove the antibiotic ointment." She brushed the pad lightly against his eye. T resisted the urge to pull his head back, thankful that the chair had a headrest. She continued to pat and dab.

When she removed most of the ooze, she placed a pad in T's hand and told him to remove any remaining ointment that may bother him, so he dabbed lightly around his eye.

T opened his eye again, searching for a focal point and instant rivulets of tears started to flow. "Is it too much light?" Ember asked. Instead of answering, he lifted the pad to his cheeks and dabbed at the wetness falling down them.

"Mr. Kingston? How is the vision now?" The doctor had worry in her voice.

His eye found Ember. "You're wearing your cross."

Ember's chin began to quiver. "It's the cross Slate gave me each time he deployed as Delta, and now when he leaves on missions with Hellforce, when he can't wear it in the field. It's his grandfather's World War II cross he wore in battle. T, if you can notice this small, ornate, silver cross, then..." Ember broke into tears that morphed into sobs.

Everything was different now. T could see.

Mitch Hayes dipped the wire brush into the bucket of solution and continued to scrub the outside wall of Hayes' Hardware store. The spray paint wasn't coming off as well as he'd hoped, but with a little more elbow grease, the brick-faced facade facing Main Street would be back to normal. The words *One of Three* would be gone by the day's end.

CHAPTER 17

After a battery of tests, T and Ember were driving to the hardware store to visit Pops. T was wearing a pair of blackout sunglasses to shield the light from his sensitive eye. The sensitivity had lessened, so the brightness indoors wasn't wreaking havoc on him, but outdoors he needed some type of protection.

He was just grateful his vision was back. It was still blurry, but the doctor assured him it would clear up with time. He had a follow-up appointment at the end of the week to check his progress and make sure no infection set in. He had antibiotic drops to put in throughout the day, just to err on the side of caution. The last thing he wanted was a setback. He wasn't guaranteed he'd have the same 20/20 vision he had before the attack and that worried him. He couldn't get back on his gun without perfect vision, but with the possibility of LASIK surgery, at least he'd still be on the team, in the field, fighting beside his brothers. That thought alone brought him peace.

Time. Time would tell what the future held.

T looked over from the passenger's seat as Ember sat behind the wheel, sunglasses on and her fiery red hair whipping in the wind coming through the open window. It was a beautiful day, and he was happy. They both cried when he mentioned her necklace. It was a miracle he was able to see with such clarity. The doctor was astonished. Most patients weren't able to see that well right after the bandages came off. That gave him hope his vision would be fully restored.

~

Ember was hopeful as well. The doctor gave him strict instructions to rest his eye when it felt fatigued and not to strain it. But, this was T-BAR. The word *rest* wasn't in his vocabulary. Ember knew the man couldn't begin to comprehend the meaning. He had patience, but his activity mode was always on high. Ember knew King would see to it that he followed doctor's orders. And, King, being King, was all the incentive a person needed and ten times scarier than any doctor's warnings. If he wanted to get back on the gun, she figured he would do just about anything.

They pulled into the lot behind the hardware store and she put the truck into PARK. It was a dirt lot where the employees parked. Customer parking was in the front along Main Street and also in the paved parking space around the corner of the building. Slate was on Pops to get better lighting in the back lot. A lone flood light illuminated it in the evening and night time, but another light would be a lot safer. Pops had it on his to-do list but it hadn't been installed yet. When the store closed, only he and the one night employee used the back lot, and they walked out together. They parked close to the building which had four, small lights attached along the back wall. It was well lit but needed improvement.

"There's my girl!" Ember's mom, Susan, greeted her and T as she walked towards them from the office into the back storage room.

"Hi, Mom." Ember pushed her sunglasses up top her hair, gave her mom a hug, and brushed a kiss on her cheek.

T removed his glasses as well.

"And, don't you look handsome as ever, Mr. Kingston." Susan raised up on her tiptoes and gave T-BAR a hug, then placing a hand on his chest, she brushed a chaste kiss on his cheek.

He raised her hand and placed a delicate kiss on her knuckles, "You look beautiful, as always, Mrs. Hayes," T's voice was sexy and lyrical with his slight British accent.

Susan chuckled, "He's not here."

"Damn!" T dropped her hand and gave a quick shake of his head, holding back the smile all the ladies loved.

The group of three broke into laughter, creating a ruckus.

Innocently, Susan flirted with the Hellforce gang It was a rolling joke that she'd be a cougar if she wasn't married to Mitch. The guys laid it on thick whenever Mitch was around, within hearing distance or in direct line of sight. Each would see who could get him to growl the loudest while they flowered her with compliments that went a miniscule over compliments but never over the line. They'd never disrespect Pops with inappropriate behavior, but they'd greet Susan with a kiss on the cheek that earned them a side eye and a grumble from Pops. Susan loved it because when Pops had enough, he'd ravish her with a deep, passionate, very inappropriate-for-public-viewing kiss that made Ember gag a little, telling the guys 'hands off.' Sometimes, he'd go as far as dipping her back to the floor, as the guys laughed, and Ember would turn away because no child, no matter how old, wanted to see their parents making out.

But, Ember adored her parents' relationship. They were always affectionate with each other. When Ember and Rhys were teenagers her parents would see how far they could push it before one of the girls would yell out, make gagging noises or literally try to pry them apart. Ember wanted a marriage like her parents. She couldn't wait to have a guy love her with all his heart and soul. A guy who was affectionate as well as a protector. She wanted to be a partner, just like her mother, who supported her husband as well as her children.

She knew it wasn't popular in today's society, but she wanted the traditional roles of husband and wife. She loved the fact that, growing up, her mom was home with her and Rhys. a homemaker with supper on the table by five. She ran the house, and worked the hardware office from home, and was always there when they needed her. Her mom was a strong, confident woman. Housewife and business partner. And, her dad pitched in as well. Her father defied gender roles before it was PC. If the dishes needed to be done and her mom was helping them with homework, her dad did the dishes. If Dad was home when it was laundry day and her mom hung clothes on the line, Dad would be hanging them alongside her. And, it worked both ways. If either she or Rhys got sick, sometimes her dad would stay home and her mom would run the store.

Ember wanted what they had. She knew the guy was out there, somewhere, she just wasn't sure how to find him, but she knew, deep down, she would.

"Where's Dad?" Ember asked.

"Oh...he's doing some maintenance."

Ember loved working with her dad. "I'll see if he needs a hand, where is he?" she asked before walking out of the storage room.

"Em, I'm sure he's got it." Her mom seemed hesitant, something Susan Hayes was not. Something was off. T straightened his posture slightly. "I'm sure he'll be in, in a bit. It's hot out. He won't be long." Susan tried to be nonchalant, but it was clear as hell she was hiding something.

"I'll take him a bottle of water." Ember headed onto the store floor before her mom could stop her, with T on her heels.

She made her way down the main aisle, past the cluttered end caps filled with things from bottle openers and wood putty, to jointer biscuits and ballcocks and around the bins where nails and screws could still be bought by the pound. Rounding the corner, she almost collided with a customer.

"Ember, how are you? Been a while since I've seen you. You sure have grown into the prettiest spittin' image of your maw'-ma." Mr. Potter stood slightly hunched looking at the joint compound. He was the sweetest old man and gave her a smile. He used to bring her and Rhys salt water taffy when they were little while they roamed around the store with their dad. Always a pink one for Rhys and a red, white and blue swirled piece for her. Everyone in town called him Old Man Potter. He was about a hundred-and-thirty-seven years old, if not a day younger. He was old when Ember was little and even older now.

"I need a quick-set compound," he began, showing her the bucket in his hand. "I'm repairing a section of drywall where the joints meet, and the gall darn stuff keeps cracking." He looked down at the mix in hand.

Ember really didn't want to stop and help. She wanted to see what her mom was hiding by keeping her from helping her dad, but Mr. Potter was...well, Mr. Potter. He was like an old-timey grandfather, and she'd known him her whole life, so she stopped to help him.

"Don't need a huge pail of it, just—"

"Mr. Potter," Ember politely interrupted him, "what you have here is putty for small patches...nail holes and wall dents. What you need is a setting compound."

He looked at the mix in his hand again, "Hmmm."

"Are you using a powder setting compound, one you add water to?" Ember's eyes caught T's with both his eyebrows raised, a smirk on his face and he mouthed the words, "Good luck," and headed out the front doors.

Ass. Ember thought internally, knowing he was rolling with laughter in his head.

As T left, Mr. Potter began to tell her about his prizewinning magnolia tree and azalea bushes.

Dang it!

∽

T left Ember with the frail, old man and headed past the registers and out the front double doors. Taking the single step down to the sidewalk, he glanced to each side spotting Pops brushing the front wall, and he headed his way. As he approached, he saw what Pops was doing; he was trying to remove spray paint from the store front. Instantly, anger rose in T's bloodstream. Someone tagged the hardware store! *What type of punk-ass-bitch did this to the Hayes store?* Everyone loved the Hayes family. If you needed something fixed, Hayes was the place to go. There was no big box store in their town. Didn't need one. Hayes Hardware had it all. The joke around town, "if Hayes' didn't carry it, they didn't make it." It was a real hardware, hardware store.

"What mothafuc—" T-BAR stopped mid-sentence, reading the words painted on the brick face. *One of Three.* T gave a knowing look to Pops, understanding who was behind this. He knew exactly what this meant. If Ember saw this, she was going to freak out. She'd been doing well since the shooting incident but was shaken up again when the mysterious, cryptic note was left by Omar Bazwar on the counter at the range. Fury and rage roiled in his gut. He was in charge of Ember's safety, and he'd be damned if anything happened to her on his watch. And, Slate would be irate if something happened to his girl while he was away.

"You have security cameras?" T barked out the question a few decibels louder than appropriate. "You need to get Matthews over here right now!"

Pops dropped the brush in the bucket of solution and wiped his brow with the back of his forearm. "Matthews has already been by. We looked through the footage from last night. It's Bazwar. I sent Matthews the digital footage, and he's going to have it analyzed and processed." Pops stood back and stared at the graffiti tag, untouched, thinking of what else he could use to remove the paint without marring or discoloring the brick. T stood next to him taking in the scene.

"This is some unusual paint," Pops huffed, wiping his brow again from the Texas midday heat, then removed the rubber gloves from his hands. "Definitely isn't regular aerosol spray paint. I've tried multiple removers, solvents and thinners. Nothing's taking it off. It's like they wanted to brand the store instead of tagging it."

"Pressure washer?"

"First thing I tried after Matthews left. Didn't remove a damn thing. Probably going to have to paint over it."

T walked up and touched the paint, wiping his finger across the brick. "You gonna tell Ember? She needs to know. Matthews is probably going to contact her. Think it'd be better to hear it from one of us before she's blindsided by a call from him."

"I want to remove it before telling her. Seeing it will send her over the edge. She needs to be protected, and I'll go to any length to do that for her." Pops rubbed the back of his neck with a handkerchief and looked down as he folded it to put in his back pocket. "Where is Ember?"

"I'm right here."

Both heads swiveled towards the sound of her voice as she

walked over to them. When she got closer she saw the bucket at her dad's feet. Realization dawned, and she turned to the three-foot high letters scrawled across the face of her family's store. Her expression transformed from confusion, to shock, to anger. She set her jaw and her breathing deepened taking in the tag. *One of Three.* The warning loud and clear, not so cryptic this time.

T expected her to become enraged or a trembling mess, but she stood stoic and controlled, never taking her eyes off the brick face.

"Bazwar." It wasn't a question.

Pops answered her anyway, "We think so." He corrected himself, "Actually, we're pretty sure."

"When did it happen?"

"Last night. We—"

"You didn't call me?" She looked to her dad. Her words had a bite to them.

He answered with the truth. "No, but I only discovered it this morning."

She shook her head in disgust and looked up at the front overhang and then at the end of each roofline. "Cameras working?"

T knew she was compartmentalizing the situation. Organizing, dissecting, categorizing and filing away each piece of information and clue. She was in soldier mode. Times like this made T question why they were all on Ember Protection Detail. She was a damn great soldier. Had proven herself over and over again, and he knew she was tough as nails. Then, he reread the graffiti tag and knew, more than ever, she needed someone at her back.

Pops answered her question. "Yes. Sent a copy of the recording to Matthews after he left here this morning."

Ember closed her eyes. "Matthews was here? Why wasn't I?" Her tone was ice. Cold, sharp, precise and crisp. Short and clipped. "So, let me get this straight," she paused, getting her emotions and thoughts in order. "You found this, this morning," she pointed to the wall, "you called Matthews, but you didn't call me?" Her words were pointed. "When were you going to call me?" She didn't give her dad time to answer the rhetorical question. "After you removed it? Scrubbed it off the wall?" She let out a breathy laugh. "Or, maybe you were going to let me find out from one of the hundreds of gossips in this town? Or, I don't know, one of the hundreds of customers that shop here or drive by?"

Mitch didn't say anything.

The door to the front of the store opened and Susan joined the huddle on the sidewalk.

"Honey," her mom reached out an arm to put around her shoulder, but Ember pulled to the side standing her ground. She didn't want to be coddled.

Pops took a step forward, "Baby girl, I—"

"Don't baby girl, me, Dad…" The words were just above a whisper and her sentence fell off.

Mitch opened his mouth but said nothing.

"I'm sick of everyone walking on eggshells around me. Everybody thinks they know what is best for me without even asking *me* what's best for me. Shouldn't I have a say in my own decisions?" She looked at her dad with sympathy, knowing he and everyone else had her best interest at heart. "I know I freaked when this whole thing went down, I still don't understand why, it wasn't like me at all. I kinda lost it. But then, everybody started making choices for me." She was frustrated, finding it difficult to express what she wanted to say. "I'm not a child anymore. I don't need coddling or a watch team." She looked at T-BAR. "Look, I'm glad everyone is concerned. And yes, I do feel safer having a second set of eyes with me, 'cuz we don't know what these crazies," she pointed to the wall, "are going to do, or where or when they'll show up. But shouldn't that be my decision? Shouldn't someone ask me what I want to do?" Disgust enveloped her and she shook her head coming to grips with the moment.

Mitch rolled his lips between his teeth and planted his hands, awkwardly, in his pocket. He was never awkward. He was always the rock when it came to decisions, issues or problems. When it came to adversity, he was always the go-to man, so to see him almost broken, filled her with unease.

"Baby, gir—" he stopped himself, "Ember, I was going to call you—"

"But, you didn't." She whispered the words almost in defeat.

T felt bad for her, seeing things through her perspective. It was true that everyone around her was making decisions for her, and no one had stopped to get her input, even though she probably would've agreed to everything, even having someone with her all the time, but no one had made her part of that decision. It was only natural to have her push back.

"T." Ember walked to him, waiting for him to look at her. "Please, don't think for one second that I'm ungrateful. I love that you've been with me this week." Her voice was gentle and he knew she wasn't giving platitudes; she was sincere. "I need you with me. Not that I *can't* be alone, but I don't *want* to be alone." She shifted her weight, measuring her next words. "But, sometimes, I think you and the guys forget that I'm not helpless."

He had to agree with her. Even though the guys had her best interest at heart, they wouldn't treat a fellow teammate this way. Her next words solidified his thoughts.

"You wouldn't be trailing King or Trip. Cy, Slate or Arctic wouldn't allow you to follow on their heels. I'm not asking you to leave or to not be with me. I *want* someone to be with me, to be my extra eyes."

T-BAR chuckled and pointed to his right eye beneath his sunglasses and raised his brow.

She smiled at his joke and continued, looking over at her father, "You and Mom raised me to be independent. Stand up for myself and others. Never to cower." Her parents nodded in agreement. "Am I pissed this Bazwar guy is fucking with me for God only knows why? Yes. Am I going to live in fear and in the shadows and let him rule my life? Fuck no! Am I going to be reckless and take unnecessary risks? Absolutely not. *I'm* going to decide the way *I* live. But, I'm also going to make my own decisions and decide what's best for me."

Both T and her parents agreed and knew she was right. Any future choices and decisions would be hers.

Her dad came to her and wrapped her in his arms. "I love you baby, gir—" he pursed his lips into a flat line.

Ember smiled up at him, giving him permission to don her with the endearment.

He continued, "I love you, baby girl. Just trying to do what is best for you, and I'm sorry if we overstepped. Sometimes I forget you're a grown woman and not the scrappy little girl you once were."

"I'm still scrappy...just not so little." He hugged her tighter and she spoke to his chest, "Love you, Daddy." He kissed the top of her head and stepped back so her mom could dote on her as well.

T's phone rang and he stepped away to answer it. Ember pulled her phone from her back pocket and began snapping pictures of the tag from different angles. Susan gave Mitch's arm a light squeeze, and she headed back inside the store.

"Ranger Matthews is probably going to get a hold of you. Let you know about this." Mitch pointed to the wall.

"At least I won't be blindsided. Glad I saw it before he called." She gave her dad a reassuring smile to let him know she was okay.

"Guys are back." T came up beside her while sliding his phone into his pocket. "Gotta head back to HQ."

"Okay. I got pics and will talk to the guys about this. After that, I'll see what Mary's up to, maybe call Maven while you man-up with the boys."

T smirked, "Man-up? What's that?"

"You know," she said with a shrug of a shoulder, "exude testosterone, measure biceps, sqqqueeze things." She curled her bicep and fisted her knuckles, mimicking the motion.

T stared at her and chuckled on an exhale. "Really? That's what you think we do when we get together?"

"Pretty much."

"Sorry to disappoint, love, but men don't become primal and flex oiled muscles while comparing man bulges when they get together."

Ember's face curled up into a sinister grin and she said, "Well, girls don't prance around in skimpy thongs and braless tanks while having pillow fights when we get together."

T face fell in sadness and he grabbed his chest, "Why would you piss on my beautiful dreams?"

"I'm outta here!" Pops grabbed the bucket and gloves at his feet before he heard more banter. "Don't need to know any of this info."

All three laughed and headed into the hardware store leaving the message on the storefront. *One of Three.*

How soon those words would become reality.

CHAPTER 18

It had been a grueling four days in Lebanon. The team worked seamlessly and got the three diplomatic aid workers back on US soil. The rebels holding them were amateur, at best. Chaotic, undisciplined and unplanned. The team referred to missions like this as *drive thrus*. Pull up, find what you want, get what you need, and home in a flash. All in a quick and efficient, timely manner.

The guys gathered their personal gear in their cages after returning their rifles and sidearms to the basement armory. All weapons and gear were turned in and logged by staff. Inventory of damaged or broken weapons and gear had to be up to date so Mary could order any necessary and needed items and replacements before the next mission.

King never skimped on tacticals. Any mods or specialty orders the guys needed or requested to make their job easier and more efficient, King would gladly supply them. He knew having the appropriate tools to make the job more efficient could mean the difference between living and dying; between bringing his brothers home whole or bringing them home beneath a flag. Slate knew King never let money stand between his guys' ability to carry out a mission and succeed. Slate appreciated that King knew how hard it was when you didn't have the equipment needed. In the military, they were supplied with what the DOD thought they needed. Even though Special Forces got a highly padded budget for the latest and greatest weapons and gear, it wasn't always available when they needed it. And, the hoops needed to jump through to get it was a mind fuck. Sometimes it was easier to go without than to go through the grind to get what you needed. King wasn't going to put his men through that. The guys wouldn't request things they didn't deem necessary, and anything he could give them to make a mission successful, he never balked. Although, Trip's request for the M1A2C Abrams tank was a bit of a stretch and above budget. Mission success of the last op had the guys on a high and the usual banter, bullshit and barbs were being slung amongst the guys when T came into the room.

"Holy hell! Smells like shit in here." T wrinkled his nose at the smell of sweat, BO and some indescribable foul, rank, stank hanging in the air. None of the guys had gotten to the shower yet, and they had a four-day funk on them.

Arctic was the first to pipe up, "Some of us have been doing men's work and smell like men, while others," he nodded to T-BAR, "have been doing delicate pansy-ass work and smell like roses." Arctic strode up and gave him a light sniff. "New bath bomb fragrance, or is your tampon scented?" The guys erupted in laughter.

T gave him a half-hearted gut check, and Arctic doubled over even though he was laughing the whole time.

"Do you need me to pull the string so you can change into a new one?" Cypher was on the other side of the room, and T hit him with a glare that had the guys laughing harder.

"Fuck off...all of you." He gave the finger around the room to each of his brothers.

Slate was the first to notice. "Hey, where's the pirate patch?" He pointed at his own eye.

"Got it taken off this afternoon."

"And…" The room went silent waiting for T to elaborate.

"And, what?"

"What do you mean, 'And, what?' Can you see?"

"How many fingers am I holding up?" Cy held up his middle finger.

T laughed and said, "The same one I used on your momma last night."

Laughter and ribbings wafted throughout the room at Cypher's expense.

Cy held up both fingers and sent two birds in T's direction.

"Yup, that's right, she especially likes double penetration." T-BAR braced for impact as Cy barreled at him from across the room. "She loves it so much, now you can call me daddy!" T egged him on, getting him riled.

Cypher crashed into him, sending T back against the wall. "You motherfucker!" Cy was laughing as he pummeled his friend, and it felt good to T to be back with his team.

"Acknowledging it is the first step." T played off Cy's poor choice of vulgarity.

The guys couldn't stop the roar of laughter that poured throughout the crew. After four days of little sleep, heat, sweat and travel, it felt good to just be themselves.

King entered the room and stopped dead in his tracks catching a whiff of the funk hanging in the room. "What the fuck?" His booming voice had everyone coming to a halt. His head pulled back and his face crinkled, "My God, smells like a cheap whore's motel room on a spring break weekend: Sweat, tang and shame. Showers, all of you!"

That put the guys over the top. The ruckus was so loud, Mary stuck her head in the doorway, concern written on her face and Ember right beside her. "What in the world is going on —" Her words cut short as she covered her nose with her hand.

Ember did the same. "Oh, my God! You boys reek!"

The guys continued spewing laughter at the girl's antics.

"Hold up, all of you!" King's voice brought the room to silence. "Where's your patch?" King pointed to T.

"Don't need it. Vision's back."

"Back completely?" King asked.

"Not completely. Not yet, at least, but I can see out of it. Blurry as fuck, but it's better than darkness."

Mary's lip quivered and she looked like she was about to cry, when King pulled her into his barreled chest.

"No shit? You really gonna be able to see?"

"You getting back on the team?"

"How long before you're back?"

The questions came from all around the room.

T spoke in King's direction, "I hope to be back in the field as soon as this heals."

King nodded. "Any idea of a time frame?"

"Not yet. Have another appointment at the end of the week. Hope they can give me a better idea of where I'm at by then."

"Can't wait to get you back." King reached with his free hand and gave him a pat on the back. "The rest of you, showers!" He motioned his thumb over his shoulder towards the door.

"That includes you, too!" Mary scolded King, pushing off his chest. "You're as ripe as them." Pinching her nose, she pointed to the door just as he did to the team.

King grinned, "Yes, dear." He gave her a peck on the lips then turned to the door, ushering his wife before him, and the rest of the guys cleared the room behind them.

Slate stayed in his cage and continued to empty his bag.

"Not gonna hit the showers?" Ember blocked the entrance, hanging onto each side of the cage and wrinkled her nose.

Slate drank her in, his eyes perusing her perfectly toned body. "That bad, huh?"

She fanned her face and shook her head. "Not as bad as the rest."

"Four-day funk. Not the most appealing way to say welcome home, huh?"

"As long as you're safely back home, I don't care what you smell like."

"Really?" Slate took a few steps to meet her, closing the gap between them.

The air shifted. An almost electric mood moved throughout the room.

Her words softened. "I'm glad you're back."

"Would've been sooner, but you know how things go."

Ember reached out, lacing her arms around his neck, not

caring he needed to hit the showers. The movement was anything but conscious, and Slate rested his hands on her flared hips.

"I was worried this time. I worry every time, but this time was more nerve-wracking than most. I think it was because I knew T wasn't at your six."

"Creed had me covered."

"But, I don't know the new guy. I know T, and I know he's brought you home to me every time. New guy," she shook her head, "...gotta build trust in him to know he'll bring you back to me."

Slate settled his weight, pulling her closer. "I'll always come back to you, Red. Always. Forever."

Their lips gravitated towards each other, a hair's width apart, allowing every word to be felt as their breaths mingled. Somehow, throughout their conversation, a magnetic pull brought them together. Her breasts heaved with every inhale, and her felt her nipples pucker beneath her bra, rubbing against his chest.

"Eli." His name blessed the wisp of her breath.

"Emmy."

Their lips brushed across one another, once then twice, and the heat of their names splayed across their flesh. An electric arc sparked between the gap of their parted lips. He fisted her hair, tangling it between his fingers, the silky strands knotting within his grip. He used the knotted strands to tilt her head to his liking and she arched, rising onto her toes, making the distance between them nonexistent when he pulled her flush against him.

"Red, I want you. I need you so damn bad..." It was a breathy decree met by a soft mewing from the back of her throat. His tongue licked the seam of her lips and she opened slightly, her tongue tantalizing as it met his.

"Your cell's been ring—" Mary's voice hitched.

The intrusion broke the fogged haze encompassing them, and Ember stepped back, dropping her arms from around his neck, causing Slate to hesitantly loosen his grip. Her locks tumbled free.

Awkwardness hit the room.

"Oh my...I'm...ah...I'm so sorry. You left it on my desk." Before

Mary could finish the apology, Ember's phone peeled out a familiar ringtone. Mary held it up, her wide-eyed stare volleying between her two friends. The phone's incessant ring now seemed obnoxiously loud in the silence that hung heavy.

"I should get that." Ember's voice quaked, and she stepped away from Slate.

She took it from Mary but the ringing fell dead. She stared down at it like it could give her the answers as to what the hell just happened. Slate watched her nibble her thumbnail, a nervous tendency. She looked up and locked eyes with him, her brows knitted with the questions she was about to ask. "Eli. I—"

"Emmy—" He could still taste her angel breath on his own. The very breath he'd felt whisper to him, night after night, in his dreams.

She looked at him with pleading eyes while bewilderment spread across her face. Before he could stop her, she disappeared from the room with the words she didn't say. He wanted to call her back, but the words were gone along with the moment. As was she.

Slate closed his eyes and dropped his head. A millimeter more, a second sooner, and he could have laid claim to his heart's most wanted desire.

His Red.

"I'm so sorry." Mary's soft voice lifted Slate from his anguish. "I had no idea..." her words trailed off.

He held up a hand and shook his head, telling her it wasn't her fault, which she seemed to understand. He pursed his lips into a flat line, rolling them between his teeth.

Slate saw the anguish in her eyes, and though it was no fault of her own, he knew she still felt terrible for breaking their moment. She gave him a stiff smile then turned and left the room.

He closed his eyes punishing himself for taking too long. Opportunity missed by his own hesitation to tell Ember the truth.

He wanted to be hers.

≈

MARY:*WHAT THE HELL JUST HAPPENED?*

EMBER:*I don't know.*

MARY:*What do you mean, you don't know?*

EMBER:*Exactly what I mean. I. DON'T. KNOW!*

MARY:*Where are you?*

EMBER:*Bathroom.*

MARY:*Going? Or Hiding?*

EMBER:*Both.*

MARY:*You need me to come in there?*

EMBER:*No.*

MARY:*You need to get out of here?*

EMBER:*YES.*

MARY:*Need a drink?*

.   .   .

EMBER:*YES.*

MARY:*Bar or house?*

EMBER:*House.*

MARY:*Yours or Mine?*

EMBER:*Yours.*

MARY:*I'll tell King I'm leaving.*

EMBER:*DO NOT tell him why!*

MARY:*Gotcha!*

EMBER:*Mare?*

MARY:*Yup?*

EMBER:*Will King give T a ride home?*

MARY:*Sure. We taking your truck?*

EMBER:*Yup. Meet you out front in five.*

.   .   .

MARY:*Coolio!*

Ember sat in the bathroom stall leaning against the cool metal. *Stupid, stupid, stupid!* What the hell had come over her? That was the million-dollar question.

One minute, she was welcoming him home, and the nex*t* —*Oh, God*—next she was about to welcome him home like she never had before. Confusion ran rampant through her mind. *Why did it feel so good? So, right? Did I come on to him, or did he come on to me? What the fuck!* She was so embarrassed; so confused. This was wrong. *Absolutely wrong.* Then, why did she tingle all the way to her core? Why did her vajayjay flame with fire? Not just fire, but an inferno. A *raging* inferno.

This is Eli. She didn't want to face him. Definitely didn't want to face the rest of the guys. One look and they'd know what had happened. Thank God for Maven's perfect timing. Her untimely phone call saved her from the sheer disaster of making a monumental mistake. *Remember last time he kissed you?* God, her mind was like a damn Dr. Phil episode. *Question. Answer. Explore your thoughts.* She needed a drink...and her girls. This was a clusterfuck she couldn't unravel by herself. She pulled her head from the cool, metal wall of the stall and huffed in exasperation. *You're so screwed, Em!*

~

"You're so screwed, Em!" Maven was not helpful at all.

"I didn't invite you over to tell me what I already know. I invited you over so you could tell me how to un-fuck myself!" Ember crossed her arms over the kitchen table and thumped her head against them.

"Margarita?" Mary brought the pitcher over and topped off Maven's glass.

Ember didn't lift her head but said, "Keep 'em coming."

Mary topped off Ember's glass then poured herself one from a different pitcher. "No fair. You get the happy juice, and I get the virg-arita."

Maven piped up without missing a beat, "Because, if you'd stayed a virgin you could join in margaritas with us. Not my fault King had to deflower you, manhandle you, and put his big ol' cock—"

"Hello, ladies!" King rounded the corner and entered the kitchen, causing Maven to halt mid-sentence. He bent down and planted a steamy kiss on Mary's lips not caring it was in front of company. Mary gave as good as he got, assaulting her husband's mouth. Definitely not PG, but just short of X-rated. Then, he crouched and placed a chaste kiss on Mary's flat belly. "Maven. Ember." King greeted them as if he hadn't heard Maven's outcry of deflowering and big cocks.

Maven smiled at him, not one bit of embarrassment crossing her face. Matter of fact, she threw King a wink and took a sip from the salted rim of her glass. King shook his head and headed to the refrigerator.

He spoke while perusing the shelves, addressing Maven. "Honey, I deflowered my wife long before she was carrying our child and long before we said, 'I do.'"

Maven gave Mary two thumbs up and threw wide eyes as if to congratulate her on the accomplishment. Mary mimicked her husband's lead and shook her head at the Maven-ish antics. Maven had no tact and pulled no punches. It was one of the many things Ember loved about her.

Ember hoped King wouldn't linger. She didn't want him to know what they were talking about; what they were here to discuss. The last thing she wanted was King to know how desperate she'd become to come on to Elijah. To know that they were microseconds away from forever changing their relationship. Letting some mysterious draw lead them to a place unknown, undiscovered and unable to be pulled from the brink. King was like a big brother to her, and she didn't want him knowing anything about her non-existent love life.

"So, you and Slate, huh?"

Ember about fell out of her chair.

King spoke from inside the refrigerator, his head buried deep inside so his voice was muffled, but Ember clearly didn't hear him wrong. He knew.

"Finally." He pulled out what seemed to be four different sandwich meats and a jar of Miracle Whip. Then, strategically balancing them below his bearded chin, he reached back in for a pack of cheese slices and a cold beer.

Ember hoped she'd been transported to another dimension where only that dimensional King knew what had happened. Maven pushed Ember's drink closer to her and mouthed the words, *Drink up*. Ember gladly did, taking two big gulps, wishing the alcohol would hurry up and carry her out of her misery. She shot Mary a look, telepathically asking her if she had told King. Mary, knowing Ember well, shook her head *no*, giving her widened eyes to emphasize she didn't tell a single soul. The room grew silent. No one said a word.

Of course, silence never lasted long when Maven was around, so she just blurted out what they were all thinking. "So, who told you these two were playing tonsil tennis and seven-minutes-in-heaven in Slate's cage?"

Ember could have killed her. The look she threw her were daggers. Huge, pointy, kill you, daggers. Maven just smiled, winked at her, and nonchalantly sipped her 'rita.

"Cameras."

"What?" All three voices rang from the table causing King to laugh.

Mary's voice took on a knowing, "Ohhhh, cameras."

"Cameras?" Ember needed to know what cameras he was talking about.

King busied himself making his sandwich that had enough meat on it to feed a third-world country. "Security feed." He took a single bite of the "meatwich," making half of it disappear and continued speaking around the mouthful. "Got them throughout the building, Except bathrooms and locker rooms." He took another bite leaving only a morsel of crust and washed it down with a long swig of his beer. "But, I do have cameras pointing at the entrances of the bathrooms and locker rooms. That's the place most criminals hide if they would ever be so stupid as to break into a joint."

Ember put her head back down to the oak table. "FML. Just F.M.L."

Maven refilled her own glass from the pitcher and topped off Ember's as well. "Need more 'rita!" She said to no one in particular.

Mary grabbed the pitcher and headed to the blender to make another batch. "Like anyone's dumb enough to break into Hellforce, babe."

"Stupider things have happened." King said, making himself a second sandwich.

"Yeah, like Em and Eli sucking face in a public place when they don't want anyone to know." Maven laughed and brought her drink to her lips.

Ember's head flew up. She grabbed Maven's glass mid-sip, sloshing some of the cold beverage onto the tabletop. "Stop! Enough."

"My 'rita." Maven looked like a kid who'd dropped an ice cream cone.

"We didn't kiss, suck face, tonsil hockey — "

"Tonsil tennis," Maven corrected her.

If looks could kill, Maven would've been six-feet under. Ember wasn't playing. She was pissed.

"Whatever. The fuck. You call it. It didn't happen!"

Maven was about to say something, when King saved Ember from wrapping her hands around her best friend's throat and strangling her if she dared to utter another syllable.

"It *almost* happened." King quipped.

Ember took a long pull of her margarita, needing all the liquid courage she could muster to get through her embarrassment. "So, who all knows? Who'd you tell?" She took another pull, making half the glass disappear.

"Didn't tell anyone." King finished making a second sandwich and put the ingredients back into the refrigerator.

Ember breathed a sigh of relief, thankful none of the other guys knew about the "almost kiss."

Mary returned to the table with the new round of drinks, filling the glasses without even asking. "See, your secret's safe. No one else knows besides King."

"Didn't say that." King devoured the rest of his sandwich. "I said, I didn't tell anyone. Not that no one else knows."

Ember buried her head in her arms again and let out a guttural groan.

Mary asked the question everyone was dying to ask. "Who else knows?"

King placed his plate in the sink and wiped the crumbs off the counter. "Don't know for sure, but Slate and Cy were in his office when I left. Both clammed up when I stuck my head in to tell them I was leaving."

"So, Eli told Cy?" Ember asked.

"Don't know, but you can't blame him."

That got Ember's hackles up. Why couldn't she blame him for telling Cypher something so personal, even before they had a chance to talk it out amongst themselves? And, she proceeded to tell King her thoughts on the matter. "He shouldn't be discussing something so personal with—"

King raised an eyebrow, the way only King could. His face could say a thousand words, without him uttering one.

Fuck!

King nodded.

Eli was confiding in Cy, his best friend, the same way she was confiding in Maven and Mary—which at the moment, she was having second thoughts about doing so. Man, the decision-making part of her brain must be off-kilter today. She held up her hands in capitulation. "You're right, I can't be mad. But, can I at least be humiliated?"

Maven jumped back into the conversation and gave a stitch or two of wisdom. "Why be humiliated? Not like it's some random stranger you hooked up with at the grocery store or local laundromat. It's Eli." Maven swiped a bit of salt from the rim of her glass and licked her finger.

"Exactly! It's Eli! My best friend, Eli." Ember's voice rose an octave, coming out shrill and forced.

Maven pushed her own drink to the side and pinned Ember with a dubious stare. "Are you fuckin' serious?"

Ember was taken aback by her tone which was saying a lot, because not too many things Maven did shocked her anymore.

Seeing Ember wasn't tracking, she said, "Look honey, I love you. Known you for too many years not to be honest with you.

I've waited around, hoping you would finally come to your senses and figure it out, but I don't see that ship sailing anywhere near the horizon."

Ember sat confused, not sure what her bestie was laying out.

"Don't say a word. God only knows you'll talk yourself in circles, and you still won't be anywhere near the truth that's staring you point blank in the face."

Ember opened her mouth.

"Naw, uhh, uhhh, uhhh. Close your trap. Fill the gap. Here," Maven shoved Ember's drink in her face. "Sit back, sista, 'cuz it's gonna be cold hard truths from here on out."

Ember searched for a lifeline, hoping to find one in Mary, but she was wrapped in King's arms, her back to his chest, his hands around her flat belly, caressing their baby. Both gave her raised brows with unsympathetic smirks across their faces.

Oh, shit! Whatever was coming, she had no allies.

She was screwed.

CHAPTER 19

Slate rubbed the back of his neck, replaying the last moments with Ember over and over in his mind. *Fuck!* Why'd they have to have *that* moment in the cage room? Why couldn't it have been anywhere but there? It was the makeshift high school prom all over again. Relegated to the friend zone for fifteen years, only to be banished back there...again. She left before they could talk, and he *knew* she was going to play the friend card...again.

Cy entered the room and headed to his cage, his hair wet from his shower. "You okay, man?"

Slate stroked his too-shaggy beard, a reminder it needed to be trimmed after a four-day trek, and debated if he should say anything to Cy. He needed to get into the shower and into the conference room to debrief, a task that could take a while. Hopefully, it wouldn't take too long, but the way his luck was having it, they'd be debriefing until the midnight hour. Knowing he couldn't spring this on Cy and then have to sit in the conference, he decided to let it ride until after business ends were tied up.

"Yeah, I'm good. Just want to get this over with, sit back and get home."

"I hear that." Cy rummaged around in his locker, pulled out a black t-shirt and slipped it over his head. Walking out of his area, he eyed Slate. They were best friends and Slate knew Cy could read him like a book. Some type of weird telepathic skill all the guys had honed over the years working together.

"Not now." Slate gave him a look that said *don't push the issue*. "After the debrief?"

Slate drew in a breath, exhaling in a whoosh. "Yeah."

"Okay. Meet you in the conference room after you get that four-day Lebanese funk off ya. Hit the shower and I'll see you in fifteen." With that, Cy left the room.

Slate grabbed a change of clothes from his locker, his shave kit, and headed for the showers.

"Ah, man!" Cy leaned back in the chair, hands rested behind his head and stared at Slate.

The debriefing had gone rather quickly and, for that, Slate was grateful. He tried to stay in sync with the guys, but his mind kept wandering. He tried to concentrate, which made him more frustrated, because he knew how to stay in the mindset of the moment but couldn't command his brain to focus. Why was this fucking with him? *Put it aside; come back to it later.* He kept repeating the mantra each time he caught himself sliding off the topic. King had noticed him slipping a few times and gave him a subtle nod telling him to stay on track. Slate was all too grateful when King wrapped up the debrief and sent everyone packing.

"So, ya just let her leave?"

Slate walked the length of his office and rubbed his freshly trimmed beard. "I didn't. *let her leave*, she's a grown-ass woman, she leaves when she wants to leave." He knew if he would've caught her before she bolted, he could've tried to talk her into staying around until after the debrief. Or, at least meet up with him later in the evening, but he had an inkling she was gone. When he didn't see Mary at the front desk when he headed to the conference room he knew she was MIA by the time everything wrapped up. He was pissed she'd left without telling him and she had no one on her six.

"Did you call her?"

"Straight to voicemail."

179

"What about a text?"

Slate shook his head. "And text her what? 'Sorry for almost making my every lustful dream of you come true. Sorry about the last fifteen years of wet dreams. P.S. Thinking of you.'"

Cy wrinkled his face in a look of disgust. "Wet dreams? Really? What are you, twelve? Don't you just rub one out in the shower or knock it out before you go to bed? Get *it* before *it* gets you?"

Slate dropped his head, not believing he was talking about spooging in his sleep and about jerking off when he should be figuring out what he was going to do next: getting a plan of action in place. He wasn't going back to the friend zone. He'd decided it was time to lay it out on the line, heart be damned. It was just the *how* part that was killing him. How do you tell the girl you've loved since childhood, since kindergarten, that she's what makes you live? Keeps you living. Keeps you breathing. Brings you back after each death-defying mission. Hallmark didn't make a greeting card for that particular occasion. God only knew, he wished they did.

"You talk to Pops?"

He stopped pacing. *Should I talk to Pops?* What could he say to Pops that he couldn't say to Ember? He knew the advice Mitch would give him. Hell, it would be the same advice he gave him at Ember's house after the range shooting. Pops had all but given him his blessing.

"I see the wheels turning, my friend. Talk it out. You do your best strategizing when we talk out a mission. The best plan comes together when we all speak out loud and bounce ideas and solutions off one another."

"I need to talk to her but not anywhere public."

"So, no restaurants."

"No restaurants." Slate repeated.

"Public places, including parks? Not too secluded, but also people not at the next table like at a restaurant."

"Park could work. Put that on the possibilities list." Slate crossed his arms over his broad chest. A park was on the right track, but still felt too public. He wouldn't want to put her somewhere she'd feel embarrassed, or a place she felt she couldn't fully express her feelings. No, a park wasn't going to be the place. "Second thought, scrap the park. Not gonna work."

"Okay, no park, no restaurant. Thought about a skywriter? 'Emmy, I'm hard for you! Love E.'" Cy laughed at his joke until he saw the frustration cross his friend's face. "Sorry, bud, just trying to break the mood."

Slate knew Cy had his best intentions in mind, and yes, the mood was tense, but he damn well was going to lay this out. Even if it meant he'd lose what he had with her. The thought sent a lead weight to his gut and a piercing to his heart. Was it worth losing what they had? Friends weren't all that bad. Until it was. Until it *would* be.

Don't wait until tomorrow has passed and you're left wanting that opportunity back. Pops' words echoed in his mind. Someday she'd find someone she thought was the one, and he'd be wishing he'd have taken the opportunity to tell her how he felt.

Sooner or later you're either going to have to tell her, or you're going to have to let her go. I would hate for you to miss the opportunity when it has always been yours.

Damn! Pops' words reverberated in his mind. But, was this the time to risk everything? Were Pops' words just sentiment? *You're a son to me, Eli. Let's just make it official sooner, rather than later.*

"Yo...Slate." The snapping fingers brought him back to his office. "Dude, where'd you go?" Slate pushed Cy's hand out of his face. "Damn. You were way off in Lalaland. No one was in the wheelhouse."

Slate shook himself from his trance, welcoming back the present, and apologized to his friend.

"What about inviting her over to your place? No fancy dinner, just some takeout or pizza, something that won't have her thinking you're trying too hard or that you are trying to force her into talking about this..." Cy paused, "your friendship."

It sounded like it could work, but he didn't want her to come to his place. That may have her thinking she'd be trapped if all this turned into a shitstorm. *Her place?* That'd be a better option. She'd be on her ground, with her surroundings, and add in the comfort factor. She could ask him to leave if she felt things were out of her control.

"Hey, bud...you're zoning out again."

"Sorry." It was a shitty apology, but what else could be said.

"Talk it out."

Slate reiterated his thoughts of going to her place instead of his, but it still didn't feel like it was the right answer. They'd spent countless hours at her house over the years, watching tv, vegging out or just being...friends. Life long, familiar friends. Could he taint the space where they'd spent so much time? Built so many memories? The place she'd held him as her friend when he'd come home from an especially difficult op in the Army, saying nothing, but being his refuge? The space where he'd held her after the shooting incident?

No. He wouldn't sully sacred ground. There had to be a better place to bare his soul.

CHAPTER 20

Eli knocked on the solid oak door and let himself in. This house was as much home to him as the house he shared with his mom growing up. The Hayes' were as much his family as were his brothers at Hellforce. He was looking for answers and the best answers always came from Pops. So, Eli found himself calling him on his way home from HQ, and as always, Pops was ready to lend an ear, dole out advice and steer him in the right direction.

Times like this had him wondering how it would have been if his father had never passed away. Would he have a close-knit relationship with the man who shared his bloodline? Would his father be the man he looked up to like the giant of a man Mitch had become to him? Would his father have accepted his choice to forego college and enlist in the military right after high school?

The morning after their "prom", he'd sought Pops out for a man-to-man talk about his future. He told Pops he was forgoing the scholarship he'd just received, a four-year ride to the same college Ember was attending after graduation, and he was joining the Army. Pops listened with an open ear and an unjudging heart. Pops weighed out the pros and cons with him and said the choice was ultimately his. No one could make the decision but him, but he warned him not to make a rash decision. When Eli laid out his reasons, Pops listened with a heavy heart, and when he decided to forgo college, Mitch gave him his blessing, told him he was proud of his choice to serve his country, but told him he could always follow his feet home. Back to the Hayes family.

But, Eli couldn't bear to spend the next four years pining and yearning for something that was so close, yet so far out of his reach.

Ember didn't love him the way he loved her. She didn't need him to breathe. Didn't need him to feel alive. No, Eli was just her friend, though her best friend. And, that's where he stayed all these years, loving from the shadows, pining from a distance, his heart never settling, because how could a heart settle where it wasn't wanted?

"Hey, you made it." Pops' voice startled him back to the present. If Pops noticed him zoning, he didn't say anything.

"Mom around?" Eli looked around the room from the foyer but didn't see her.

"In the kitchen. Watch out, she's going to force-feed you. She just made a batch of those caramel-walnut-brownie cookies," he patted his stomach, "gonna put me in the gym an extra three hours this week."

Pops was fifty-seven but didn't look a day over forty. He still had a rock hard physique, and the man could PT the living daylights out of any of the men at Hellforce. He was as solid as his character. If Eli could become half the man Mitch was, he'd be one lucky son of a bitch.

"Can we take this somewhere private?" Eli took in a heavy breath, wanting to get the burden off his chest and out in the open. He wanted to hear what Pops' words of wisdom would entail.

"Sure. Take a walk."

The pair walked through the kitchen where Susan had about three dozen paper plates laid out, each piled high with cookies. Eli took one from the plate closest to him and bit into the delectable sugary goodness. *Divine.*

"Mmmm, my God, Mom." Eli spoke between bites and

around the bits of gooeyness that were melting in his mouth. "These are amazing. Best cookies ever!"

"That's because," she eyed his toned body, "you never eat cookies. And, even when you do, I bet they are store-bought, processed, manufactured garbage." She shoved another cookie into Eli's hand and turned to pour him a full glass of milk.

"Thanks, Mom. You're the best." Eli popped the remaining bite of cookie in his mouth and drank the ice cold milk down in one swig.

"Mustache." Susan wiped her finger across his upper lip, removing the milk left behind clinging to the hair of his actual mustache. "Never too old for Mom's pampering."

Mitch grabbed a cookie from the plate Eli had eaten from and Susan smacked his hand with a spatula so forcefully, Pops jerked it back and held it with his free hand.

"What was that for?"

"Those are Elijah's."

"But he has a whole plate full."

"Those. Are. Elijah's.' She enunciated every syllable of his name.

"Guess I'll just take one of these." He reached for the plate closest to himself and received another slap on the hand.

"What the—" He stopped himself from cursing a blue streak and looked at his wife.

"Those are for the fire station. Those will be going to the crew on shift tomorrow.'

"And these?" He pointed to one of the other dozen plates of cookies.

"Sheriff's department."

"These?"

"Police department."

Pops knew it was a losing battle, but he continued to point at random plates set out on the granite countertop. All the while, Eli, continued to eat the brownie confections off the plate deemed *his*.

"Nursing home…library…church bazaar…ER hospital crew...Police & Fire 9-1-1 dispatchers…animal rescue shelter..."

Finally, he pointed to the last plate.

"Oh, that one's for you." Susan bust out in tears, laughing at the stunned look on Pops' face. Eli had no choice but to laugh along. Pops squinted his eyes, giving her a glare that became primal as she continued to laugh, wiping her tears as they fell from her eyes. Pops straightened and his military alpha mode made an appearance. Predator-like, he walked up behind her and whispered something into her ear, making her back stiffen and her eyes widen. Eli couldn't hear what Pops said, but he was getting a strong idea of what was being murmured. Mitch grazed his wife's ear as he whispered, and her breathing became erratic. Then with one last word in low tones, Susan's eyes flared and her breath hitched. She cleared her throat and excused herself from the kitchen, scurrying up the banister stairwell.

Seeing Mitch's satisfied look on his face, Eli stopped mid-chew. Suddenly the cookie didn't taste as delectable as it did a minute ago.

"Did you just pleasure Mom with sexual banter?" The words could barely form in his mouth. He set his half-eaten cookie on the countertop.

"No. Pleasure's all mine. Punishment is all hers."

Oh, god, he was going to be sick. Blood-relation or not, he didn't want to envision whatever sexcapades were going to be taking place after he left. Thoughts of pristine, pure, saintly Mom doing anything nasty was just blasphemy. Pure, unadulterated sainthood was where Susan Hayes' pedestal stood.

Mitch smiled, grabbed a cookie from one of the forbidden plates, slapped him on the back, and headed towards the door that led out to the pastures behind the house.

Eli followed, though now, he was mentally sick.

They walked towards the nearest fence line, past the paddocks and the barn, over a rolling hill, and leaned against the white split rail fence. Neither spoke for a while as they watched the sun setting behind the farthest hill, dipping low to send parts of the world into slumber. The sky was ablaze with radiant light. Purples, yellows and the most brilliant blazes of red-orange, the exact shade of Ember's hair, blessed the sky.

Is it a sign?

The thought caught Eli in the gut. Of course it wasn't a sign. It was the wonders of nature, the same wonders that blazed orange and shone each evening. There were no signs casting into the universe tonight.

"How'd she get such blaze orange hair?" The question came out of nowhere. It wasn't the question he was planning to ask, but somehow, it felt like the right way to start the conversation.

Mitch's hair was black and Susan's was more a lighter shade of strawberry-blond than the orangy-red of Ember's locks and far from the crimson red of Rhys.

"Susan's side of the family are Scots, who mixed with the Irish. Their hair is unnatural. No shade on earth matches the blaze of reds, coppers, and oranges that run in their bloodline. The color just plain doesn't exist."

Eli thought about that and it was true. No color did match the fiery tones in her hair. He always tried to pinpoint the exact color, but when he would find a dazzling shade of orange—fabrics, leaves, sunsets, nothing compared to the intensity of her locks.

"You came here to talk about hair?"

"No."

"Lineage?"

Eli shook his head and answered in the negative.

"Come here to talk about my baby girl?"

Hearing Mitch refer to Ember as his baby girl put into perspective the fact he wasn't going to let his daughter go to anyone he didn't deem worthy. Someone who wouldn't protect her and treasure her like the rare and precious gem she was.

Mitch waited in the quiet of the evening. Quiet that included cicadas, crickets, Chuck-Will's and bullfrogs. All the sounds of a Texas summer night. Mitch let the quiet magic pull the truth from Eli.

"I'm ready to tell her."

Those five words caught Mitch's attention, though he nodded like he already knew.

The duo stood in silence, again letting the sun sink lower and the horizon disappear.

"You know what this could mean, right, son?"

Son. Pops had called him son for as long as he could remember. It wasn't until after high school, specifically the day he left for basic, waiting to board the bus, after all the goodbyes were said, that Mitch leveled him in the eye and told him he'd never been prouder to have him as a son. DNA didn't matter. He was seeing his boy go off to become a man. He was sending him out to a world that would break him, mold him, build him up to a man of honor, dignity and fortitude. Resilience would live in every bone of his body and valor would reside in his soul. He was most likely sending his boy to war, a hellish nightmare Mitch knew all too well. He would be boarding that bus barely a boy, but would return a man. Mitch would be even prouder to lay claim to him; His son.

The memory faded and Eli was once again grateful that Pops had taken him under his wing. "Will she run?"

The question hung like the hues in the sky. Barely there hints of colors that were there one minute and gone the next. If a metaphor was ever exact, this one was all-encompassing.

"Will you chase her?"

Mitch's question stung, because Eli knew the answer would kill him.

"No."

Bomb. Detonated.

Mitch turned his head, keeping his body against the rail, foot resting on the bottom slat, but said nothing. Eli kept his gaze ahead, willing the sickening feeling churning in his stomach to dissipate. He wasn't a person to experience anxiety, but he could feel his chest constricting, tightening and forcing the air from his lungs.

He wouldn't chase her. Each word stabbed his soul.

Eli lowered his head but didn't turn to match Pops' stare.

"You won't chase her?" Mitch's words hurt Eli just as much as the words echoing in his own soul.

"No." Shuddering on his exhale, he continued. "I won't chase something that's not mine. If she stays, she's mine. If she runs, I gotta let her find her dreams….even if they don't include me."

"Friends?"

It hit like thunder. "Nope." The single word sliced his tongue. "I've been in the friend zone for so long, I can't stay there any longer. I can't stay here waiting and watch the day she pledges her vows to another man. I can't stay here and witness her give birth to his children. The sight of her rounded with another man's child—" His voice broke and the lump in his throat wouldn't go down. After a minute, he went on. "I'd die a thousand deaths if I had to see her, watch her from the bleachers, every time she set another milestone that I wasn't setting with her." The thought made bile rise in his throat. "I want her to be happy. Happier than anyone on earth. I love her. And will 'til the day I die. But, I can't love her without leaving her. I'd die a little every day if she only wants a friend."

The sun had disappeared below the horizon. The wisps of color, gone from the dusk sky. Blackness encroached upon the pasture as far as the eye could see. It was the same level of darkness that Eli felt in his soul. If he had to leave her, that darkness would never dissipate, would never blaze with the signs of the dawn of a new day. He would be desolate. Empty. A wasteland. Void. But, he'd withstand it if it meant she could find her dreams. Her happiness. Her someone who wasn't Eli.

A lone tear escaped his eye. It caught in his beard at the corner of his lip. The bitter taste of sorrow. It scared him to death to think that if she ran, this would be his reality. An island of one. Desolate. Alone. Empty. Emmy was his, but he may not be hers. He'd never love another. It was a solemn vow. How could he give his heart to another when his soul was stitched to hers?

"If you love something set it free. If it comes back, it's yours. If not, it was never meant to be." Mitch's smooth timbre broke the air.

"Can't force someone to love you." Eli's words were a whisper.

"She'd be a fool to run, son. An absolute fool. And, I don't say that lightly, because she's my daughter and I live for her happiness. But, if she's blind to what's in front of her, it's going to tear me apart."

Eli finally turned his gaze to Pops. The sight stopped him cold. The big, strapping, hulk of a man, the giant Eli knew, was crying. Tears coursed down his cheeks. Eli had never witnessed his hero shed a tear.

"You're my son, Eli. No matter what Ember decides, you *are* my son." Pops wiped the wetness from his face with the shoulder of his t-shirt and sniffed back a few times. "If she doesn't run, there's no man I would want next to her other than you. You raise my baby girl up to heights no other man would ever raise her. I'll be on my knees tonight begging the Lord to grant her wisdom and clarity, 'cuz only the Lord works miracles. And, I'm gonna need a damn miracle if she doesn't seize the moment when you put yourself out there."

Pops let the deafening silence lie, clapped a single hand on Eli's shoulder, then turned and headed for the house. Eli didn't follow. He stayed in the darkness as the constellations appeared in the void of the night sky. He followed a shooting star, closed his eyes and wished a prayer like he'd never prayed before. "My true love, let her be. Not meant to be, I'll set her free."

CHAPTER 21

Her legs quaked. Her breasts rose and fell with every shuddered breath. A glistening sheen of sweat misted across her body. Her nipples were tight. She felt them pull as they puckered. His beard tickled the swells of her breasts while his luscious lips caressed and ravished them, bringing a likeable pain to the tips as he bit and nibbled on them, pulling them just beyond the point of pain. The wetness left behind glinted in the soft light. She watched the taut nubs redden as the blood rushed back to each battered tip. Her back arched as she silently begged for more. More of what, she wasn't sure. Just, *more.*

His tongue traced a river from the swollen bite he placed on the crest of her throat, down the curve of her neck, and through the valley of her breasts. He nipped and kissed the farther he trailed. A suck on her navel brought a shiver, then his tongue dipped inside, circling the hollow from inside. He traced lower, his tongue leaving a wake of fire, leaving nothing untouched, unscorched, unscathed. He burned across her body. Lower. Lower. *Yes, lower.* He disappeared.

The pull of his teeth across her sensitive lips brought a moan from deep in her throat. A cry that went unheeded. She heard his intake of breath as he inhaled her scent, her arousal doubling at the thought of him between her thighs. His tongue was sinful and it was torturous. Lashing and licking, plundering her clit while she rode the precipice.

She couldn't hold on any longer, although she wanted to hold out, make this glory last all night. The tightening and throbbing was too much to hold back. She grasped the sheet, twisting it in her fists, willing him to push deeper. The world went silent; only her panting and the rush of her heartbeat could be heard. It was a symphony, building into a crescendo. She couldn't hold it. His face buried deeper. Her hands tangling in his all-too-short hair. She wanted to cry out but her voice was lost as her breath hitched.

Oh, God. Oh, God. His fingers pushed in to the hilt, and she—

The alarm blared from her phone.

She was panting, gasping for air. She shuddered, and breathed in staccato. She squeezed her thighs together. Bare. Empty. Desolate. Panties...drenched.

She silenced the alarm wanting ten more minutes of sleep. Ten more minutes of dreams. Wanting ten more minutes of Eli.

Errg! She flopped back to the mattress wanting to crush the phone or chuck it across the room, but she withheld her anger and set it on her bedside.

Fuck! Just, fuck!

Her core pulsed as she lay sprawled out in bed. Grinding and gripping. Trying to find something to leech on to and release the pressure deep within. *Fuck!* That's right...Fuck! Fuck Maven. Fuck Mary. And fuck King. They were dead to her. This was all their fault. Every. Thing. Their. Fault. *F.M.L.*

Throughout the night, Ember lay in bed, tossing and turning, wrestling with the blankets, and finally surrendering and throwing the covers back. *Ahhh!* She let out a frustrated scream. She lay sprawled like a starfish, staring up at the ceiling. The room was dark but she could see shadows cast by the moonlight spilling through the window. *Damn!* She'd checked her phone. 3:25. *Ugh! Five hours!* Five hours she'd been struggling to get to sleep. She'd gone to the kitchen to get a glass of milk. Not warm milk, *ewww*, but a glass of thick, rich, whole milk. Unhealthy. Saturated fat. *Delicious.* Having something comforting in her belly always put her to sleep.

She stood in the silence looking out the kitchen window into the darkness and replayed the day's events. Maven and Mary conspiring; seeing things that obviously didn't exist. *What the fuck!* These were *their* dreams in her head. Yes, Maven and Mary were to blame. She threw King in there, too, just for good measure. Her mind was jumbled, swirling with the noise of the evening's gathering. They were all crazy. Insane. They were seeing things that simply weren't there and now they had her dreaming things from their imaginations.

Eli, in love with me? She let out a huff of exasperation. *Were they mad?* That's what it was. Her whole circle of friends had gone insane, collectively. She couldn't kick Mary's ass because she was with child, and it would be a futile attempt to toe with King. But, she was going to *kill* Maven!

Now it was morning and she was even crankier than last night. *Eli? In love with me?* It was the craziest thing she could imagine. They were friends. Right? Just really good friends? Best friends...yup, best friends. Eli was her...her what? Her...rock. Her...confidant. Her life-long friend. Councilor. Mentor. Shelter. Shield.

Ugh!

But, that dream. Ooooh, that dream. It was a figment of her subconscious psyche.

But, would it feel like that with him? With his hands roaming my body? And, oh, the things he could do with his mouth. Her breathing increased. *Oh, his writhing body over mine. The quaking in his breath fanning across my breasts. My nipple pulled taught between his teeth. The pain. The pleasure.*

She pushed aside the soaked gusset of her silk panties and caressed the smooth outer shell of her lips. Her fingers slid across the moistened fold to the center of her core. The heat from her dream was still there. She eased the tip of her finger into her sheath. Warm. Wet. Silkiness. She pulsed once, feeling the muscles tense around her lone finger. She pushed it deeper, just as "dream" Eli did. Her breath hitched when she curled her finger. *Oh!* Her thumb caught the nub of her swollen clit and a zing welled deep within, curling her toes. Pushing another finger into her wetness, she tightened. And pulsed. Then clenched again and again. She undulated her hips, writhing as her breathing turned into rapid pants. Her mouth was dry; her core was not. She pushed and curled her fingers, delving deeper in rhythm and pulling them out to the shallow. *Eli.* She pumped faster. *Oh, Eli.* She heard his muffled pants as he bit into her thigh. *Eli...Eli...*

"Eli!"

Her scream broke her from her erotica. Her breasts heaved and her lungs burned, starved of oxygen as she held her breath, pushing herself over the edge, past the point of no return.

Oh, God. Have mercy.

She was screwed. Not just by her fingers. She was screwed because Eli was no longer her friend. He was the focus of her wildest ride. *Eli.* She had never orgasmed like that in her life. In fact, she'd never orgasmed. Her mini clitoral vibrator tried. Yes, Clyde tried, but never delivered.

She reached between her thighs and, yup...she'd orgasmed. She gushed and leaked. She let loose. Her inner thighs were coated and the sheet beneath her was wet. Really wet. Like, Niagara Falls wet.

Fuck!

She was screwed.

After she cleaned and showered, Ember turned the dial to cold, needing the chilliest shower in the history of showers. Yet it did nothing to squelch the burning within her, only bringing shivers as the showerhead dumped freezing water over her body. It was no use. She slapped the knob harder than necessary, bringing the unsuccessful icy downpour to an end. Ember's teeth chattered. Hair wrapped in a towel, turban style, she stood facing her reflection in the full-length mirror. She turned her body this way and that, examining it from different angles. Her breasts were full and sat high on her chest. They didn't sag or part but sat close together, making natural cleavage even without a bra. She guessed they were nice boobs. She had small areolas and dusky pink nipples, contrasting against her ivory skin. She turned to see her ass, an ass she usually thought was unappealing. In her jeans it looked underwhelming. But, bare, it had an appealing curve to it, rounding nicely to the flare of her hips down from her narrow waist. It was nothing Kim Kardashian would write home about, but she thought it was nice. Then again, *she* was nothing to write home about.

But, it was her body. Her. Body.

Would Eli like her body?

Stop! What the hell's wrong with you? With everybody? She shook her head hoping to clear it of the one thing she couldn't stop thinking about. Eli.

Fed up with the thoughts, like a petulant child she stomped her way to her bedroom, stopping at her dresser and reaching into her underwear drawer. Utilitarian underwear. Some would go as far as to say Granny panties. Ember called them comfortable. She pulled out a pair with tiny windmill prints. Whimsical. Cute.

Childish?

She frowned at the thought and studied the underwear, contemplating comfort verses sexy. Ember would never consider herself sexy. She was...Ember. Plain girl. Smart girl. Sexy siren?

Nope.

But, her dream came back to her. Oh, that dream. Inhaling, she watched the swell of her bare breast rise. Not thinking the better of it, she fingered her nipple, plucking it as *Dream Eli* had. Ooh, the tingle made her nipple erect. She pinched just the tip and the thought of *Dream Eli*, with it gritted between his teeth, sent shivers down her spine. She pinched harder.

Oh!

Her knees buckled and she caught herself coming out of her stupor.

What the fuck! Get a hold of yourself! What's come over you? Stop.

Ember brought her hands to her face, growling into the cups of her palms. She'd never thought of Eli as a lover.

God, isn't that incest or something?

He was like her brother.

She paused, contemplating the situation. *Friend Eli* was

sweet, thoughtful, always there when she needed him. He teased her and tortured her just like a little sister, though they were the same age.

Tortured her.

That thought triggered *Dream Eli*. Oh, the torture he gave, and she submitted.

Stop!

Maybe she just needed to feel sexy? Just for the day. That could be the answer. All this erotica needed an outlet. She spent her time in jeans, t-shirts and utility boots. She wore the same clothes to the range that she wore outside of work. She strode to her closet. It was a small walk-in—a tiny walk-in if she was truthful—but it was functional. As was her wardrobe. She thumbed through the hangers holding her t-shirts, stopping on her favorite one. It was faded and worn. Comfortable. It had a pair of tattered angel wings and the word REBELS across the wings. A halo sat above the word REBELS, though the font was anything but holy. It had more of a biker vibe, tough, tumbled, yet resilient. On the front left breast the words: *REBELS Tattered, Not Battered.* She returned it to its spot and pulled out another. It was the same angel wings and halo, but the tag on the front said, *REBEL GIRL Resilient. Always in the Fight.*

She pulled the hanger from its place and turned to her jeans. They were neatly folded, stacked on a pile. All the same denim blue, some worn and faded a little more than others. Those were the good ones. The ones that were broken in and moved with you. The same jeans. The same t-shirts. The same Ember.

She stared at the jeans...and then at the t-shirt. Today felt different. Did she want to be the same boring girl? Or, did she want to feel as sexy as she did in her dream? She eyed the sundress hanging in the back of the closet. Back in the section of clothes she bought thinking they were cute, but most of the items were crap that Maven convinced her to buy on her many, many forced shopping sprees.

Ember bought her clothes at Walmart or the outdoor and wilderness shops. Clothes made to take a beating. She worked at a gun range for Christ's sake. Maven thought sequins and cutesy was what Ember should wear. But, almost every item she bought now resided in: *Closetville, Land of the Unwanted Garments.*

She wouldn't be at the range today. She had a ton of paperwork and orders to fill, so she'd be working from the office at Hellforce. Jeans and a tee would be efficient, but not necessary.

She stared at the sundress. It was cute. A mostly white dress with sporadic groupings of red and pink blossoms. The chiffon material was light, so the skirt was flowy. The bodice had a V-neck wrap, the material of each breast overlapping at the waist. The shoulder straps were thin so she couldn't wear a bra, but the dress had built-in cups. It was short, mid-thigh, but not prudish. Ember ran her hand over the delicate fabric. The silkiness played beneath her fingers and the image of the sexy *Dream Eli* came to mind.

Would she want Dream Eli to be with her every time she felt the material graze her body? The thought exhilarated her. It was just a fantasy. *Right?* It wasn't like she wanted the *real* Eli. And, the real Eli wasn't even at the office today. He had an appointment, so T would be picking her up. The thought of having the silkiness against her body tantalized her.

Yup, making a final decision, this was what she would wear today.

Disaster! Her decision-making skills must be lacking. At first, when she slid the dress over her head and it skimmed her body, she felt sexy. Something new and exhilarating. When she went to put on her panties, the ones with the whimsical windmills, she hesitated. She wanted her undies to feel as sexy as the dress. She ditched whimsical and reached to the very back of the drawer. Her fingers hit pay dirt.

She pulled out a lacey, pale pink thong. She hesitated. *Can I be daring enough to wear it? Would it be comfortable?* She'd always heard of the dreaded thong wedgie. The only reason she even had the thong was of course, Maven. She'd convinced Ember that she *needed* it. Said every woman should have raunchy delicates. Ember begged to differ, but as usual, Maven's relentless badgering had Ember buying the damn thing just to end the conversation. Which it did.

But, now...*should I wear it?* No one would know but her; no one would be the wiser. She wanted to feel sexy. Be sexy. The barely-there lace felt soft on her fingertips. It would probably feel even softer against her skin. Before she lost her courage, she slipped the scant lacy material up her legs. And, waited. She jiggled her hips from side to side waiting to feel the dreaded wedgie. It didn't come. She even did squats and lunges, bent over and touched her toes, but nothing seemed to wedge.

Huh? She walked back to the en suite bathroom and stared at herself in the mirror. *Whoa!* Who was that looking back at her? *Sexy siren!* The thought made her giggle, the sound echoing off the walls.

She twisted her body, causing the skirt to swish, to flow care-free, emulating the way she was feeling in her new digs. Her body actually had a shape, something that was hidden by the normal tees and jeans she wore. She had side boob! Her natural cleavage looked sexy in the V-neck, pushed together firmly by the cups of the dress. Her stomach was flat, making the flare of her hips that much more noticeable. An hourglass. *Was that always there?* She turned her back to the mirror and craned her neck. *Damn!* She had back! Junk in the trunk. *What was the name of the type of ass guys loved? Voluptuous?* Well, she had voluptuous. Turning to face the mirror once more she shook her hair out, tousling it in her fingers and let it settle around her face. Her wild, untamed mane was everywhere. Damn, she felt sexy.

Ember dabbed a bit of perfume behind her ears and on each wrist, a move she'd seen her mom do a million times. Mom always said perfume was for your man, not the masses. Ember hated when women doused themselves. And, it was never pleas-ant-smelling perfume. It was always musky and rank, the kind that overloaded the senses and made her want to gag. Church Perfume is what her dad called it. The kind little old ladies, whose nostrils were as bad as their eyesight, donned.

She never wore much makeup, which Rhys deemed a mortal sin. Rhys had enough makeup to open her own cosmetics store. She'd shown Ember how to apply it, giving her dark smokey eyes and heavy-handed contour, but it never seemed to turn out the same when she applied it herself. She looked more circus-clown-meets-Alice-Cooper sideshow freak, than cover-model perfect.

Less is more, her mother said. She applied a light pink eyeshadow and a little eyeliner to the upper and lower lid, then added a light stroke of blush and a coat of mascara. She filled in the natural arch of her brow and finished with a lipstick that complimented her hair. Ten minutes later, Voila! She was done. She stood back and admired her handywork. *Not bad.*

From the depths of her closet, she dug out a pair of white sandals—again, a Maven purchase—and slipped them on. She felt cute as she swished the skirt around her legs, her toenails peeking from the tips of the sandals.

T should be arriving any minute. She couldn't wait to see the shocked expression on his face. Frumpy, practical, boring Ember was now Cinderella.

She heard his truck pull up and raced to the door wanting to shock him before he rang the bell.

She felt damn sexy. Really sexy. That was, until she threw open the door.

Shock and horror met her face-to-face.

Shit. Damn. And, fuck.

Her eyes widened and her body went stiff.

T wasn't standing on her doorstep.

Eli was.

CHAPTER 22

What. The. Fuck! Why was Eli here? She stood frozen in place unable to slam the door shut. Her mouth hung open and stayed agape. Eli looked shell-shocked. His million-dollar smile fell along with his jaw. His eyes rounded and his brows disappeared into his hairline. He didn't blink. Just stared. He wasn't breathing either—the rise and fall of his chest was absent.

Oh, God, this is a disaster!

Eli couldn't catch his breath. *What in the fuck just happened?* He must have died and gone to heaven, or not awakened this morning, because the gorgeous beauty in front of him was the same one that haunted him each night in his dreams. No longer a figment, but of flesh. A scorching flame burned across his chest and a tightening in his ribs had him wondering if he was having a heart attack.

But, it wasn't a heart attack; it was his lungs. They were on fire, burning because he wasn't breathing. He choked in a satisfying breath and the burning subsided. His heart slammed against his chest, frantic to feed his starving lungs. A few more breaths settled him, but he couldn't take in enough of this bombshell. His mouth felt parched and he tried to swallow, but the knot in his throat wouldn't go down.

"Em?" was all he could choke out.

One syllable.

He drank her in from head to toe. A hint of makeup accentuated her flawless features. Her eyes were wide, and her mouth—oh, that mouth just begged to be ravished. Her tousled hair framed her face and fell below the gorgeous rounds of her breasts, curling just under the swells sitting front and center. Her exposed cleavage lifted perfectly with each of her breathy pants, leaving just enough to the imagination before disappearing into the V of the dress. He wanted to grasp her flared hips and leave his imprints behind. He followed her legs down to her dainty toes peeking out from under her sandals' straps.

She was gorgeous.

She was always gorgeous, but today, God, there were no words to describe her, except to say, she was *absolutely gorgeous!*

"Why are you here?" Her voice cracked the air.

Blinking, his lids felt like sandpaper across his eyes and they began to tear because he hadn't blinked since she swung open the door. The question took him aback and he slowly began to regain his senses.

"I'm here to pick you up," he continued to blink, "like I do every morning."

She still looked shocked finding him on her doorstep.

"But, you're not supposed to be here. You said you had an appointment and wouldn't be in today." She leaned out a bit from the door jamb and looked around. "Where's T?"

Whoa! Alarm bells sounded. Red flags.

The hair on the back of his neck prickled and he resisted the urge to rub it down.

Reality sunk in. She was expecting T. He gritted his teeth.

"I texted you." He kept his tone level and his anger under wraps. For now.

≈

My phone! She remembered her phone on her bedside table and mentally slapped herself. Without wearing jeans, the phone that would normally be in her back pocket sat in her bedroom. Without saying anything, she turned and hurried down the hallway to her room.

Oh, God! Why is Eli here? He wasn't supposed to be here. She picked up her phone from the bed and saw she had two texts. She opened and read them.

ELI:*On my way to pick you up. Appointment got canceled. T's with King. Laters.*

    ELI:*Plans later this evening? Need to get your input on a matter.*

She bit her thumbnail. *Should I change? Put on my regular tee and jeans?* She glanced at the clock. She had enough time.

"Gonna be late!" Eli's voice sounded from down the hall.

She didn't want to change. She felt pretty. Sexy even. But, there was no way she could stay in this dress all day if Eli was with her. She rubbed the chiffon material down her torso, reluctant to take it off. It caressed her skin, instantly bringing the image of *Dream Eli* to her mind. Her core muscles clenched and the lace of the thong parted her supple lips.

Oh, God. There was no way she could stay in this getup.

"Be right out." Her voice shook. She headed for her closet, scrambling to find the REBEL t-shirt she chose earlier. *Got it!* She tore it off the hanger then grabbed a pair of jeans from the pile. Didn't matter which pair just as long as the material didn't feel like the dress. She turned to bolt from the closet but bounced off a wall. A wall of Eli.

Shit!

"We're going to be late." He saw the clothes in her hands, "What are you doing?"

Momentarily stunned, she looked from Eli to the clothes. "Changing."

His brows met. "Changing? Why?"

If she wasn't mistaken, his voice became a little harder.

"Because," she couldn't think of an excuse, so she went with the truth, "because, I want to." It was such a third-grade comeback.

He took the garments from her hands. "You don't need to change."

"Eli, give them back." She reached for the jeans but he swiveled and held them out of her reach. "Eli, I'm serious, give them to me."

"Emmy, you do not have to change. We're running late."

"Elijah Michael, give them to me. Right. Now."

"Oooh, you're middle-naming me now. You must want these pretty bad." He chuckled and held them even farther from her reach. "Seriously, we don't have the time."

"Fine. Doesn't matter. I have a whole closetful of things to wear." With that, she turned but Eli stepped in front of her, his bulk making it impossible to get by him.

"Are you serious?" She was trying to be stern but her voice betrayed her. With each move, the silken fabric caressed her legs and passed across her hips, making her think of *Dream Eli*, only now it was worse, because *Real Eli* was standing in front of her.

Eli looked her dead in the face. "Why do you really want to change?" He bit down on his back teeth.

"Does it matter?"

"Yes."

She swore his eyes turned a shade darker than their normal gorgeous slate color. She couldn't tell him the truth.

"Em?"

She surrendered. "Just fuck it! We don't have time for this." She started to walk away, but he caught her arm. Shivers traveled from his hand throughout her body.

His eyes searched her, trying to read her, so she looked away.

"Emmy. Why?"

He wanted her answer but there was no way she was going to tell him.

"Are you disappointed I was here to pick you up today?"

Ember's eyes narrowed, "No. Why would you think that?"

"Just seemed you were awfully eager for T to be on the other side of the door." There was a bite in his tone.

For a moment, her breath hitched in shock. "Did you think I dressed up for T? Is that what you're insinuating?"

He looked sick to his stomach when she said T's name.

"You think I dressed up for T." She said the words with glee. Her smile widened. Her lips pitched up, spreading a Cheshire Cat grin across her face and she did nothing to suppress it.

"Why, Mr. Ryan, are you jealous?" She added a little Texas twang to her voice.

He stayed stoic but his cheeks reddened.

Ember let out a gut-wrenching laugh. It bubbled from her toes.

Ember walked to the bathroom to check her makeup in the mirror, making sure her tears weren't ruining her mascara. Finding everything still in place, she went back into the bedroom.

Eli wasn't there.

"Eli?"

He didn't reply. Picking up her phone, she called out again, "Eli?"

She walked to the living room and saw him exiting the front door. *Is he really mad? Damn!* Grabbing her purse from the kitchen counter, she hurried out the door.

It was the longest day in history. First, the drive in was horrible. Eli finally admitted he thought she'd dressed up for T and apologized for the accusation. She wanted to rub it in, but she could tell his embarrassment was genuine. She also felt a little bad. She wasn't sure if she sensed jealousy coming off him or if it was the heated awkwardness between them escalating her hyper-sensitivity to his proximity. She'd never felt like this around him. She didn't know if it was unnerving or exhilarating. Her dress was still sending zings to newly awakened regions.

She thought the worst part of the day was over until she stepped into the office.

Hellforce lived up to the hell in its name.

Ember felt like a bug under a microscope. Eyes. Eyes followed her everywhere.

At first, she thought it was her imagination but she would catch one of the guys looking at her then quickly see his head turn or his gaze fall when he noticed her noticing him. Eli was the worst of the bunch. His eyes were constantly on her, tracking her everywhere. He seemed almost hungry.

She'd never admit it, but she kind of liked it.

Even tucked away in her office, it was going to be a long day.

"Shut. The. Front. Door!" Mary practically sang the words when she saw Ember in the break room. "Guurl!" She circled Ember. "What the fuck! You are *smokin' hawt*!"

Ember gave her wide, strained eyes, telling her silently to shut the fuck up.

"Shut up!" Mary bellowed again.

Ember shut the door behind her and pinned her with a glare. "This is all *your* fault." She thrust her finger at Mary and whisper-shouted the words trying to remain quiet. "You and Maven with your fucked-up ideas." Ember pushed past her.

Mary's expression fell to confusion. "It's *our* fault you look sexy as sin? Like sin-on-a-stick." She ripped the corner of a package of saltine crackers with her teeth then plucked one out and nibbled on a corner, eyeing Ember up and down. "Fuck, I'll gladly take credit for this. Ember Hayes in something other than a t-shirt and jeans." She cupped her mouth and practically shouted, "Fuck yeah, I'll take the credit!"

Ember was not amused and rolled her eyes. "What the fuck! You want to bring all the guys in here?" Ember paced like a pent-up bull. "This is all your fault."

"Again, how is this," Mary motioned up and down Ember's new digs, "my fault?"

She went all-in. "You made me dress for *Dream Eli!*"

Mary's brows drew in. "What?" She looked genuinely confused.

Ember huffed as if it should be obvious, then whisper-shouted, "Because Real Eli wasn't supposed to be here, but then Real Eli showed up at my house this morning while my dress was making *Dream Eli* come alive, and now Real Eli is looking at me, making me think about *Dream Eli*, and now I can't even take a step without something zinging, because *Dream Eli*, is Real Eli." She breathed heavily as she waited for Mary to say something.

Mary stood, frozen with a saltine perched between her teeth. "What?"

Ember threw herself down in a chair and buried her face in her hands. "I'm so screwed!"

Mary sat down beside her. "Honey, I'm supposed to be the one with the hormonal, emotional outbursts."

Ember didn't laugh.

"Okay." Mary straightened in her seat, "Who is this," she hesitated, "*Dream Eli?*"

Ember buried her head deeper into her hands and let out a low growl, then proceeded to recount the events of last night's dream and this morning's erotic self-induced encore.

It was going to be a long day.

"You masturbated to *Dream Eli!*" Mary practically shouted, enjoying the shocking moment.

Ember was afraid the guys could hear her all the way across the building. "God! Can you yell it any louder?"

Mary was so giddy and enjoying her friend's misery way too much. "So, you got it bad for Eli."

"No!" Ember's voice was a bit shrill.

Mary's twinkling eyes and rueful grin said she wasn't buying it.

"Mary, Eli's like my brother."

Mary thought for a moment. "But, with that logic, *Dream Eli* would be your brother, too."

"Ewww!" The grossness factor jumped tenfold. "No, that's not how it works."

Mary cocked her head. "How does it not?"

"'Cuz Eli is real, and *Dream Eli* isn't."

Mary looked like she was trying to solve quantum physics. "But, they're the same person."

"How are you not getting this?"

"How are *you* not getting this?" Mary echoed back.

"You know what...just forget it. It's FUBAR'ed and I can't deal with this right now. Will you please take me home so I can change?"

Mary stood and Ember followed. She was going home to change into comfy jeans and a ragged tee. Soon, *Dream Eli* would be only a figment of her imagination.

Mary took her by both hands and gentled her with a motherly look. Ember was grateful to have her as a friend.

"No fuckin' way am I letting you change. Nuh-uh! Eli makes your panties wet, take them off. Eli makes you want to pant and do the two-finger-tango, there's a storage closet off the loading dock. Bite on a towel if you're a screamer, but let *Dream Eli* work your fingers to the bone. Do what you gotta do, but, damn girl...ain't no way I'm letting you pass up an opportunity to make Real Eli sweat. You're a sex-on-a-stick popsicle, and Eli is the July Texas heat...no way you two aren't puddling on the floor by the end of the week." She dropped Ember's hands, picked up a cracker and brought it to her mouth, nibbling on it like she didn't have a care in the world.

"Wha—"

Mary interrupted, "Oh, and knock before you use that storage closet, because Eli will probably be using it to stroke the salami, 'cuz, you're gonna get him bad. Get him so worked up, he'll be pantin' and gruntin'...two minutes, tops." Then she added, "Oh, and knock also, 'cuz King and I may be occupying it. His open door office policy is a killer with my prego-hormones kickin' in. Storage room is our go-to now."

Mary opened the break room door and sashayed down the hallway like she didn't just conjure an image in Ember's head she couldn't shake. She'd definitely be steering clear of the store room closet, today and every day, in the future.

The ride into work was torture. Complete and utter hell. First off, the embarrassment of admitting he thought Em had dressed up for T was hell and tore him up. But, the realization she hadn't was such a relief, it made him physically drained. Like an adrenaline dump after a mission. He'd gotten it in his head that the four days she and T spent together while he was in Lebanon may have lit a spark between them. When she about doubled over in laughter, the absurdity of it made itself known. Still, the thought of Ember snagging someone's attention, made it crystal clear what he needed to do. It was time to rip the Band-Aid off. Seeing her in that dress, the material hugging her body and the skirt brushing against her thighs, he couldn't stay in the Zone any longer.

And, second, if he had to see her all day, breasts propped up and cleavage peeking, he was going to blow his load where he stood. His dick was hard as nails, the skin of his shaft so tight, it was about to peel open like a hotdog in the microwave too long; split right down the center. The minute he got himself under control, the thought of her got him rock hard again. God, almighty. He'd been stuck behind his desk all morning, afraid if he got up, the guys would get one look at him and the ribbing would be relentless and never-ending. He didn't care if they ribbed him, but there was no way he would chance Ember overhearing the guys' crude jokes and innuendos and double entendres. It would embarrass her and he wouldn't allow that. So, desk jockey it was.

He tried to concentrate on the report King sent him but his mind was not on the subject matter. His mind was on Ember. *Those legs. Oh, how he'd love to drape them over his shoulders and —Stop!* He chastised himself, taking a deep breath, exhaling and turned his focus back to his computer. *Thump...Thud...Pulse... Thump.* He could feel his heart rate in his cock. *Damn!* He was never so thankful he'd worn boxer briefs today. The restrictive material kept his erection from tenting and held his cock tight against his body.

He pushed back in his chair trying to relieve some of the pressure. *Thump...Thump...Pulse...Thud.* The new position wasn't any better. He rubbed his palm across the bulge, praying for relief.

Just when he thought things couldn't get worse, she walked

into his office, laptop in hand. *Oh, God, Lord in heaven...why are you punishing me?*

"Got a minute?" Ember sauntered innocently over to his desk, hips swaying beneath the flowy hem of her dress.

Eli swore his dick doubled in size. He didn't think she was sashaying on purpose, but her swaying hips had him stirring.

"Um, I'm having a problem connecting to the server." She seemed a bit nervous. "This isn't my normal laptop, so I don't have it configured to King's network. Cy isn't here to help, so I was hoping you could get me hooked up."

Hooked up...He would love to get her hooked up.

She set the laptop down adjacent to his and braced herself against his desk. She hesitated.

"Everything okay?"

Ignoring the question, she bent forward and started typing. By the way she was leaning, he had a clear view of her cleavage. Her breasts rose and fell. He was used to seeing a tee hiding them, but in that dress, and at that angle, her perfect mounds were on display and the crease of her cleavage just begged to have him—

"...and when I entered the user code, it said it was restricted because the network is restricted."

Eli didn't catch a single word. He cleared his throat, coming back to the conversation.

"I don't know if you can get me on the network?" She bit the corner of her lip, letting it slide between her teeth.

"Sure, let me take a look."

He slid the laptop closer. God only knew he didn't want to leave his chair. He was safe as long as he was discreetly rolled under his desk. He clicked a few settings, checked the network, and within a few seconds she was connected.

"There you go, Emmy." He slid the computer to her side of the desk.

"Thanks. I was worried I'd have to wait for Cy." she bit the pad of her thumb, showing her nervous tick. "I got a crap-ton of things to get done."

Eli wanted to be that thumb. He could watch her nibble it all day long. *Thump... Thump... Thud.* Shit, the heavy pulse was back.

"Everything all right? You look...um, uncomfortable."

Shit. "Yeah, I'm fine. Just have some aching muscles that need to be worked out." *No statement was ever truer.*

Ember rounded the desk and began kneading his shoulders. She'd done it in the past, especially after a mission or a grueling PT session, so it wasn't anything out of the ordinary between them. And, he'd often returned the favor when she'd had an exceptionally hard day, but now, at her touch, he stiffened even more.

"Wow, you're really tense." She ran her hand over his back and shoulders, kneading the specific muscle groups and worked her fingers deep. *God! I'm going to die!* Every touch was torture.

"God, you're so hard." She squeezed his neck, grinding her palm against his traps. "I gotta rub this out if you want any relief."

Yup, she was killing him, slaying him. She had no idea the double entendres she was speaking. Eli craned his neck to the side and leaned forward, causing Ember's hands to drop.

"That's ok, Em." He tilted his neck from side to side, "I think I'll be all right. I got tons of stuff I need to get back to." He pointed at his laptop. "King needs these back, pronto." He was more tense than before.

If Ember was aware of his discomfort, she didn't say anything. Walking back around his desk, she collected her laptop. "Well...thanks." She gestured the laptop towards him and gave a genuine smile.

"You're welcome, Emmy."

She opened the door, her ass swaying in sinful rhythm, each hip taunting him, when she turned around. "Eli?"

"He looked up from the report. "Yeah, Em?"

"Um." She swallowed. "What did you want to do later?" Her thumb made its way back between her teeth and so many sinful thoughts came to his mind. Her question had his brow knitted.

"Your text. You asked if I had plans?"

Had her breaths increased, or was he imagining things? She almost seemed nervous. "Oh, that." He almost chickened out. Was going to make up an excuse of wanting a late supper, but he forged ahead. "Yeah, um...I need to get your input on a decision I'm making."

She took a few steps back into his office. "Oh? Anything I can help you with now?"

If she only knew.

"Nope. Nothing now." *Liar!* "I thought we could get supper and then," he paused, "then, just go somewhere special and talk."

She shifted her weight, "Okay...guess it's a date then."

He gave her a nod and a stiffened smile. She sauntered out the door and he inwardly groaned, then leaned back in his chair. His hands laced behind his head, and he let out a sigh.

Like it or not, things were going to be a whole lot different come morning.

Ember left his office and just about collapsed against the wall. Her legs were trembling as she hurried to the bathroom. She pushed open the door and about lunged into the stall. Something was drastically different. When she'd touched Eli's shoulders, an electric *zing* took over her body. She almost reared back, but remained still so Eli wouldn't question her. And, if she was reading things right, it seemed as if he'd felt it too. She shook the thought from her mind. Just because she was having midnight fantasies didn't mean he was too. Her thoughts turned back to *Dream Eli* and her inner muscles pulled and kneaded, looking for any type of relief. Oh, God, this was unnatural. Something had to be wrong with her. She held her breath, trying to stave off the pulsing. No luck. She felt a gush between her clenched thighs and instantly regretted wearing the thong and not the whimsical windmill panties. The thong held nothing back.

Fuck!

Real Eli affected her just as badly as *Dream Eli*.

Maven entered Ember's office and threw a pair of panties on her desk.

"What the hell?"

"You're welcome." Maven sang the words like she was Oprah Winfrey.

Ember got up to shut the door, her office being between King's and Slate's, since Maven had no filter. Better they not overhear whatever Mavenisms she was about to spew.

"Girl—"

Ember held up a finger and said, "Not a word."

Maven pouted.

She was about to latch the door when Mary barged her way through, saltines in one hand, Slim Jim in the other. Ember wasn't even going to ask.

"Don't start the party without me!" Mary sing-songed the words louder than Maven a few seconds ago. She plopped into the extra chair next to Maven and the two stared at Ember expectantly, like she knew why they were in her office.

Ember closed the door, holding her back against it as if warding off anyone else who may possibly want to join this shit-show. "What?" Ember deadpanned.

"You tell me." Maven had a Harley Quinn grin plastered across her face.

"Tell you what?" Ember made her way back to her desk. "And these?" She picked up the panties.

Maven tipped her head to the side like a Valley schoolgirl and twisted a lock of her hair around her finger. "*Dream Eli* made you cum!" Her voice was loud and giddy, singing like schoolgirl in her Georgia twang, giving it all she had.

Ember's eyes practically popped from their sockets and her jaw hit the floor. "Shhhh-Shhh-Sshhhhh!" The sound came out in short bursts. There was no telling how thick the walls were and Ember knew both guys were in their offices. Her eyes flew to Mary.

"Oh, yeah," Mary nodded repeatedly, "I called her." She was immensely proud of herself.

Ember wanted to kill the two friends in front of her. Make that *ex*-friends in front of her. She held up the sinful red panties, mouthing the question, "Why?"

"Got plenty of them. Thought you may need a spare, so I got

'em out of my emergency stash in the glove box. You're welcome."

Ember threw them back at Maven in disbelief.

"Deets girl. Spill 'em." Maven took a bite off the beef jerky stick Mary was holding and they both settled back as if this were a Lifetime movie event

Fuck my life and my friends!

CHAPTER 23

Eli was nervous. He kept the outward signs from showing but his stomach was doing somersaults and backflips. The moment of reckoning was upon him. Either he and Ember would be forging forward, exploring a new relationship, or he'd be losing the most precious thing in his life. He kept telling himself it was for the best, that he needed to carve a new path...hopefully, one that included her.

"Where're we going?" Ember asked from the passenger's seat of his truck, still in the sexy-as-sin dress, the hem of which rose past her mid-thigh now that she was sitting, legs crossed over one another, enticing. Eli craved to reach over and run his hand up her creamy ivory flesh.

Eyes on the road, bud. "Someplace special."

Ember tilted her head. "Going to give me any hints?" Her voice was all singsong, bubbly and bright as she was. The nervous undertones he'd picked up on earlier were gone.

"It's a place we've been before." He bit his inner lip, keeping his concentration pure and innocent, warding off the scandalous, delectable and indecent things he'd like to do to her.

She scoffed and wrinkled her forehead. "That's a shitty clue. We've been everywhere together, Eli. Think you could narrow it down a bit?"

Wasn't that the truth? And it hit him square in the gut. They *had* been everywhere together. *Every* adventure. *Every* milestone. *Every* turn of events. It was Eli and Emmy; *they* were Eli and Emmy. They were two parts of a whole. He could hear the smile in her voice without taking his eyes from the road. When he didn't elaborate, she reached over and laced her fingers with his.

His hand gripped the wheel tighter as a jolt shot through him and it took everything within him to keep the truck on the road. He wondered if she felt it too, because she jumped like a cat on a hot tin roof. Maybe his mind was conjuring things with his emotions heightened, but whatever happened from here on out was beyond his control and the fates would make whatever happened, happen.

The country road meandered and they drove in silence. Not that they didn't have anything to say, but because everything had been said before. They didn't need meaningless words to encompass what was them. They'd driven this path a thousand times if only once. The familiar scenery passed them by and everything felt as it did a thousand times before. Comfortable. Content. Safe. Easy. Everything Emmy and Eli.

"Um, seems like we're heading to my parents?" She looked over at him, "Are we going to my parents?"

Eli let out a chuckle. "Kinda."

"Kinda? That's your answer?"

"Yup."

"Care to elaborate?"

"Nope."

Ember huffed in mock indignation, and Eli let her stew. Suspense always killed her. Birthdays and Christmases were her kryptonite. She could keep a secret but it was always on the tip of her tongue wanting to burst forth. He knew she was dying to know what he had in store and the longer he could keep her guessing, the better. He tightened the grip on her hand, keeping his eyes straight ahead, not daring to glance over at her in that dress. Damn, she was *his* kryptonite.

Nearing the house, he slowed the truck.

"Sooo," she drew the word out, "why are we here? Dad and Mom are both at the store."

Eli knew this because he'd spoken to Pops earlier. He

215

couldn't think of anywhere better to have their talk. He didn't pull into the driveway; instead, he took the gravel access road around to the backside of the house and put the truck in PARK. Ember looked at him, confusion marring her features.

"Stay." At the single word, he opened his door.

"I'm not a dog." By her laugh, he knew she wasn't mad.

"Be right back." He shut the door before she could protest, taking the back steps two at a time, and disappeared into the house.

Ember sat wondering what he was up to. After the whole bathroom incident, and the humiliating talk with Mary and Maven, her mind was still reeling over what exactly happened.

She couldn't believe Mary called Maves. Shaking her head, she felt the embarrassment wash over her again. She loved her girls, and wouldn't trade them for anything, but some days...some days she just wanted to strangle them both, today, being one of those days.

Maven had been her usual boisterous, over-the-top self. She bounced and fluttered around the office, no filter in place, her voice carrying like a damn megaphone. It would be a miracle if King or Slate hadn't heard her every word. Ember guessed it didn't matter if King heard, because Mary's big trap would probably be spilling the minute she and King were on their way home. Ember slumped in her seat. *How humiliating.* Facing King was mortifying enough. But if Eli heard, she'd be devastated.

The door behind the driver's seat opened and Eli put something on the floor. She didn't get a look at what it was, still lost in her own thoughts when he came out of the house. He shut the door, opened his, and settled into his seat.

"Ready?"

Ember flattened her lips. "I don't know. What am I supposed to be ready for?"

Eli just smiled, put the truck in gear, and they were off.

"The barn?" Ember scrunched her nose and threw the question at Eli, "Really?"

He mimicked her face but said nothing, coming to a stop outside the barn doors, then shut the engine down.

She repeated her question. "Why are we at the barn?"

"You ask too many questions." Eli opened his door then turned back to her. "Sit."

She rolled her eyes. "Again, not a dog!" She knew the drill. *Stay in the truck until he opens your door.* The whole thing was silly. She could open her own damn door. She'd fought in war for shit's sake, so a door was no feat. But secretly, she loved it. Her dad had the same chivalry with her mom and that was probably where Eli had learned it.

Her door opened and he held out a hand to help her down. A pure gentleman. Just like her daddy.

"Can you tell me why we're here?"

"Don't you know patience is a virtue?"

"Don't you know the not-knowing is killing me?"

"In that case, if you keel over, I know CPR. You're in good hands." He shot her a wink, laced their fingers together and headed back around the truck. Never dropping her hand, he opened the rear door, grabbed a large blanket from the seat, and threw it over his shoulder. Then he picked up a picnic basket from the floorboard, shut the door with his hip, and they set off for the barn with long strides.

She eyed the basket. "You have this all planned?"

"Mom helped. Told her we needed supper and she had it covered."

Ember smiled at the thought of her mom packing them a picnic. It was such a Susan Hayes thing to do. Mom loved Eli, so Ember knew he didn't have to twist her arm. Knowing her mom, there was most likely a seven-course meal in the basket. Susan Hayes, always giving the most to her children. The thought made her smile.

Eli slid the large door open and what awaited them was nothing short of a wonderland. There were strings of white lights hanging across the rafters, setting the barn in a dimly-lit glow. To the side atop a few hay bales was a five-gallon bucket of ice chilling what she assumed were about a dozen or so juice boxes. There was a platter of cheese and crackers, and another with an assortment of cut-up fruit. Beside that sat a Bluetooth speaker.

Ember laughed at the memory. It was their makeshift prom night all over again. Hopefully, this evening wouldn't end in disaster like last time. There would be no kissing beneath the stars. She vowed to herself that wouldn't be happening. With last night's dreams and her body zinging the way it had today, kissing Eli would be deadly.

Eli motioned for her to proceed and he slid the door shut behind them. The strings of lights shimmered in the darkness of the barn.

"You do this?" She pointed to the lights.

"Ah...no." Eli rubbed his neck, looking up at the rafters and the lights in question. She shot him a look only to see the surprise on his face. "Pops must've done it. I did everything else, though."

"This looks familiar." Ember walked over to the bucket, smiling at the juice boxes. "And, look, fine hors d'oeuvres also...minus the paper plates this time."

"Hey, I was on a teenager's budget back then. I couldn't afford silver platters, so paper plates had to do." He laughed as he set the basket down and started to unfold the blanket. Ember grabbed the opposite end, helping him lay it over the hay-littered dirt floor.

Eli couldn't keep his eyes off her. His nerves were on a hair trigger. He just had to get through the evening, and tomorrow everything would be different.

Better?

Worse?

He didn't know, but if it was the latter, he'd already put a plan in motion and discussed Ember's safety with Pops. Pops would join her at the range each day while Susan ran the store. It would be tough, but Pops told him they'd make it work. If she turned him down, he'd have to sever ties. He loved her too much for it to be any other way. *If you love something, set it free...* It would be the death of everything that made him whole, but for her sake, for her future happiness, he'd do right by her. She may not see it in that light at first, but over time, the truth would make itself known. He couldn't stay in the friend zone any longer. She held his heartstrings and, hopefully, she wouldn't be tearing them out.

"Whoa! How huge is this thing?" Ember's amazement drew him back. She was looking at the pillowy blanket, which was more of a monstrosity than what was usually a small picnic throw. "Guess we'll dine in comfort. It's so cushioned, our butts won't know there's hay and dirt beneath us."

Ember kicked off her sandals and knelt on the blanket, making sure to be lady-like and keeping her knees together. She ran her hand over the pillowy softness of the blanket as her eyes widened. Goosebumps broke out all over her skin.

"You cold?" Eli sat beside her, pushing a straw into a juice box and handed it to her.

"Cold?"

"You got goosebumps." He grazed his fingers over the erected flesh and the feeling went straight to his dick. *Zing!*

She flinched, then rubbed her arm, brushing his fingers aside. "That's weird. Guess it's cooler in here compared to outside." She took a sip of her juice box and he unwrapped the platters of cheese and fruit.

"Mom sure went all out." Ember popped a few grapes in her mouth.

Yeah, 'cuz this could be my last meal. The thought ran through his mind, as he started to unpack the basket.

"So, what'cha want to talk about?" Ember mumbled around a bite of cheese and crackers, "Gotta be something big if you went through all...this." She motioned around the barn.

"Eat first." Eli set a paper plate in front of her and then himself. He continued pulling things out of the basket until it was empty. A smorgasbord laid out before them: sandwiches, sides, salads, desserts; Susan didn't skimp.

"How long does mom think we're going to talk? There's

enough food here for a family of five..." Ember looked over the feast, "...for a week!"

Ember must have caught something that unsettled her in Eli's gaze. "You okay?" Her voice broke his stare and he started unwrapping a sandwich, taking a bite without completely removing the wax paper.

"Eat, Emmy." He pushed her plate towards her and they ate in awkward silence.

~

Both done eating, Eli packed the leftovers back in the basket and gathered the garbage in a trash bag. Ember sat with her legs curled to the side, fiddling with the hem of her dress; the flouncy skirt lay lazily around her. The contrast of the scarlet blanket beneath her ivory thighs made him audibly swallow.

Stunning.

She was gorgeous. Absolutely beautiful. Her head dipped slightly, staring blindly at her fingertips as she incessantly fingered the sheer material between her thumb and forefinger. What was she thinking about? He could see her mind working, concentrating on what, he wasn't sure. Probably obsessing and guessing what he wanted to discuss with her. Her curiosity was getting the best of her. She was nervous and so was he, though he didn't outwardly show it. Years of conditioning by the military had taught him to stow his emotions, but he was all nerves beneath his laid back, relaxed facade.

This was Ember. The girl next door. The girl in his dreams who lay beneath him with a mane of fiery curls cascading over her shoulders. Ends of her red hair curling beneath the curves and swells of her breasts...

"Eli?"

...for endless nights he dreamt of her writhing beneath him as he made passionate love to the girl of his dreams...

"Elijah?"

Ember's voice broke his reverie of last night and so many nights before. Hearing his given name pour from her lips sent chills over him and his cock twitched, but he controlled himself.

From the lengths of her ivory thighs his eyes roamed up her body and met her sky blue eyes. *How many nights have I stared into those eyes?*

"Elijah, is everything alright? You haven't said anything in a while, and you're strangling that trash bag like it's going to get away."

He looked at his hands, and yes, he was gripping the trash bag mercilessly. Relaxing, the bag fell loose.

"Where'd you go?"

Eli drank in her eyes, looked to a place so deep within her, and answered, "To a place only you live."

She creased her brows and pulled her lips flat. Confusion guarded her eyes. "Where do I live, Eli?"

He spoke from deep within as his words poured out of his soul. "My dreams. My nights. My days. My heart, mind and soul. You're in me so deep, Emmy. You're with me everywhere. Every day. Every night." He took a deep breath and continued, "I'm so drunk on you, Red, that I can't exist without you.

"My body screams for you. You're my drug. My passion. My grounding rod. You've been with me in the sandy deserts of Afghanistan. You're my constant companion on lonely nights. You stand sentry on the starless nights as I lie awake and dream of you. You've been with me in the sweltering heat of Iraq and Somalia. I've taken you to places no sane person ever wants to see. And, because you were with me, I knew I had to bring you home safely." He paused. "I needed to see you in the flesh again, Red. The thought of never seeing you again pushed me to survive those shitholes and carried me back to you. Every. Time."

Ember was speechless. Eli had never been so poetic. Never so raw and open to her. She'd never seen the depths of his soul like this and she knew he meant every word he spoke.

"If you need the words, Em...I love you. I've loved you for as long as I can remember. I go to sleep each night with you in my mind. I see you in my dreams and I wake up with you in my memories. I brought you here, Red, to tell you I love you. I don't know where that will lead me...us...but I can't hide it any longer. I don't know how *not* to love you."

There. He'd said it. He loved her. He meant the words with every breath, every beat of his heart. It was simple. And, it was true. She was *the one*. His One. He put himself out there and laid himself bare. The moment was hers. Fight or flight. His hands trembled, which never happened. He'd seen war and his nerves were always steel. For a moment, fear gripped him. Would this be the moment he'd look back on and know he'd lost everything? Or, would it be the moment he gained everything, the world, his Red?

Time hung between them. Ember sat motionless, her eyes wide and mouth agape.

"Please, say something."

CHAPTER 24

Please, say something.

Ember heard his words. They were a whispered plea. She didn't reply. What would she say? Could she say? No words seemed big enough, or strong enough, to say what was buried deep within her. Just now a revelation, a realization bubbling to the surface, percolated in her soul.

This was Eli. This was her childhood friend. The boy who knew her deepest secrets, the man who knew her deepest wounds. The man who held her after deployments and the man who comforted her in her deepest misery. This was the man who would go to the ends of the earth for her and the one who would protect her with his life, if need be. This was Eli.

She met his eyes, seeing turmoil running deep within them. She needed to answer him. Actions spoke louder than words, so before she could think better of it, she lunged forward into his space and plastered her lips to his. He loved her. And at that moment, she knew she loved him, too. Always had. She was blind to it until he opened her eyes. Tore open his soul. Melted her heart.

Yes, she loved him.

The force of her body crashing into him knocked him back. He threw his arms behind him and caught himself, then settling back against the corded muscles of his shoulders.

223

Ember adjusted her body to his, straddling him, her skirt pulled taut over his muscular, steely thighs. She'd caught him by surprise but after she settled in, he brought his hands to her face and wove his fingers into her hair. She cupped his jaw, feeling the prickle and softness of his short, trimmed beard beneath her fingertips. Foreign carnal wanting bubbled up from her soul and into her kiss as she cupped his short hair and fisted the neck of his tee.

At first, their kiss was closed, drawn out, her mouth pressed firmly against his. But, his tongue swept across the seam of her lips, begging for entrance, and she obliged. The kiss deepened. Tongues dueled for urgency, sliding over one another. He gripped her hair, using the ember locks to turn her head this way and that to his liking. She moaned from the back of her throat, lighting up her senses and pushing them to the brink of passion. Things escalated, heating quickly, and need raged between them. They were lost, wrapped up in each other, both giving and taking equally.

"I love you, Eli." She barely broke the kiss and her words came out on a breathy cry. "I love you," drenched in lust, love and need, "my God...I love you." Each word hitched. Truth reigned.

He pulled back and saw tears in her eyes, identical to the tears pooling in his. Their heavy breaths mingled. His breath was hers, and hers was his. At that moment, there was no one else, they were one. Time stood still and he swore....no, he vowed, until his dying day he would remember this very moment. The moment his Red loved him back.

Eli slowly lowered back onto the blanket, using his arms to steady them both until he was lying flat. The sight of Ember astride him made his blood burn like fire. He trembled with every breath. Every heartbeat sent passion raging through his veins. He pulled her chest to his and she willingly went; his arms enveloped her body and cradled her tenderly. His lips brushed against hers keeping their kiss light but her salt laden tears traced the curves of her swollen lips and he tasted each one.

He sucked her tongue that sinfully teased him and she didn't hold back. Hands roamed freely, each grasped for the other when the kissing wasn't enough.

Eli turned them with ease. He lay atop her, settling his body between her splayed legs. Her skirt rode high but the flouncy material covered her decency. His arms caged her and he rested his weight on his forearms, careful not to crush her. He knew she could feel his erection between them. His cock throbbed with his racing pulse. He pulled back and stared into her eyes. She stared back. They both knew where this was heading, and neither wanted to stop.

Eli's hand crept beneath the hem of her dress. His fingers caressed her bare skin, grazing her panty line. She closed her eyes, waiting for his fingers to cross the line.

"Say you want this, Red." His words were breathy, each word fanned across her face as he tipped his forehead to hers. "Tell me you want me," he panted. "Tell me you need me."

Her eyes closed.

∾

His words were a prayer. A prayer she needed and wanted.

Opening her eyes, she saw his were still closed. His jaw clenched, holding back his desperation. He lowered his head, resting it in the crook of her neck. "I can stop now. I won't push you to do anything you don't want to do or anything you're not ready for."

She ran her hands through his hair and he thrust his head up. She whispered to his soul, "Take me with you." She locked her lips over his and he tasted like heaven. Everything she never knew she wanted was contained in that kiss. She reached beneath her skirt and pushed her fingers alongside his. She looped her thumb beneath the elastic string of her thong and shimmied a fraction before Eli lifted his weight enough that she could pull the elastic over her hip.

Eli didn't waste time. He propped himself up, sat back on his heels and assisted her removing the pesky thong. The material skimmed down her legs and she pulled her feet through the almost-nothing lace then spread herself before him. Eli brought the panties to his face and inhaled. Ember went still, lay frozen, staring up at him. The thought of someone sniffing her panties should have appalled her, but the sight and sound spurred her on.

He lowered the pink thong and deftly shoved it in the pocket of his jeans. He pushed the button of his jeans through the buttonhole and pulled his zipper slowly down, as if giving her time to tell him to stop. His eyes never left hers and with a single look she silently told him, yes. Yes, she was wanting, and yes, she was willing.

He fisted his tee behind his neck and pulled it over his head in one motion. The his glorious chest muscles appeared and he was absolutely gorgeous. No two ways about it. She'd seen him without a shirt before. Countless times, he'd been bare-chested at her parent's house, in the pool or helping her father with chores, splitting wood, baling hay or working in the yard or barn. But now, seeing him in a new light, his pecs on display, he was mesmerizing. A god of Eli. A god to Ember.

She explored. His skin felt like velvet. Smooth. Silky. Steel. The cords of his neck flared and ran flawlessly to his shoulders. The tips of her fingers tracing his skin left behind lines of acid fire, her tips burning with each inch she explored. She trailed down his breast bone, between the furrowed muscles of his pecs, his skin taut and strained over each curve of his chest. She traced a divot on his shoulder and one on his side, the puckered scars of old wounds. There were many to explore, some deep, some small, but now wasn't the time to find and explore each one. He was a gorgeous sculpture of perfection hovering over her.

As she took her time, his arms shook with the strain of holding himself while she perused and trailed the back of her hand over his rock hard abs. Sculpted. Chiseled. A masterpiece. He was exquisite.

The excitement made the group of muscles quiver with each of his anguished breaths. Her eyes fell and followed the trail of hair starting just below his navel. It was fine and sparse and disappeared beneath the open button of his jeans. His muscles quaked and her hands shook as she slid them lower and met the coarse parted material. She paused, meeting his eyes before delving eagerly beneath the waistband of his boxer briefs.

Smooth, warm, velvety skin met her fingers. She encircled his cock head, caressing the softness then drew her hand lower. She gripped his shaft. It pulsed and wetness moistened his slit. The coarseness of his pubic hair brushed the back of her hand and she wanted to explore lower, feel the weight of his balls, but the restriction of his jeans and boxers, coupled with her hand's awkward angle between them, made the task nearly impossible.

Eli groaned as her flesh met his. His hardened length pushed up and it felt like she was strangling him. He could feel himself leaking onto the tips of her fingers and knew she could feel it too. He needed to best the situation before he embarrassed himself like a prepubescent teen. He wasn't going to blow. Not before he had her screaming his name. But, when Ember pulled her hand from his cock, fingers wet with his precum and brought it to her mouth, he did everything within him to hold back his release.

Holy, Mother of God!

He lost his mind when her tongue teased her fingers and swirled around the dainty tips. Then, she sucked them between her lips and pulled them out clean. Curiosity and satisfaction written all over her face.

God, almighty, have mercy.

Ember pushed against Eli's chest, her legs still splayed to him. He arched back, as she continued to push until he came to rest flat on his back again. Straddling him, she stared down, and he caught the fire in his eyes. She unsaddled him and pulled at the waist of his jeans, tugging, trying to pull them free. Eli complied. Sitting up, he unlaced his boots, took off his socks and removed his jeans, leaving his boxer briefs on. She grabbed the hem of her dress, crossed her arms and pulled it up over her body, letting her full breasts bounced free of their confines. The dress fluttered to the ground behind her and she shook out her ember curls like a ravishing beast.

Eli's dick pulsed and he took a few needed deep breaths. She was a goddess of beauty; his Aphrodite and Venus. A blush reddened her skin but she had absolutely nothing to be embarrassed about. When she went to cover herself, he caught her wrists, revealing her breasts and she opened her arms, exposing herself to him once again. He rubbed the back of his knuckles over her gorgeous nipples and she shuddered. He did it again, then pinched the tips lightly. She moaned and pulled back but not far enough to lose his grip. He added more pressure, and when she closed her eyes and moaned wildly, he couldn't control himself.

"Ember." Sitting up, he leaned in and put his mouth over her beaded nipple and sucked. She let out a whimper and watched him gently tongue and suckle the hardened bud. Her breathing sped up. He sucked and nipped, pulling her taut nipple between his teeth, just like he did in his dreams. The voyeuristic sight had her panting when he went from one breast to the other, all the while teasing and plucking the exposed nipple while swirling his tongue around the one he feasted on.

Eli pulled back, his breathing just as erratic as hers. "I can't do this." He panted the words between breaths.

"What?" Her hand came up and covered her chest.

"No, no." His breaths were heavy. "Not, *'I can't do this,'*" he gestured between them, "I can't do *this*." He pointed to her chest. "If I keep this up, I won't last...and God knows I want this to last."

Ember went from humiliation, to a temptress grin, and pushed Eli back down on his back. "My turn to play." She stopped straddling him and pulled at the waistband of his boxers. "Off," she commanded. He lifted his hips, sliding and kicking them down his legs, which probably wasn't the sexiest striptease, but urgency beat flare.

Her confidence was shaken when she saw his size. His purple cock head lay heavy against his stomach, almost reaching his navel. She steeled herself and stared at his cock. It was huge. It was the only cock she'd ever seen in person. He was never going to fit. Her vibrator, Clyde, was only a clit stimulator. No wonder it was a novelty and had never made her orgasm. Nothing ever penetrated her. She started to hyperventilate.

"Red, come back to me." Eli's voice brought her out of her panic. "If you want to stop just say the word and we'll stop." He propped up on one elbow.

She didn't want to stop and shook her head. "Lay down, Eli." She was going to do this; wanted to do this. Eli's gaze measured her, making sure she was good, then laid back. She straddled his lower thighs.

With trembling hands, she gripped him and heard his intake of breath. She felt a surge of power; she was in control. She lightly stroked him, watching the taut skin move and slide with every push and pull of her hand. Eli laid his head back, his eyes closed, concentrating. He was letting her explore. She watched the head of his cock drip with precum when she brought her hand to the tip. It swelled and the mushroom head darkened a deeper purple.

She wanted to taste him. She'd seen it done in videos. Hell, Maven talked about giving head more than she'd like to remember. She even gave Ember a tutorial using a burrito, showing her the ways to caress, suck, tantalize, and hide her teeth. And, how to always, *always*, pay special attention to balls.

Men liked their balls.

Liked to have them sucked, caressed, teased, fondled and slightly tugged. Ember wasn't sure about that last one, but didn't dare to ask Maves to elaborate; God knew she'd be off on a tangent. She was a plethora of information.

Pulling up, she watched a bit of precum well to the surface, then leak down the head onto her hand. She got a small taste earlier and decided she was just going to go for it. If she was doing it wrong, Eli would tell her.

She bent forward and licked the tip with the flat of her tongue, and his taste exploded in her mouth. Every taste bud opened and enveloped his essence. It was erotic as hell, spurring her on.

Eli bucked his hips when she covered the head with her

mouth, making sure her teeth didn't touch. His moan filled the air, and she felt herself pulse and moisten. Could this turn her on as much as him?

"Em…" His voice was heady.

Ember looked up at him using only her eyes, his head still in her mouth. She felt him pulse, bringing more saltiness to her tongue. It seemed he was hanging on by a thread. His legs trembled and every cord in his neck strained.

"Red, you don't have to…I'm not going to last."

She pulled off him with a powerful pop and Eli dropped his head. She saw his fists grasping the blanket.

"You don't want me to?" Her voice held dismay.

"Em, please, I'm begging you…if you don't want me to cum, babe, have mercy…please." He sounded almost frantic, "Baby, please."

She swore she could see his soul as he looked at her with pleading eyes. She grabbed the base of his cock, opened her mouth, and pushed him to the back of her throat. Eli's moan was mournful, and she gagged, but didn't let up. She had no idea if she was doing it right, but she kept on, pulling her lips all the way to the head, sucking in the wells of her cheeks, and pushing down against the resistance. Her gag reflex eased, and she took him as deep as she could. What she couldn't go down on, she stroked with her hand, pushing the base towards his sack as she drew up to the head. His balls hung loose but heavy. She repeated the motion a few more times and saw them draw up under the base. His thighs tightened and his butt clenched. She felt him tapping on the back of her head but she kept going with more vigor. She felt like a goddess, holding him at will.

"Em…Emm…Emmy, pull off, I'm going to cum!" His voice begged, so she pushed down all the way, as far as her throat would let her, taking him deep, then swallowed, constricting his engorged head with the muscles deep in her throat, vicing around his cock head, then she gently squeezed his balls.

He let out a guttural roar and exploded like a cannon. A rope of cum shot against her throat, pushing the soft tissues, causing her to gag and pull off his dick. She pumped him with her hand while she spit. His hips pushed up with the next spurt and

Ember was mesmerized. She went back down, swallowing just his head, and felt another rope dance across her tongue, salty and warm. He went slack and his legs continued to quiver. She lapped at him, twirling her tongue, staying only at the head, afraid if she went down she'd gag again. When she licked him clean, she dropped his cock then trailed the stream of cum that jetted onto his stomach and chest.

Eli lifted his head and watched her tongue trail along the line of his cum.

Having him watch her was sexy as hell. So erotic. So taboo. She felt herself clench and gush.

Oh. My. God.

Her wetness coated Eli's thighs, and suddenly she was embarrassed. Pushing herself up, still straddling his thighs, she met his eyes. His normally slate-blue eyes were dark as sapphires. For a moment she was unsure what he was going to do, but when his lips crashed against hers, she melted in his arms.

Deep thrusts of his tongue had her begging him to take her. Do anything; she didn't care. All she wanted was for him to touch her, to be inside of her. She moaned, but with his mouth on hers, he ate her passionate shriek. When he broke the kiss and lowered them to the blanket he cradled her close to his chest and hitched her leg over his.

They lay in silence listening to each other's breaths, coming down from their high.

"Where did you learn to do that?" Eli's voice broke the stillness, wonder and humor in his tone.

Ember tucked her head into the valley of his arm and asked, "Do you really want to know?" The apprehension in her voice was clear.

Silence.

He stiffened. "Please don't say a word if it's another guy's name."

Ember felt a spike of anger. Didn't he know she'd never been with a guy before?

"You know, I've never been with, um...I'm—"

"I'm not insinuating you've been with someone, but I'm

praying there is another way you learned how to make that luscious mouth into a sinful vixen."

"Maven."

The silence was deafening.

Ember raised her head to look at Eli but his eyes were already fixed on hers.

"Maven?" He raised his eyebrow, a trait of his she loved, and she giggled. "How is that girl making her way into the most mind blowing moment of my life with the girl I love?"

The girl I love. The words fluttered like butterflies in her soul. He was still waiting for her answer. She suddenly felt embarrassed. Five minutes ago, she was shameless, and now she was blushing.

"Well," she swallowed, "it was Margarita Monday—"

"Oh, God, that explains it." He let out a low laugh that rumbled in his chest. "Any story that starts out with, 'It was Margarita Monday,' has to end badly, especially with Maven in the mix somewhere."

"True, but you should probably be thanking her." She took in a deep breath for courage. "She was telling me about her, um... 'exploits'...and, um, was telling me the 'procedures' she uses to, um, getaguyoff." She buried her head into his side.

Eli kissed the top of her head and, again, he let out a rumble of his laughter.

She continued, "Well, I wasn't sure exactly what she meant, so Maven was *Maven*, and showed me her *technique* on the Grande Burrito."

A laugh erupted so deep in his chest it made her cheek bounce on his pec and it was a glorious sound. He had an amazing laugh. Deep and husky, almost like a song when he let loose.

"She didn't hold back either. Got right into it." Ember laughed at the memory.

"Did it leave money on the edge of the table before it left."

"No, but she got her meal for free...and the waiter's number."

That did it. They lay there laughing, both naked as the day they were born.

Eli played with the strands of her hair as they came off their high. He repeated the words she would never get enough of, "I love you, Red."

He flipped her to her back and laid feather-light kisses along her neck. She craned to give him access, reveling in the moment. Never in a thousand years would she have ever thought she'd be here. The man she was looking for, praying for, was with her all along.

He made a necklace of kisses across her throat and then in the swell of her breasts, causing her body to zing.

His shoulder muscles quaked as she ran her hands over his taut skin and she heard the undertones of his moans as he explored her breasts. Her skin burned when he licked a path through the valley of her cleavage and buried his head between the mounds, pushing them together and feasting from nipple to nipple, never leaving one unattended. He nipped and bit at one while rolling the other between his fingers, tugging until she winced. He was like a maestro, tuning an instrument to perfection, coaxing and playing with mastery. Watching him worship her body made her euphoric. Eli left no flesh untouched, kissing every inch of her. He nipped the underside of her breasts, then licked a pathway down the center of her stomach. He nestled in her trimmed curls and she held her breath when he slid his nose down the apex of her thigh, first one side, then the other. She blushed, but the intimacy of it turned her on.

He parted her legs farther apart, applying light pressure to each inner thigh until she opened wide enough to accommodate his large frame. Then she draped her legs over his shoulders. She could only see the top of his head. Her heart thundered against her chest and she waited for his next touch, but when it didn't come, the anticipation was both exhilarating and almost painful. Then, she felt it. A light wisp of air as he blew across her most sensitive place.

Holy shit!

How could something so light, feel so magnificent? Again, he wafted his breath over her clit and she felt herself dampen all over again. The flat of his tongue lapped her from ass to clit causing her to grasp the blanket like a lifeline, twisting it in her fists. Eli laid his hand above her mound and gently pushed down holding her at his will. He used the thumb to pull back her protective hood and volleyed between tonguing her clit and licking her folds, nibbling each side and licking straight up the center. Then, he speared his tongue in deep.

The sensations overwhelmed her. It was like a symphony of instruments being played on one body. Each area a single sound, but together, together it was a musical masterpiece. With the need and want rising to a crescendo, he pushed his broad middle finger into her center and she flew. His finger was thick, pushing and receding, repeating the motion with one drawn out pull and then a quick upward thrust where he held it in the deep. She felt his four remaining fingers splayed snuggly against her ass.

Oh, God. I can't breathe...

"Breathe, baby. I need you to breathe." Eli murmured against her thigh, gingerly placing small pecks here and there as he spoke.

She took in a few panting breaths. Eli was so attuned to her he could read her thoughts, knowing what she needed before she did.

"Deep breaths, baby, come on....deep breath for me." His words would have been calming, if he would've given her a reprieve, but he kept pushing and pulling, ratcheting up his speed as he coaxed her.

"Deep breath...good girl, that's good." He breathed the words over her clit, then lashed it a few times for good measure.

Her mews and whimpers became moans of ecstasy within minutes. The gates of rapture called to her. And, when he pushed in a second finger, scissoring to stretch her, she gushed with wetness, dousing his hand. He added a third and latched onto her clit and she lost it, convulsing again, and bringing another gush, then three. He was relentless and drank from her like he was dying of thirst.

She thrashed and cried with passion and he relented, pulling his fingers from her and unabashedly licked them clean, hungry for her taste. He brought her back to earth whispering against her temple, coaxing her from her euphoria.

She didn't care. She was shameless. Weightless. Sated.

She loved Eli and Eli loved her.

CHAPTER 25

He was hard and still had her scent on his face and her taste on his tongue. It wouldn't matter how many showers he'd take in his lifetime, he would never lose her scent. He'd never forget the sight of her splayed for him—pink, ripe, and ready. He'd never forget her taste.

He settled between her thighs and opened her wide enough to drape her legs over his thighs. She was still wet, but he still fondled and played.

"You like that?" He swiped his hand against her weeping juices.

Ember arched her back, "Take me, Eli." She practically begged.

He spread her swollen lips, making sure she was ready for him.

"Eli."

A feather-light touch grazed his shaft and her delicate fingers lingered up and down his length.

"Careful."

"I am."

He let her rub from base to tip; the pressure was just right and he let out a feral growl.

"You sound like a wild bear."

"I'm about to become wild if you don't stop."

She squeezed his girth.

"You little minx!"

She smiled and mouthed the words, "I love you."

"Love you, too." He placed a kiss between the valley of her breasts. Reaching for his jeans, he took out his wallet and pulled out a foil packet.

"You came prepared." He saw something wilt in her eyes, though she didn't change her demeanor. He knew exactly what she was thinking.

"If you think I came expecting this to happen you're absolutely wrong." He held up the foil packet wanting to tear into it. "The only reason I have this," he trailed off, feeling embarrassed. "I carry it because none of the guys know I'm...a virgin." It sounded strange to admit it out loud. No one knew except Cy.

Ember's eyes widened.

"Don't look so surprised. I'm not a man-whore like some of the others."

"But," she had trouble processing the thought, "but, you're...Delta."

That made Eli laugh. "And...non-virginity, that's a prerequisite?"

"No, but..."

"As much as I'd love to sit here and talk about my soon-to-be-non-existent pure, celibate lifestyle, there's more pressing matters I'd like to get to." He ran his fingers up the center of her folds and she shivered. "You ready, baby?"

She sucked in a breath and let it out on a whoosh, "Ready."

He tore the packet open with his teeth and his hands trembled a bit when he placed it on his swollen cock head, squeezed the tip of the rubber, and tried rolling it over the engorged head. He struggled but it wouldn't roll down.

"What, are these extra small?" He tried again, but the circumference of the rubber didn't match his girth.

Ember watched with bated breath. "Wow, I thought you were big, but now I'm thinking you're huge."

"As much as that makes my ego flare, it's not me, it's the condom."

"Oh, usually it's the, 'it's not you, it's me...' adage." She giggled.

Eli was frustrated and getting pissed. "I can field strip a gun in pitch blackness, but I can't roll on a fucking condom?"

Finally, the rubber let loose and he rolled it down his length. It felt dry, but he'd never used one before, so maybe that was normal. "Ready?"

"Yes." Her following words showed trepidation, "Please...Eli...go slow."

Leaning forward, Eli planted a chaste kiss on her lips, stoking the fires. "I will, baby. Tell me if anything hurts or if you want me to stop and I'll stop. The last thing I want to do is hurt you."

"Okay." The word was said on a breath and he knew she was nervous. He could feel her legs trembling.

"Love you, Red." He kissed her forehead, lingering before pulling back.

"I love you, Eli."

With shaking hands, he grabbed his shaft and it pulsed beneath the rubber.

Ember pulled her knees back, lifting her feet from the ground, giving him a beautiful view, willingly offering herself.

He ran his thumb over her clit and rubbed his shaft against her, coating himself in her arousal. Aligning himself with her opening, he slowly began to push inside. When he met resistance, he pulled back, then pushed in again.

"You ok?" His breath was shaky.

"Yeah."

He pushed in until his head disappeared between her folds.

Ember winced.

Instantly, he pulled back.

"Em?"

"I'm fine. Just a little pinch...and a lotta pressure. I'm good."

He pushed in, sinking the head again, gaining half his length, and he felt something give

Ember let out a screech and bit her lip.

He stopped.

Eli felt the tear and knew exactly what it was. He'd taken

Ember's virginity. And, in turn, she took his. Though he didn't want to hurt her, it filled him with overwhelming joy and honor that she gave herself to him. She chose him. The feeling was branded on his soul along with a million other memories from today.

He continued to feed her with slow measured thrusts and kept watch over her. Her eyes were closed and she started to writhe against him, lifting her hips, meeting his forward movement, silently begging him to go deeper. He pushed deeper and with a little more force, meeting her then retreating. He was a little more than half seated when she dropped her knees to the sides, widening herself, giving into his thrusts.

"Fuck, Emmy, you're so fuckin' beautiful."

She opened her eyes and his heart melted at her smile.

He gained more ground. His balls swayed, almost touching her ass.

"Just a little more."

"I don't think I can take any more," she said on shaky breaths.

"You can take it, baby," he rocked a little harder putting more force behind his thrust. He widened her legs, pulling her ass a little higher onto his thighs. "That's it, baby."

"Eli..."

He sunk to the hilt, his balls pressed against her ass, and he held himself there letting her adjust to him.

"E…"

"I'm in."

"E…"

"Yeah, baby?"

"I'm…"

She shattered, coming with a gush.

He gritted his teeth as she tightened around him. *Holy shit!* He pulled back, fighting against her muscles all the way to the tip and sunk back to the root. He went down to his elbows pinning her beneath him.

"Take me, Eli."

That was all he needed to hear. He let loose, pumping his hips like a piston. She was begging him the whole time. He did it again and again, over and over.

He was hard as steel.

"Faster, Eli…" she panted.

He pulled back so far he slipped out of her and she moaned at the loss of him. He was shaking, wanting to get back inside her. He reached for himself.

"Fuck! The condom broke!"

The latex ring still held tight around his shaft, but the rest of the condom was split from head to base. "Fuck!"

"I don't care, Eli," she pleaded, "I don't fucking care. Take it off and fuck me."

He saw the pleading in her eyes, almost rage. Not the rage of anger, but of want. Need. Of primal prey.

"Em."

"Elijah, please."

Hearing his given name roll from her lips was all it took.

"I can pull out."

"Yes…pull out, just get in me."

She rubbed herself against his hands as he pulled the destroyed layer of latex off his shaft.

Grabbing hold of the base, he slammed home. Her scream mingled with his moan and he began to pound into her, ruthlessly, grabbing her hips and firing home. Slam, after slam, after slam, he rocked into her.

When she locked her legs behind him, he knew the gloves were off. He sat back on his heels, grabbed her hips, and pulled her to meet every thrust. God, it was primal. Grunts and moans filled the air mingling with sex and sweat.

His balls drew up and he commanded. "Get there, baby."

On cue, she exploded, lost to the intoxicating ecstasy. She was beauty in its rawest form.

He rode high. Ten-feet tall and bulletproof. *He* did that. Brought out her sexual beauty.

He had no idea they could wield so much power over one another, hold each other captive with a stroke or a touch.

She shivered, quaked, not in control of her own body.

Euphoria. Utopia. Ecstasy.

Eli pumped, resisting the convulsing of her inner muscles and swore he saw stars as he let loose. He felt two ropes of cum shoot out his cock before he remembered to pull out. He pulled out and lunged forward, spilling his seed onto her stomach. His cock pulsed between them.

Eli squeezed his eyes shut.

CHAPTER 26

Fuck!

I came in her!

That was Eli's first thought when he returned to planet earth. He was draped over Ember, both panting, sweat-laden and spent. He rolled off her, coming to rest on his back. Sprawled out, he brought up his forearm, letting the crook settle over his eyes. *I fucking came inside her! Shit!* Panic hit his gut.

Fuck! Fuck! Fuck!

The condom. The two-year-old condom. *Fuck!* He should've known. When it wouldn't roll on, he *should. Have. Known.* Granted, he'd never used one before, but common sense. God! *The rubber was dry.* He shook his head and mentally berated himself a million more times. He was supposed to protect her, but instead...*Fuck!*

"I can hear you thinking. Don't harsh my mellow."

In his fucked-up panic, that made him smile. "Harsh your mellow? Pauly Shore? Encino Man?"

"No, but you would think."

He tabled the thoughts of the condom, hearing the exhaustion coming from her as she lay almost comatose next to him. The tender mewling and tiny whimpers had died down. With his eyes closed, he could still see her and she was absolutely beautiful.

God, I love her!

He needed to touch her. He didn't know how he would survive without her touch. She was right next to him but seemed miles away. Closing the distance between them, he pulled her to him. She came willingly, curling into his side, head nestled to his chest, leg hitched over his and her arm draped over his cum-ridden stomach. She didn't care. She just burrowed into him and he loved it.

His world was complete.

He had Red in his arms and nothing, *nothing*, was going to tear her away. He'd die before he'd let anything happen to her. Burying his face into her head of ember curls, he laid down a chaste kiss.

Her hand slowly caressed his stomach, running over his abs, and gliding through his cum. Her touch was light and she lingered in his essence, rubbing in concentric circles, working his seed into the flesh.

The thought of her relishing his cum was not only erotic as hell, but made him want to beat his chest like a caveman. He'd marked her. She was his.

"You pulled out." It was an observation, not a question. Her fingers kept tracing his abs.

Fuck!

He had to be honest with her.

"Baby," he searched to find his next words. "Baby, I tried." Her finger continued to trace, and she flattened her palm, coating more of his stomach, the distraction keeping him from concentrating.

"Tried?" She swirled some more. "Seems like *Mission Accomplished* to me."

Concentrate. "Babe, I...think..." He corrected himself. "I know I didn't pull out soon enough."

Her hand stilled.

He held his breath.

She had every right to be angry. He was angry. She trusted him, and he failed her. That stung. He braced and could deal with whatever her reaction would be.

"Hmm." She continued her circles on his stomach, now almost dry.

He laid his hand on top of hers, stopping her from caressing him. "Did you hear me?"

"Umhuh."

"I didn't pull out in time."

She hesitantly nodded against his side.

"I came *in* you."

She nodded again.

What the fuck? He rolled to his side and pushed up onto one arm, looking down at her still curled into position.

"Em."

She craned her head to him, but stayed curled up.

Staring at each other, he waited for her to...to, what? Say something? Yell at him? Get angry? Burst into tears? Just something. He needed her reaction.

She waited a moment then raised herself to her elbow.

"Em—"

"It happened. We can't change it. Freaking out isn't going to help. I just had mind blowing sex for the first time, with the man I love, and I just want to bask in it. Savor the memory. Live in the moment."

"You're not freaking out?"

"Oh, I will be later. I most *definitely* will be later, but right now, I just want to be with you. We can deal with this but not right now, please, Eli." she begged him with her eyes, 'Please?" Without another word, she lowered herself back down.

He rubbed the back of his neck and let out a sigh. She was right; freaking out wouldn't help. It wouldn't change the fact that he failed her. Betrayed her trust. He laid down next to her and settled her into his side. It was getting late, but he didn't want their time to end. There was only one first time and she was right, he should bask in it. Did he want the memory of him holding her in an aftersex glow, or of her worried and crying? He had his girl in his arms, and that's what mattered. Again, he buried his face in her mane of curls and inhaled.

His girl.

Every prayer he ever uttered was answered. *All the wishing, wanting and pining for her are over. I'm never letting go.* He made a silent, solemn vow to God; he would never take her for granted. He would spend every minute of every hour of every day earning her love. He would cherish his woman and make every moment count.

They lay together in the barn that held so many of their memories, now holding one more. All too soon, he'd drive her home and tomorrow would start a new chapter in their lives. They were now an *us*. He closed his eyes and held her close. *Us*. A single word was never sweeter.

The sound of a rumbling engine woke him from the greatest dream. He and Ember. Together. *Damn.* Then, the smell hit him. Unfamiliar, but memorable. Musty grass? Hay? He peeled open his eyes but the light streaming through the window was piercing causing them to slam shut. His dream was so clear. Sex-laced Ember writhing with him. *Damn.* It was amazing!

The sound rumbled again and he tried to clear the fog from his head. Then, she stirred. His eyes popped open again and he took in the most beautiful sight; a dream come true. Ember Hayes laying in his arms. His Red...in his arms. If a grin could crack a face, it was the one plastered across his from ear to ear. He was going to die a happy man.

They'd fallen asleep in the barn.

She stretched like a languid cat, arching her back, pushing her naked breasts against him. *Shit!* His morning wood became redwood. Tall, towering and massive. He buried a kiss in the tangled mane. "Morning, beautiful."

She let out a joyful sigh with a hum. "How did I never know I wanted you?" She spoke the words into his ribs. "In less than a day's time, I know I'll love you forever." She was curled up, cradled in the apex of his shoulder and pec, arms pulled in with her hands in prayer under her chin. She was beautiful. She fluttered a light snore and he had to smile.

"Never another, Eli. I'll marry you." In a sleepy mutter, she uttered the words. Her brain was not awake yet, but her subconscious spilling her truths.

He stilled at the thought. He, Ember, and forever. Nothing was more perfect.

"Hey, baby." Another kiss to her hair. "We fell asleep in the barn. Think we need to get up before we're discovered."

"Uhh-uhh." The sound of denial breathed through her nostrils. She kept her eyes closed. "Wanna stay right here." Her creaky morning voice was heady and sexy. She burrowed further into his side.

She was so cute, curled up like a kitten, molding herself to him. He, too, wanted to stay curled up with her.

The rumbling of a diesel engine drew nearer. He placed it as a tractor. More specifically, Mitch's tractor. *Shit! Pops is close by and we're naked!*

"Babe, gotta get up...now!" He pulled his arm from under her, causing her to stir.

"Can't we lay a little longer?"

"Your father is outside the barn."

That caught her attention. Her sleepy eyes popped open, and she took in her surroundings.

"Come on, Red. Gotta scoot." Eli was standing, already gathering his clothes.

She sat, a lazy grin crossing her face.

"Babe...Naked. Dad. Shotgun. Marksman. None bodes well for me. Why are you grinning?" He voiced his thoughts while pulling his tee over his head.

She motioned with her head to his morning wood, standing tall, proud and erect. "You. Are. A. God. You wield that thing like a master."

He shook his head, pulling his boxers up over the masterpiece of discussion.

She frowned. "I wasn't done looking." She added a pout.

Just then, the idling engine roared back to life.

Both heads swung to the barn doors.

They froze, listened, staring as if they could see through the wooden planks of the doors. The sound became louder. Pops was closer than they thought.

That triggered a frenzy. Both scrambled to clothe themselves. Eli picked up her dress and pulled it over her head. She struggled to find the straps and he yanked his jeans over his hips, careful to pull his zipper up over his subsiding hard on, then he grabbed his boots.

"Panties. Where the fuck are my underwear?" Ember yelled in a whisper, searching the blanket and the surrounding area.

Eli laughed at the sight of her desperate search, on the hunt for the scrap of lace. He pulled her thong from his pocket and dangled it from his fingertips. "I was hoping to keep this as a souvenir."

Ember caught his pose and laughed, swiping them from his hand and pulling them over her ivory legs. "Or, a trophy." She pecked him with a kiss.

Though time was short, he pulled her to him and spoke into her hair. "To the victor goes the spoils." He bit her earlobe then nestled, loving the scent of her shampoo mingled with the smell of sweat and sex. It was a drug he would get high on each time she'd give herself to him. "I want to ravish your mouth right now, but morning breath and all, I'll settle for the chaste kiss."

She dipped her head and rested it on his chest. "I can think of other places your mouth can go, morning breath or not."

A growl rumbled deep in his chest, matching the growl and rumble of the tractor outside the barn.

It got them moving. He bent to grab the scarlet blanket and noticed their stains from last night.

"That needs to be burned!" Ember reddened with embarrassment.

"Fuck, no! I'll frame it. Hang it on my wall so I can look at it every day."

"Ew, Eli, that's gross!"

"Nothing gross about it, Em."

She put her hands on her hips, trying to look feisty, but it just made her more adorable. "Yeah, hang it where you can see it...along with my father when he comes to visit?"

The mention of her father had him bunching the blanket and grabbing for her hand.

"Goes in the burn pit!"

"That's what I thought!"

They headed for the doors, hand-in-hand, fingers laced as always, but this time it was different. Just like their fingers were intertwined and melded together, so were their hearts.

They were both grown adults, fought in war zones, lived on their own, but both felt like teenagers sneaking home from a date after curfew. Were they really doing the walk of shame? Eli reached for the door, praying the tractor would be nowhere in sight. *Please, God, don't let Pops be anywhere in sight.* He whispered the prayer as he slid open the heavy door.

Fuck.

Pops was across from the barn using a small backhoe to pull a broken fence post.

Eli's truck was in front of the barn door. He pulled open Ember's door and she quickly jumped up into the cab. He made his way around the truck when the tractor's engine shut down, and Mitch climbed from the seat.

Fuck!

For a second, Eli thought about opening his door and gunning out of there, but he wouldn't disrespect Pops like that. Obviously, Mitch had spotted his truck this morning and he wasn't stupid, he had to know they'd spent the night together. Eli's stomach churned.

But, why? They were two, grown, consenting adults. He wasn't ashamed. There was no crime in spending the night with the woman he loved. So, then why did he feel like he was about to face a firing squad? He'd been in some tough spots in his life but nothing put a pit in his stomach like facing Ember's father. Because this wasn't Pops, his mentor and hero, this was Mitch, father of the girl he just deflowered...in his own barn...on his own property.

Shit!

Eli would take his lumps and face Mitch like a man.

"Mornin'." Mitch had a casual swagger that was all his own.

Eli turned to face the executioner.

Mitch just stood with a shit-eating, knowing smirk across his face.

Double fuck.

"Beautiful mornin', wouldn't you agree?"

Bastard! He was reveling in Eli's discomfort. "Sure is." Eli held strong, not letting Mitch goad him.

"Susan's got breakfast going. Coffee brewed. Looks like you could use some."

Susan, not *Mom.*

The smirk turned into a grin. A knowing grin that had him pinned, and Eli just had to take it.

"Long night." It wasn't a question nor a statement. It was put there to tell Eli there was no secret. *They* were no secret. Mitch was shameless.

Silence hung between them, a technique used by interrogation experts to hone more information without asking for it. Eli knew the tactic; hell, he'd used the tactic. Time trickled past. Both men held their own. Neither willing to crack. But, it was Eli who broke first.

"I love her."

"I know."

"She loves me."

"Know that too."

"It's not a fling. It's the real thing, Mitch. I love your daughter. Every breath. Every heartbeat."

"Always knew that, son."

If Mitch was going to beat his ass, he'd take the beating. She would be worth every blow. He loved her.

Holding his stare, Mitch held out his hand. "Take care of my baby girl."

Eli was momentarily stunned, though he shouldn't have been after their talk at sunset. So much in that one sentence. Trust. Hope. A warning. His blessing. Pops was trusting him with his baby girl.

"Always." He grasped Pops hand and shook it. "Forever."

Pops found Ember's eyes as she sat in the passenger's seat and mouthed, "Love you," and threw her a wink. Ember smiled back at her dad, blushing profusely, and mimicked a kiss. He then gave Eli a nod, turned, and swaggered to the backhoe. Eli knew he had Pops' blessing before, but getting it under the circumstances of the morning, made it all the better. Mitch trusted him. But, he also knew Mitch would hunt him down and kill him if he ever hurt his baby girl.

CHAPTER 27

"Is he as hung as you'd hoped?" Hopefulness rang in Maven's tone. "He's not bent or crooked, ya' know, like any deformities or growths?"

Ember hung her head. *Why?* Why would any sane person ask that question. The answer stared back at her. Maven. Maven wasn't sane.

Sometimes, Ember wondered if there was an undiscovered gene or chromosome that made Maven...Maven. Maybe it would be named after her? Although, it would be a gene mutation, something that would baffle scientists, and would be studied and dissected by great thinkers and great minds. The diagnosis would be as shocking as cancer or some other terminal disease. *"I'm sorry to inform you, you've contracted...the Maven.* And people would wallow and wail and hold benefits for the ill-stricken person. Masses would come to grieve. It'd be awful!

Maven had rushed over when Ember called and told her she'd spent the night with Eli and they'd had a mishap with a condom. Maven didn't even say goodbye, just ended the call and was banging down her door thirty minutes later. Without Ember knowing, Maves stopped at the pharmacy and got her a Plan B Emergency Contraception pill. Ember wasn't sure if she should take it, but Maven told her she had five days to decide.

Maven wanted all the details, a play-by-play of the "good parts" as she called them.

"It's bent, isn't it?"

"What—" Ember lost her thoughts and tuned back into her friend.

"You didn't answer, so that means there's something wrong with it. Is it gross?"

"No, it's fine, it's—"

"That's ok hun, you can work around it. Maybe there's medical treatment." She picked up her phone and started to google, speaking out loud, "Crooked wangs..." She started to scroll.

Ember pulled the phone from her hand and said, "It's fine."

Maven pursed her lips and raised a brow, "Just fine. Oh, honey, I'm so sorry." She put her hand on Ember's knee. "Well...at least he's cute."

Ember closed her eyes and shook her head. *Why? Dear, God, why?*

"Nothing wrong with his...wang. It's absolutely perfect."

"Does it—"

"Conversation ended. Not talking about it." Ember got up, walked to the kitchen, opened the freezer, and swapped out the bag of peas.

"Hold up. You *finally* lost that V-card you've held onto for thirty-some years—God knows I've tried to get it cashed for you —you cash it at the Bank of Eli, a guy that's loved you for...like forever, and now you're not going to tell me the deets! That's brutal, bitch!"

"Bitch. Really?"

"Shoe fits."

Ember came back to the living room, threw down the bag, and sat in the overstuffed armchair.

"Shit! Cold, so cold."

"Bet, you're thanking me now for that little trick." Maven pointed to the peas and gave her a sassy *you're welcome* look and laughed.

Ember didn't reply, just nestled the bag of frozen peas between her thighs and sat back in sweet relief.

"Probably hurts because of the bend. Does it have a knuckle?"

Ember couldn't hold back and she split with laughter. Laughter so hard it hurt her swollen vajayjay.

"No," she said through her laughter. "No knuckles, no bends, no deviations, no kinks."

"Speaking of kinks—"

Eli walked in the front door with Cypher and Ember was never so grateful for the interruption. Seeing Eli, she felt her heart swell. Thank God for great timing. Then, she remembered the crotch peas and was mortified. Not only would Eli see them but Cy would too. *Oh, God of mercy!* She closed her splayed legs, hoping they hadn't seen them.

Eli made a beeline to Ember.

"Babe." His face was all one big smile. He held out a hand for her to stand but instead, she grabbed it and pulled him to herself. He kissed her hard, not caring they weren't alone, and then nipped at her ear.

Oh...my, God! Her libido rose one-hundred and ten percent. She swore her loins just boiled the entire bag or frozen peas. He lingered at her ear, inhaling her, then Cy cleared his throat.

"We'll come back to this," he whispered in her ear before nipping once more.

"Get a room!" Maven feigned disgust.

"It's my house." Ember shot back.

"Room!" Maven pointed over her shoulder, behind the couch, to the hallway. "Use it."

"Guess we're going to be seeing a lot of this." Cy stood next to Maven who was eyeing him up and down, examining him as if she were buying prime stock at a stud show. She knew Cy. He hung out with Eli, who hung out with Ember, who hung out with Maven, so they weren't an official "group," but they were a gang. Also, his brother, Channing, ran an investment firm and Maven was his personal assistant. "What's your shoe size?" Maven blurted out the question to Cy.

"Maves!" Ember gave her a stern warning with one word.

Maven ignored her bestie and continued her perusal, stopping, again at his shoes.

"Well?" She twisted a lock of her hair, putting the tip of it in her mouth. Today, she was wearing her *innocent* ponytails. Not the adult version banded below each ear. No, Maves had the *third-grade, pull-my-pigtails-naughty-schoolgirl* kind, banded on each side of her head, complete with red satin ribbons. The *I'm-waiting-to-be-punished* kind. She could turn on Sex Kitten or Sex Slave like a switch.

"Twelve-and-a-half."

Maven raised her brows to her hairline and bit her bottom lip, still nibbling on her hair ends. "Narrow or wide width?"

Cy sent her a sex laden smirk that dripped sin. "3E."

Maven nibbled her lip some more, then took out her phone and began typing. A few swipes, and she studied her phone screen.

Eli started talking, "Gonna grill out. We bought steak and chicken. Picked up a few salads—"

Maven gasped and the hair she was nibbling fell from her lips. The trio stopped talking and all eyes went to Maven.

"Problem, darlin'?" Cy laid on his Texas accent, hitting the *'R'* low and sultry. Ember knew he spoke ten languages, so dialect and accents were second nature to him. He wasn't a Texan. He was actually from southern California, but you'd never known it by the southern drawl he used on her.

"Ah, I gotta, ah...go to the bathroom." She was down the hall like a shot.

All eyes followed her down the hallway, then Eli finished his thought. "Picked you up some chicken breasts, and I'll make some of that honey glaze you love. If you're hungry, we'll get the grill started."

Ember squirmed in her seat because the frozen peas were freezing the same area since the guys walked in. "That'd be wonderful. I can whip up something for dessert."

Eli sat on the armrest of the chair, holding Ember's hand. He lifted it to his mouth, placing a kiss on her fingers, causing her to break into a giddy, girly smile.

Cypher took the seat on the couch Maven had just vacated. "Just want to say, I think this is really cool." He motioned back and forth between Ember and Eli, "Really happy for you two."

Eli and Ember exchanged looks and grinned back at Cy.

"We're happy, too." Eli stole a second glance at his girl, "It's a long time coming."

"We all knew it would happen sooner or later." Cy looked down the hallway then back at his friends. "There's someone for everyone, right?"

"Just can't believe you all knew it." Ember closed her eyes and shook her head.

Cy rolled his lips, "Kinda hard to miss, Em. If his 'doe-eyes' didn't give it away, his uber over-protective *don't-touch-her-or-I'll-kill-you* attitude was a dead giveaway."

Eli glared, "Doe-eyes my ass!" He shot back.

Cy tilted his head and made an exaggerated, dopey, wide-eyed, lovesick stare that had Ember giggling.

"Fuck off!" Eli shot the barb at Cy with a laugh. "I don't do that."

"Oh, yes you do!" Mave's voice carried from the hallway. She walked around the couch and took a seat next to Cy, so close she could have practically been in his lap.

"We all talk about it." Maven gave them a *duh* expression, while Cy nodded his head in agreement. "We've watched him pine over you all these years like a lost puppy, and you just patted him on the head thinking he was just there to be a companion, when he really wanted to be your lap dog. Ya know, hump your leg and jump you so hard we'd have to break him off you with a firehose."

Cy let out a roar and three shades of red covered Ember as she tried not to laugh, hiding her head in Eli's side. Slate gave his teammate the finger.

Ember feigned a pout and glared at Maven, "Would've been nice to know."

"Telling you he wanted you would be like telling someone the sky's blue. Well, no shit Sherlock! How you were so oblivious to him is absolutely mind boggling."

"Well, fine, laugh all you want, he's mine now and it's a forever thing...not a fling." She caught Eli's eye.

"Never gonna leave, babe. This," he motioned between them, "is forever." The passion in his voice was sincere. He leaned over and gave her a smoldering kiss. Ember didn't care that Maven made a gagging noise.

"How 'bout we get those steaks on the grill." Cy broke the lovesick moment.

"Sounds like a plan." Eli pulled Ember from the chair.

Fuck!

"Peas?" Eli's focus went from the soggy bag of melted vegetables to Ember's mortified face. His raised brows and smirk as he made the connection made her want to crawl in a hole and die.

"Impressive, man." Cy slapped his friend's shoulder and he headed out the patio door to fire up the grill.

"That knuckled wang of yours ravaged the hell out of her coochie. Thing probably looks like a rabid beaver, all foaming mouth and snarling teeth." She started to walk away, "She's one lucky bitch!" Maven laughed and went to join Cy on the deck.

Eli turned back to Ember, a grin stretching his face coupled with a smug, cock-sure gleam in his eye. To say Ember was embarrassed was the understatement of the year. If the earth would split and swallow her whole it would be nothing short of merciful. He leaned over, brushed his lips to hers, then whispered, "I don't know about the knuckle, or whatever, but if you're not too rabid, I'm hoping you have an entire case of peas, because I'll be ravishing you later. Ice up now, 'cuz it's going to be wild!"

Holy hell...I'm one lucky bitch!

CHAPTER 28

He waited, and he watched. Omar Bazwar was a patient man. A quality that served him well as he planned his next move. She was always with someone. She was smart enough to switch up her routine. She was a creature of habit, small mundane tasks, but her training had taught her the value of being unpredictable, changing her driving routes to work, never eating at the same restaurants, things of that nature. But, she'd slipped up.

She left the hardware store with her father through the back entrance when she closed the store with him, although that wasn't a set schedule. She always left the security business in the evening, at the same time, always with the guy at her side. The father and boyfriend were going to make things more difficult.

His younger brother, Husani, thought he got rid of the guy at the gun range, but he shot the wrong man. It was a stupid misjudgment on his part. Mistaking Gabriel Dorian for the devil woman's boyfriend was a crucial mistake. They looked similar, extremely close in makeup: same build; same height; same hair and beard. If he'd had his binoculars and hadn't followed them on foot, Husani probably would've made the discernment. But, what was one more American casualty? If anything it was a blessing. One less infidel.

Now, Omar would have to finish his brother's retribution. Retribution for the death of their eldest brother, Khalid.

Khalid found the devil woman in Mosul. Or, she found him.

But, it was Husani who portrayed himself as an Iraqi/US counterpart in Mosul and found her again. It was his lucky break, getting the intel that she was a sniper, that led him to find her in the States. Now, she would pay, and there would be no mistakes. Omar would take two of hers for one of his. The two that were her world.

Husani was in a jail cell, awaiting murder charges for the botched murder at the gun range. Khalid lay in the ground as his mother wailed. All at the devil woman's hands. Omar vowed she wouldn't walk away. Soon her mother would wail as well.

After the cookout, Maven offered to drive Cypher home so Eli and Ember could have the evening to themselves. Even though it was Saturday, Eli had to report to the office earlier in the morning. King had called the guys in. Ember knew he couldn't discuss his work, but she knew it was most likely something to do with a mission they'd be leaving on soon, or at least prep work for an upcoming mission. Being former military, she knew what dedication it took to plan an op. Missions didn't care if it was the guys' day off; any new info had to be discussed and gone over. Mary told her King had been taking more government jobs, something that he didn't care to do, but it meant a bigger payday for Hellforce and the guys, and they could do more pro bono cases for private families, something King put high on his priority list.

Now that Cy and Maven had left, she and Eli needed to talk and for some reason she felt awkward. He sat next to her on the couch, her head resting on his chest, his arm around her shoulders playing with a wayward strand of her hair, absently curling it around his finger.

"I'm sorry," he started, "I didn't say it last night or this morning, but I want you to know how sorry I am. I'm sorry I wasn't prepared and even more sorry I didn't pull out in time." He spoke to the top of her head without breaking their hold.

Stupidly, she felt better not looking at him directly. Like somehow the pretend veil of anonymity would give her courage to speak without staring at his beautiful slate eyes. She felt the uptick in his heart rate.

"I know you are." And, it was true. She knew he was sorry for trusting the condom and also, he felt absolutely terrible for getting caught up in the moment when he came, not pulling out in time.

He let the moment settle before speaking again. "That condom was well over two years old. I should've never used it. Arctic gave it to me when a girl was hitting on me at the bar." He felt her tense. "It was a joke. Obviously I didn't use it, but I put it in my wallet and kept it there, I don't know...I guess as a sort of ruse for the guys."

"A ruse?"

"Yeah, none of the guys, except Cy, knows I'm...well...*was* a virgin. It's stupid but I kept it hidden, knowing if the guys would have known, my nick would have been changed to Priest, or Saint or even go as far as nicking me Virgin." He chuckled. "Wouldn't have wanted that call sign to go out over the comms before getting ready to breach." They both laughed.

"Yeah, that would be brutal." Ember knew monikers could be given to humiliate a fellow soldier. A soldier didn't choose their nick, it was earned, a play on their name or it was a joke all the others could relish at the person's expense. So, she knew why he didn't dare let the guys know he'd never taken a woman.

"In my wildest dreams, I never expected anything to happen. If anything, I thought you'd shoot me down and I'd lose you forever."

That had her sitting up. "Why would you lose me? That doesn't make any sense."

Eli's expression softened and he gave her a half-hearted smile. "Em, I've been in the friend zone for as long as I've known you. Every time I thought I could step out of the zone, I was sent back before I could blink. So, I thought when I told you how I felt you'd banish me back there. I couldn't stand not to have you so it was all or nothing when I laid myself out there."

Ember took in the thought. Eli would have left if she hadn't reciprocated his feelings. The thought pained her. The thought of Eli not in her life was unimaginable. "Well, we don't have to worry about that anymore."

He kissed the top of her head and she melted into him. A few minutes passed. "We have another matter to discuss." His voice was low, something Ember knew meant he was deep in thought.

Her reply was quiet, "I know."

"You have choices."

"Don't you mean *we* have choices."

A moment passed when he answered. "I would say yes, but society would tend to differ."

"We aren't society, Eli." Her voice was soft but not a whisper. "It's not just my say."

Eli kissed her head again and rested his lips in place. Just as he was going to speak, her phone rang. She let it go.

"You going to get that?"

She glanced at the screen lying beside her. "It's my dad." She hesitated. "Don't know if I want to take that." The memory of her dad's presence at the barn that morning was too fresh in her mind.

Eli knew what she was thinking and consoled her. "He's your father. He loves you. He's not going to lecture you and he's not going to think any less of you. You're a grown woman. If he can deal with the knowledge of Rhys' sexcapades, he can surely deal with us."

"Sexcapades?"

"Do you know your sister?" The dripping sarcasm only punctuated the fact they all knew. Rhys was cute and sexy as sin. Her liking of—or some would say addiction to—sex was known by all.

"True," she paused. "But, I'm his baby girl."

"Call the man back. He's calling for a reason. If he was angry with you and wanted to yell, you know he wouldn't do it over the phone."

Eli was right, so she reached for the phone that had since gone silent.

"Gonna use the bathroom." Eli got up and headed down the hallway as she called her dad back.

~

Eli zipped his fly and turned to the sink to wash his hands. He reached for the towel and noticed a box on the countertop. Curious, he picked it up.

"Plan B?" He read the box, "Emergency Contraceptive. One tablet. One step."

Whoa. His eyes rounded. Had Ember taken the pill? He saw that the box was unopened but still, the thought made his stomach flip. She'd made the decision by buying the pill, a decision that made him sad. He didn't know anything about cycles and woman things, but he had heard Mary talking about "fertile days," and how she must have conceived during that time, so for all he knew Ember could be carrying the beginning of life.

A baby. Their baby. He looked at the box again, wondering if she was going to tell him she'd bought it. He'd assume she'd tell him. Again, a feeling of sadness came over him and his stomach filled with lead. *Damn.* He inhaled deeply, trying to quell his stomach. He tried to reconcile that she would be the one going through body changes and God, the same hormonal imbalance Mary was going through, and that was a lot to consider if she didn't take the pill and became pregnant. Everything physically rode on the woman. But he was he hoping he could be by her side if she became pregnant. He wanted children. Lots of children.

Get a grip and deal. He had to be okay with whatever she chose. *Could I be?* It was just the way things were. Father or not, no say. He told himself he'd be okay. He lied. Because, no matter how small the lie was to swallow, there was no way it was going down. He knew, in this day and age, it was supposed to be a woman's choice, but it felt wrong. He was sad for something he didn't even know if he had. He'd have to somehow come to grips with it. He felt nauseated. He shook his head because he could never come to grips with it. He sent up a prayer, put the box back on the counter, and left the bathroom.

He walked back into the living room where she was scrolling through her phone.

"Called Pops back?"

"Yeah." Before he could ask what he wanted she continued, "He wanted to invite us to Sunday dinner tomorrow."

Eli felt his stomach flip again, this time for a whole different reason. "He's going to kill me, isn't he? Wants to give me a last supper before he acid-washes my body and no one ever finds my remains."

"What happened to we're adults and he won't think less of us? Didn't you just tell me that before I called him back?"

Eli digressed, "Lies. All lies. Complete and utter bullshit!"

Ember laughed at his over-exaggeration. "Actually," she continued, "he said he and Mom want to celebrate...*us*."

That thought of *'us'* made his stomach flip again, but this time with joy, not dread.

"Really?"

"Yup."

"Us?"

"Us."

"You happy with us, as an 'us'?" Eli asked.

"Think I answered that question last night." Her mouth turned up into a grin.

Eli leaned over her, caging her with his arms on the back of the couch, "Sure did, babe." He gave her a chaste kiss that threatened to become more if he didn't pull back, which he did. Thinking of their pending discussion, he sat down next to her. Again, dread crept into his bones causing his stomach to unsettle.

"So, you're taking that pill?" His question was light and he tried to keep his voice from quaking. He wanted to be strong for her and stand strong for her decision.

"What pill?"

"*The* pill...in the box....on the counter...in the bathroom." He was trying to keep his thoughts in order, but they were coming out in short segments. "That Plan B pill?" He wasn't sure why it came out as a question, but he pushed forward. "You're taking it?"

≈

Shit!

Ember had asked Maven to put it in the vanity drawer but she must've put it on the counter instead. She mentally slapped herself.

She met his questioning stare. A visceral reaction made her swallow. Was she going to take the pill? Did she want to take the pill? *Does* he *want me to take the pill?* The question ran through her head. She knew her answers but she needed to know his.

"Do *you* want me to take it?" A surge of anxiety rolled her stomach.

Eli sat splayed, forearms resting on his thighs, wringing his hands.

"Eli?" Her voice came when his didn't. "I need to know." And, she did. Her worry may be for nothing, but then again, it was coming up to the twenty-four hour mark since they had sex; unprotected sex. He was taking the blame and it was weighing heavy on his shoulders. She knew he was punishing himself, but *she* had been the one to beg him to continue after the condom broke.

She begged him. He obliged. Both caught in the moment of bad decisions. Both held the blame. Would he ask her to take the pill? Could she take it?

"Babe." His voice was quiet.

Ember felt the anxiety rise within her and she blurted out, "No. I'm sorry, Eli." Calming herself, she continued, "I can't take it." She shook her head and added, "I won't take it." Her face was caught in anguish. "I'm sorry, but I just can't." Her feelings welled to the surface and she vomited the words, "I won't ask you to do anything if you don't want...if I'm pregnant. I'm not trapping you...I'd never do that to you but then, I don't even know if this is even happening...so, I just...I just...can't...I'm sor—"

Eli let out an exhale, relief sounding through the action. The breath he'd held released in a gush, "Thank God." The words were quiet, but Ember raised her head.

"You're okay with that?" She was surprised so she clarified, "Okay if I don't want to take it?" Her voice went from questioning to very small. "You're not going to be angry, are you?"

Eli stood and knelt before her, looking up into her eyes.

"Angry? Babe, I don't want you to take it. I really, really, desperately don't want you to take it." He parted her knees and knelt between them and his hands wrapped around hers. On his knees before her, it was as if he was praying the words. "Em, if this...our first time...us," his words were jumbled but she understood every sentiment, "if we created a life..." He lost his words again, then continued. "I love you, Emmy, and if...a baby is the result of our first time together..." His voice cracked.

She slid from the cushion onto her knees and wrapped herself around him, telling him with her body and soul that she too wanted to accept any result of them coming together. With eyes welling, she whispered, "I love you, Eli."

Happiness, relief and anticipation. Three in one.

He wrapped himself around her and they both cried with relief.

CHAPTER 29

Three weeks had passed since "The Barn" as it was now dubbed, and Ember couldn't be happier. Things with Eli were great, as with all budding relationships, but it seemed different than the others. They'd known each other forever so it felt like they were a seasoned couple. They already knew each other's quirks and habits and it felt...easy. There was no tiptoeing around each other trying not to let too much of themselves show before the relationship settled in. No, they knew the good, the bad and the ugly and nothing ever felt sweeter.

"Did you get that last box of shut off valves put into stock?" Mitch asked Ember while he stocked the pipe fittings.

"Yup. Got the aisle stocked and the reorder scanned for tomorrow."

He finished putting the last fitting in the bin and turned to his daughter. "Thanks for helping out tonight. Mom needed a break and I knew she wouldn't ask for one."

"Sneaky Dad. How many invoices did you take home yesterday just to get her to work from home instead of the office?" Ember shot him a rueful smile.

"No idea what you're talking about." Mitch feigned unknowing.

"Right, Dad...no clue. Weak story."

"Doesn't matter if it's weak. What matters is your mom is home relaxing." He tousled her red curls.

"Dad!" She ducked her head to the side. "Tousling, really?"

"You're adorable. lil' girl."

She patted down her hair. "Like it's not unmanageable enough." She huffed indignation but pulled back her smile.

"She *is* adorable!" Eli walked up behind her and wrapped his arms around her, placing a kiss on her lips.

"Okay, you two. I'm all for your relationship but none of that mushy stuff. A dad has his limits."

"Oh, please, you and Mom are the randiest couple I know! You're not subtle at all." Ember made a gagging noise.

"Healthy, adult, sexual relationships are what keeps a marriage strong."

"Don't want to hear this."

"We are in the prime of climaxable pleasure, and we—"

"Not listening." Ember covered her ears and hummed to block out the sound.

Eli laughed as Pops continued talking, holding Ember in her agony with the thought of her parents nude and in the throes of passion.

"...and your mother is the most limber she's ever been. Early Senior Yoga has taught her positions I never knew were possible."

"Okay...Okay, Pops. As much as I love you torturing Emmy, it's torturing me too. I want to be able to look Mom in the eye next time I see her."

Mitch laughed and stopped the in depth explanation of their frisky sex life.

"God, I think I'm going to be sick." Ember clutched her stomach.

"Nothing wrong with it. Perfectly natural for two people in love to have a healthy sex life."

Ember grinned at her father. "Well, in that case, you should see how Eli can bend me over and—"

"Whoa! Whoa!"

"Em...*Stop*!"

Both Mitch and Eli were shouting before she finished any more of her sentence.

She posed a look of confusion. "What? I thought it was perfectly natural and healthy—"

"Em, your father's store has hatchets, knives, saws, and wood chippers. I am susceptible to all of them. Please, for the love of God, do not continue that sentence." Eli caught Mitch's eye and saw all the humor had left his face.

"But, Dad said…" She egged him on.

Mitch's voice fell flat. "Your dad does not want one more word to cross your lips."

She held back her laugh.

Mitch turned to Eli. "I'll pretend I know nothing because I'm sure there's nothing to know, right?"

"Absolutely nothing, sir." He tagged the formality to the end of his sentence, letting Mitch know he knew the hierarchy of where he stood in the family.

Mitch nodded and walked up the aisle to the registers.

"Are you insane?" Eli's eyes couldn't get any wider. "That's your father!"

Ember laughed. "If you only knew how much torture he and Mom put Rhys and I through."

"Yes, but it's not your balls that are on the chopping block." Eli wrapped her in his arms. "Please, your father likes me and I'd like to keep it that way and stay in his good graces."

Ember went up on her tiptoes and gave him a peck on the lips. "I'm very bendy, too, ya know."

"Good God, woman. You slay me." Eli planted one more kiss on her lips, this one a little heavy to be given in the middle of the workplace, but he got lost when she returned the kiss. "Gotta get going, Red."

She put on a pout. "Really?"

"Yup. Gotta go over a few things that just came in. King is set on taking this case and he's been examining each lead and leaving no stone unturned."

"Sounds personal."

"Don't know, but if it is or isn't, either way he's determined to get a mission set."

Ember memorized his eyes as she did a thousand times, the grey-slate taking on more of a steel-blue today. "Love you."

"Love you, too, babe."

She gave him one more chaste kiss on his lips, then he gently placed a kiss on her forehead.

"I love when you do that."

"What?"

"Kiss my forehead."

"Oh, yeah?"

"Yeah." She felt his smile against her skin. "A kiss on the lips says, 'I love you,' but, a kiss on my forehead says, 'I like you.' It's playful and makes my heart smile."

He kissed her forehead again.

"Eli?"

"Yeah?"

"Stay safe."

He pulled back. "Stay safe? Why'd you say that?"

She looked up into his beautiful eyes. "I got a bad feeling. Not just in my stomach but in my bones. It's chilling me and I can't shake it."

"Babe, I'm not leaving on a mission yet, just going to discuss whatever King's discovered."

She took in a breath. "I don't know, I just have this horrible feeling. Something's— "

"I'm safe, Emmy. Alert and strapped if anything happens. Which it won't." He patted his Glock, concealed and holstered to his side. "I'm good."

Ember's gaze scanned the store, worry settling in her eyes.

"Red?"

"Can't shake it." She shook her head. "I know this feeling." She scanned once more before meeting his eyes. "It's battle-wary."

She could tell that raised his attention, though he didn't show it in his demeanor.

"Maybe I'm hyped, I don't know, but it's in the air."

"You want me to stick around? I can call King if it's that strong."

"No. That's absurd." She tried to steel herself but failed

miserably. "King and the guys need you. Just, please, be extra vigilant."

Eli stared her down. "I will. I promise." He pulled her to him. "Nothing's going to happen to me."

"Something's going to happen, Eli. I just know it."

His voice was low. "You carrying?"

"Always." She patted the HK beneath her shirt.

He kissed her head. "New holster?"

"Uh-huh. Just got it."

"Good choice."

He kissed her forehead and she pulled him tighter, whispering a prayer for safety.

Omar watched as the guy walked from the store to his truck. Not only had the devil woman dropped her guard, but the guy had slipped as well. He had no idea—once he left in his truck, he sealed his fate. Omar's patience had paid off. Waiting in the shadows, lying low and out of sight, he would finally reap his reward. Retribution was due and Omar would see to it. The tears and screams, the begging and mourning, would flow from *her* eyes and lips, just as they did his mother's. Dusk was settling, and Omar watched as the truck pulled out of the lot from behind the hardware store. They guy never saw Omar pull away from the curb and follow him down Main Street. He was headed to the security company. Omar would follow at a distance to make sure and then his plan would be in motion.

CHAPTER 30

Blistering pain came from Ember's temple and the metallic taste of blood filled her mouth. Opening her eyes, she saw blackness. Nothing. Not a sliver of light. She checked her faculties, mentally running a checklist, ignoring the throbbing radiating from within her head. She was lying on her side and felt like throwing up. *Concussion?* Anxiety consumed her. She tried to suck in a breath but couldn't.

She worked her jaw. *Fuck!* Her mouth was taped shut. She inhaled through her nose and a putrid stench hit her. She felt the bile rise in her throat and tried to swallow it down, but instinct won out. With nowhere else to go, the vomit shot from her nostrils. She instantly gagged and choked.

Panic overtook her and she flailed, but her hands were bound, zip-tied behind her back. Whoever tied her was not gracious. The plastic bit into her flesh, zipped so tight her hands were numb. The sensation of choking on bile burned her lungs and throat. Her eyes watered profusely. Her cries, muffled by the tape, were of no use and she strained to see anything she could in the pitch blackness.

Control yourself. Soldier mode kicked in.

First, she had to control her breathing or she'd pass out. As best she could, she inhaled deeply through her nose, then blew out as hard as she could, clearing any remains of vomit. She sucked in another breath, this one deeper than the last, and got the much needed air into her lungs. It was difficult, but she controlled her heart rate, something that was usually second nature to her. She tried to take in her surroundings again. The coolness of metal pressed against her cheek. Only the sound of silence filled her ears. *Concentrate.* Still, nothing. No distant sounds, nothing familiar. Nothing. That's what she heard. Nothing.

She rolled to her back, her hands digging into her spine, and lifted her knees as high as she could to her chest. She pulled her shoulder blades together and pushed her bound hands below her butt and wiggled each cheek over her wrists. She pulled and strained, hoping the plastic ties would give and break under the pressure, but it only made the skin of her wrists tear. She gritted her teeth. The burn was tolerable and the wetness of blood let the ties slide and the bite wasn't as bad. She succeeded in getting her hands below her thighs. Ember rocked herself into a sitting position, then brought her leg into a figure-four and slid her knee beneath her elbow, pulling her elbow inward and bringing her wrist over her foot.

Success! One leg free.

The pain from the ties was now excruciating, and she felt the slickness of blood oozing onto her hands. She didn't care. She needed to free herself. Repeating the same motion, this time it was easier to maneuver and she got both legs through and her arms in front of her. She immediately tore the tape from her mouth.

Son of a bitch! Duct tape did not come off like a Band-Aid or as easily as in the movies. It stung and instant heat seared her lips. She spit the vile remains of the vomit from her mouth. It was heaven to be able to breathe freely again. The blood from her wrists ran down her forearms, and even in the pitch darkness, she knew the damage was bad.

Ember lifted her wrists above her head and in one fast, swift motion, she brought them down over her abdomen, pulling her wrists to each side, using her body as a wedge. Instantly, the ties severed and fell to the ground. Even with her adrenaline pumping and her hands tingling with numbness, the pain was intense. Her skin sliced and tore some more, adding to the already gruesome damage to her wrists.

Patting herself all over, the phone she kept in her back pocket wasn't there. *Shit!* Then, she lifted the hem of her shirt and reached for her Glock. Gone.

Fuck. Fuck. Double Fuck! No phone. No weapon. *Damn it!* With arms stretched out in front of her in the darkness, she had to learn her surroundings. She took a few shuffled steps hoping to feel...something. Nothing. She shuffled some more, waving her hands into the void. Still nothing. She knelt to the ground and coolness met her finger tips. *Metal.* She wanted to stay quiet in case her captors were near, so she hummed low and soft. Listening, she heard the reverberation. She shuffled forward and once again, coolness met her palms. She ran her hands up and down and side to side. The wall was metal too. She slid her hands along the wall and shuffled her feet quite a distance then came to a corner.

I'm in a box. A crate. Some sort of container. Despite the throbbing in her head, her thoughts were clear. She walked the perimeter and stumbled over a raised section. Running her hands over it, she knew it was a wheel well. *Fuck! I'm in a box truck, a moving van. This isn't good.*

Centering herself, trying to remember how she got here and what had happened, made her head pound. Nausea built again. She staved off the bile threatening to come up. *Think.* She squeezed her eyes shut, willing her mind to conjure her memory and thoughts. *Please, remember. Pleeease!*

Gun shots! Rapid succession. The sound filled her memory. *Two, then three.* Ember smelled the gunpowder. She had fired the shots. *Why?* Thoughts overwhelming her, she crumpled to the ground, the pain intense in her head. She cradled her head, not caring blood was smearing her forehead. Images flashed, jumbled, not making sense, making the throbbing worse. She took a cleansing breath. *Control yourself. Calm yourself. Clear yourself.* The mantra she used as a sniper centered her being.

Her mind cleared.

The hardware store.

Her memory materialized.

~

"Got the lights." Ember flipped the breaker and the lights in the hardware store dimmed, leaving only the night safety lights glowing.

"All right, got the deposit and I'm good to go." Mitch shut the office door turning the handle a few times, double checking to make sure it was locked, and met his daughter at the back door. "You're always on your phone."

She sent the text.

"Eli?" He pointed and she smiled. "Ah, young love." He placed a hand on his heart. "Oh, to be young again."

"You're still young, Dad."

"Not as young as I once was."

"Fifty-seven is still young. You don't even look your age, let alone act your age." They both laughed knowing it was the truth. "You're fit. You're spry and not in the grave yet. So that's a bonus!"

"All things to be grateful for." Mitch dug his keys from his front pocket while he punched in the code to set the security system. "We're hot! Set and ready."

Ember turned the knob and pushed open the door with her shoulder, leading her dad into the parking lot behind the store. The door shut behind them and he pulled the handle to double check that it latched and locked.

Mitch fell to the ground, twitching and convulsing as a rapid, repetitive snapping sound cut through the air.

"What—Dad!" Ember's yell pierced the night when she saw two leads stuck in her dad's arm and back.

A taser. She stopped herself from touching him and spun around, drawing her gun from its holster, pulling it level, ready to fire. And, she did. Two shots exploded in a millisecond. One person dropped, the two others flanked her.

Fuck! She tracked the one closest to her, firing two more rounds. As she squeezed the trigger, the third shot fired and a flash of white pain met her temple. As her body fell, pain enveloped her. Then, as fifty-thousand volts slammed into her body she convulsed.

Her earlier intuition came to fruition.

≈

"Thanks, Maven. I'll let you know when I know something." Eli disconnected and dropped the phone onto the coffee table. He rubbed the back of his neck. "Where are you?" He asked the question to no one.

Ember hadn't come to his place after work like they'd planned. It was going on ten-thirty, only ninety minutes after the hardware store closed, but he was worried. It wasn't like Ember to be late. Ever. And, on the few occasions she was ever late she called, even if it was a ten-minute delay. Something wasn't right. Eli picked up the phone to dial her mom, when his phone rang.

Mom 2. Susan Hayes' picture displayed across the screen.

"Hey, Mom. Are they there?" Eli's voice sounded hopeful.

"No," she paused, "Eli, I'm getting really worried."

Susan was Eli's first call when Ember didn't arrive an hour after closing. It wasn't unusual; sometimes things came up and she and her dad would stay later, so an hour late wasn't alarming. But Ember always called him, just as Mitch would call Susan. But, now, an hour and a half late was worrisome.

"I'm going to head to the store. Maybe—"

"*Do not* go to the store." Eli cut her off with the direct warning.

"But, El—"

"Absolutely *do not* go to the store. I don't need you out traipsing around in the dark. I'll go check things out."

"I don't want you alone. I can meet you there."

Eli was already formulating a plan. "No, Susan." *Susan, not Mom.* He stressed her name. "I'll get the guys to meet me and I'm sending someone over to your place, too." He'd call King's friend, Chase Jackson, to go to Susan's and stand guard. He needed the rest of his team with him. The hair on the back of his neck tingled and the taste of something foul brewed in his gut, turning his stomach. The same churning that happened when doom lurked in battle, or when an op was about to turned bad. "Where's Rhys?"

"Rhys? Um, probably home at her place."

"Call her and let her know I'm sending someone over. Not to let anyone in without them knowing the password."

The *password* was a safety word Mitch and Susan derived when the girls were little. If anyone came to school, home, or anywhere the girls were, wanting them to go with them, the person would have to know the password so the girls knew it was legit to go along.

"Fighting Irish." Susan repeated the password they'd used.

"Yup. I'll let Trip know."

"Which one's Trip?"

Eli knew Susan was on edge because she was familiar with the team, but he answered anyway, "It's Jayson. Jayson Reeves."

"That's right, Jayson Reeves," Susan repeated. "Do you really think it's necessary to send someone to her townhouse? I don't want to alarm her...I mean, they could just be running late." Susan didn't believe it, just as much as Eli wasn't buying it.

"What's the address?"

Susan rattled off Rhys' address.

"Stay put, Mom, and I'll call you as soon as I know something."

"Okay."

He was just about to hang up when Susan's voice called him. "Eli?"

He brought the phone back to his ear. "Yeah?"

He heard her swallow, "Be safe. Be smart..."

"...Come home." He nodded even though she couldn't see him. "I know, Mom. I will." He hung up.

Be safe. Be smart. Come home. It was what she told him each time he deployed. Whether it was in person, over the phone, letter, text or email, it was always something that bought him comfort. Susan's little way of telling him goodbye, without saying it.

Eli dialed Cypher. He could track Ember's phone, something that he should've done right away when he first realized she was late, but he didn't want to be *that* boyfriend. With the hair on his neck still standing on end, he made the call.

Next, he called Trip and gave him the info on Rhys. Climbing into his truck, he called T-BAR, who would alert Arctic and Creed, knowing they would meet him at the store even though it was late. He didn't call King. With Mary pregnant, Slate didn't want him to leave her and have Mary worried. He had enough backup with the guys.

Ember felt around what she assumed was the back door to the truck and felt for a latch or handle, anything that would open it. She found a thick, heavy nylon loop, meant to pull the overhead door down, but when she pulled up on it hoping it would lift the door, nothing. Nah-da. *Damn it!* She pulled harder, yanking the tether with all her might, feeling pain radiate in her wrists. No way out. She was screwed. She couldn't get out. She'd have to wait until someone came in.

CHAPTER 31

The blows kept coming. From the left. From the right. To the face and the gut. Over and over, the sounds of flesh hitting flesh met the stifling air. Thankfully—if it was something to be thankful for—the blood running from his broken nose made the blows glance off his cheeks.

"Hayes. E-eight...one—"

Whack! A blow from the left.

"Haye—"

Whack! Another strike to his jaw causing his teeth to bite his inner cheek. The tang of more blood hit his tongue.

"Work him over good." A woman's voice with a Middle Eastern accent came from behind him. "Don't kill him, yet. Death is too merciful. She needs to see him and suffer."

Ember. Where is she? Are they torturing her like they are m—

Thud! A fist to the gut. Mitch lost the air he didn't know his lungs held and the exhale spewed blood from his mouth and busted lip. He couldn't inhale. The stifled air caught in his gaping mouth. Nothing in. Nothing out. *Name. Rank. Number.* He would neither scream, nor beg. He wouldn't give them the satisfaction of knowing his agony. *Name. Rank. Number.* His Army identification only crossed his lips.

Another jab to the ribs had him curling against the blow, wanting to cradle his side and comfort it, but his hands were bound to the arms of the chair along with his feet. He was at their mercy, of which they had none.

Crack!

Fuck! That was bone. His torso burned in agony.

"Hayes..." He sputtered, gasping and forcing out each word, "E—"

A blast to his temple gave sweet relief and darkness overcame him as he passed out.

∽

Empty. That's what they found when they barreled into the rear lot of the hardware store. Mitch's truck and Ember's SUV were abandoned. The store was locked up and they were nowhere to be found.

"Fuck!" Slate roared into the night. "Where the fuck are they?" His rhetorical question put the pit in his stomach into a ravishing churn.

"Calm down, Sla—"

"Don't tell me to calm the fuck down! She's gone. Missing. We know who has her. Fucking Bazwar!" The cursing rolled off his tongue like he was still enlisted in the Army. He'd curbed it somewhat after being enlisted for eight years, but it was a second language now. "Where the fuck do we start looking?" He turned to pace.

"Calm. The fuck. Down." King's voice permeated the still night air and commanded the resulting effect. Everyone stood stock still. They hadn't heard him pull up while Slate was lost in his fit of anger.

"Chase called me."

"Bastard. He wasn't supposed to bother you...with Mary—"

"When your friend goes missing it isn't a bother, it's a fucking nightmare. And, I'm pissed that you didn't call me but we'll deal with that later." King was taking control of the situation. "Trip picked up Mary and Rhys and took them to Susan's. Maven's there, too. Chase is with Susan." King's voice turned from concern to ice. "SITREP."

Arctic began to fill King in with the little information they had, which in all, meant nothing.

"Blood!" T-BAR's voice held venom. He was beside the back door in a shadowy area dimly lit by the poor lighting.

The guys gathered where T was standing, all of them pissed and stirring with anger.

"The night deposit." Cy toed the bank bag with his boot, not wanting to pick it up and disturb any evidence.

"Search the lot," King said as he headed to his truck. "I got flashlights for anyone who needs one." It was an empty offer because each guy had a flashlight in their EDC, Every Day Carry bag, stowed in their trucks.

"Keys." Creed crouched a few feet in front of the back door.

T and Arctic walked over to him.

"Slate, are these Mitch's or Ember's?" Arctic asked.

Slate wasn't in the huddle. The guys all looked to the middle of the lot where Slate was staring at something in his hand.

"Buddy...we got keys. Whose are they?"

But Slate didn't answer, didn't move an inch, didn't acknowledge Arctic's question. He curled his fist and brought it to his lips, pausing before he brought it to his heart.

T was the first to come to his side. "What is it, Slate?"

The others gathered, too.

He uncurled his fist and held his palm under the light coming from King's flashlight.

"Fuck!" T's roar was echoed by King, Arctic and Cy's expletives.

In the light shining through the darkness, in Slate's hand, laid his grandfather's World War II battle cross. The one Slate wore and gave to Ember every time he deployed. The cross that Ember now wore daily, never taking it off even to shower.

It was bathed in blood.

Slate said nothing. The guys said nothing. The anger level hit ten. They all knew that things had just turned from bad to worse. Ember wouldn't take off the cross. It would never leave her body—only by force, or by death.

All prayed it was the former.

Which was worse, the blinding darkness or the deafening silence? Both were driving her mad. She waited what seemed like hours, but without a watch, her phone, or the shadows of nightfall, she couldn't gauge time. Plus, how long had she been unconscious? It could be daylight now. Though Ember doubted that because with the hot Texas sun her box of blackness would become an oven by mid-morning.

The thought sparked another spike of fear within her. She had to get out, though she knew that wasn't possible. If she couldn't get out, she'd have to make someone come in. She had to attract her abductors. That was her only hope of getting out.

Are they near? Is the truck abandoned in the Texas plains, in the middle of nowhere? Shit! Only one way to find out. She took in a breath for courage and hoped it worked. She'd have to gain the element of surprise when the door opened. Ember released the breath, filled her lungs again, covered her ears and let out a piercing scream. Her ears, though covered, rang at the shrill banshee cry reverberating off the metal walls and floor, making her wince. She held the scream for as long as she could until her lungs burned for air.

Next, she began to bang on the metal walls, feeling them give and flex with every beat of her flat hands. Again, she yelled and screamed, making enough noise to wake the dead. When she exhausted herself, she waited. Waited and listened. The silence was maddening. What she thought was deafening before was mere lulling compared to the absence now.

When her fit brought no one to the truck, she settled in for a second round, this time kicking at the side walls, causing claps of thunderous noise to echo in the box. Again, she stopped and waited, listening for any faint sound.

There! Her breath hitched and she strained to hear. Was her mind playing tricks on her, conjuring up sounds, just to appease her ears? *There. Again! Talking.* She put every ounce of effort into her ears. Yes. Voices, now louder. *Louder means closer, right?* She prayed it would only be one person, maybe muttering to themselves, but she didn't lie to herself. There were most likely two, hopefully not more. It would be difficult, but not impossible. Being five-foot-three, she was usually underestimated. She was small, but she was fierce. She'd mastered hand-to-hand combat and was ready.

Ember backed herself against the farthest wall from the door. She would make them come to her. Her placement would force one, if not both, to get inside the box of the truck after opening the door to pull her out. She second-guessed her plan. *Should I wait at the door and jump them before they realize I'm there?* No, she shook off the plan. If it was one person, the plan would be brilliant, but if there were two, or heaven forbid more, she'd be offering herself up on a silver platter. *Better stick with plan A. Hide in the back. Make them surrender to you.*

The voices were right outside the truck. Her heartbeat raced though she was trying to calm it. *God, can they hear my heartbeat echo in this tin can?* Adrenaline readied her. There was no flight; just fight. And she was ready to fight. But, not ready for what happened next.

She heard the heavy, metal latch of the door fall from its confines. She widened her stance. Metal against metal, the rollers of the door rumbled as it rose less than a foot. Then, a light tinkling sound of metal hitting metal echoed against the floor.

Fuck! She knew that sound. The heavy metal door came back down, bathing her in darkness once again, but she bolted to it anyway. In the same instant, just as the sounds registered, the fumes of noxious gas spewed from the metal canister and rolled to the center of the box.

Fuck! Shit! Fuck! She instinctively held her breath and covered her face, knowing it would be no use. Her eyelids slammed shut as the gas erupted into her eyes and every pore of her nose. A deluge of snot poured down her face, mingling with her non-stop tears. She couldn't wipe any of it because her coughing spasms caused her to clutch her chest.

Control yourself. You've been trained, you've experienced this before.

Her body betrayed her mind. Instinct had her banging and kicking at the sheet metal door while gagging on the gas and her own bile. She heaved but nothing came up. Again, two, three, four rounds of stomach-crunching heaves and she fell to her knees. *Fuck!* She was going to die. This was it. Bazwar won. She wouldn't stop fighting even through the agony she was experiencing.

Never stop fighting!

She balled her fists tighter and threw them against the door along with her body, again and again, over and over, never stopping, never giving up, pain radiating through her.

"Open. The. Fucking. Dooooor!" She screamed each word and punctuated each by slamming a fist against the hard metal. The darkness in the truck matched the darkness overcoming her as she fell to the floor. The metal floor pooled her spit and vomit. Gagging, snotting and tearing, she still fought to stay conscious. Her lids cracked open and shut again, but not before she heard the metal rollers and a blinding glare shot into her eyes.

But, *her* darkness overtook her.

"King." Tex's signature twang came over the speaker of King's phone. "What can I do for you?"

"I need a trace on Ember's phone."

Tex's voice steeled on the other end and deepened at the mention of Ember's name. "SITREP." His command was heavy and direct.

King laid out the situation. He could hear Tex clicking away at the keyboard he always seemed to have in front of him. For a fleeting moment, King thought about Tex's wife and family, wondering if they ever got a moment together, with him helping so many teams.

The silence on the line was agony and King knew personally every second mattered when the one you loved was in the grasp of a madman.

"I've got a lock on her cell."

"You found her?" King's eagerness got the better of him, but before the words were out he already knew Tex's reply.

"Didn't say that. All I can guarantee is that her cell is pinging off the tower near Rolvan Flats," he paused, "about an hour away from the old, abandoned Timmack mineshaft."

King knew the area and his heart sank to his stomach. The landscape surrounding the Timmack mineshaft was desolate. He only hoped they would find Ember and not just her phone pinging in isolation.

Tex came back on the line and rattled off the coordinates, "Keep me in the loop. Keep safe."

Before King could thank him the line went dead.

Tex never held on the line long enough for thanks and gratitude, though King knew better than to attempt the gesture.

~

Six burly guys were crammed shoulder-to-shoulder in King's truck and were speeding out of town, blowing through red lights and pushing the speed limit beyond safe.

Now, approaching their target, the truck barely stayed on the road as it careened through the back roads while their GPS guided them to the middle of Bum-Fuck Nowhere. Pavement was no longer an option and the road was now dirt. Only headlights, and the night's full moon, illuminated their pathway.

"I'd welcome a multi-cruiser-police pursuit right about now. We could use all the law enforcement when we get to their destination," King muttered.

A pealing chime echoed in the cramped cab and Chase's voice came through the Bluetooth.

"I have Zion on standby if you need. My guys are ready and willing to go to bat if need be."

Slate, though filled with anger and hatred at the moment for Bazwar, felt a calming peace come over him at Chase's words. Though King's friend, Slate barely knew Chase, but not only was he willing to help him and put his team at risk, but his team was willing to stand at the ready. The brotherhood. It spanned ranks and teams and companies. It was a bond like no other.

Slate couldn't conjure the words with the lump in his throat but King answered the call. "Thanks, buddy. You got a marker."

"No thanks needed, but will keep that marker on the back burner. Never know when it'll be needed."

The call disconnected before Slate could ask about Susan and the girls, but he knew it was futile because Chase would protect them as if they were his own men.

They approached the area about a mile away from the GPS location near the ping of Ember's cell and all prayed that tracking the phone meant finding Ember and Mitch and not an abandoned electronic in the desert.

King turned off the headlights, not wanting to alert anybody of their approach. With no trees or buildings to mask their arrival, King didn't chance that the headlights would give them away. The full moon was more than enough light to navigate closer through the desolate desert. King killed the engine a half mile later, and four men strapped themselves to the teeth by the light of the moon. Everyone had their go-bags with enough guns and ammunition to hold off a small army. None hoped that was the case, but if so, they were prepared.

King pulled a stash of M4s and two M16s from the underbed compartment of the cab's back seat along with extra loaded magazines. He rounded the back of his truck, dropped the tailgate, and slid the concealed storage compartment from beneath the faux truck bed liner.

It was a tactical wet dream.

King drove a roaming armory and no one was the wiser. Vests, helmets, gloves, NVGs, comms, and an array of close combat tools: KA-BARs; SOGs; Leathermans, chem sticks. Every gadget that could attach somewhere, King had multiples. They were heading into war, to rescue their own, and King was prepared. Slate knew why. Suiting up brought back memories of Mary's tragic rescue and the unpreparedness of the guys.

Luckily, Mary's nightmare ended with the team coming home alive, which wasn't quite the case for King. The man cheated death so many times, he and the Reaper were probably on a first-name basis. King almost came home beneath the Stars and Stripes with a twenty-one gun salute. To think King and Mary not being, "King and Mary," had Slate thinking of himself and Ember. Their "us" had barely even started being an "us."

He'd be damned if anyone was going to take that from him. He'd be unstoppable.

"M4 or 16? Your choice." T held two rifles, gesturing for Slate to choose which one he wanted if they had to go "balls out" on this mission. *This mission.* The two words snapped Slate into operator mode. He was no longer *the boyfriend,* he was Alpha-three, take no prisoners, bad-ass motherfucker.

"M4." Slate nodded towards the rifle.

Arctic handed him a vest and helmet. He strapped the helmet on, attaching the NVGs, and secured the vest over his shoulders and on the sides, pulling the straps tight. The MOLLE straps were filled with gadgets, things he knew King strategically and meticulously placed on each. He knocked the chest plate and reached for the rifle T held out to him.

Slate slung the carbine over his head, pulling the single-point sling into place, cleared the chamber and slapped the thirty-round mag in place, then chambered a live round.

"Locked and loaded."

And the mission began.

They were dragging her. Literally dragging her through the dirt and grassy patches. Face down, arms outstretched above her head, pulling her along. Destination? She was uncertain. She was conscious, but between the gas burning her eyes, her lungs on fire from the retching and coughing, she was unaware of her surroundings. Add all that to the excruciating pain coming from the two people pulling her by her ravaged wrists, she was definitely not taking in her surroundings.

The dirt turned to gravel. Stones scratched against her stomach, digging into her flesh. She tried to arch her torso, but the way she was being "transported," it was a losing battle. Her tee rode up, exposing her belly, allowing the ground to be merciless against her flesh.

Ember stayed calm, acting weak and docile between coughs and spasms, waiting for a chance to overpower her captors. Letting them think she was weaker than she was, would give her the element of surprise if the time came. *When* the time came. But, the million dollar unanswered question: How many more were there?

Her body bumped against the rise of two steps and they dragged her across a wooden porch. She heard the door open and her blood ran cold

"Hayes...E-eight…"

Dad! His grunting sounds came after every blow, but when Ember craned her neck to see what was happening, her swollen and tearing eyes prevented it. She was dumped in a heap on the floor at her father's feet.

"Daddy!" She was able to croak out the word between hacks.

"Emmy! Are you okay? Stay quiet...don't let them—"

Ember heard flesh hit flesh and her father stopped talking.

"No! Stop!" Ember knew not to cry out. It was one of the first things taught about resistance in SERE training. Showing any response would spur them on and they would use him against her. But, it was her father; the cry was involuntary. The man continued to work her father over, landing blow after blow.

A bucket of water was dumped over Ember's head and she frantically wiped her hands down her face to cleanse the burn from her eyes. Then, a second bucket was dumped, and again, she washed when the water dribbled over her face. It didn't help the fiery sting, but at least she could see better. Before she could catch her bearings, she was rolled to her stomach with a knee jabbed into her back and her wrists were held to be bound. The man pulled one arm behind her, then up between her shoulder blades, and she yelled out in pain. But she got her other hand free from the woman helping to hold her down.

It was time to fight. She bucked wildly at the older Middle Eastern woman kneeling on her back, who she assumed was the mother of the other two. Ember pushed her body upward with her freed hand and rolled in the opposite direction her captors had her pinned, causing both to roll off her. With her arms free, she jabbed an elbow into the woman's face, feeling a satisfying crunch. The cry of agony told Ember she'd planted it exactly where she wanted; dead center to the nose. Ember jumped to her feet, though she had to steady herself and was off-balance from the gas.

Control yourself. Calm yourself. Clear yourself.

She had to use fast, critical tactics: groin, knees, throat, eyes, any vulnerable areas she could assault to subdue her attackers. There were no movie theatrics to be played. She was in it to win it.

Adrenaline seared through her veins. The pain from her previous wounds evaporated.

She met familiar eyes and panic flooded her. Eyes that were burned into her memory. A distant memory.

Omar Bazwar? It wasn't his eyes but his brother's, Husani Bazwar, the shooter from the range, that scorched her soul. Another memory flashed. Almost the exact same eyes from years past now haunted her present. They belonged to Khalid Bazwar, a terrorist she'd taken out years earlier, who planted an IED along the roadside. His eyes haunted her through her sniper scope, now they haunted her again as she stared into his brother's.

Omar charged at Ember but she side-stepped and kicked his knee. He wailed and buckled to the ground, temporarily taken out of the fight. He'd be down, but not for long.

Next, she spun to face her third attacker, a younger Middle Eastern woman who had nothing but evil in her eyes, matching her brother's. The woman lunged at Ember but she jabbed a throat-punch followed by a quick straight punch, again connecting with her throat. The woman grabbed her neck so Ember followed up with a left hook to the jaw, sending the woman stumbling into the wall. She slumped at the waist. Ember wasted no time and sent her knee into the woman's face. She collapsed to the ground, legs splayed haphazardly in front of her, and let out a muffled scream as she clutched her nose. Ember powered through with no mercy, bringing her booted foot down with brutal force, obliterating the woman's kneecap. Gurgled screams split the air, and with her knee destroyed, she rolled to her side and passed out. All this happened in less than a minute, too long for Ember's liking, but only because she was still feeling the effects of the tear gas. She bent to catch her breath and clear her head.

Omar got up, testing his weight on his injured leg. Ember noticed a blood-soaked spot on his arm, the shot Ember had taken in the parking lot that brought one of her assailants down, but it wasn't enough to keep him out of the fight. Now, seeing it was Omar she hit, Ember wished she'd have gotten off a second shot and ended his miserable life.

He lunged to Ember's blindside, taking her off her feet, and both fell to the ground. She was forced onto her side, but rolled to her back, wanting to be face-to-face with Omar.

His eyes seared her soul.

Those eyes.

Omar overpowered her with his weight, straddling her, and he let loose on her. Holding her down with one hand, he drew back his fist, planting a punch to her temple as she turned her head. Not at all a trained fighter like her, he made contact but it was a glancing blow. Pain bloomed and Ember's grunt was involuntary. She'd taken worse during training, but still, it hurt like a motherfucker. Ember saw his mother get up and come straight towards the fight.

Ember and Omar grappled until he got one of her hands pinned to the floor. She raked her nails across his face and he let out a howl, but it wasn't enough to loosen his grip.

Next, his mother reached for Ember's free arm but she flailed, trying to keep it out of her reach. They brought her wrists together and both were bound. His mother sat on Ember's calves, then zip-tied her ankles, pulling the tie tight enough to cut into the skin. Omar stood, stared down, and spat on her.

She was bound. She was fucked. And she couldn't do a damn thing about it.

They dragged her back in front of her father. Still tied to the chair, he fought against his restraints with all his might when he saw his daughter. Scalding anger fumed from him. Father and daughter faced each other. Each helpless. Each speaking with their eyes. Ember, telling him to be strong; Mitch, telling her to fight until the end.

The mother grabbed a roll of duct tape, tore off a piece, and covered Ember's mouth. She tried to resist, but it was hopeless with Omar holding her head. Two more pieces were placed over the first. Then, they did the same to Mitch. The tape held loosely over his mouth because of the amount of blood on his face, but his facial hair kept it in place.

The mother lowered herself to Ember and spoke in broken English. "You are devil woman. Took my son!" She spit in Ember's face. The vile action made Ember sick and she was helpless to wipe it from her face.

Ember thought she was talking about Husani, the man who shot Gabriel Dorian at the gun range and now sat in jail, but the mother went on.

"Khalid was warrior."

Khalid. Ember knew exactly who Khalid was and he was *no* warrior. He was vile, scum of the earth. Scum of the earth who could no longer hurt anyone because he was dead. By her .338 round straight between the eyes, eyes identical to his mother's.

She continued, "His father was warrior, too. He kill American infidels. Died honor in homeland. Khalid fight in father honor. Kill many American soldiers. Make mothers weep of sadness. I rejoice. Happy and praise."

Ember studied the woman's haunting, hate-filled eyes. The eyes of Omar and Husani.

The eyes of Khalid.

Ember was transported to a memory years earlier. One minute she was staring into the mother's abhorrent eyes, the next, she was on the hot rooftop of an abandoned shell of a building, laying prone, looking through the scope of her rifle into the carbon copy of the same eyes.

The Ranger squad was clearing the village, moving from house to house, looking for insurgents and finding caches of weapons. Ember remained their eyes above, overseeing their movement and the activity around them. She looked for threats: approaching cars, motorbikes or people, anything that could be a target against her team. Suicide missions were routine with ISIS, and smaller radical sects trying to show their allegiance to the terror group. Ember scanned ahead of the troop and across the rooftops, looking for anything out of place, anything that didn't belong. The squad broke through the door of a ramshackle home when Ember spotted a young man behind one of the rows of houses, walking alone, a rifle slung in front over him. His head scanned from side to side, trying to stay hidden among the debris and rubble, but she could see his every move. She watched and waited.

Hanging from his side was a satchel no bigger than a shoebox and across his chest hung a rifle from a bygone era. He clutched it close to his body and, again, swung his head to see if he'd been spotted.

He was spotted...by Diamond.

She radioed the squad, but the comms crackled in her ear, dead to the attention of her team. She tried again with no response then called into base reporting the possible threat, needing clearance to dispatch the target.

The Rangers advanced closer to where the man hid as they entered another house and cleared it of any occupants. The village was abandoned and all residents had cleared out weeks ago. Anyone still occupying the buildings and homes were insurgents and dealt with as such. She tracked the young man, adjusting her sights. He moved swiftly over what was once a home and towards the remains of a burnt shell of a car. She called in to the squad again with no reply, and once more to base for approval. The moment hung waiting for a response. Sweat beaded on her forehead and trickled down her temple. She didn't move to wipe it. Zeroing in on the man, she waited.

Move on. Move on. Don't do anything stupid.

Ember hoped he'd abandon whatever mission he'd been assigned. She counted her breathing, slowing it and her heart rate. Approval came through her earpiece. Nestling her cheek to the riser of her rifle, Ember switched the safety off.

Control yourself. Calm yourself. Clear yourself.

The young man edged closer to the car. Ember categorized and chronicled every movement. She heard the faint crackle over the comms. She'd taken out many targets, men and women alike, didn't matter. In her book, any threat to her brothers in the squad was a threat against her.

The man scurried to the rear of the car and reached into the satchel, pulled out a cylinder, and placed it behind the rear tire. He paused with his hand still on it.

Pick it up. Don't leave.

His fate rested in his next move. *Pick it up.* But, he didn't.

Fate had decided.

Ember released her breath, counting as she exhaled, and her finger moved down the trigger guard resting in place. With his profile in view, she zeroed in, seeing the beads of sweat glistening from his black hair and tan forehead. It was as if he were standing a foot in front of her. She eased her finger against the trigger, feeling the resistance of the pull.

The man's head turned and his eyes widened as if he could see her. *Those eyes.* Eyes of contempt, bitterness and hatred. The eyes of evil. They scorched her soul; burning into memory.

Controlled. Calmed. Cleared.

She broke the wall of the trigger.

Thwat. The stinging slap brought Ember out of the past and staring into the same eyes of hatred. Of evil. Khalid's mother's eyes burnt into her soul.

Ember had killed her son.

CHAPTER 32

Slate and the guys crept silently under the light of the moon towards what looked like an abandoned shack. A box truck parked out front and light from the front window were the only signs it wasn't abandoned. Other than that, the place was dilapidated and looked like something out of a ghost town.

King's truck was about a half mile back and they hiked the rest of the way in to keep the element of surprise.

The land was barren and they were sitting ducks out in the open. An occasional isolated tree or scrub brush wouldn't provide them any cover if needed. They moved swiftly across the plain and spotted a small thicket of trees about a hundred meters from the shack. They regrouped and went over the plan to rescue Ember.

"I want point," Slate said, "but I can't do it objectively. Someone else has to take it." His voice was low and it pained him to say it. "I swear I'll blow every motherfucker to hell if I breach and see they laid one finger on her, and considering the circumstances, we all know that's likely the case." This was his mission but the guys clearly understood. It wasn't said but King's vengeance during Mary's rescue was running through everyone's mind. Though King was Alpha-One, always the lead and owner of Hellforce, it was the one time the guys wished they would've defied orders and pushed back. Slate was right not to take point.

"King?" Slate posed the question without asking.

King nodded. "Order as usual." They would take up the usual sequence, falling in behind King. The team quickly devised a plan. This was not a scheduled op, but because they worked seamlessly together, it was old hat to the seasoned team. They started to fan out in sequence and headed towards the shack.

As they set out, a young boy, maybe six or seven years old, came running across the open clearing right towards the team. Instantly, all rifles were up and aimed at the approaching threat, halting every man.

"Easy, boys." King gave the low command over comms.

"Could be a trap." T-BAR followed up.

King stepped forward and the boy stopped, throwing his hands in the air, and falling to his knees in the dirt. "Please, help me. Save me." Though he was terrified, he kept his voice quiet, and tears washed over his face. "Please!" He whispered, followed by a sobbing hiccup.

"Cover," was all Arctic said when he eased forward, rifle still aimed and at his ready. He approached the boy searching for any small movement that could spell disaster. The team knew damn well it could be a ploy.

"Please. Don't hurt me. Don't leave me. Please, help me." It wasn't the words anyone wanted to hear from the lips of a child. The boy was trembling, waiting to see if he'd be hurt, but he must've been more scared of whatever was going on in that house if his odds were better to trust six, bigger-than-life strangers, armed to the teeth in the middle of the Texas desert after midnight.

"Show me your hands." Arctic's order wasn't his normal harsh command. The boy immediately raised his hands higher but still sobbed. The rest of the team approached slowly, ready to assist. Arctic lowered his rifle and stepped behind the boy, securing his hands in his own instead of using his flex cuffs.

The little boy's voice quivered, "I didn't hurt them. I need to get help for them. Please, don't hurt me. Don't take me back." His oversized, brown eyes, rimmed with unshed tears, were heart-wrenching. Usually, the guys were rescuing children, taking them away from danger, not subduing and cuffing them.

Arctic pulled the boy back into cover under the copse of trees.

"What's your name?"

"Rafi."

"Bazwar?" Arctic gentled his voice but still held an authoritative tone.

"You know me?" Rafi craned his little neck sending the question behind him while Arctic padded him down, though it was almost useless considering the boy's clothes looked more thirdworldly, rag tagged, tattered and dirty than what a typical young boy would wear.

"I have her phone.'

Slate stiffened.

Arctic pulled it from the boy's waistband and finished the pat-down. "All clear." The two words had the team easing their rifles. He swiped the lock screen and it lit with a picture of Ember and Maven, proving the phone was Ember's. She was in the house.

"Where did you get that?" The question came from T.

"It's the lady's. Momma had it on the table. I took it when I hid. I wanted to call for help, but I don't know how to use it."

Slate took a step forward but King halted him with a hand to his plate carrier. Slate was pissed and wanted to storm the house.

King brought his hand to his beard, smoothing it down his face, "Well, this throws us into a clusterfuck." He knelt eye level with the boy. King was huge next to his small frame, intimidating. The kid's oversized eyes rounded larger. King pointed towards the house, "Who's in there?" His low tone was hard and demanding and the kid cowered.

"King." The word came from Arctic.

King tried to look gentle but it didn't work. Still crouched, King leaned forward. The boy looked scared to death and his lip quivered.

"Fuck, King!" Arctic crouched beside the boy placing a hand on his shoulder, "Is your family in there?"

He locked eyes with Arctic and nodded.

"Who? How many?"

"Mama," without turning his head, he glanced back at King, then back to Arctic, "my brother and sister."

"Who else? You said, them. Who's them?"

"The lady and man. I hid. They need help. I ran to get help." His body shook with panic.

Arctic glanced up at Slate and T-BAR. Cy held back with Creed in case this was still a ploy.

King stood to his full height. "We can't breach with him alone out here." He smoothed his beard again.

Creed stepped up, closing the distance between his post and the group. "I'll stay with him." It was what the team needed. They had to rescue their own. If Creed had been with his own team, he'd want to be the one storming the castle.

King and Slate gave Creed a chin lift, Slate grateful for the man's offer.

Arctic took Rafi's hand in his. "You were brave to come to us. Really brave. We're here to help them but we can't all stay here with you and help them." The boy's face tightened. "I know you're brave; we all know you're brave. Can you be brave a little longer and wait here with our friend while we go help? It's the only way we can help them."

"Will you come back?" Although it wavered, it was his bravest voice.

"Yes."

That was all the promise he needed. Rafi nodded and looked at the towering men around him, "Okay." Rafi raised his skinny arm and ran it across his face, smearing his tears onto his dirty cheeks. He sniffled. "Promise you'll be back?"

"Promise we'll be back." Arctic made the promise for the second time.

"You may hear things, scary things, but we need you to stay here, no matter what." King was gentler but still stern.

Rafi nodded, "I will. I'm not going back."

Arctic squeezed his little fingers and stood.

"Don't send me back there." It was barely a whisper.

No one acknowledged the little boy, but Creed swore under

his breath, then crouched to be at Rafi's level. He put his hand on his scrawny shoulder, reassuring him he wasn't alone.

"Well, boys." King clicked his coms open, "It's zero-hour."

Ember watched in horror as her father was bludgeoned once again. She cried out in terror behind the duct tape when his head fell back, losing consciousness. She'd lost all composure and resolve to remain stoic seeing him tortured. Mother and son took turns torturing both of them. Ember had multiple cuts to her biceps, running from shoulder to elbow, and she could barely see through her swollen eye from their punches. Omar's mother took glee as she sliced down the length of Ember's flesh.

Omar sneered down at her. "Death's too good for you, bitch. When daddy wakes up, the real fun will begin." He unfastened the belt from his pants, handing it to his mom, then straddled Ember's knees and unbuttoned her jeans.

Ember trembled in fear. No training could have prepared her for this degree of terror. She prayed the guys would find her, but without her phone, she was on her own. She strained against her bindings when he yanked apart the denim of her jeans, tearing the zipper.

Her dad's awakening moans had Omar standing and walking over beside the chair. He slapped Mitch's face to wake him. "Daddy is in for a treat."

The chaos that erupted happened in less than a heartbeat.

The door was obliterated, falling from the hinges, and all hell broke loose.

Five massive men stormed the house.

Omar spun towards the commotion and pulled Ember's gun from his waistband. He fell to the floor before he got off a round. A perfectly placed hole in the center of his forehead trickled blood. His haunting eyes glazed over.

His mother screamed and lunged for the gun.

"Pick it up, bitch...give me a reason to match you to your son." T-BAR's voice was deadly, begging her to flinch so he could make good on his promise.

She put her hands up in surrender and Arctic moved forward to restrain her. Before he made it two steps, she reached for the gun and T cashed in on his promise.

One and done.

She crumpled beside her son's body, a matching hole trickled blood down her forehead.

King was at Mitch's side as soon as she was down. He pulled out his knife and cut the ties. "Call Tex, we need his medical evac." He examined Mitch's hand before removing the restraint, swearing when he saw the extent of the damage.

Ember stared into Slate's blue eyes. "Muuhmmhuum!" Her frantic cries were muffled behind the tape.

"T!" Slate's yell brought T-BAR to his side.

"Fuck."

"Need you to get pressure on her arm. Hang on, baby, I'll get those ties off." Slate rolled her enough to cut the ties from her hands. T pulled his blade and cut the ties from her ankles in one swift motion. He unfastened his plate carrier then ripped his shirt down the middle, pulling it off his chest. Ember cried out when he lifted her arm to tie the cloth around the multiple slices down her biceps and applied pressure to staunch the flowing blood.

"Sorry, doll." T winced in sympathy, then shot her a wink.

Only T would flirt while in the middle of a rescue. The thought broke her terror and brought her back to herself.

"Hang on, babe, this is going to hurt. I'm sorry." Slate started peeling the tape but Ember tore it from her face She let out a sob. Slate leaned over and cradled her, but she pushed at his torso, fighting against his hold, scrambling to get to her father. "Dad!" she wailed and twisted in Slate's grasp. He held her in place preventing her from further hurting herself. "Let me up! Dad!"

"Sssshh, baby. Red...he's good, he's good...King's got him."

Relief flooded her when Slate turned her to see he father. Seeing his battered state, she let out a shrill cry and Slate cradled her to his chest.

Arctic entered from around the corner. "Stiff's in the other room." King and T-BAR threw him a questioning look. "Throat's bruised. Crushed larynx." He motioned to Slate and Ember. "She got her good. Looks like she crushed it with one blow." Ember noticed none of the guys looked surprised. "Gonna go back to get the kid." Arctic stepped over the door lying in the entrance and joined the night.

Cy and Trip stood sentry waiting for medical to arrive, and King and T aided Mitch as he groaned, until they could get him to medical evacuation.

CHAPTER 33

When they arrived at the hospital, Ember wasn't sure how she was going to explain her bruised and battered state without raising alarms and having the staff call the authorities to report the unexplained injuries. She knew if they were called, she couldn't tell them what happened, risking the guys getting arrested, but Eli said not to worry about it.

How am I not supposed to worry about it?

The explanation came in the form of King. King worked with a lot of liaisons and his connections were immeasurable. She was nervous when the doctor came to examine her, but was surprised when she didn't ask questions or try to pry information from her.

The doc was cheery and pleasant and acted as if Ember was an everyday patient. As much as Ember wanted to know what kind of facility this was, how King had finagled a safe haven, she knew she'd be better off not knowing.

She learned later that after she and her father left, King called the cleanup crew and the Bazwar family was removed and disposed of. And, the remote, isolated shack was now a smoldering pile of ash.

In a few hours, Husani Bazwar would succumb to injuries from his suicide in his jail cell.

Yes, King's reach was as extraordinary as it was chilling.

Ember knew he wielded power in the circles of his trade, and being one of the top forces he could get things done that didn't seem humanly possible. What she didn't know was Hellforce was renowned for its contacts, markers and privy to the ears and favors of those most powerful in the US and foreign governments.

King was no small fish in a pond.

He was king fish in an ocean.

After a call to Tex, Rafi was taken to a special family center, a place that King and his contacts used in cases like this, a sort of WITSEC for kids of horrendous crimes. Tex made sure someone was on scene within the hour to take the little boy. Rafi would be placed in the care of a family, and recovery treatment and therapy would be available to him. It was a godsend Rafi ran and hid and didn't witness the demise of his family. The team was sure he knew what his family had done and what was ultimately their fate.

Rafi had begged and pleaded not to be taken back to his family, and the sweet boy clung to Arctic until the agency came to take him away. He begged Arctic to come with him; he didn't want to go alone, and it tugged at Arctic's heartstrings to see the little boy, alone, scared and reaching out for him when he passed the clinging boy to the female agent.

Before Rafi was placed in the backseat of the black, tinted-out SUV, Arctic tore the Velcro patch from the front of his Kevlar vest, the one embroidered with the Hellforce logo, and gave it to the little boy. "You were brave. Whenever you feel scared, this patch will remind you of how brave you really are." Arctic's heart broke for the little boy, but swelled a bit when Rafi wiped his nose and tears with the sleeve of his tattered shirt and said, "I'm brave...just like you."

King would closely monitor the boy's progress in the program, to see if he'd be placed with one of the families within the program, or if a relative would come forward to claim him. If he was claimed, King needed to know the new faces appearing on his radar. King and Arctic both secretly prayed no one would come forward and Rafi wouldn't be claimed by his family. The little boy deserved a better start.

Ember sat up in the hospital bed, waiting for the nurse to return with an update on her father. The doctor had seen her earlier and decided she needed to stay the night for monitoring.

The effects from the gas inside the box truck had worn off, and even though she protested, Slate made it clear she would stay the night. Her arm was sutured and bandaged and she had cold compresses on her swollen face. The swelling around her eyes had gone down, and she could see a bit better, but she still resembled a marshmallow puff. After a blood work panel, and enough IV fluids to make her almost wet the bed, she was ready to go home.

"Please, I'm fine. I just want to go home. To *our* home, to our bed, to lay next to you. I need to be next to you.

Eli stared at her and cocked a lopsided grin.

"Stop staring...I know I look horrid."

He leaned against the bed with his hip and twirled a tendril of her hair, then brushed another from her forehead. "You're beautiful, Red."

Ember scoffed.

He lowered the bedrail and Ember scooted over, careful of her IV. With his bulk, it was a tight fit, but Ember nestled into his side when he wrapped an arm behind her neck.

"Do you mean it?" He continued to absently curl a tendril.

"Mean what?"

"*Our* home. *Our* bed."

The Freudian slip made her smile and she winced when her split lip began to bleed. Eli grabbed a tissue and held it to the open wound.

"Thanks." She held the tissue to her lip a moment, then brought it to her lap, fidgeting with the edges. She waited a beat then asked, "Do you want me to mean it?" She fidgeted some more. "Because, I think I want to mean it...I know I want to mean it."

Eli took her hand, bringing it to his lips. "Yeah, Red. I want you to mean it." He picked up the tendril again and wove it between his fingers, "I really, really want you to mean it."

"Then, I mean it." She choked back the emotions welling

within her. "I'm so grateful you all came for me. I thought," she started to cry, " I thought—"

"No, no, baby, none of that." He grabbed another tissue, dabbed at the corners of her eyes, then caught a rogue teardrop sliding down her swollen cheek. "I'll always come for you, Red. Always. Every. Single. Time." He kissed the top of her head.

She wiped her eyes.

He pulled back collecting his thoughts. "I know we just became an, 'us,' but we've been an 'us' for as long as I can remember," He paused, "Since—"

"Since I punched Tommy Fleck in the nose in kindergarten." She chuckled and they both laughed at the memory.

"My Emmy. Always a fighter. Always fierce and strong. I've loved you since that moment. The girl with the fiery red hair."

He placed a kiss to her hair and wound another tendril around his fingers. "Em, I will never, ever, take you for granted. Not one day, one hour. Each minute, every second that I am given to be by your side, I will cherish you." He ran his thumb over hers. "I can't imagine my life without you in it. Honestly, I can't."

He softened his tone, "I've been scared, Em, I mean really scared. On the battlefield, on missions and ops, but tonight, I wasn't scared." He swallowed. "I was truly and utterly petrified...terrified that I would never be given another second to be with you." Eli swallowed harder. "I want to wake up to you for as long as I draw a breath. I knew it before today, and I know it now. I want to marry you Emmy, have babies with you, have fights with you...make up with you." He winked at her. "Fall in love with you all over again. I want to grow old and moldy with you. Even when these turn silver." He held up a lock of her ember hair, "I will love you all the same...and even more. Every bit of you."

His voice went husky. "Marry me, Emmy."

She pulled away from his side. Her chin quivered and her swollen eyes welled. He kissed her cheek as an errant tear escaped.

"Are you just asking because you're scared?"

Eli shook his head and propped himself up, adjusting to face her. "No, Red, I'm asking because I love you and don't want to go one more second without knowing you'll be mine, and I'll be yours and that we'll be and *'us'* for the rest of eternity." He rubbed the back of his neck.

She blurted, "Yes, Elijah! A million times, yes!" Ember threw herself into his arms, ignoring her pain. "Yes!" She cried with joy into the crook of his neck, and he kissed her head, whispering I love yous deep into her masses of hair.

"But, only if we can get married in the barn."

Eli smiled.

"It's where we will officially became an 'us.'"

He pulled back and gently brushed his lips across hers with feather-light, angel whisp kisses. "Anything for you, Emmy. Whatever you want, where ever you want...all I want is you. Just give me a date and time, and we'll officially be 'officially us'." Again, he lightly brushed his lips across hers.

She wasn't having it. She pushed forward, crashing her lips to his, and ignored the stinging cuts masked by the zings of their ardent love.

"Em," he tried to pull back, "I don't want to hurt you."

"Shut up and kiss your fiancée." She leveled him with another hard kiss, then tilted her head, pouring the pent up passion, fear, heartache, joy and happiness into their kiss.

A throat clearing from the open doorway had them hesitantly pulling apart.

"Daddy!" Ember tried to leap from the bed, Eli stopped her gently when she saw her mother wheeling Mitch into the room followed by Rhys, Mary and Maven.

"Stay where you are." Her mom pushed the wheelchair to the bedside.

Ember settled back but was practically hanging off the edge. "Daddy. Why are you here? You shouldn't be out." Her dad looked horrendous.

"I had to see with my own eyes that my baby girl was all right."

Mitch was in bad shape. The strong, stoic Goliath they all knew was reduced to a bruised and battered man. Nothing ever held Mitch Hayes down and his perseverance would hold him through a long coming recovery.

Mitch's doctor followed behind the group. "He wouldn't take my word for it. Threatened to sign himself out AMA. Didn't want that to happen, so we negotiated; he'd stay the night if he could come and make sure you were all right."

"Daddy!" Ember scolded, admonishing him with what was supposed to be a stern look, but wasn't quite working with her swollen face. "You are not leaving this hospital against medical advice! I'll have the guys stand guard if need be."

A knock at the door stifled his rebuttal. "Guess the party's in here?" King stood in the open doorway backed by six hulking guys, "Is it okay if we come in?"

The doctor hesitated but seemed to sense they all needed this moment together and motioned them in. Soon the small room felt like an office cubicle filled with wall-to-wall muscle and family. King, Chase, Cy, T, Arctic, Trip, and Creed barreled their way into the already cramped room.

Mitch ignored Ember's attempted harangue and picked up where he left off, "You must be doing well seeing you two can't keep your hands off each other."

Ember brought her fingertips to her lips "Did you ask him?" She whispered to Eli.

"Ask him what?" Her attempted whisper wasn't as whispery as she thought, because her father pinned her with a stare.

Eli kissed Ember's hand then took in each of his teammates, then his soon-to-be in-laws. "I've asked Em to marry me...and she said yes."

The room erupted in cheers and whoops of excitement not fit for a hospital with ailing patients, as rounds of "Finally" and "Congratulations" sounded throughout the group. The doctor winced at the commotion, probably second-guessing his approval.

"Wait, wait...wait a minute." Mitch's voice, though weak, quieted the bunch.

The room stilled, everyone waiting to hear what her father would say.

"You asked for her hand?" His timbre was low and serious.

"Yes, sir."

"And, you said yes?"

Ember nodded, "Yes, Daddy."

Mitch flipped up the foot-paddles with each foot and struggled to stand, ignoring the protests from Susan and the doctor. Eli stood to steady him. He cradled his casted broken arm and his face contorted in pain even with his nose bandaged up.

"Daddy?"

"Pops."

Mitch turned to Eli and rested a firm hand on his shoulder. "I've watched you grow as a young boy into a young man...seen you fawn over my baby girl." He grinned at Ember. "She, never noticing, oblivious to your attempts to woo her." He looked back to Eli. "And you ultimately accepted that she wouldn't return the sentiment. But, you still watched over her, protected her and loved her from a distance...there for every milestone from a gangly, wild-haired girl, into a beautiful young lady and now a beautiful young woman.

You're a man of honor and integrity, Eli. You fought for your country and now you fought for my baby girl." He cleared his throat, washing away the emotion welling in his voice. "She'll always be my baby girl. Remember that." He placed a kiss on his daughter's cheek and wiped her joyful tears. Turning to Eli, he stuck out his hand. "Finally, and officially, welcome to the family."

Eli grasped his hand and Mitch pulled him into a hug. It wasn't the normal side hug men gave one another, it was the embrace of family. In his low timbre he spoke, "Welcome to the family, son."

Eli closed his eyes and Ember watched the emotion wash over him from the man who took him in and raised him up...and became his mentor and hero. "Love ya, Pops!"

The embrace was a little longer than normal and Mitch squeezed Eli's shoulder. "You have my blessing." Then to his daughter he added, "But he treats you wrong, guaranteed, you're going to be a young widow."

The room broke into laughter. Mitch leaned in and said, "I've always been proud of you, son, but you taking my daughter's hand makes my heart beam that she's in the place she was always meant to be. Take care of my baby girl."

Eli swallowed and pledged, "I'll always protect her, you have my word." Mitch nodded and Ember knew that was good enough for him.

The heartfelt moment was broken by a voice coming through the crowd. "Wow! Didn't know there was a convention going on." Ember's doctor was making her way through the throng to her bedside.

Eli helped Mitch back into the wheelchair, then settled back in Ember's bed.

Looking around, the doc announced, "Visitors are supposed to be family only." She winked.

"Oh, they're definitely *all* family," Ember acknowledged.

Lighthearted laughs and chuckles came from the group.

"I have your test results." She glanced at everyone around her. "Would you like some privacy?"

Ember looked around the room and knew whatever was said could be said in front of everybody...her family. "No need."

"Are you sure?"

She nodded.

"I really think...I would advise that this would be best discussed without an audience."

"I'm good. Whatever you tell me, I'll just have to repeat to them. Two birds, one stone."

The doctor took a deep breath, studied the tablet in her hand, then looked back up at Ember. "You're pregnant."

The room stilled into silence. Nobody moved. Mouths fell open and all eyes were on the soon-to-be-parents.

Eli leaned into Ember, a breath away from her lips, and smiled. "Congratulations, Mommy." He kissed her gently and she could feel his smile against her lips.

"Congratulations, Daddy!" Both were locked in the other's love.

All eyes went to Mitch.

"I'm going to be a Papa!" Mitch's booming announcement sent the room into another eruption of cheers.

Ember and Eli kissed, letting the others' exuberance fill their souls. They knew there'd be time to celebrate later, but for now, only the two of them existed.

The doctor raised her hand to quiet the room. "Unfortunately, I've got some concerns."

The room went silent again.

CHAPTER 34

Eli handed her the cup of herbal tea but she shook her head, so he placed it on the bedside table then sat beside her and ran his hand over her blanketed hip.

Neither felt like talking.

It was a waiting game now. *Wait and see* was the advice they were given. Wait and see; hope and pray. A week had passed since she'd been kidnaped and she was now four weeks pregnant. At least, that's what they hoped.

Eli climbed over her legs to the other side of the bed and spooned her to his chest. She cradled herself in his arms wishing the world would go away and time would stand still. That she could stay in this moment forever and still carry their child. But, sometimes fate was cruel. Unpredictable.

"I keep waiting for something to happen, cramping or spotting, something...anything. And, I know stress isn't what I'm supposed to be putting myself through, but how can I feel anything but that?" Ember held tight to Eli's arm, pressed against her chest. Sorrow ripped at her heart. "I just want to get it over with; if it's going to happen, I want it to just happen. But, then I fill myself with guilt and grief and hatred for even thinking like that, wanting to hold on to this precious little baby every second I can." She cradled her flat stomach, willing their child to hold on.

～

Eli lowered his hands to her belly as if he could protect the little bean from harm. He couldn't see Ember's face but he heard the tears in her voice and felt them wrack her body as she sobbed. He had to be strong for her. Be the rock he always was and not let her know he spent every morning and evening sobbing silently in the shower. It was the only place he could let loose and cry the anguished tears of the unknown. He let the wetness of his tears wash over his face and mingle with the droplets of water from the shower head. He suffered in silence so he could be her stronghold.

After the overwhelming joy of hearing Ember was carrying his child, the world came crashing down around them with the force of sobering truth. Although the lab results verified she was indeed pregnant, the trauma from the tasing in the parking lot may have ended it. It was too early to hear a fetal heartbeat, and though an ultrasound could show the proof of an embryo, no heartbeat could be detected until five-and-a-half weeks at the earliest, to know for sure if it was still a viable pregnancy. That was a week-and-a-half from now. So, for the last seven days, Ember was trying to stay calm and stress-free, which was nearly impossible. Eli knew if he was feeling the range and roller-coaster of emotions weighing on him, she had to be feeling them ten-fold.

He felt her shoulders shake and she curled even deeper into him. "Shhh, Emmy. It's okay," he spoke into the crook of her neck. "Don't get yourself worked up. Remember what the doctor said." It was the same thing he told her every time she crumbled and needed reassurance.

She tore back the covers with force and peeled out of bed. "I know what the fuck the doctor said, Eli. I was right there with you!" She began to pace.

"Em, come on, sit back down, have some tea," he motioned to the cup on the nightstand, "don't get worked up. Remember—"

She stopped and stared him down. "Are you serious right now?" she deadpanned. "Do you hear yourself? Have some tea?

Really?" Her voice rose along with her anger. "Tea? Fucking tea! You think *tea* is going to make this better?"

"That's not wha—"

She huffed and resumed her pacing, then stopped to address him again. "Do you even care, Eli?"

That had him out of bed in a flash, standing toe-to-toe with her. "How can you even ask that?" His anger was rising.

He was standing so close, she had to crane her neck to see him. Normally, when he towered over her, she smiled up at him. But now she took a step back. "I don't know, Eli. How can I ask that? Let's see, the fact that you haven't shown one ounce of emotion since we got home. Um, the fact that you walk around here doing day-to-day, mundane tasks like our world isn't about to shatter."

His anger bubbled to the surface and he wanted to scream back at her, but held himself in check knowing that was the last thing she needed. He bit his tongue and ground his teeth. His molars were going to crack from the force of the pressure so he loosened his jaw. "That's not true. I've cr—"

"Maybe you're happy," she said. "Maybe you're cut off and cold-hearted because this is what you really wanted. Having second thoughts about fatherhood? This could be your out?" The verbal diarrhea wouldn't stop. She kept catapulting and slinging it at him. "Maybe starting a family right off the bat isn't ideal, so you're wishing—'

He grabbed her by the arms, something he'd never normally do, but he needed to get her attention and stop her tirade.

"Stop, Ember! *Stop*...Enough!" He held her upper arms, forcing her to look up at him until she winced. He loosened his grip, remembering her sutured arm. The anger on her face melted into confusion, then into sorrow. Like a veil being lifted from her eyes, the realization of her words, the devastating blows she dealt him materialized, and she crumpled into his chest. Collapsing her weight against him because she couldn't stand on her own. She sobbed uncontrollably. He buried his head in her fiery curls and sobbed as well. Two broken souls finding solace in sorrow.

"I'm sorry, Eli," she said between sobs, "I don't know what

came over me. I didn't mean it. God, I didn't mean it. I'm so sorry."

He held her just as he did in the hospital when the doctor told them the news, until her wails and sobs turned into silent shudders. He pulled her to the end of the bed and onto his lap, murmuring into her hair while his tears fell onto her mass of curls.

"Baby...it's okay baby...Get it all out...I love you...I love you so fucking much." He rocked her as he spoke through his tears. "I love our baby. God, Emmy, I love you. Hold on to our baby."

Finally, when they both couldn't cry any longer, Eli spoke. "I cry every morning, Em, and every night in the shower...so you don't see me break. You can't see me weak, or else I can't stand strong. It kills me and brings me to my knees. I pray and curse God on my knees, hoping I haven't caused this to happen with all the blackened marks on my soul. Praying He isn't taking a life for the lives I've taken. Punishing me—" Tears he didn't think were left trickled down his cheeks.

"Elijah, no!" She stared him in the eyes. "No, Eli. You didn't do this, God wouldn't do this. Evil did this. The same evil you banish. You're light, Eli! Ridding the world of the worst of the worst and protecting the innocent who have no hope. You're their Hope, Eli. For every piece of shit you take out, you save countless people from a life of hell." She grabbed his face, looking at him through tearstained eyes, forcing him to look down at her, "This. Is. Not. Your. Fault. Get that out of your head. You're light, Eli! A light for good."

Eli nodded, sniffing back his tears. He had so many questions. Questions he hadn't asked her to keep her from worry.

King had called a few days ago but he kept the conversation short, causing Eli to wonder if King was thinking the same things he was, seeing as King and Mary were ten weeks further along in their pregnancy than they were. Mary was fifteen weeks now.

If Ember miscarried, would King and Mary feel guilty when their baby was born and their baby would have followed a few months behind? Would each milestone cause either couple to live in guilt or resentment, seeing what milestones they would never experience without their baby? Would they be able to rejoice in the birth of their friends' first born, standing by idly, knowing their child's life would never share in the same joys?

Would the loss be a blessing in disguise, because they needed time to be an *us* before starting a family? Would it be too much for them to handle as a couple? Would it tear them apart? Or bring them closer together? Would the waiting for the unknown make them discover a deeper, undying love and devotion to one another? Would discovering Ember was still pregnant make them cherish the pregnancy and the baby even more once it was born, knowing how precious life is and how easily it can be lost?

How was he supposed to burden her with all those questions when he was supposed to be her rock? By not voicing them, she thought he didn't care, which caused her more stress and worry. Could his never-ending questions actually bring them together?

They had to be open to each other's worries and fears. So, for the next few hours, they stayed in each other's arms and laid all their hopes, worries and fears, finding comfort that they were both worried about the same things. Though there were no answers to the uncertain questions, knowing that the other was experiencing the same uninhibited fears, brought comfort to their hearts in its own twisted way. Waiting would still be unbearable, but at least they could bear it together.

CHAPTER 35

Ember watched as Eli stepped off the last rung of the ladder and admired his handiwork.

"Are you sure pale yellow was the right choice? Maybe we should've gone with the tea green pastel." Ember bit her thumbnail, second guessing the paint scheme.

"Yellow is beautiful. Cheerful. Revitalizing." Eli stepped behind her and rubbed the emerging six-month baby bump beneath her oversized sweatshirt. "Every day our child wakes, they'll be greeted by the color of a new day."

She wrapped her arms over his cradling her belly. "Yellow is fine for a girl, but it doesn't exactly scream baby boy." She worried her thumb between her teeth again.

Eli pushed her hair to the side exposing his favorite expanse of skin. She craned her neck, opening an invitation for him to indulge. Nuzzling her ear and peppering kisses down her flesh, he nipped at the juncture of her neck and shoulder, causing a moan to rumble from her throat.

"Girl or boy, either way, the room will be fine." He nibbled her lobe and she shrugged him away with her shoulders. Turning in his arms, she laced her arms beneath his and caressed his sculpted back below his worn tee. He did the same to her, but his hands followed her flesh to the nape of her neck, pushing the sweatshirt up and over her shoulders.

"Eli! What are you doing?" She feigned exasperation but didn't object to him undressing her.

"I'm examining my wife." He eyed her ample breasts and licked his lips.

Wife. The word falling from his lips brought shivers along her spine. That, and the kisses venturing lower into her newly engorged cleavage, had her pushing into him.

"I love your baby-tits, baby." He kissed the rising mound, licking down a path into the cleft of her cleavage and biting the other rounding mound as he emerged. "I loved your tits before, but good God, I could feast on these beauties all day."

Ember looked down at the him between her breasts. Her dusky pink nipples stood stiff and enlarged, like plump little raspberries poking through the black lingerie bra. It had nothing in the area of support, but the intricate lace pattern made her feel sexy as her ever-changing body began filling out in places she'd never carried weight. Eli ran his finger below the straps and over the ridgeline of each cup and it brought back the memory of the morning she cried because her favorite bra made her expanding breasts look like rising bread dough in a too-small pan. Eli came home that evening carrying a little pink boutique bag that held a matching bra and panty set. She was shocked he'd shopped at her favorite lingerie store. When he admitted Maven had given him her measurements, but he picked out the scandalous set himself, she could have kissed her friend. She immediately modeled the set for Eli, which was pointless, because the show lasted all of five minutes before he stripped them from her body, worshiping her while the lacy set lay in a crinkled heap on the floor. The memory brought a pulse to her inner muscles.

He pulled at her budding nipple through the lace and the shock brought her to the present. He explored, never leaving either unattended, sucking her nipple through her bra and pinching the other between his fingers. They were oh-so-sensitive and each flick of his tongue, pull, or pluck of his finger was like lightning splaying jolts of pleasure throughout her lady bits and sanding surges of need to her clit, dampening her panties.

Eli pushed the cups of her bra below each breast, surging

them higher onto her chest, tweaking one nipple and biting the nib of the other. A shriek erupted from her steady crooning when he bit a little too hard, and she felt his smile against her flesh as he kissed the sting away. He didn't let up. Panting, she grasped his tee and pulled it over his head. He released her reddening nipple with a pop and she begrudged the loss. He pushed down her leggings and underwear with one push of his hands over her luscious ass and down her legs. She stepped out of the pooling fabric as Eli removed his jeans and boxers with urgency.

The sight of his heavy cock, glistening with precum, had her wanting to swallow the head and swirl his salty essence over her tongue. A shot of want throbbed deep in her pussy. Eli wasted no time when he pushed two fingers high into her tight sheath, causing her to clinch around his thick fingers, as he delved deep, pumping them in and out. The rhythmic sound of suctioning wetness should have embarrassed her but only spurred her on.

"Eli, I'm going...I'm going...Elijahhhh!" She belted out his name and he held his fingers deep within her spasming walls until the tightening muscles let loose with a gush of cum that pooled in his palm and trickled down her thighs.

"My God, baby. You let loose like a canon." He removed his fingers, bringing them to his mouth. Her musky tang sprang from his fingers, and at the sight, she wanted to taste him more than ever. She went down on her knees, grasping his shaft, feeling its pulse in her hand. She caressed his heavy sack with her palm, rolling his balls in her hand, then gave a slight pull. Eli's head fell back as she slid him deep into her mouth until she felt him bump into the back of her throat. She'd learned to suppress her gag reflex, allowing her to deep throat him, holding him deep.

"Em, I can't—"

She loved to hear him beg, so she pushed him even deeper, past the group of constricting muscles, and swallowed, causing them to squeeze his engorged head. He was no longer in her mouth, he was deep in her throat.

"Baby, please, I'm begging you, I don't want to cum in your mouth."

She pulled him out of her throat, leaving a line of saliva trailing from her tongue to his shaft, then licked the underlying rigid vein from root to tip, slathering his head with a flattened tongue and her remaining spit. She purposely dragged her teeth over the sensitive head.

Eli let out a groan. "Fucking vixen." He fell to his knees, pushing her back and lowering her to the plush carpet. "You're going to regret that."

"I'm hoping so." Ember gave him a devilish grin and he took her hard, pushing his tongue into her mouth, not waiting for an invitation. He wanted her and wanted her now. He pulled back tugging her exposed nipple, causing her to scream.

"Naughty girls get naughty punishments."

God, she loved how they played, opening them to a new world of sexuality. He knew just what she liked. He constantly pushed her boundaries, but never pushed her too far.

Eli nestled between her legs, pushing them beyond their normal spread to accommodate his broad thighs, and hauled her ass into his lap. He looked down her body and his eyes locked on her rounding stomach. A moment of reverence hit him when he glided his hands gently over her skin, settling them over the round bulge. The urgency he was just experiencing halted the moment he felt the firmness beneath his fingers. He leaned over, bringing his forehead to her navel, kissing the swollen flesh, lingering in worship of this woman he called his own.

"Eli?" Ember's call met his ears, but still, he stayed planted to her midriff. "Um, babe...kinda feeling antsy." The urgency in her plea had him smiling against her flesh. She got to feel their baby every minute of the day, but he reveled in wonder each time he could worship her womb, and his heart stopped every time he felt a small flutter or faint kick beneath his palm.

"Elijah, if you don't get a move on, I'm going to have to finish this myself."

As if that's a threat. He loved to watch her masturbate. The way she arched and writhed, sprawling and humping to the rhythm of her own fingers or toys. It was like every holiday and birthday rolled into one. As tempting as it was to watch her go to town on herself, he wasn't passing up the opportunity to take her where she lay.

"Daddy's going to help Mommy. If you hear dirty cuss words, it's just Mommy being a bad girl. Just ignore her filthy tongue." Ember swatted him on the shoulder as he kissed her stomach. With unmatched affection he then whispered, "Daddy loves you, little one," and he ran his hands down her sides. He didn't know what he did to deserve this woman and child in his arms, but he would spend forever being their protector.

Then he worshiped his woman like the goddess she was.

Her body went lax. She was floating. There was no ground. There was no ceiling. She hovered in space where time didn't exist.

"Come back to me, babe...come back, Red...." She heard Eli's voice but she didn't want to acknowledge it. She wanted to stay in the ether of sexual bliss.

""Babe..." his voice crooned...Red, baby..."

His voice was lulling her to sleep. She answered him with a pleasant little grunt.

"Emmy, girl...come on."

She felt him lift her body from the plush carpet, not even caring if she had rug burns on her back or ass. She loved the feel of his naked torso against her cheek as he carried her sated body to their bed.

"Is it terrible we just had sex in our child's nursery?" She mumbled the words into his bare chest.

"Go to sleep, Red."

"But, we need to finish the crib and table...the rocker..." The words trailed off when he laid her in bed and she settled her back against him. Eli spooned her from behind, his hand cupping her baby bump. She knew once and for all her was their protector.

EPILOGUE

"One more time, baby."

The crack of his palm lashing her rounded ass made her release squirt onto his balls. She was ready to collapse, but he'd pinned her thighs with the bar, so her surrender was not her own. She saw nothing but blackness. No light peered through the covering hastily tied over her eyes, causing all of her other senses to heighten. He lifted her sagging head, fisting her hair in his grasp, looping the tangles around his hand, and pulled her hair back like reigns. She cried out. She arched her back, trying to relieve the tension on her neck, but it was drawn back as far as he could pull it, all the while he pounded relentlessly into her from behind, giving her no reprieve from the last orgasm, causing her to call him filthy names. Each word spurred him on, sending each jetted thrust against her spine and causing her to bark out a yelp in rhythm with his thrusts. She was going to lose consciousness, her labored breathing made her mouth run dry and she was having trouble swallowing.

"You're a dirty girl, who deserves dirty girl things."

She felt the heat of his breath against her ear, and she shivered when he licked the side of her face.

Lord, Jesus, help me! Her prayer was ripped from her soul, as he lashed another four cracks, in succession, over her tender ass, and this time she knew welting bruises would remain.

"Who's riding this?" His voice bellowed in her ears.

She wasn't sure how long she could endure this punishment.

"Who?" He demanded her answer.

She held her breath, and the burn in her lungs pushed her further.

"Say it! It's not going to end until you say it."

Oh, God! Her impending orgasm was rippling to a climax. She couldn't hold it, but she didn't want to let it loose and give him one more ounce of satisfaction. She panted and silently swore. *Oh, fuck! Oh, fuck! Fuck! Fuck! Fuck!*

"*Say it, Maven!*"

"*Monty!*"

ACKNOWLEDGMENTS

First, and foremost, I have to thank Susan Stoker for allowing me to play in the Aces Special Forces Operations Alpha world and giving me the opportunity to hobnob with your amazing characters. Though fiction in the world of literature, these characters have become real and cherished by your readers, and I hope I've done them justice. Thank you for your words of advice and encouragement. Writing in your Stoker Universe has been an adventure, and I am forever grateful for the experience.

To Riley Edwards, I thank you (and apologize) for the endless lists of questions I bombarded you with, on an almost daily basis. Words are immeasurable for my gratitude for the insightful advice you always lend. It sounds cliche, but is ever true, I could not have done this without you. You've taken an unknown, untried, newbie author under your wing, mentored me, guided me, and supported me before I got through my first manuscript. And, even when I didn't believe in myself, you gave me the encouragement to succeed and a kick in the pants when needed. I will forever be grateful for your support, and I hope to one day be able to return the favor to a newbie.

To Anna, my "Hand Twin," thank you for mentoring me. You've made this venture worthwhile and navigated me through the dark side of writing that I know nothing about and the things that lie beyond, "what happens *after* you write a book" journey, the depths of hell I didn't know existed. Thank you for giving me your time that I know is so precious to an author. Like you said, our likeness is uncanny and I am blessed to call you friend. Your time and advice is a treasure trove, and I am forever thankful. Thank you, Hands.

To my "Smutties," yes, you know who you are! This dream envisioned, first as a practical joke, blossomed into an unimaginable dream come true for me. I couldn't have done any of this without your love and never-ending support.

Becky, you are literally my lifeline on speed-dial and video chat, 24/7, to *every* crazy and unimaginable question I could throw at you: from medical opinions, to coffee bar menus, down to the choice of a character's underwear color. Thank you, a million times over, for not unfriending me...or calling the authorities.

Anne, many times you have talked me off a ledge when I wanted to give up, pack up, and never wanted to write another word in a manuscript. Your push and encouragement kept me afloat in desperate times and for that, I am forever thankful.

Jo, your mad reading skills are a gift to me, and I am honored that you take my written words to heart and grace them with your intellect. You've encouraged me from the start to chase the dream, grab it, and never let go. You're a force to be reckoned with, my Cyclone Jo. So, to each of you, there are no words that can express my gratitude. Words are inadequate. Hellforce would not exist if not for this group of Smuts! I know I've driven each one of you bonkers at one time or another, but you kept me grounded, going, moving forward, AND gave a dose of cold hard truth when needed. Though miles of land and even oceans divide us, you've woven a dream come true for me. I love you all with the depths of my heart.

To Nicole thank you for believing in me way before I believed in myself. You are a constant cheerleader and a forever optimist. Thank you for allowing me to invade your Messenger with every question that this newbie author could fathom. You are a gem in my host of treasures, and I am unbelievably grateful for your time, understanding, and patience. It takes a village!

Rebecca, I am humbled by your gift of editing and the eye of an eagle. Without you, literally, none of this would be a reality. Thank you for muddling through Slate and Emmy's manuscript...that most likely had you turning to the bottle. It's unbelievable how you can take my mass of words and somehow make a coherent masterpiece. You are truly a talent unrivaled. You know my depths of gratitude, and I will never forget the gift you have bestowed upon me. My words are short, but my gratitude is unending.

Lori, again, thank you for gracing the cover with the prime cut of alpha meat! I know they say, *Don't judge a book by its cover*, but you make that adage fly out the window! Your artistic eye makes a difficult job look easy, but I know with my vision of romantic eye-candy, most likely had you rolling your eyes and wondering how you got roped into making Slate a reality. Forever, I am humbly grateful.

And, finally, TO THE READERS: Thank you for taking a chance on me, a new author, and this second book in the Hellforce series. Thank you for giving me a few hours of your precious time. You don't know how much your support means to a newbie, and I'm honored that you chose to join the pages of Hellforce.

Love, peace, and hugs,

Rayne

ALSO BY RAYNE LEWIS

Hellforce Security: Alpha Team

Justice for Mary

Saving Emmy

ABOUT THE AUTHOR

Rayne Lewis is a lover of all things books. On an ideal weekend, you'll find her curled up in a comfy chair, cup of tea brewed, binge reading a good series. She loves a happily-ever-after romance and also a good "who-done-it" mystery. Baking is a passion and her favorite sweet is her Mandarin orange-pineapple cake (or anything that'll curb her sweet tooth). Though a novice, sewing is a hobby. When she isn't in the kitchen, she enjoys evening walks with her husband and spending time with their furry doggo at the dog park. She's a Midwestern girl and loves her family.

*There are many more books in this fan fiction world than listed here,
for an up-to-date list go to www.AcesPress.com*

*You can also visit our Amazon page at:
http://www.amazon.com/author/operationalpha*

Rose Smith: Saving Satin
Jenika Snow: Protecting Lily
Lynne St. James: SEAL's Spitfire
Dee Stewart: Conner
Harley Stone: Rescuing Mercy
Sarah Stone: Shielding Grace
Jen Talty: Burning Desire
Reina Torres, Rescuing Hi'ilani
Savvi V: Loving Lex
Megan Vernon: Protecting Us
LJ Vickery: Circus Comes to Town
Rachel Young: Because of Marissa
R. C. Wynne: Shadows Renewed

Delta Team Three Series
Lori Ryan: Nori's Delta
Becca Jameson: Destiny's Delta
Lynne St James, Gwen's Delta
Elle James: Ivy's Delta
Riley Edwards: Hope's Delta

Police and Fire: Operation Alpha World
Freya Barker: Burning for Autumn
B.P. Beth: Scott
Jane Blythe: Salvaging Marigold
Julia Bright, Justice for Amber
Anna Brooks, Guarding Georgia
KaLyn Cooper: Justice for Gwen
Aspen Drake: Sheltering Emma
Emily Gray: Shelter for Allegra
Alexa Gregory: Backdraft
Deanndra Hall: Shelter for Sharla
Barb Han: Kace
EM Hayes: Gambling for Ashleigh
India Kells: Shadow Killer
CM Steele: Guarding Hope
Reina Torres: Justice for Sloane
Aubree Valentine, Justice for Danielle

Maddie Wade: Finding English
Stacey Wilk: Stage Fright
Laine Vess: Justice for Lauren

Tarpley VFD Series
Silver James, Fighting for Elena
Deanndra Hall, Fighting for Carly
Haven Rose, Fighting for Calliope
MJ Nightingale, Fighting for Jemma
TL Reeve, Fighting for Brittney
Nicole Flockton, Fighting for Nadia

As you know, this book included at least one character from Susan Stoker's books. To check out more, see below.

SEAL Team Hawaii Series
Finding Elodie
Finding Lexie (Aug 2021)
Finding Kenna (Oct 2021)
Finding Monica (May 2022)
Finding Carly (TBA)
Finding Ashlyn (TBA)
Finding Jodelle (TBA)

Eagle Point Search & Rescue
Searching for Lilly (Mar 2022)
Searching for Bristol (Jun 2022)
Searching for Elsie (Nov 2022)
Searching for Caryn (TBA)
Searching for Finley (TBA)
Searching for Heather (TBA)
Searching for Khloe (TBA)

Delta Team Two Series
Shielding Gillian
Shielding Kinley
Shielding Aspen
Shielding Jayme
Shielding Riley
Shielding Devyn (May 2021)
Shielding Ember (Sept 2021)
Shielding Sierra (Jan 2022)

SEAL of Protection: Legacy Series
Securing Caite (FREE!)
Securing Brenae (novella)
Securing Sidney
Securing Piper
Securing Zoey

Securing Avery
Securing Kalee
Securing Jane

Delta Force Heroes Series

Rescuing Rayne (FREE!)
Rescuing Aimee (novella)
Rescuing Emily
Rescuing Harley
Marrying Emily (novella)
Rescuing Kassie
Rescuing Bryn
Rescuing Casey
Rescuing Sadie (novella)
Rescuing Wendy
Rescuing Mary
Rescuing Macie (novella)
Rescuing Annie (Feb 2022)

Badge of Honor: Texas Heroes Series

Justice for Mackenzie (FREE!)
Justice for Mickie
Justice for Corrie
Justice for Laine (novella)
Shelter for Elizabeth
Justice for Boone
Shelter for Adeline
Shelter for Sophie
Justice for Erin
Justice for Milena
Shelter for Blythe
Justice for Hope
Shelter for Quinn
Shelter for Koren
Shelter for Penelope

SEAL of Protection Series

Protecting Caroline (FREE!)

Protecting Alabama
Protecting Fiona
Marrying Caroline (novella)
Protecting Summer
Protecting Cheyenne
Protecting Jessyka
Protecting Julie (novella)
Protecting Melody
Protecting the Future
Protecting Kiera (novella)
Protecting Alabama's Kids (novella)
Protecting Dakota

New York Times, USA Today and *Wall Street Journal* Bestselling Author Susan Stoker has a heart as big as the state of Tennessee where she lives, but this all American girl has also spent the last fourteen years living in Missouri, California, Colorado, Indiana, and Texas. She's married to a retired Army man who now gets to follow *her* around the country.

www.stokeraces.com
www.AcesPress.com
susan@stokeraces.com